Also by Cheryl Benard

Moghul Buffet

Turning on

THE

Girls

Turning on

T H E

Girls

C H E R Y L

B E N A R D

Farrar, Straus and Giroux

N E W   Y O R K

Farrar, Straus and Giroux
19 Union Square West, New York 10003

Library of Congress Cataloging-in-Publication Data
Benard, Cheryl, 1953–
    Turning on the girls / Cheryl Benard.— 1st ed.
        p.   cm.
    ISBN 0-374-28178-5 (alk. paper)
    1. Women—Fiction.   2. Man-woman relationships—Fiction.   I. Title.

PS3552.E5363 .T8   2001
813'.54—dc21

                                                    00-056050

Designed by Jonathan D. Lippincott

My thanks to Elisabeth Kallick Dyssegaard, an editor who knows when to be flexible, when to show her muscle, when to step in with a saving idea, and when to simply count to ten and be a saint;

to Joe Regal, for so much substantive help and creative input, but especially for his heartening indignation in the face of bizarre and distressing gender events;

to Elaine Chubb, especially if she will just kindly hand over 10 percent of her wonderful logical brain;

to Charlotte, my real and virtual mother;

of course to Zal, Charlie, Alex, and Max, my once and future men; and to Griffin, who possesses all the virtues of Mac, but greatly exceeds him in beauty

Turning on

THE

Girls

Lisa returns to her office, fifteen minutes late and not very happy. Pushing aside a stack of books and slumping into the chair, she locates her prompter. She stares at her compuscreen and at the paragraph she was working on before lunch; no, it has not miraculously turned brilliant during her absence. She picks up a book from the side table; it is a copy of Pauline Réage, *Story of O*. Lisa throws it hard, it flies forward and hits the door. Being a paperback, it fails to make the kind of satisfying thud that a hardback would, but even so it has made a noise, and the door opens. A young man sticks his head in, inquiringly. "Coffee?" he asks.

Okay, time out, I need an introduction and I might as well put it here. The first thing you have to know is that, in my story, women have just taken over the world.

My main character is going to be Lisa, whom you have just met, and she will work for the Ministry of Thought, Department of Values and Fantasies, Subdepartment of Dreams.

The female persons who are now in charge of everything believe that a revolution has to change your thinking, otherwise, before you know it, you will be right back where you started from. So they put a very large staff in charge of women's brains and how to, you know, kind of launder out the sediment, iron out the kinks of centuries of oppression.

Well, oops, come to think of it, I guess they wouldn't like my metaphors, laundry and ironing. See how these things creep in? See how you automatically think in domestic terms when you think about women?

But back to Lisa. Lisa works for one of the many bureaus dedicated to the mammoth task of mental revolution. She is supposed to help straighten out the warped thinking, the retrograde dreams and politically incorrect fantasies, of her gendermates. Specifically, Lisa has been assigned to work on sex. Which doesn't sound so bad, I wouldn't think. In fact, though, as we will discover, working on sex is no bed of roses. Not when your boss is Nadine ("the Nazi") Schneider.

But I fear I am getting ahead of myself. You, of course, are still asking yourself, "Goodness me, how did women happen to take over the world?"

I can see that you won't just let me assume this happy scenario. I can see that you are going to force me to give you some kind of explanation of how it came about. It won't be a very likely story, I can tell you that much right now. You're just going to have to swallow it, suspension of disbelief and all that. You're just going to have to indulge me on this one, otherwise there's no story, and you'll never find out what happens to Lisa, and worse yet, you won't get to read all those excerpts from the pornographic texts which make up her working life, and with which I intend to spark your interest throughout the book.

And furthermore, I want to say that if you are going to let George Orwell get away with a bold premise, and Aldous Huxley, then you should extend me the same courtesy, I really think. If you are going to let barnyard animals be in charge of the world, then women shouldn't be that much more of a stretch.

Now, changes in power, even from one gender to another, are not an entirely absurd idea. Although I wouldn't hold my breath waiting for this one, frankly. Nonetheless, numerous academics, especially fanatical radical probably lesbian feminist ones who will never get tenure, believe that such a gender-related shift in power happened at least once before, that things used to be matriarchal until one day the guys said hey, screw this, we're bigger than them, and made a revolution.

The matriarchal period of human history, herstory, whatever—Nadine would undoubtedly make me say herstory—is generally described by nostalgists as being really very nice, with lots of over-weight, berry-gathering herb-brewing ladies in charge, ladies who made statues of themselves that have names like the Venus of Willendorf, which you can now see in a museum in Vienna, in the Naturhistorisches Museum, which I have been to, and it is a pathetic place full of moth-eaten stuffed wolves and dusty dead snakes with all their scales gone, and should you find yourself in Austria, I advise you to give it a miss and go skiing.

But anyway, in the descriptions, matriarchy sounds—except for the part about women being fat, of course—a great deal like Southern California, with lots of psychic energy zooming around and everybody really in tune with, you know, nature and their bodies and stuff. The men are said to have meekly gone along with all of this because they believed women could make themselves have babies all by themselves, by magic, whenever they felt like it, and if you made them mad the human race would die out or, worse, they would specifically get rid of *you* in particular, because they were just keeping you around out of the kindness of their hearts and for your entertainment value. Actually, the revolution is thought to have started when the guys somehow figured out that, hey, on the topic of making babies this was not quite the whole story.

My point is, I could probably develop a remotely plausible story for how the power shifted back, since some paranoid people think this is happening already anyway. But then I would have to write a really well-researched historical tome, which would be about a thousand pages long, and who do I look like, James Michener? I don't think so.

So let's get past the part about taking over the world, and the most painless way to do that is going to be for you to join me in imagining a cataclysm. It could be an environmental disaster, it could be a war, it could be some kind of international terrorist extravaganza, it could be a total economic collapse, it could be all of the above, and I ask you to imagine that as it begins to unfold, people feel there has been a colossal bit of global mismanagement and poor judgment on the part of those in charge, who happen to be men, and that maybe it would not be such a bad thing to let a different gender take a shot at it, women, for example. Actually, all of this could happen sort of incrementally, with more and more really competent and ambitious women gradually inching up higher and higher and looking better and better compared to the male power-holding individuals of poor judgment, bad morals, a lack of regard for the law, an affinity for purchasing extremely expensive instantly obsolete weapons systems, a penchant for involving themselves in highly embarrassing public sexual escapades with interns and press secretaries, and a thundering lack of interest in the well-being of the normal people they are supposed to be working on behalf of. Let's imagine that everybody starts to get seriously annoyed about this, until all that's really required for women to take over is a nudge. Let's imagine that the mind-set of a fresh young millennium, and a combination of the above disasters and annoyances, provide the nudge. And if you want a longer version, you can read the novel *Dryland's End,* which chronicles in exhaustive detail how women come to power, but I warn you that it is BO-RING and, on top of that, has a sad ending.

So why don't we do it my way and just say that here we are, and women are in charge of a fine, upstanding, democratic, justice-and-equality-oriented, security-minded, peace-seeking social order, which they call the New Order, and are striving to erase all signs of what came before, which they call AR, which stands for ancien régime and shows how erudite they are.

Now, it's not that easy to set up a new order. There is much to do, just to keep things running and to prevent a backlash. And you've got to change everything: the schools and the toys, the books and the language, the television programs . . . everything. The rules. The world. The women. The men.

Now, some of you may be familiar with men, and may have an opinion on how easy that last part of the enterprise is likely to be, and just how enthusiastically we should expect men to go along with a program designed to trim their sails, rinse the starch out of their shirts, renovate, domesticate, demystify, democratize, and overall improve them. I mean, yes, it's a full-fledged government program, but is it that different from what women have been trying to accomplish for centuries on the more modest scale of home-grown cottage industry? I'm skeptical. But let's wait and see. Maybe they'll surprise us.

Lisa is a child when the Revolution happens, and now she is twenty-three. The New Order has put down some roots, laid some groundwork, but it is still young, still in its fragile, uncertain beginning.

Everyone has a task, and here is Lisa's: she is supposed to start updating women's sexual fantasies. Most of these fantasies are bad, bad, bad for you! They are either sickly-sweet and romantic, making women simper their lives away over some stupid notion of love, or, worse, masochistic-misogynist, filled with self-hate. This kind of stuff just has to go.

Yes, centuries of exploitation and oppression, of pornography and prostitution, of discrimination and intimidation, have left their mark everywhere, resulting in an incredible amount of garbage for the new regime to shovel away. Lawyers and psychologists and soci-ologists and artists and media specialists and musicians are all hero-ically erasing the perfidious remnants wherever they are to be found, rewriting books, redrafting rules, designing behavior modi-fication programs and curricula and exercises. This is a massive Cultural Revolution, after all; it is not enough to focus on the exter-nals. All aspects of behavior and thought have to be reexamined and revamped.

Lisa is a little cog, a tiny dedicated little cog in the machinery cranking out the bits, parts, and pieces of a brave new world. When she applied for her work-study assignment and got accepted by the Ministry of Thought, she was deeply honored and very excited, of course, but she had no idea which exact project she would be working on. Specifically, she is to collect material for a program to "eradicate women's romantic and masochistic fantasies and replace them with more appropriate images."

"More appropriate," that's what it says in the goal statement and that's all Lisa has to go by. It certainly sounds worthwhile, no doubt about it, but at the same time it seems a little slender. What *is* "more appropriate"?

The most difficult part of her assignment is that she feels so alone with it. Eventually, no doubt, once they've cleared their schedules of the more pressing, existential matters of social reorganization, psychologists and psychoanalysts and educators and media experts and all sorts of brilliant people will devote their important minds to this, but it's her database they'll be drawing on, her survey they'll use, and the weight of that solemn responsibility rests heavily on Lisa's shoulders.

There is a monthly meeting, but Lisa would feel stupid confessing her lack of direction to such a large forum. There are morning meetings in her branch office, chaired by Nadine, but nobody else in that office is part of her particular endeavor, and the meetings in any case are devoted to manifold administrative matters and rarely touch on substance.

Lisa's titular supervisor, the brilliant but distant Dr. Mazzini, works in another building and is rarely seen. Even when she is, she moves about within a rarefied aura of distraction. Tiny and slender, with one sternly chic braid down to her shoulder blades, no makeup, severe clothing in expensive Italian fabrics, a military bearing, and a constant worried frown, she seems somehow electrified; you worry about wasting her time, and getting shocked for it. You worry that if you were to accidentally bump into her, in the hallway, she would give off little sprinkles of IQ like dust or pollen; or like dandruff.

On those few occasions when Lisa got up enough nerve to approach her with a question, she was rewarded with an abstracted glance, a glance that missed Lisa entirely and veered off into outer or probably inner space, and a reply that sounded like something out of Luce Irigaray, whose texts Lisa remembers sweating over in her women's philosophy seminar. Or, worse, something from Hélène Cixous. There is little concrete assistance to be expected here. At most she will receive an Italian rebuke and feel yet more stupid.

Her own morning committee, to whom she finally confesses her problem, initially responds to her plea in a disappointing fashion.

What is "more appropriate" sexual imagery?

"It's got to turn you on but not be sick," Rebecca explains, speaking slowly, as though it were obvious, as though Lisa were an idiot. "*You* know." As she is sitting next to Lisa, she completes her contribution by nudging Lisa in the ribs with her elbow and winking encouragingly.

Nadine frowns disapprovingly at this distasteful display and offers her own guidance instead: "You vill consult ze data. Ze material vill speak. You vill be thorough in your research and you vill find ze proper dirrektschun. Good, useful, and strengthening fantasies to take ze place of ellienaschun," she goes on, alarming the others with this uncharacteristically rhapsodic display, and leaving Lisa with a somewhat scary image of an ecstatic female Hun throwing off her breastplate and taking a deep breath of frosty Alpine air before leaping gymnastically onto someone named Lars.

The image is rudely interrupted by Eva, simpering out a sweet little rebuke. "You're being too linear, Lisa, that's masculine," she whispers. "I worry that your whole approach is completely wrong." Such a dear little voice, just the kind of dear little voice Lisa remembers as the bane of her childhood, the voice of girls who detest you and are planning to do something horrible to you. Eva smiles a comradely, helpful smile, and her voice is ever so soft and sisterly, and Lisa simply hates her.

Yes, Lisa hates Eva, first because she has always hated sweet-voiced back-stabbing femininity of that sort, and second because Eva is invariably on the opposite side of any issue and debate. And Eva isn't even her real name. The world is suddenly full of Evas: you can change your name if you want to, and Eva is a popular choice. Most of the new Evas had names like Henrietta or Alexandra or Roberta or Charlene before, names that show you were supposed to be a boy, but in this particular Eva's case, Lisa has reason to believe that her name used to be Tiffany.

But after this initially disappointing response, the committee rallies to Lisa's aid. They will help her, of course they will. Rebecca, the computer person, prepares to send out all-points bulletins to peripheral agencies, universities, institutes, and other possible sources of intellectual support. Nadine promises to assign Lisa her own personal assistant, who is to fetch and carry and scan and copy and do anything else that may ease her burden. And Lisa is to remember that hers is a pioneering work. They are sending her into the wilderness! She is exploring new frontiers! She should not expect too much of herself. She is merely to blaze the trail and plant the initial guideposts. Others will follow.

I'm not sure I would have chosen Lisa's particular nook and cranny of the New Order. It's an interesting place to work, but chilly, and very cerebral. If the New Order were a kitchen, which it definitely isn't, but if it were, then Lisa's office would be the refrigerator, or maybe the sanitized disinfected stainless steel work surface. If it were a hospital, it would be the operating room, or maybe the morgue. If it were an amusement park, it would be the dingy little room where the cables connect and the switches run—well, you get the idea. The ideologues, technocrats, and politicians run the show here, with only the barest nod to all that female spirit running lush and rampant everywhere else. Elsewhere things are warm and fuzzy, and getting warmer and fuzzier by the hour, but in the offices of the New Government there's work to do. It's Rosie the Riveter. The office they assign you to might be more spacious and more gracious than before, but they still expect you to store your heart in a cubicle.

When Lisa's friends talk about their workplaces, she is sometimes beset by doubts and envy. On the other hand, it's undeniably thrilling to feel the heartbeat, to breathe the air, to walk the halls of power. I mean, Ministry of Thought . . . how cool is that?

Yes, Lisa is a fortunate young woman. She lives in an attractive new apartment building equipped with all the modern amenities. The Ministry pays her a good salary, and in all likelihood will hire her permanently once she graduates. She owns nice things. She has friends. She travels to work on a public transportation system that is clean, uncrowded, and free—no, it's better than free, she gets paid to use it, as an ecological incentive. Her children, should she one day have them, will blossom in luxuriously endowed, lovingly staffed facilities. She'll never have to do laundry, she'll never have to lug groceries, she doesn't have to cook, except as a relaxing hobby. Little vans do it all—take her dirty things and bring them back ironed, folded, and fragrant with her choice of herbal sachet, deliver groceries, rush her any sort of meal she could want. Should she feel ill, health care of all varieties will be urged upon her— holistic, traditional, homeopathic, Ayurvedic, with a week at the spa thrown in to regenerate her.

There's money for all sorts of good stuff, all of a sudden. There is tons of it, an ocean of it, enough for any social program you can dream up. The government is swimming in it, my dear, and do you know what? It always has been. Amazing, how much money they used to spend, without you or me getting any pleasure out of it.

Bills, taxes, that kind of nasty stuff still exists, but you barely have to deal with it. Your personal finance counselor pays your bills, she oversees your investments, and she talks to your boss in no uncertain terms to demand that raise for you, because she knows how hard you work, honey, and you shouldn't have to trouble your- self with aggravating things like that on top of all of your other responsibilities! It's like having a cross between your mother, Lara Croft, and J. P. Morgan managing your financial life.

And if all those benefits and luxuries aren't enough to make her happy, Lisa's also got love to keep her warm. Love in the shape of Brett, who would formerly have been termed her boyfriend but now is known less coyly, more maturely as her Significant Relation- ship, SR.

At age thirty-four, he is markedly older than Lisa. Still, he's a suitable partner for a new woman; in fact, he's quite a catch. When the Revolution hit, Brett was a young psychologist working with men's groups, and the author of a popular book, *Suffering in Silence: Understanding the Pain of That Man Who Won't Talk to You*. Revolutions don't scare someone as flexible as that. Brett barely missed a beat, and is now an acclaimed lecturer and educator on the Reshaping of Masculinity.

And he's not bad-looking, either. Yes, he has a great number of attractive features, each and every one of which he is acutely aware of.

Does Brett love Lisa? Maybe, in his own way. Anyway, unless you're her mother, it's a bit too soon to seriously love Lisa— she's not herself yet, whereas Brett, frankly, is as much as he'll ever be.

Does Lisa love Brett? Well, she didn't mean to. What she visualized was a sort of heroic partnership; a passionate couple doing Important Works together. And that could still happen. Things could still work out.

Well, not according to her counselor. According to her counselor, Lisa needs to commit herself to serious work on her "archaic symbiosis fantasies" and start doing her "individuation exercises" every day so she can begin "phasing out of" the "dependency relationship" with her current "autonomy surrogate" in order, after a healthy interlude alone, to start looking for that "equivalent growth partner," male or female, who will "more appropriately integrate" with her "psychodynamic boundaries."

In other words, she's supposed to break up with Brett pronto. Which is why Lisa hasn't been to see her counselor for almost two months.

But, ladies, if all we were planning to do was obsess over our romantic attachments, we didn't need to have a Revolution. No, relationships are merely one component of a productive life, and a secondary one at that. Lisa knows this, and she takes it to heart. Anyway, what with her work, her classes, her improv theater group, her Womanpower-Girlpower Transgenerational Neighborhood Sports team, her Holistic Health Imaging appointments, her mentoring, her meditation, her mediation, her bionutrition consultations, her social service, and, of course, her bonding sessions with neighbors and with co-workers, Lisa is a very busy young woman who has no time to mope.

Well, very little.

And here she comes right now, just entering her office. She checks the ergo-display on her way in, to make sure it was properly reset after Lammas, the August holiday; there have been problems lately, and there's nothing worse than being blasted with the wrong mood-inducers. Like that morning last week when nobody could properly get going, just couldn't shake off the lethargy, and it turned out that, after a horribly contentious interoffice meeting the day before that had called for radical affect deescalation measures, all the diffusers had accidentally been left on Stress Reduction mode and were lulling everyone with soporific blasts of clary sage and lavender, instead of perking them up with citrus and spearmint. But no, things seem to be in good order this morning. Her thermostat, her humidifier, her personal diffuser, and her white-noise levels are all set to her morning preferences, and she's ready for a productive day.

Lisa has just spent a week in Visual Records, fast-forwarding through their stored porn movie discs. That was pretty dull. Mostly, you saw a lot of women arching their backs and playing with their own nipples while running their tongues slowly around their lips, over and over again. Watching them made Lisa's lips so dry that she went through three ChapStick tubes in just the one week. The only real excitement came from importantly signing for the restricted materials, and having them handed over by solemn librarians. But she hadn't expected to get any real insights here, anyway. She knew that women never went for those kinds of visual stimulants, but thought she'd better have a look, just to gain an understanding of AR erotics.

After that she wasted another full week in Archives, plowing through piles of musty paperbacks featuring stern headmistresses, stepmothers with canes, sulky sultry pupils, and cotton underwear referred to as knickers. Well, nobody's interested in that sort of thing anymore; might as well read the Rosetta Stone.

For her next step, she's decided to concentrate on fundamental texts. Build on the classics, and you can't go wrong.

For starters, Lisa has selected *Story of O* and *Nothing Natural*. She chose these books because they are classics in the genre of erotic literature, because the authors are women, and because they're said to be "upscale."

This latter criterion, a bow to her own squeamishness, is one that Lisa has already come to regret. All it seems to mean is that, besides slogging through the same lot of bizarre bondage she would find elsewhere, she must also suffer through many painful paragraphs of abstruse philosophizing. Her copy of *Story of O* even has a foreword by Georges Bataille, full of all sorts of French leftist psychobabble, but she's not going to read it. Twenty pages into *Story of O,* she decides she isn't going to read *that,* either, it's just too stupid. She decides that Pauline de Réage is a nom de plume, and that Georges Bataille probably wrote the whole damn thing. She decides that instead of reading it, she is going to use her copy of *Story of O* as her official tranquilizer; whenever she feels tense, she will throw it at the wall.

Quickly, so the day won't be a total loss, she turns to her next book, the Jenny Diski. At least it seems to have an actual story. Well, that's an improvement. She skims her way through the plot. Girl meets boy at dinner party. Girl—Rachel—is a divorced schoolteacher, sexually adventurous and unconventional. Boy—Joshua— is a youngish businessman with a provocative sort of charm, though he is "not all that attractive." A woman friend, who introduces them, has previously described him to Rachel as "strange, odd, someone who messes people up." On the basis of this commendation, Rachel decides to pick him up. (Lisa frowns disapprovingly, but then recalls her college psychology seminar where they learned that dangerous men used to be attractive to women, in those sad old days. Feeling scholarly, she writes "DIM" in the margin of the book, DIM for "disturbed image of men.")

Okay. Rachel is still at the dinner party. She unambiguously comes on to Joshua during dessert and then takes him home, where, as they chat and get to know each other, he indicates that he has an ever so genteel, you know, fondness for a bit of sedate S and M, nothing extreme.

Which is fine with Rachel, who confides that her fantasies circle around "oh, the usual rape and violence stuff."

With so much in common, Rachel and Joshua begin their relationship. It will consist of occasional assignations, short intellectual conversations, and demeaning sexual scenarios designed by Joshua, and played out in Rachel's apartment around the dinner hour.

. . . She beat oil and vinegar together to make a vinaigrette . . . Joshua got up and moved toward the kitchen . . . Joshua's wrist lifted the weight of the skirt as his fingers stroked the inside of her bare thigh and moved up to feel her crotch. Rachel worked on the already well-amalgamated dressing . . . Joshua said, "Bend over the table." His voice was calm but firm, he was giving an order . . . Suddenly he began to smack her, short, sharp slaps, pausing for a second between each. Six, eight smacks, hard enough to make her draw in her breath.

Frowning, Lisa flips the book over, and feels enlightened to discover that the author is a Brit. Of course. Brits had that whole spanking thing going, she remembers, it's a known fact; something to do with their boarding schools and the bad weather. Also the way Rachel doesn't mind that Joshua hits her, but is miffed because she thinks they should have eaten their dinner first, and is annoyed with him for causing the roast to char . . . that's very proper and very English. And probably you're supposed to keep your pinkie extended when you smack people, Lisa conjectures wryly.

Cultural insights in place, she whizzes through the first few chapters, then begins to turn the pages more apprehensively, because she can sense what's coming next. No, not the whips and belts, she's resigned to those. What she dreads is the Deep Underlying Philosophy. The New Order's fondness for acronyms is in her blood, so she calls it the DUP.

Joshua, the DUP informs us, had an "ogre" of a mother and was sent to boarding school at age four, which broke his little heart and turned him nasty. Rachel, meanwhile, suffered a series of abandonments until she was finally adopted at the advanced age of twelve, and has been trapped in a series of destructive love affairs with cruel men ever since, because she is desperately trying to get a mean daddy to finally love her.

But then, as she makes her way dispiritedly forward, the plot takes a sudden turn. Rachel, reading the newspaper one day, comes across the account of a rapist who has just attacked a young girl in Scotland. There's a police sketch of him, based on the victim's descriptions. And the sketch looks exactly like Joshua. And it just so happens that Joshua is vacationing in Scotland at this very moment. Can it be? Can Joshua, tired of mere games, be branching out into genuine assaults? On children?

Rachel is disturbed, but decides not to think further about it. Joshua returns from his holiday. Things go on as before.

But then. All the weird stuff begins to take its toll on Rachel, who anyway suffers from depression, and she falls into a deep gloom. Joshua deigns to hand-hold her through one particularly critical night, but after a short while his empathy is exhausted and he leaves, though not before pleasing himself one final time with the suicidal, semicomatose woman.

Rachel emerges alive from this pills-and-booze, doom-and-gloom night, to realize that she is angry. Very angry. Because Joshua's conduct proved to her that incredibly, even after three whole years of unfeeling, arbitrary, sick sex, he still doesn't love her. And in a blinding moment of insight she realizes that she wants him to. She *thought* she wanted eccentric thrills and humiliation, but now she realizes that she has actually been searching for TRUE LOVE.

Joshua laughs that off. Tough luck, kiddo. They had a deal, and he never promised her anything more. Still, he can see that Rachel is upset, and wants to cheer his playmate up. She thinks he's being too bossy? She thinks all the rules are his? Not so, and in order to prove to her just how equitable and fair-minded he really is, he invites her to script their next rendezvous. She can design the interlude to suit herself and he will comply.

So she tells him that she wants him to come as a burglar. She wants him to sneak in the back door, just before midnight. He is to fall upon her as she sleeps, then tie her up and have his way with her.

Joshua listens attentively. He doesn't say anything, but she can see that he likes the scenario, that, in fact, he is hooked. So the very next day, she visits her friendly neighborhood police station and reports that someone is stalking her. A strange man is staking out her house, and she is ever so frightened!

The police are sympathetic. They promise to keep an eye out for her on their neighborhood patrols.

On the appointed evening, Joshua breaks in, tippytoes into the bedroom without any clothes on, tippytoes over to Rachel, ties her up, and BOOM! In come the police, and he is UNDER ARREST!

And when they book him, they will discover that he is the rapist of the Scottish moor, and lock him up and throw away the key.

THE END.

Lisa puts the book down thoughtfully. Okay, the guy gets it in the end, but otherwise Lisa cannot say that she is pleased with this piece of literature. She leans back in her chair. Joshua never pretended to be anything he wasn't; Rachel liked him *because* he was a pervert. But then she discovered that what she really wanted wasn't, as she had thought, the thrills, the handcuffs, the leather whatnots, but a Relationship. A Commitment. True Love. Lisa sighs. So the message would be: no matter what it might look like, all women are ruled by their emotions, love-starved, monogamous? And if the men won't commit, the women get nasty and take a sneaky devious revenge?

She studies the back cover again. "Jenny Diski was born in London, attended University College and then did two years toward an advanced degree but dropped out and wrote *Nothing Natural* instead," she reads. That's all it says, no pets, no children, no steady job, no fleshed-out life with verifiable details, and would any adult woman actually call herself Jenny?

Lisa takes herself sternly to task. No. Surely there once lived a real Jenny Diski, a real woman who really wrote this book. This won't do. She can't go on jauntily dismissing one book after the other, concluding that they were secretly written by men passing themselves off as women, like so many reverse George Sands. No, she is going to have to take these books at face value. She will just have to believe that women, in fact, authored these volumes, and that these contents represent their fantasies.

Or perhaps one could read it as a socialist parable? The workers signed a contract, true, but it was an unfair contract, based on their desperation, their ignorance and powerlessness. But then they rise up, and the greedy capitalists are trodden underfoot. Lisa mulls this over. Okay, so then Joshua, representing patriarchy, is ultimately overthrown by Rachel, representing oppressed women, and their prior fling represents false consciousness . . .

But why is she bothering to interpret? She's not writing a term paper. She is supposed to find material for fantasies. And what might those be? Joshua and Rachel on the kitchen counter while the roast burns? The burglar, breaking in? The lover, dressed—well, undressed—as the burglar, being hauled away by the police?

Lisa conjures up these images in turn and forces herself to hold each one to a count of twenty, to see if anything appeals. A burglar, perhaps? Burglaries are so rare these days that it's hard for Lisa even to imagine such a person. Burglars—weren't they men from undesirable social backgrounds, often addicted to drugs, riddled with mental and physical illness, armed with lethal weapons? How would it be thrilling to get assaulted by such an individual?

But no, she's looking at this the wrong way. Joshua wasn't a real burglar; Rachel was just playing a game with him. Okay, try that on for size. Let's say Brett were to dress up as a burglar, on a prearranged night, for the novelty. Would that be stimulating?

Lisa tries to visualize this scenario but gets entangled in the logistics. It would be really tough to organize. First she'd have to talk Brett into it—Mr. Equity, Let'sdiscussit, Isthisasgoodforyou-asitisforme Brett. That won't be easy, but let's assume he could be persuaded, in the interest of science and research. Then next you'd have to get Circumference Security to go along with it, so you would somehow have to explain to them that you wanted your Significant Relationship to come shimmying through the window armed with a rope, and they shouldn't detain him, please. Well, this is a conversation that Lisa simply cannot imagine having, ouch. But okay, she reprimands herself, don't be so literal, it's a fantasy, so assume that it could be worked out.

Lisa closes her eyes. She imagines herself in her bed, imagines Brett climbing through the window, in a stocking mask, under the indulgent gaze of a forewarned Video Surveillance . . . Collapsing with giggles, Lisa chides herself. Come on now, give this a serious chance. Pressing her eyes shut again, more firmly, she wills herself into the story. He's lean, he's mean, he's silent, he leaps through the window dressed all in black. She is asleep, pretending to be asleep. Silently removing his clothes, Brett creeps over to her bed and grabs her wrists, his famous empathetic lecturer's voice reduced to a menacing growl as he ties her up . . . She laughs. Okay, forget that one.

Lisa scrunches her eyes closed, determined to make progress. What about the kitchen scene, then? She's in the kitchen, she's throwing together a salad dressing, Brett comes up behind her. Of course, the scene needs to be modified; obviously he can't hit her, that's out of the question. He wouldn't do it anyway, nor would she recommend that he try it, not unless he wants to spend the rest of the evening combing vinaigrette out of his hair.

But what about the setting? There wouldn't be a roast in her oven, of course, how disgusting!—but let's say a vegetable lasagna. It's in the oven, she and Brett get carried away. Let's see. If you leaned forward against the counter, like Rachel, wouldn't the edge dig into your rib cage? Or if you bent backward, your vertebrae?

Nor could you lie down on top of it, it's too high and too narrow, not to mention hard, cold, and slippery. Plus, the time Lisa burned that vegetable casserole, the stench was overpowering, and she and Brett spent an hour scraping charred bits of broccoli from the sides of the oven . . . But what if they leaned up against a wall? They're in the kitchen, they start to kiss, they clutch, they are overcome, no time to seek out horizontal quarters. The food is in the oven, but they don't care, the bedroom is right next door, but that's too far. They grab, they cling, they find frantic support against the kitchen wall. Giving herself up to the fantasy, Lisa feels the heat, she feels the kiss, she feels the wall. She feels her hipbones and the back of her skull banging against the wall while Brett scrambles for rhythm and balance and oily, acrid black smoke curls from her grill . . . It's no good. Unable to detach her brain from culinary and other details, Lisa shakes her head. It's just no good.

She sighs. She rests her head in her hands, massaging her temples with two fingers.

"Are you okay?" a concerned voice asks. Startled, Lisa opens her eyes. A young man is hovering uncertainly in her doorway.

"Oh," she says. "Yes, I'm fine, thank you." She looks at him inquiringly.

"My name is Justin," he says. "I'm here about the job, on the project? As your assistant? I don't know much about it," he goes on when she still doesn't say anything. "The CC office sent me here. They said you needed somebody with a background in literature? And I can do programs, too."

Justin is getting a little nervous. Why doesn't she say something? Of all the positions currently offered at the Consciousness Center, this sounded like the most interesting. They told him the job has something or the other to do with literature and psychology, and both of those fields intrigue him. He wants this job. In order to get it, he plans to apply the strategy that has served him well during the prior steps of his reeducation process: go with the flow, keep your cool, and don't ask too many questions.

This Lisa woman, his potential boss, seems okay. She appears to have a headache or something, and she's not real talkative, but she doesn't seem hostile or unfriendly and he likes the way her frizzy brown hair, which she has gathered into a tight ponytail, bushes up kind of horizontally behind her, against gravity. You're not supposed to judge people by their appearance, especially not women, he knows, but hair is androgynous, so he figures his thoughts are okay.

The owner of the coiffure in question is still not speaking. She is thinking. When Nadine promised her an assistant, she didn't say that she meant to assign her a re-ed. Isn't that too much of a responsibility? What might she be getting into? She studies Justin covertly. He looks all right. He is tall, lanky but graceful, dressed conservatively but well. His face is open, unguarded. He appears somewhat anxious but cooperative. What should she do? Will the guy be helpful, or is he just one more headache?

Lisa has an idea. "Read this," she says, reaching into her desk drawer and handing him *Story of O.* "You can take your time. I'll be here all day."

Appearing a little surprised to be faced with a test, Justin accepts the book without looking at its cover.

"The office right next door is vacant today," Lisa says. "You can sit there."

At four-thirty he reappears in her doorway. "Done," he says.

"And?" Lisa inquires.

"Not bad," he says.

Lisa keeps her face impassive. Let him dig his own grave, fine. "Oh?" she says, without apparent interest.

"I only found three misprints," he offers. "I put slips between those pages, and I circled the misprinted words in pencil and put checkmarks in the margin."

Lisa still doesn't say anything. She is trying to decide whether he is putting her on. Can that be his only comment? Lisa, whose teeth began clenching and whose heart began palpitating with rage before she even got to page 20, finds his detachment barely credible. Can he possibly—in the face of this sick AR fantasy of compliant women delivered half-naked by taxi to become the abused sex toys of a bunch of arrogant sadistic men, in the face of a forbidden document immeasurably more explicit than anything her applicant could, in his sheltered postrevolutionary young life thus far, ever have encountered—have thought he was merely supposed to exhibit his skills as a human spell check device?

His face, earnestly turned to hers, appears devoid of either guile or black humor. Lisa toys with the idea of asking him some substantive questions about the book, just to trip him up, but then she goes with the moment. "Excellent job, Justin," she says. "Can you start tomorrow?"

The Nazi is ranting. This occasions amusement among her subordinates who, in heavy German accents, mock Nadine and her work ethic behind her back. Ve must vork harder! Feminism does not mean slautsching! If you vant to sit on ze fat behind and somebody support you, you are in ze rrrrong decade!

Nadine wants to see results! She wants to see some action here. She wants to see that consciousness, rising.

Lisa, who is engaged in a mammoth task, is treated with greater lenience. "You must be surrow in ze research," Nadine admits, frowning over the slender results of Lisa's project.

Her goodwill extends to Justin, too. She calls him "Lisa's little azubi," which Lisa at first thinks is a kind of Japanese bean but which she has since learned is some sort of obnoxious German acronym for a white-collar apprentice. The first time Nadine uses this term, Lisa loses half a valuable working hour trying to clear the Japanese bean out of her head. What the hell *is* it called? Wasabi? No, that's the mustard. Azuki, that's it, that's the bean. Azuki. Of course.

Assistant or condiment, Justin is settling in nicely. He's starting to relax a little and be himself. The assignment strikes him as weird and unnecessarily complicated. In his humble opinion, any project about sex that causes you as many headaches as this one is causing

Lisa has to be way off track. And why work so hard at it, anyway? They're in charge now, aren't they? They should simply dump out whatever offends them and enjoy the rest. But his is not to reason why, hopefully they know what they're doing, and as for him, he keeps himself motivated with a little project of his own.

Justin is trying to disprove a bit of lore about women, which is that they have no sense of humor. His teachers and mentors have repeatedly warned him that the line between acceptably funny and horrendously offensive is not just thin but, to all intents and purposes, completely invisible to the male eye, but Justin doesn't believe them. He thinks that women probably do have a sense of humor, just one previously uncharted by men. He amuses himself by thinking of it as a scientific endeavor, as a principle. "If there's gravity, there has to be levity" is his hypothesis. He is using Lisa as his gauge, and the study is going well so far. He hasn't stepped on any land mines yet. Sometimes she looks startled, but in the end, so far, he's always gotten her to laugh.

Lisa, while unaware that she is the subject of an experiment, is satisfied with her new assistant. It's a lot more companionable to work with someone else, and Justin is turning out to be an excellent teammate. Plus, there is much enjoyment to be gotten out of really bad writing when you have a partner to spoof it with. The bad news is that they are turning up zip. One trail after the other dissolves in puffs of ridicule, one book after the other proves to be rich in material for Justin's satiric monologues but poor in erotic content.

So I should tell you a little bit more about Justin. He's a re-ed, as I mentioned, which means that he is completing his social reeducation program in preparation for attaining full citizenship in the brave new world so recently established. Everyone has to complete such a program. There is no discrimination here, although of course women need an entirely different course of mental restructuring than men do. Women's courses are divided into four components, mental, physical, social, and political, and it's very complicated: depending on your ideological affiliation you can certify yourself in very different ways. There is a much higher degree of standardization in the men's program, since men fall into only two schools of thought regarding the New Order: for, or against, and against is illegal.

Justin needs five certificates. He has four already. He has passed successfully through the course for Self-Reliance Skills, which means that he can cook, at least theoretically keep a toddler alive for seventy-two hours, and do many of the things girl scouts used to win merit badges for in the bad old days. He has completed his Violence Aversion Training, and will probably throw up if shown a video clip of soldiers storming a beach and have an asthma attack when viewing a rape scene. He has undergone Biographic Enrichment to realize how shortchanged he was by his gender-stereotyped upbringing and to get in touch with the unhappiness of his parents with their enforced gender roles. Lastly, he has attended Contemporary Interaction School, where he learned what to say and do and what to avoid in his future dealings with ethnic minorities, the handicapped, women, youth, the aged, persons with sexual orientations different from his (mind your own business), and red meat (don't eat it).

Only one hurdle or, as the architects of the reeducation program prefer to see it, one enrichment opportunity remains, and Justin will be a certified and attested, accredited male citizen of the New Order. He will be able to rent his own apartment and leave the ridiculous dormitory where he now resides. He will be able to get a real job. Women will consider going out with, maybe living with, eventually reproducing with him. All he needs is this final credit, showing that he has constructively contributed to a better society. If he acquits himself well, this should only take nine months. Everything takes nine months nowadays, and it behooves Justin not to roll his eyes at this, lest he find himself flunking his Awareness Review.

Justin lives in a place called the Residential Suites, a fancy name for what is really a cross between a college dorm and a halfway house. Every resident has completed at least two evaluations. Everyone has his own bedroom and living room, but kitchens and bathrooms are shared by six units. No woman ever enters the premises, ever. Approaching the issue from very different angles, the Men's Bureau and the Ministry of Gender Affairs in rare unison came up with this inflexible rule, though for different reasons.

The ideologues believe that these men, having completed their course in self-reliance skills, deserve a period of time to practice the domestic arts, without women busily interfering, without counterrevolutionary habits leading women to take over most of the domestic chores and men to cede them. Here, among themselves, equipped with new skills and knowledge, men together will happily and efficiently keep house, they believe.

The pragmatists believe no such thing. They believe that men, slothful by nature and scarcely touched by a few resentfully completed home economics courses, will quickly revert to filth and inertia. Their residence will be disgusting, so disgusting that they will long to leave it and live with women again; this, they think, will motivate men for the rest of their reeducation.

As a casual glance would immediately inform you, the pragmatists were right; they usually are. Justin's housemates have not been transformed into skilled homemakers. Justin, who has a fastidious streak, keeps his rooms clean and organized, but the communal kitchen! Worse yet, the shared bath! There is mold between the tiles, and a scummy brew of toothpaste, soap, and hair bastes the edges of the sink, tub, and shower. In the interest of keeping our lunch down, we will not even discuss the condition of the toilet.

The contribution of most of Justin's housemates to collective housekeeping is restricted to oral reprimands, usually obscene in nature, of everyone else. Who left the goddamn towels on the floor! All right, which asshole took the last frigging beer!

Justin is not a happy resident of the Residential Suites. His motivation to leave is very, very good.

Even as you read these lines, Justin's domestic discomfort is about to be increased greatly by the introduction of Mac. A few months ago, the dormitory inhabitants were subjected to yet another psychological screening, this time to determine their "nurturing competency." At the time, it seemed like just one more of those tests their counselors were so fond of, but it seems this one had a practical purpose. It was designed to determine the kind of "dependent living thing" upon which the men will be given the opportunity to exercise and expand their care-giving skills. "For centuries, little girls honed their maternal skills through play, with dolls and nurturing games," the counselor explains in the house meeting. Men are very disadvantaged in regard to their parenting skills! In compensation, they are all going to take their first little step into modern fatherhood! Everyone is to receive a pet.

Justin is discouraged to hear this. He remembers reading that the Nazis used to issue pets to their concentration camp guards— cute little puppies. The guards fed, played with, and grew fond of these adorable, trusting little animals; then, one day, they were ordered to cut their throats. The purpose of the exercise: to kill their capacity for sentimental attachment. Justin finds the analogy depressing, even if this current exercise ostentatiously has the opposite intent. The men are to be given something small and alive to care for, in order to stimulate their fatherly qualities. The test was to make sure that no one will be stressed beyond his capacities, but will be matched with an appropriate creature. Hugo, for instance, the taciturn, short-tempered guy on the first floor, has been teamed up with a hermit crab, which makes no noise, requires little care, and is practically impossible to kill. Some receive fish, or a bird.

Justin has done really well on his test. The counselor dispensing the results grants him a special, benevolent smile as she informs him of his score. Yes, Justin has attained the most responsible outcome possible on this test: consequently, he has been allotted a dog. Since he lives in an apartment building, it is to be a small dog.

"Small," the sociologist says, adding chattily, "but not silly." She smiles at him conspiratorially. "Not a poodle. I picked out something very masculine for you!" Then she signals her assistant, a large fellow in a veterinarian's jacket who disappears briefly into the next room and emerges with a small carrier from which he lifts Justin's new roommate. The dog is indeed small, small and fat, and belongs to one of those enormously ugly, wrinkly breeds who look as if they have accidentally been issued twice as much skin as their body warrants; who look as if they have been first stepped on with a boot until their little legs collapsed into their bellies, then stretched lengthwise, and finally stuck in a compressor, face first. The animal, in a word, is hideous.

Justin looks at the dog and then at the counselor. He suspects her of mocking him, but no, she is practically exploding with condescending benevolence. He can read her thoughts on her face, each and every patronizing one of them, as clear as day. She thinks she knows all about the atavistic male ego; she is determined not to offend him with a "cute" pet; she thinks he will feel more at ease with something ugly; as in the old nursery rhyme, she is mentally pairing him with frogs and snails and puppy-dog tails to put him at his ease and accommodate his nasty male nature.

"He's called Mac, and I know you're going to take wonderful care of him," she adds encouragingly.

Mac growls.

Mac and Justin hate each other on first sight. Justin doesn't want a dog to begin with. If he has to have a pet, a fish would be okay; he could live with a parakeet, but what he really wants is a cat. Since the tester seems so friendly, he asks if he can have a cat instead of Mac. But cats, it seems, are not part of the project. A little taken aback by his request, the tester explains why not. Cats, it seems, are too independent. "You can't learn nurturing with a cat," she confides. "There just isn't enough direct interdependent affect," she explains, adding, in case that went above his head, "A cat doesn't show that it needs you. You won't experience emotional growth. I think you'll *like* having a dog, once you try it."

And right about now, some of you are starting to disapprove, aren't you. How evil, you're thinking. Those women are so mean! So manipulative and condescending, making nice people like Justin live in dormitories while they have enlightenment shoved down their throats. And I say: Get over it! Did you pay any attention at all during history class? What were you doing, filling looseleaf pages with manic loopy scrawled fantasy signatures showing what your new name would be, if you could get your dopey high school boyfriend to marry you? Allow me to brief you on Revolutions 101: what we have here is the genteel, fastidious parlor version. These women are being extremely civilized and this revolution is very nice.

Most revolutions start with a bloodbath. The mob takes to the streets, slaughtering, lopping off heads, locking people into dungeons, chasing them into churches and setting them on fire, placing their heads on stakes, constructing towers out of their skulls. Then comes the neighborhood cleanup, during which you can denounce anyone you don't like and see them dragged to the guillotine. Whoever makes it through that part should take a deep breath, because here comes the Cultural Revolution! Time to stand you up in front of lots of people and humiliate you. Time to rewrite history, burn some libraries, ban some books, destroy some major artwork, search your home in the middle of the night, and train your children to spy on you.

You're thinking that these women are mean? Check out the French Revolution, the Chinese Revolution, the Iranian Revolution, and then we'll talk. This is nothing. I say Justin should take his ugly new dog home and be thankful.

Lisa doesn't have a dog, though she might be better off with one. Dogs are loyal, they say.

It's nine o'clock at night. Brett was supposed to come over right after work, but he is two hours late. He must have been detained, his seminar must be running late. Lisa decides to leave a message for him, but when she calls his home, he is there.

"Oh, you're there!" she exclaims, surprised. "I thought you were coming over."

Appearing before her on the compuscreen, he looks a little disheveled. Was he asleep?

"Oh, hello, darling," he says. "I was going to call you. That's right, I was planning to stop over, but something came up."

As he speaks, Lisa can see the Something in the left corner of the screen, sashaying across Brett's living room. The Something is slim, incompletely dressed, and definitely female.

"Oh," Lisa says, "you have company." She's satisfied with her choice of words, but not with her voice, which has come out kind of squeaky and sad and pitiful. Damn, she thought she had gotten over that.

Brett's voice, by contrast, is relaxed and factual. "Yes, I do," he replies. "That's Sylvia. Sylvia and I are coordinating the next seminar, and as we were preparing today, we kept getting distracted by these powerful physical vibrations between us, so we thought we should get that resolved tonight before it starts getting in the way of our work."

"Oh, right," Lisa says. "Sure, I see. Well, then."

In the past, this would not have been Lisa's response. She does not like to remember how she acted, in the early days of their relationship. A sarcastic comment about powerful vibrations and what he can do with them would have been the least of it. Such a response, as she has learned, is unwise. It will get her one of Brett's famous, acclaimed lectures, free of charge and just for her. In a compassionate voice, he will examine her complaint, tracing it back to an outdated—but deep-seated! and perfectly understandable!—AR feminine insecurity—for which she is not to be blamed! which he will be delighted to help her work on! But he doesn't want to push her! Maybe she'd prefer him to back off, to give her more space?

It is really much better not to say anything.

Brett has been waiting, but now he is satisfied that there will be no scene. "We'll talk soon," he promises nicely, in reward. "I really want to hear how you're doing with your fascinating project. Have to go now." He smiles, waves to her affectionately, and disconnects.

And that's fine. Perfectly fine. He never lies to her; she likes that. Obsessing over personal relationships was a distortion of women's emotional makeup brought on by societal conditions, the double standard, and economic dependence. Fidelity is an option later, in committed monogamous living arrangements, which are only one choice out of many possible lifestyles. Lisa smiles the aloof smile of a modern woman who is above and beyond the quaint, antique feelings of her mother and grandmother, relaxes gracefully into her sofa, and pounds her fist into a large batik cushion with a shout of rage.

Justin enters Lisa's office. His face has the eager expression of the star pupil, advancing to the blackboard in expectation of praise. "I, ummmm, might have found something," he says.

"Oh?" Lisa replies, a little absentmindedly.

He is carrying a book, an old-fashioned hardback book with a burgundy linen cover. The book, Lisa sees by glancing at the spine, is in German. The author, she notes, is Bertolt Brecht.

Lisa frowns, but Justin is excited, entirely engrossed in his mission. He sits down on the opposite side of her desk, leans on his elbows, and begins leafing through the book.

"Ummm, a friend mentioned this book to me," he says. "Well, actually, one of my former professors. And he loaned it to me. And I've been studying it carefully. It's poems, actually. Some of them are"—Justin pauses, searching for the correct term and finally settling on one—"typically AR," he says. "Hetpat stuff," he adds, disapprovingly, with a slanted eye to Lisa, to see how he is doing.

Heterosexual patriarchal, he extends the acronym for himself, wondering why it makes him feel a little queasy in a funny, not altogether unpleasant sort of way.

Lisa appears interested. So Justin goes on.

"Some of them are, I think, borderline. Borderline cases. One of them is about sex in a sauna."

"Brecht?" Lisa repeats, incredulous.

"Yeah, I know," Justin murmurs sympathetically. "A male author, it's not ideal. But, you know, he's been dead for a long time."

"That's not what I mean!" Lisa snaps. Really, sometimes she could swear that Justin is being deliberately dense, just to mock her. As if being dead for a long time had anything to do with it, really!

"What I mean is, the only Brecht I know is that German guy, the big literary hero, the Communist intellectual one," she explains impatiently. "Are you telling me that Mr. Self-righteous Hero of the Socialist Revolution wrote pornographic poems? That might be useful for our assignment?"

"These poems," Justin explains in a murmur, "were long suppressed by Eastern European officialdom. Buried in their archives." He is happy to know this. He has been waiting for her to ask these questions, just waiting to triumphantly give this answer.

There is a brief silence, while they ponder Communist archives and Brecht, stuffy anticapitalist Brecht, writing forbidden poems about sex.

"The sauna," Lisa reminds him.

"Right. Well, the sauna one has, you know, a traditional kind of motif. It also uses some objectionable terminology for the, umm, reproductive, ahh." Justin clears his throat. He hasn't quite gotten used to this job yet. "And the man is definitely in the, mmm, active role, although, of course," he adds solemnly, "everything is completely consensual."

It occurs to him briefly that he has hardly done justice to Brecht's playful description of events in the steamy, pine-paneled room. He doesn't want to get into this one any further, though, because he is pretty confident that Lisa will not like the part where the woman runs the man a hot bath and scrubs his back. He consults the text to be sure, and the phrase "In the manner of our forefathers, she serves him in the bath" glares out at him. No, he is quite certain that this is far too geisha for the New Order.

"But," he continues, brightening as he moves to the next stanza and safer ground, "then, right after that, the woman takes over the active role! She . . . well, she takes these birch switches and she . . ."

The look on Lisa's face is not encouraging. Justin speeds forward.

"Well, as I said, that one's definitely borderline. Then," he says, "there's the next one, which is called 'The Ninth Sonnet.'"

Lisa leans back in her chair. Justin, looking earnest, works out a translation.

> *"First I taught you to make love, forgetting me*
> *to take your share of pleasure from my plate*
> *and to love making love, not me . . .*

"Okay, it's not perfect," he interjects quickly, carefully, "with the guy acting like he's the teacher and so on, and why is it *his* plate, but I thought the part about avoiding romantic delusions might be good . . ."

Lisa shrugs. Sounds like the tired old Triple L, the lame leftist line to psych you into thinking that promiscuity is liberation . . . and when they talked about this very thing during a recent group session, her counselor gave her a meaningful look . . . Lisa squirms in her chair.

"And then," Justin continues, unaware of her discomfort, "there's the one about the angels."

His voice has softened; he leafs gently through the pages, looking for angels, Brecht's pornographic angels. Lisa sees that the literature freak has come to the foreground, and sighs. Oh God, here comes the great intellectual socialist sex poem.

Justin is oblivious to her skepticism. "'On the Seduction of Angels,'" he reads. He says the first line in German, his voice tasting the words. "'*Engel verführt man gar nicht, oder schnell . . .*' I wish I could have found an English translation," he adds, "a really good one. But I don't think there is one, this is from a really obscure publishing house that found these poems in the archives after German reunification and—"

"Yeah, right," says Lisa, heading off the summary of boring last-century European events with a crisp "Just give me the basic idea, never mind the classroom stuff."

"It's really much better in German," Justin says. "He uses vulgar expressions, but they sound different in German. The whole language is so guttural, so it all sounds very coarse, you know, and that way, the individual expressions don't sound so aggressive, if you know what I mean. And he plays with that, the words and the sounds, and it makes this powerful contrast to the idea of angels. I don't know how to do that in English."

"This isn't a goddamn seminar!" Lisa shouts, exasperated. "You wanted to show me something? So show it to me already!"

"Well . . ." Justin concentrates, frowns. "It's got a lot of, umm, very explicit stuff in it. I left that out in my rough draft . . ."

Lisa rolls her eyes.

"Okay. And, ummm, I couldn't make it rhyme," he says. Lisa jumps up menacingly.

Justin begins. "Okay, okay, so here's how it basically goes: 'You must seduce an angel quickly, or not at all. Push him into a doorway, kiss his mouth, and when you think he's ready, turn him against the wall, pull up his skirts, and fuck him. Make him move against you, then hold him while he falls with you through the chasm between heaven and earth. Just don't ever look him in the face, and his wings, man, don't crush his wings.'"

Justin pauses, frowning in disgust at his inadequate translation. "'*Und seine Flügel, Mensch, zerdrück sie nicht,*'" he adds, to himself, in a whisper.

"Well," Justin says, brisk and businesslike again, "I just thought you ought to know about this, as it's a rather arcane source you might not otherwise happen across."

Then he clutches the book to himself and rushes out of the room. He is terribly embarrassed. He liked the poem, well, he loved the poem, but he's not confident of his judgment. Maybe it's tacky, vulgar, and really bad. Maybe Lisa will now think he is disgusting.

Lisa stares at the door that has closed behind him. The poem is entirely inappropriate. First of all, it is clearly a homosexual poem. Both actors in this poem, human and angel, seducer and seduced, are male. The references to casual, anonymous, faintly violent sex, taking place in doorways, fit Berlin, though not, she would have thought, the prim and stodgy former socialist East Berlin, home of the Worker Hero and Mother Courage. She now suspects Brecht of sneaking through Checkpoint Charlie in drag in order to frequent slummy West Berlin gay bars.

And yet, and yet, Justin is not entirely off the mark. Even in his bad, inhibited, self-conscious translation, there was a kind of . . . something. There's something there, in that mix between shoving someone into a doorway and worrying about their wings, making free with their body but respecting their face . . . Something, something . . . but the insight eludes her, flitting around her, just beyond her reach.

Instead, other thoughts intrude. What, for example, is a religious image doing in a socialist sex poem? If religion is the opiate of the masses, then what is an angel? An angel, moreover, who is open to wild assignations on dark streets? It's so confusing.

As she muses, her thoughts begin to wander. Actually, Justin looks a little bit like an angel, she thinks, not the curly-haired insipid kind but a lean, sort of Germanic one, the kind Brecht maybe had in mind. A nervous young angel, who doesn't know his own strength yet and is unaware of his beauty and if you should find yourself alone with him in a dark deserted doorway, it might occur to you to startle him with a kiss . . . Startled out of her reverie by this appallingly inappropriate thought, Lisa shakes her head and turns back to her papers.

Religion. It always messes you up.

If there's one thing Lisa is maybe a little short on, it's family. She doesn't have many relatives, and the ones she has are very busy. Her widowed mother, formerly a sedate nutritionist, was energized by the Revolution and swept away to Sun Valley, Idaho, on a tide of enthusiasm to manage a Transgenerational Recreation complex. And indeed her relationships with an ever-changing series of aging ski instructors, Lisa has at times been moved to reflect disapprovingly, sound amply recreational.

Her older sister, Theresa, lives closer, right in the adjacent suburb as a matter of fact, but she is equally busy with her own affairs, affairs of science in her case. That leaves Cleo, Theresa's well-loved but much-neglected ten-year-old daughter. Lucky for Cleo that Lisa is such a devoted aunt.

Most Tuesdays, Lisa and Cleo spend the evening together. This allows Cleo's mother to teach an evening class, and it gets Lisa Nurturing Exchange Credits that, since she has no children as yet, she can bank for later use. Since Lisa enjoys being with Cleo and rarely misses a Tuesday, she has considerable savings already—enough, she sometimes jokes, to have her first three children raised entirely by others. It's only half a joke. Cleo's mother, for instance, is deeply, deeply in debt, owing about three thousand hours' worth of taking care of other people's kids, pets, or seniors. Given how busy her sister is, Lisa cannot imagine how she will ever find the time to pay off this debt, not to mention the accruing penalties—no, wait, the term is "enhancements." Nor would Lisa like to be on the receiving end of Theresa's services, if and when she finally does cough them up. Nurturing is not what Theresa does best.

Lisa tries to make those Tuesday evenings into quality time. Homework will usually have been finished in school, but if Cleo's drama class is performing a play, they might rehearse the lines. Projects, too, usually require some polishing up at home, as do reports. And today, apparently, is one such day. Cleo answers the door looking bedraggled, gives an elaborate sigh of exhaustion, and falls backward onto the sofa to show Lisa just how unbelievably worn out she is, because she has been slaving over this *report* she has to give, which is due *tomorrow,* and she still isn't really happy with it, and won't Lisa *please* help her fix it up?

"What's your topic?" Lisa asks, amused as always by her niece's youthful flamboyance.

"Inventions. I have to do a report on inventions," Cleo explains. "The teacher gave me some sources, but there's *so* much stuff in them, and I did a search, which turned up *twenty-five* pages of entries. I've been working on this for *a week*!" Cleo says. "We have to give these reports at assembly, and I want to get a good score for

Anne, you know, our teacher. Last semester, she only got an 85, because our reports weren't that good. Which wasn't fair, because the other class had lots easier topics. But anyway, so we want her to do better this semester, because she really deserved way more points, she's totally estro and a really good teacher."

Cleo's bright little face, with the pointy chin and the playful monkey expression, makes Lisa smile, as does the openness with which she relays her worries and the obvious didactic success of making the children feel responsible for their teacher's grade instead of being graded themselves.

"Why don't you read it to me," Lisa suggests. "It's probably very good already, and if it isn't, we can polish it up a little bit."

Cleo unfolds herself from the sofa and scampers to her room for the report. The girl who returns is Cleo in a very different manifestation, Cleo the Orator, walking with the self-confidence of three years of rhetoric classes and radiant with self-esteem. She strikes a pose in front of the ottoman, settles her face into solemn lines, and begins.

"An invention is a good idea that you have when you see a way to do things better, or to solve a problem. *You* can invent something, too, by just looking at the world around you in a creative way. At our science fair last year, our class received three prizes for good inventions and four prizes for innovations. An innovation is when you take somebody else's invention and make it better, which is important, too."

Cleo breaks stride to explain gleefully to Lisa that this statement is aimed at the parallel grade, who think they are such hot stuff because their teacher got a 92, so they should remember that they didn't win a single prize at the science fair last year.

Returning to her stentorian tone, Cleo continues: "Long ago, before the New Order, women were not allowed to invent things, or if they did, their ideas got stolen and other people took the credit for them. Do you think I should put 'stolen by their husbands and other men,' or would that sound too hostile?" Cleo asks her aunt, peering over the pages of her report with a worried frown.

"Well . . ." Lisa considers. "How does your teacher usually handle that? What would she say?"

Cleo thinks about it and then brightens. "I can say 'stolen by the AR men of those olden times.' That can't bother anybody." She scribbles in the correction and continues.

"So. If women invented something and applied for a patent, which is how you register your invention, then it was issued in their husband's name instead of their own until the late 1800s. Also for a long time they were not even allowed to go to school, and when they finally did, everybody told them that they were bad at math and science. But, even with all of these obstacles, women invented important things that play a big role in our lives. For example, a woman invented the brown paper grocery bag which is flat on the bottom, an item which we use practically every day. This replaced the bag which did not have a flat bottom, and which would easily tear when you put in grocery items that were heavy or pointy, like pineapples or cans, and not as many things would fit into those bags, so you needed more of them, which was environmentally bad and used up too much paper. That part wasn't in the source, I thought of it myself because Anne says to always keep the environment in mind," Cleo adds proudly.

"This invention was by Margaret Knight in 1871. Before that, in 1858, women invented the plastic tube to put ink in when you use a fountain pen, which we don't use anymore, but in the olden days that was practically the only thing you could write with, and some people still have one at home. And her name was Susan Taylor and she invented it in 1858. And women invented the fire escape, which is by Harriet Tracy in 1883, and she also invented syringes for giving shots, well, they used to make holes in your arm with needles and then shoot medicine in." Cleo shudders, member of a generation that, if holistic medicine, massages, steam treatments, and the like fail, receives her chemicals painlessly by patch, spray, eyedropper, or inhalation.

"Mary Anderson invented the windshield wiper in 1903. And Eva Landman invented an improved umbrella in 1935. There was something called Liquid Paper that got invented, but I don't know what that is," Cleo explains, in an aside to her aunt. "Plus and, I left out some things like diapers, galley kitchens, dishwashers, and low-calorie chocolate, because those are, I don't know"—Cleo wrinkles her nose—"not really things I would like to invent, I think."

Lisa has to agree. Diapers and kitchens and dishwashers and calories, too classic. Her niece is right.

Cleo takes a deep breath, winding up for her grand finale. "Women also invented things of special benefit to men," she says. "That was in our guidelines for the report," she explains. "At the end, we're supposed to make sure our presentation promotes gender empathy."

Lisa nods approvingly.

"We're supposed to put in something that was done especially for the welfare of the other gender, but all I could find was in 1991 Linda Dixon invented the anti-snoring pillow. Mom thought I could use that, because she says men snore more than women. What do you think?"

Lisa mulls this over. It's a bit of a stretch. Even if it's true, doesn't the anti-snoring pillow help the man's bed neighbor, often a woman, more than it helps the man himself?

"Let me hear the rest, and then I'll decide," Lisa suggests.

"Okay," Cleo agrees. "We're almost at the end, anyway. The end is just some more of the gender part." In a benign singsong voice, she finishes up, "Not *all* inventions were by women. As I said in the beginning, anybody can invent, it's easy if you try. And men also made inventions, for example, electricity."

Cleo gives a businesslike nod, to show she is finished.

"On the men part," she tells her aunt, "they invented some other stuff, too, but I left out the bombs and nuclear thingies and missiles and other bad things, because we just talked about that in our Chronics class, and it was a real downer and made everybody feel sad," she says.

Lisa nods. "I think it's a fine report," she says. "I like it, and I'm sure the class will like it, too. Good job, Cleo. What about working on your herb garden?" she suggests, and Cleo nods happily.

"I think the lavender's going to bloom," she says, "even though it isn't supposed to until the second summer!"

And they spend a contented hour on the balcony, tending to lavender, yarrow, and chamomile, rubbing the leaves between their fingers to release pungent smells, reviewing the medicinal uses, and considering what they will tie the dried sage bundles with, for smudge sticks in the fall. At the end of the evening, Lisa has three more credits in her time account, some twigs of peppermint for her bath, and peace in her heart.

Lisa and Justin are two diligent little workers. It's a holiday, but they have agreed to meet in the office anyway. Might as well be comfortable, so they have appropriated the seminar room. It has two chintz chairs and a sofa, lots of plants, and soft prints on the wall. Here Lisa and Justin have set up headquarters for the day. Lisa's hair is twisted on top of her head and Justin is wearing a black sweatsuit. The coffee table before them is piled with books, a mountain of books, and they are reviewing them one by one. Many of them have been marked and sent in by the helpful public, apprised of the ministerial effort through press releases and via the communitynet. Others were shipped up by the Research Department.

Anne Rice has been sent in many times over. There is clearly no way around Anne Rice, she is obviously their most promising lead, so Justin and Lisa have decided to tackle her today. Bending their heads over twin stacks of the Beauty Trilogy, they flip through the pages in silent review of highlighted passages.

Lisa, reading these volumes for the first time, is taken aback.

In Rice's version, Sleeping Beauty is saved from her spell-induced coma by a handsome but perverted young prince, who awakens not only her but also her taste for S and M. He then carries her off to a castle run by his even more sadistic mother, who keeps hundreds of princes and princesses in more or less willing captivity as playthings for her assortment of cruel aristocrats. If these captives cause problems, they are turned over to sadistic peasants in the nearby village, kidnapped by sadistic pirates, or sold to sadistic sultans.

Lisa is finding the text to be a repetitious blur of boots and whips and medieval instruments of torture applied against a variety of backdrops from the pastoral to the Disneyland castle to the Orient. The first cursory skimming leaves her astounded and tentatively appalled. But thousands of women have mailed this in, as their suggested raw material for a new emancipated fantasy life, so there must be something to it, and she owes it an attentive reading.

Well, it's true that Rice is an equal-opportunity flagellist. Princes and princesses are maltreated with equal fervor by merciless ladies as well as lords. So that part is okay, Lisa doubtfully supposes. But where, in this crowd of sad and sadder specimens, will she find the dream lover, the key erotic image for a new age?

Perhaps in the village, where princes are used as horses to pull carriages and plows? Where, in order for them to appear more horselike, they are outfitted with ornamental tails attached to their bodies by being plugged into their nether orifice.

Lisa puts the book down and returns to the preceding volume, where the protagonists are still prisoners of the castle. A castle, that's romantic. Maybe she will discover a pleasing scenario there. Let's see. We have the slaves in the tapestry-hung private quarters of their Mistresses, naked and performing household tasks while moving about on their hands and knees, only permitted to use their teeth. We have the slaves in the palace gardens, scampering naked across the lawn to retrieve golden apples in their mouths while being flogged for greater speed. We have the slaves hired out to do chores and having their payment, in coins, stored in the same place that will later hold the horse's tail. Lisa winces. As official imagery for the Revolution, this just isn't getting her anywhere. Not that the book isn't interesting. I mean, how long *would* it take you to put a bedspread on a bed, using only your teeth? Would an employer really *want* money that had been transported in that kind of wallet? Rice is thought-provoking but not, so far as Lisa can see, terribly suitable as a futuristic aphrodisiac.

Still, there must be *something* to be harvested from these volumes. She can't bear to have wasted an entire day. Glancing at Justin, she sees that he is deeply immersed in Volume 3, face inscrutable. Lisa returns to Rice with new determination.

> Quickly I was stood up against the wall and chained with legs and arms in the form of an X and left there . . . Just as I was dozing off, I opened my eyes with a start to see the lovely face of my dark-haired Mistress . . .
>
> She had several small black leather weights in her hands with clamps like those I had worn on my nipples yesterday, and as the maids talked on behind a closed door, she applied these clamps to the loose skin of my scrotum. I winced. I couldn't keep still. The weights were just heavy enough to make me painfully aware of every inch of the sensitive flesh . . . She worked thoughtfully, pinching the skin . . . When I flinched she took no note of it . . . The touch of these things, their movements, were unendurable reminders of these bulging organs, this degrading exposure.

No, that won't do. Flinching along with the hero, Lisa searches on. Even if someone liked that, it's too hostile, and would never pass the Gender Amity Review Board.

"Well," she offers finally, "what about here, page 144?" She reads aloud:

> " 'I've come very far,' he said. 'I've been taught. And I owe it to Mistress Lockley. If it hadn't been for Mistress Lockley I don't know what would have happened to me. Mistress Lockley bound me, punished me, harnessed me, and took me through a dozen forced tasks before she expected any-thing of my will. Every other night I was paddled on the

Public Turntable . . . and only after a good four weeks of that was I unbound and ordered to light the fire and set the table. I tell you I covered her boots with kisses. I lapped the food literally from the palm of her hand . . . I worship her,' he said. 'I shudder to think what would have happened if I had been bought by someone softer.'"

With furrowed brows, they both study this paragraph. "Well?" Lisa asks, after a few moments. "What do you think?"

Justin shrugs. "I . . . well, I really don't know. Yeah, I guess. Maybe."

It's nine-thirty, Lisa has sacrificed a whole precious day to this effort, this is their meager harvest, and she gets a tired maybe?

"You're no help!" she shouts. "I might as well be doing this by myself! You're just not helping at all!"

Justin is angry, too. He's been here all day as well, just as long as Lisa, patiently perusing texts about men having disgusting things done to them by Amazons. So okay, there's a measure of historical justice here but still . . . to be asked his opinion in a nice parlor voice and then get reprimanded for insufficient enthusiasm, that's going too far. It shakes him out of his usual measured goodwill and allows him to forget, for a moment, that all he really wants here is a signature, Lisa's signature, at the conclusion of the nine months, on his final piece of paper.

"Why are you asking me anyway," he yells right back. "You're the ones with the messed-up heads! You're the ones who need the government to find new fantasies for you because your old ones were so sick! So you tell me, does this do it for you or not? Does Mistress Lockley fix your lousy self-esteem or doesn't she?"

Lisa slams the book down on the table with so much force that it bounces right off again, striking Justin on the knee. It's an accident, but Justin is beyond such fine distinctions. "I don't have to put up with this!" he yells, leaping to his feet. He would like to rip the book into a million pieces and throw it in Anne Rice's or, barring that, at least in Lisa's face. With superhuman effort, he controls that impulse. Turning on his heel, he storms out of the office instead, slamming the door, setting the monitors abuzz, and startling the after-hours watchperson, who leaps up to bring his dramatic departure to an ignominious halt.

Lisa remains on the sofa, lost in thought, waiting for the inevitable ring of in-house security.

"Lisa," a nasal voice asks, moments later. "This is security? What's going on? I have a re-ed here without his pass, he says he was working with you? I saw him slam the door on the monitor and I was on my way upstairs when he flounced by me. Whatya want us to do with him?"

Lisa sighs. "It's okay," she says. "My mistake. I forgot to give him his pass back. We, umm, we were reading a scene to see how it plays. We were just, um, testing a presentation. That's why he slammed the door. It's okay. Let him go."

So Justin, steaming at the indignity of his departure and even more at the ignominy of being charitably bailed out by Lisa, is released from the security booth and permitted to make his way home.

Home to the Residential Suites. Home to the grimy kitchen, the slimy bath. And home to Mac.

For a month now, Justin has been trying to decide if Mac is mean or just dumb. I say he's dumb, because if he had any sense at all, he would not choose this particular evening to greet Justin with a snarl or to latch on to his pants leg with his nasty, drooly little mouth. Because on this particular evening peaceful, agreeable Justin snarls right back. Then he kicks Mac with a measured blow of his sneaker, while growling, "You try that again, you miserable mutt, and you're hamburger!"

Whimpering reproachfully and feigning a limp, Mac slinks off into a corner.

The door to his neighbor's apartment closes with a gentle snap, but in his fury Justin is unaware that there was a witness to this entirely incorrect treatment of his paternal bonding object.

An hour later, feeling only slightly calmer, Justin is lying on his bunk with his headphones on. He doesn't hear the knocking right away. He rises reluctantly, yanks open the door, and barks out an angry "Yeah, what?"

The man facing him is about thirty-five, chunky, and big. He is one of the men that Justin usually gives a wide berth to, the kind of guy who in the old days would have been called a redneck and who, even in the nice new days, has not had the mean glint reeducated out of his eyes yet. "Came to getcha, pal," the man says.

Justin stares at him in bewilderment.

"Heardya kick the mutt," his visitor goes on, and for an incredulous minute Justin has to conclude that this man, this lunky Old Order man of all men, is going to turn him in for insufficiently empathetic behavior to his surrogate baby.

"Filthy mutt," the man elaborates, and Justin relaxes. It seems he is not going to be denounced. But then what does this visitor want from him?

"Come on, good buddy, time's a-wastin'," the man mysteriously says, punching Justin lightly in the solar plexus. Then he turns, and it is clear to Justin that he is expected to go with him.

Justin follows his new friend down the hall, down the stairwell, into the basement. In a gray concrete room, lit too brightly by a long fluorescent tube, nine men slouch on worn-out sofas and armchairs. "Here he is," his guide announces, adding, as soon as all eyes are on Justin, "the man we have been waiting for."

And there stands Justin, gulping heavily as ten muscle-bound guys nod at him with avuncular warmth. Waiting for him for what? Waiting to have him for dinner?

"I know he don't look it," his pal goes on, "but he's A-okay. Aaaaand, he works where? On o-fishull business, in the la-di-da big-mama Ministry, that's where."

And that is how Justin ends up in a counterrevolutionary cell.

Lisa enters her apartment to the smell of soap and pastry. Vera. Her heart sinks. It's a small problem, as problems go, but a constant one. She walks into her kitchen apprehensively, and with good reason. She knows what she will find there, and sure enough: there it is.

This week, it's worse than usual. It is huge, sitting on her counter under the ridiculous acrylic dome Vera gave her for her last birthday. It appears to be some kind of meringue concoction this time, with yellow sticky stuff dripping out from under a huge frothy top. Besides this monstrosity, there is also a message from Vera on the compuscreen. "Hi hon!" it says. "Let me know how you like my new recipe, lime cream pie! ENJOY!" It is signed with a heart and three X's.

Lisa chooses RESPOND and composes her reply immediately, before she can forget. "Vera! You shouldn't! That must have been so much work! The pie is absolutely scrumptious, yum! Big hug!"

She studies her note. Are there too many exclamation marks, even for Vera? Is there any way to avoid the "yum" and still sound warm and appreciative? No, it has to stay. She adds a smiley face and orders SEND quickly, before she can change her mind. Damn, she's hit the pad too hard.

"That felt impulsive!" the computerized voice of her screen is saying. "Did your finger slip, or is that really your command?"

Lisa flexes her fingers to relax them, and repeats the motion more gently. She times the message to transmit in an hour, enough time to make it plausible that she has come home, changed clothes, made tea, and eaten some of this horrible gook. Vera pays attention to details like that, as Lisa knows from bitter experience. Anything to avoid another of those you-didn't-really-like-it-you're-just-saying-that-to-make-me-feel-better conversations.

Then she cuts two generous slices, places them in the refrigerator in case Cleo comes to visit, and studies the remainder for a moment, thinking hard. Senior Mother McNeill, down the hall? No, she's so nutrition-aware, she'd never eat this. Break time at the office? No way. They shrieked in horror when she tried to feed them that apple pie a few weeks ago—they'd go into sugar shock just looking at this baby. Justin? Men still eat stuff like this, but she can't be bringing her re-ed slices of homemade pie, how would that look? Regretfully, Lisa dumps the sticky thing into the organic bin of the disposer.

The next expression of Vera's personality awaits her in the bedroom. Everything looks wonderful and smells delightful. Homemade potpourri releases its fragrance from a ceramic bowl on the dresser. The bed is freshly made, the window is open just a crack, and the vacuum has fluffed up the carpet in neat parallel lines. Well, not everywhere. In the middle of the room there is a circular island where the machine has detoured around an obstacle, a pair of dirty, crumpled argyle men's socks. Lisa smiles in spite of herself. Of course. There is no way that Vera is going to pick up after "some man," as she puts it, and certainly not after the particular man Brett, whom she has met and taken an immediate, deep dislike to. Shaking her head, Lisa remembers the one, the only, the awful encounter between Brett and Vera. He had spoken to her very nicely, tried to engage her in conversation, but Vera had just studied him coldly for a few minutes without replying and then snapped at him to bug off. She had called him a "condescending meathead," if Lisa recalls correctly.

Lisa peeks into the bathroom just to confirm what she already knows: that Vera will have left everything sparkling, clean towels folded and draped artistically over the rack, all the better to accentuate Brett's boxer shorts and sweaty T-shirt, still slung over the rail beside them. Lisa collects these delinquent items and throws them on the floor of her closet; he can retrieve them the next time he comes over, whenever that may be.

Not for the first time, Lisa wishes she could just use a cleaning service. But that's out of the question, you have to show social responsibility, you can't just think of your own comfort, especially not when you are a government official. Somebody has to employ the displaced homemakers, somebody has to allow them to express their caregiving needs, and it certainly wouldn't be safe to unleash these intense individuals on just anybody. Lisa shudders. It is frightening to think that, instead of whisking the children of such women into the healthy environment of a public educational facility, they actually used to leave helpless toddlers alone with people like Vera, in the confinement of a single-family dwelling! Yes, cruelly, women suffering from Domestic Obsession Disorder used to be pent up with only small children and cleaning supplies for company, which of course thrust these poor, compulsive individuals into a frenzy of spraying and hovering and scrubbing and nagging and fretting.

Today this illness has almost been eradicated, and the remaining sufferers have been placed within a wider community of stable adults who have the maturity to handle them, who can accept their constant incursions into the personal space of others and the greedy desperation of their emotional needs and still maintain boundaries. And Vera isn't as bad as some, not by far. The stories Lisa hears at work! The meddling, the tears, the paranoia! The hideous, unsolicited macramé hangings that appear without warning on your living room wall. The sulking and the scenes if you don't leave them in place. The women who wait for you to get home, no matter how late, and won't leave until you notice and remark upon every little thing they did that day. The ones who sulk for weeks if you forget their birthday. In short, Lisa is well off with Vera's notes, lengthy and saccharine as some of them can get, and her pies, inedible as they are, and she knows it.

And it's important to count her blessings, because she's been feeling pretty down. Work is turning into a grim and tedious affair, as she chugs along unproductively at her assignment. After the unhappy interlude with Anne Rice, Lisa has decided to take a break from practice. "I need more distance," she tells the morning meeting, and everyone agrees. When you think about it, it makes sense that any erotic thought produced within patriarchy will be completely tainted, whether written by a man or a woman, for men or for women. Hopefully, an excursion into theory will put things in better perspective.

And maybe her friendship with Justin can be salvaged, over time. She hopes so; they were getting to be buddies. Things have been awkward since the Rice incident. She feels guilty about the way that day ended. She blames herself for overlooking Justin's state of mind. She is supposed to be his mentor, and working for her is supposed to help him in his personal growth, not make him miserable. She has not been sensitive enough to Justin's feelings. Since he is so agreeable, she has started to think of him as a fellow woman, so to speak, but of course he isn't. One good thing came out of the scene he threw: it helped her notice him as a real person with a life and mind of his own. What is it like to be Justin, Lisa wonders.

She knows the rudimentary biographical facts; he's told her. His parents are elderly. They live far away. Their lifetime of petty squabbles and arguments over whose fault what is having neatly survived any broader societal changes, they are still together, living in a condo on the other side of the continent. He has no siblings. From his remarks about how he spends his weekends, Lisa can tell that he has plenty of activity partners, but none of them sound like very close friends. He's just a nice, average young guy, waiting for his education to end and his life to begin. But what Lisa really would like to know about is his mind. Does he share the goal of a happy, equal future for everyone, men and women, or does he secretly wish for the past? Does he resent the loss of old entitlements and privileges? Maybe he secretly hates her. Maybe he sees her as another Nadine, bossy and humorless.

Weeks ago, the Research Department sent up a box; Lisa had opened it at the time, found nothing but heavily annotated, cumbersome translations of endless passages about Minoan double axes and symbolic marriages and fertility rites, and shut it right back up again. After the Rice incident, she pulls it out of storage and hands it over to Justin. Let him take his funk to ancient Crete, and good luck to him. She really can't deal with his developmental problems right now.

Every second Sunday, Lisa gets up early to join Mother McNeill for a hike. She doesn't need the credits, strictly speaking, but still, it wouldn't feel right somehow to rest her entire account on Cleo when she gets so much enjoyment from her company. Mother McNeill can be interesting, too, and likable, but she definitely requires an effort, starting with her insistence on taking her morning hikes at 6 a.m. And of course she repeats herself, as elderly people will, so that you have to hear over and over again about how lucky you are, and what a struggle things used to be, and how you just can't *imagine* what it was like in *her* youth, and how you should count your blessings. And that's fine. When your Fostering Transgenerational Understanding credits show up on your Social Growth Evaluation, at least you'll feel that you earned them.

And there she is now, the indomitable Mother McNeill, in her signature purple sweater and matching leggings, with the large orange-and-gold earrings that complete her Autumn Equinox ensemble, her hair cut spiky as a wheat field after the harvest, and her feet already padding rhythmically up and down in a runner's warm-up, knocking impatiently on Lisa's door. She looks kind of cute, Lisa has to admit, and makes her smile, even at 5:45.

"Let's go, girl, let's go," she says, still jogging in place, and Lisa grabs her own gray jacket and they're off.

They aren't actually going to run, Mother McNeill really isn't up to that anymore, at age seventy-four. It's not the early rising, and certainly not the exertion, that makes these outings tedious—it's Mother McNeill's lectures about safety. "You girls don't know how lucky you are," she'll say, and then you're in for it. In her day, you couldn't just roam about at dawn in deserted parks and expect to come home again in one piece. In her day, they didn't have the wonderful, the marvelous HUE band to protect them. In her day, if you were alone on a jogging path, the sight of a man in the distance would make you nervous.

Lisa tries to be patient. Sure, the HUE band is a good idea. All of the older women love it; the younger ones grew up with it, and don't give it a thought, any more than they think about wearing underwear or shoes. To Lisa's mind, it's almost more of a fashion accessory than a security device. Violent crime is nearly unheard of, in her world. She is accustomed to going where she pleases, any time of the day or night. She's never looked over her shoulder on a dark street, never quickened her pace at the sound of footsteps, never forgone her Walkman in order to better hear the approaching mugger or rapist. The mugger and the rapist aren't here. They've been counseled, medicated, and reeducated into a remorseful stupor and are as tame as little kitty cats. Or they've been judged irremediable, and sent far away to Zone Six, and they're not coming back.

"I tell you, honey, the HUE band is the best thing that ever happened to women," Mother McNeill is saying now. Lisa nods politely and strokes her own band absentmindedly. It is an iridescent, rainbow-colored strip of plastic, rather pretty. Aptly named, too, Lisa reflects. It certainly would be a Highly Unlikely Event to be assaulted anywhere, city or country, night or day. Lisa has friends who have had occasion to activate the CIO, or Check It Out, button, which you are not only encouraged but practically begged to do by the security people in their annual Personal Safety Update seminars. "If anything seems the slightest little bit suspicious, push the button, *please.* That's what it's there for. Do it for us. Do you have any idea how boring it is to sit around all day and never get even a CIO call?" Lisa remembers the lecture, at last year's event. Lisa knows they were just trying to overcome everybody's reluctance to set off a false alarm, though she supposes it truly *could* be boring to sit at your monitor day in, day out, and never get a call. Lisa tries to think whether she knows anyone who ever used the actual red alert button, but she doesn't.

Mother McNeill leaves Lisa with the admonishment to be grateful, to count her blessings, and to consider herself lucky. The next morning, in the office, Lisa remembers the advice with childish resentment. Talk is cheap, isn't it? How can she be happy? Where's this so-called luck? Her love life is going nowhere, and neither is her career. When all you ever get from your SR is empathy and a lecture, when you've got co-workers like Eva stopping by in mock concern because "it sure looks like you're blocked," then a cheap plastic band around your wrist and the freedom to go jogging in the stupid forest at stupid goddamn dawn are cold comfort.

Lisa takes a deep breath. One has to keep things in perspective, she knows that. But the project is really getting her down. It's hard not to feel a wretched sense of personal failure. Drawing a total blank on sex, that's not very ego-enhancing. Obviously, she's the wrong woman for this job. Probably she is too literal for it, she reflects. Too uptight. Too conventional.

"Feminists' view of sex is naïve and prudish," she reads, in the volume of Camille Paglia now before her. In her current mood, the sentence goes through Lisa like a skewer. Yes, probably she is naïve and prudish, exactly right, and that is why she must fail at this project, why someone as brilliant and worldly as Brett is bored by her, why her life has no core and no direction.

"Leaving sex to the feminists," she reads, "is like letting your dog vacation at the taxidermist's." Lisa flinches. She can't say exactly what that's supposed to mean, but it feels very cutting.

"The sexes are at war," she reads. Hmmm. Now Paglia is starting to sound like Nadine. This is confusing.

"Aggression and eroticism are deeply intertwined." Lisa clicks on highlight and the sentence reappears in luminous pink. Okay, this might be pertinent after all.

"Hunt, pursuit and capture are biologically programmed into male sexuality. Generation after generation, men must be educated, refined and ethically persuaded away from their tendency toward anarchy and brutishness."

Well, sure, that's the point of the whole reeducation process, of the five evaluations, though you're not supposed to put it as bluntly as all that. You're not supposed to say it's biology, that's too hostile and too discouraging to men. Lisa frowns. This woman is all over the map, she can't seem to come down *any*where. She goes after feminists, she goes after men, she goes after biology . . . Of course, Lisa reflects tolerantly, women in those days had no real political home. An intelligent woman could easily end up just flailing around in despair.

"Sex," Paglia is noting now, "is a turbulent power that we are not in control of; it's a dark force . . . It's the dark realm of the night. When you enter the realm of the night, horrible things can happen there . . . It's like the gay men going down to the docks and having sex in alleyways and trucks; it's the danger. Feminists have no idea that some women like to flirt with danger because there is a sizzle in it," Lisa reads. "We can't consider that women have kinky tastes, can we? No, because women are naturally benevolent and nurturing, aren't they?"

Not fair. Lisa is perfectly willing to confront kinky tastes; what else has she been doing lately, day in, day out?

"What women have to realize is their dominance as a sex," Paglia concludes. "Women's sexual powers are enormous. All cultures have seen it. Men know it. Women know it. The only people who don't know it are the feminists."

Well, she certainly has a bug in her bloomers over the feminists, doesn't she. Her mother must have been scared by a feminist while pregnant with little Camille.

And her writing is very dated. You couldn't write like this today, not so much because of the feminist business, that just wouldn't make sense to anyone, but the stuff about men is way too deterministic. Not that lots of people don't *think* it, but it really isn't the done thing to say it or write it. You can't say that men are nasty by nature. You don't want to discourage them, and besides, it would be discrimination. So the only thing she really takes away with her from Paglia is a nagging fear that she is a prude.

The morning meeting is enlivened, for once, by a new event. Nadine has entered, she has muttered her Germanic greeting out of narrow lips, rustled her papers, disapprovingly noted the absence of one of the participants, and begun the day's business when the door opens again to admit a tardy Xenia. When you are late for a meeting, you usually just go to your seat, but Xenia seems to be dawdling deliberately, waiting to be noticed. The others glance her way, and she pulls herself up straighter, like a bird showing plumage. Nadine frowns. Xenia sashays slowly to her chair and sits. There are large blue spots on her upper arms and her wrists when she leans— ostentatiously, Lisa thinks—far forward on the table. Nadine clears her throat, preparing to read out the next item on the morning agenda, but Xenia drawls out a "Sorry I kept you waiting." Nadine nods abruptly, but Xenia isn't finished.

"I overslept," she says. "What a night!" she adds. Her voice is lighthearted but provocative. "We tried some bondage. It got a little rough. Then this morning, just thinking about it, we got so turned on! So . . . we seized the moment, and I'm late."

Oxygen consumption in the room drops abruptly as everyone present briefly stops breathing. There are bright red patches on Nadine's cheeks, but she is not a leader for nothing. Picking up her papers, she says, "Fine. Now. Conserning our conference next mons, we should . . ."

At the conclusion of the meeting, Nadine says only, "I see you in wan hour, Xenia, please. Also you, Lisa."

When Lisa enters the office an hour later, Xenia is already there, relaxing on the sofa. She is sporting, besides her already famous bruises, a smug smile. Instead of spending the intervening hour on productive pursuits, Lisa has been trying to guess how Nadine will open this conversation. Will she be therapeutically neutral? Angry?

Will she transfer Xenia to a different bureau? Remand her for psychiatric treatment? Give her a lecture?

"So!" Nadine booms, when Lisa is seated. "Xenia, you vanted our attention, you haf our attention, so please! Your point is vat?"

Lisa thinks this is pretty subtle, for Nadine.

But Xenia just gives an exaggerated sigh. "That, exactly *that,* is my point, Nadine. *You* are too obsessive, constantly looking for deeper meanings everywhere! *Why* do men do this, *what* does it mean, *why* do women like that, *what* is the deep political significance of it . . . So I'm here to tell you, Nadine, loosen up and bug off! Some of us have rich, sensual lives, beyond the little boxes you want to stick everything into."

"Dere is nothing liberated about masochism, Xenia. It is a psychological disorder usually showing zat ze person has a disturbed relationship to zeir own identity and to power. Dere is nothing free or sensual about it. You are having a problem and I am liking to help you."

Xenia snickers.

"Ze old forces have a strong pull, ve are dealing wiss centuries of ellienashun, but, Xenia, and I spick also for Lisa, ve help you."

Xenia squares her shoulders and smiles pityingly at Nadine. "Some of us, Nadine, are still living in the past. But *others* are ready to explore *all* aspects of the psyche, and to *open* ourselves up to every experience, including the darker side of eros."

"You sink zis is freedom, Xenia, but it is not freedom vat you are getting involved in," Nadine says, sadly.

Xenia laughs scornfully. "You're talking about your politburo freedom, Nadine," she says. "But I'm interested in *my* freedom."

Nadine sighs deeply. With a tired wave of the hand, she gives the floor to Lisa, who is here in her role as resident expert on sexual consciousness.

"I can fully understand this," Lisa says.

"You, Lisa, understand zis?" Nadine repeats, looking truly dumbfounded. What? Another betrayal?

"Yes," Lisa says, ever so nicely. "I can well understand Xenia being beaten up by her lover. Whenever I'm with Xenia, I usually feel like slapping her, too. To be honest with you, Nadine, I think it would be a real turn-on for me just to slap her silly face, and if I were actually allowed to beat her with additional implements, I think I would be beside myself with pleasure."

There seems little to add to that, and she has achieved her goal of at least wiping the stupid smirk off Xenia's face, so Lisa simply gets up and leaves.

Of course, the matter is far from over. Nadine's attempt at damage control, by removing the issue from the public meeting and dealing with it privately, in her office, was well intentioned but doomed. Everybody in the meeting, and soon everybody in the building, is talking about what happened.

Even Justin has overheard snatches and picked up rumors. Two days later, he finally has something really interesting to report to his basement gathering. His story is a success. At least twenty minutes are spent elaborating on exactly how they would like to accommodate Xenia if given the chance. Another fifteen minutes are devoted to the idea that the rest of the women in the Ministry would enjoy the same sort of treatment, if delivered by the right guy.

Yes, Justin is an enormous social success tonight, in his new little club. They have always been nice to him, but tonight he feels truly liked and really accepted.

Perplexingly, when he returns to his apartment, Justin does not feel good at all. Maybe he is coming down with something! Maybe the flu! He feels a little queasy, a little ill. He drops down onto his futon to read, but can't focus on his book. He feels quite sick, really, and when he discovers that Mac has made his uninvited home on the futon right next to him, he is too tired and dispirited to kick him away. Tonight, if she could take a peek, the sociologist would be delighted by the tableau presenting itself in Apartment 9D. A chastened man, reaching over absentmindedly to pet his nurturing object on its ugly head between its asymmetrical ears. And a nasty yappy territorial male dog tasting the sensation of human affection for probably the first time in his life and finding it, if his asthmatic wheezing purr is any indication, tentatively to his liking.

The Xenia episode has unfortunate repercussions for Lisa. It makes the celestial Antonia Mazzini deign to remember Lisa's existence, and inspires her to provide guidance for the research.

Mazzini is with a group of exotically dressed women, a delegation of some sort, on her way to somewhere important no doubt, but she smiles thinly when Lisa, answering her summons, appears before her office door. "Ah, LisA," she announces, putting an accent on the final vowel. She takes Lisa by the lower arm, maternally, we may suppose, but her fingers dig deeply into Lisa's flesh. "Thank you that you come. I look at your Call for Data. I look over the lists of your content analysis. Good, good, but I suggest something to you. The most important is missing. You must grapple with Sade," Her Brilliance admonishes. She has to tilt her face upward to look at the very much taller Lisa, but somehow she appears supremely aloof even in that posture. Her small, cold blue eyes rest on Lisa as she nods. "The key is Sade." She pauses, studying Lisa intently. "And of course his commentators," she adds, and Lisa's heart sinks deeper still.

Her posture, as she slinks back to her office, is dejected. "Sade," she says to Justin, in passing. "Sade is the key." He grunts sympathetically but barely glances up; Lisa has been in a bad mood for quite some time now.

Lisa decides to do this part on her own. She knows what will happen if she reads Sade with Justin. They will crack up. They will make a few jokes, dismissing the message as stupid, and she will be back where she started, at zero. She touches her lower arm at that thought, as though insistent Italian fingers were still clawing her. No. If Sade is the key, then bygoddess she will give her attention to Sade.

She marches to her desk. She has Sade, of course she does, on her Classics shelf. She just didn't read him, but now she will. She will do a total immersion in Sade. She has *Justine,* she has *Juliette,* she has *The 120 Days of Sodom*. She has a couple of biographies. She has, alas, some commentaries.

So who is this guy, anyway? Okay, so basically he's a psycho who spends most of his life in jail or in the loony bin. He is arrested several times for hiring people to beat him. He starts life as an aristocrat, a perverted aristocrat whose fault none of this probably is, after all that inbreeding, and then he loses all of his property and his title in the French Revolution. During those years, blood flows and a lot of heads roll, more even than in his gory books. Maybe he's not so crazy after all, to spend those years safely tucked away in jail cells. That's where he writes his books, sometimes actually composing his manuscripts on toilet paper. What would Justin say about that—but no. Lisa is determined to apply herself to this oeuvre alone. Total immersion, she reminds herself. The key is Sade. She *will* be open-minded, a resolution severely tested during the following days, as she totes his books, bound in their bright yellow warning jackets, around the office building with her for continuous reading. She even has him propped in front of her over lunch in the cafeteria, dipping her celery grimly into the burdock dip while Sade's heroes roast children for their cannibalistic dinner. They deliberately infect their own mothers with syphilis; they torture and murder toddlers, but never mind. Lisa reads on calmly, reflectively. Rape, sodomy, necrophilia unfold before her; she remains unmoved. "Sade is the key," she murmurs, her new mantra. "The key is Sade."

Justin starts to worry about her mental health. "Hey, Lisa, don't let that stuff get to you," he calls out to her, concerned. "It's crap."

"The term is coprophagy," she corrects him cheerfully. "And we should keep an open mind about it."

Yes, she's going a little crazy.

Lisa's resolve lasts for nearly a week before it collapses. Okay, some of the earlier books, maybe you could get just the tiniest little twinge of a thrill out of them. Not always from an image or a paragraph that you would like to, you know, publicly own up to. But here, confronted with the *key,* her odometer's in the deep freeze. Ugly men, vile women, doing gross stuff, most of it only distantly related to what most people would even consider sex. So there's one little feminist passage in *The 120 Days of Sodom,* much touted by his biographers; big deal.

> Charming sex, you will be free: just as men do, you shall enjoy all the pleasures that Nature makes your duty, do not withhold yourself from even one! Must the more divine half of mankind be kept in chains by the other? Ah, break those bonds; nature wills it.

It seems this paragraph was lifted from the rest of the text and circulated among the French revolutionaries to encourage the *citoyennes* to join in the uprising. The passage had been discovered, a nugget of political gold in the muck, by Saint-Simon. Lisa can just imagine the meeting where Mr. Brilliant Philosopher presented this find to his buddies.

"I happened on this proclamation on page 86 of *The 120 Days of Sodom* totally by chance, when I picked it up purely by accident, mistaking it for Voltaire." Sure! What a creep.

To hell with that. And to hell with her own resident philosopher, too. Let Her Brilliance find her own damn key.

"Charming Lisa, you shall be free!" she calls, throwing the collected volumes of Sade back into the Interdict case and kicking that out into the hallway for Archives to pick up.

It's only eleven, still time for Stimulate, but, witnessing this outburst, and just to be on the safe side, and even though clary sage makes him slightly nauseous, Justin creeps silently to the ergo-display and manually sets it forward to the soothing afternoon Rebalance mode.

The satisfaction of pitching Sade wears off quickly. The afternoon seems endless to Lisa. She fiddles with her notes, checks her mail, updates some files, then wanders up to the sixth-floor Archives to find Justin. It annoys her to see him sprawled comfortably in an armchair and totally absorbed in some stupid old anthropology book.

"Justin," she calls, "helloooo, you can come back to the twenty-first century now. It's almost five, let's call it a day."

"What?" Justin asks, startled out of his concentration.

"I said, I've had enough for today, haven't you? Let's go home."

Justin looks like he is about to disagree, but then he shrugs. Lisa has already started to clear away the books. Reluctantly, he gets up to help her, his eyes still glued to the page. Still reading, he half-heartedly shuffles the books in front of him into a sloppy pile; finally, he tears himself loose, reluctantly puts his book aside face-down, and rises.

"You could take those two boxes by the door, and I'll get the rest of the stuff," Lisa suggests.

She starts to stack the remaining volumes. But first, out of idle curiosity, she turns over Justin's book to see what so held his attention. Printed in an unappealing, archaic script on shiny tissuey paper, it's just some moth-eaten old study of Minoan society. Fragments of ancient texts and poems are interspersed with lengthy, tedious expositions by translators and archaeologists. Dutifully, Justin has highlighted their explanation of the Minoan social order as an egalitarian one in which women held high positions. But can that have been what absorbed him? He has also circled a segment of original text, which appears to be the fragment of an antique love poem. She reads, "He put his hand in her hand, he put his hand to her heart, sweet it is to sleep hand in hand, sweeter still to sleep heart to heart . . ."

Well, that's very charming. And four thousand years old, too; very nice. Lisa tosses the book unsentimentally into a box, forgetting the passage immediately.

Not so Justin. It is still on his mind when he gets home.

Justin is thinking that spending his nights beside a woman would be infinitely superior to the way things are now, when a periodically snorting, less than fragrant dog is his only nocturnal companion. It gives him some comfort to know that men four thousand years ago felt the same way. And that, if things go well, a mere seven months separate him from the pleasant possibility of seeking out the kind of roommate preferred by men since the days of King Minos.

Even Lisa unexpectedly finds her thoughts returning to the ancient paragraph. She'll be sleeping alone tonight. Brett usually stays over on one or two weeknights, and sometimes on weekends, but tonight he has other plans. Again. He isn't that great a bed partner anyway, if truth be told. He insists on keeping the window open, somehow always manages to wad up her duvet inside its cover, and sets the alarm for five, even on Sundays, to accommodate his elaborate morning meditation and exercise ritual. His Express Your Feelings lecture series is a crucial component of the Men's Program, so Lisa supposes it must be her fault that he acts so cold sometimes, that his touch seems so cerebral.

Even when he's in her arms, even when he's as close as close can get, you never really feel that you are touching his heart.

She actually sleeps a lot better without him.

Is that a rebellious thought? Is Lisa attaining a measure of detachment? Does Brett sense this? Or is he just noticing that a certain Justin comes up more and more often in her conversation? Does he have a rival? Can a lowly re-ed possibly be competition for lofty him? It certainly seems highly unlikely, but it's causing Brett an occasional restive moment nonetheless.

If your universe is not in order, how can you concentrate? And one of the fundamental principles of Brett's universe is that his momentary main squeeze, currently Lisa, ought to be there when he wants her. True, lately that has been less and less often, but he's a busy man. When the sun is busy, do the planets just go off and entertain themselves elsewhere? Of course not. They stay in their orbits where they belong. So Brett would like to be certain that Lisa is properly rotating, and that this Justin person is just some harmless cipher in her workday life. Or could this individual possibly be exerting some sort of rival gravitational pull? Finding himself free and in the neighborhood one Sunday morning, Brett decides to check this guy out.

There is a call from the foyer, informing Justin that he is wanted downstairs. He isn't expecting anyone; puzzled, he proceeds to the lobby. A man is standing by the window, looking out; he turns when he hears Justin approaching. "Justin?" he asks. Then he smiles. "I'm Dr. Martins," he introduces himself, offering a handshake. "But please call me Brett. You don't know me, Justin, though you probably know *of* me. And I have heard *so much* about *you*."

The sentence is cryptic, but the voice is collegial, and Justin does not know why it is setting his teeth on edge. So he just says "Oh?" in a neutral tone of voice.

It must have sounded hostile anyway. The man raises his eyebrows slightly, but his smile doesn't waver. "Yes," he says. "Lisa talks about you a lot. She mentioned that you were living here. I happened to be passing by, so on an impulse I thought, why don't I drop in and say hello, see how Justin is doing. Hey," he adds, as though on a sudden inspiration, "why don't I buy you a cup of coffee?"

Justin is confused. Who the hell is this weird-talking guy? "Dr. Martins," he says, frowning, "I'm actually kind of busy—"

"No, no, call me Brett, please," the man chides, and this time it clicks. Brett, oh yeah, Lisa talks about him, he's her SR and some kind of big shot.

"Of course you're busy, that's urban life, right?" Brett is saying, soothingly. Justin feels like a patient. "But that should never get in the way of our human connections. We men have traditionally had problems with that, haven't we? Priorities. Have to set priorities."

Justin shrugs. They go to a shop down the street, where they talk for a while about nothing in particular, leaving Justin at a loss as to why he has been visited. What did this guy want? He feels like he's been checked out, and has passed muster; he also feels that passing muster with Brett is not a compliment. And he can't explain any of those feelings, which makes him very cranky.

Shrugging it off, Justin spends the rest of his day playing tennis with one friend and helping another move some furniture. He's pretty tired that night, almost ready to hit the sack when he hears the knock on his door. He knows that thudding knock by now; it's his neighbor, Will. Not another basement meeting, please! He slouches to the door without enthusiasm; a meaty hand shoves him backward. "Hey!" Justin protests as Will's burly body follows his hammy fist into the room and his large shoe kicks the door shut. Then the giant hand grabs Justin by the shirt collar.

"What!" Justin yells, flailing at his assailant.

"You're hangin' out with the snitch, and don't deny it!" Will barks accusingly. "What did you tell him! What did you tell him about us!"

"What the hell are you talking about!" Justin yells back, his voice not as firm as he would like. Will's grip on his collar is tightening, it's hard to breathe. Justin is getting angry: this guy is a nut. He's getting a little scared, too. He tries to land a stomach punch, but his position is bad; he is trying unsuccessfully to shift for better leverage when Will lets out a sudden yelp and jumps backward, releasing him and cursing wildly. He continues jumping crazily, shaking his leg. Justin looks more closely, and laughs. Mac has clamped his teeth onto the pants, and evidently into part of the calf, of his assailant.

"Get that goddamn mutt off of me before I kill him!" Will yells.

Still laughing, Justin shouts, "Down, boy, that's a good dog, down now, boy."

Mac retreats, still growling, looking about as menacing as you can look when you are barely a foot high. Justin is touched, but first he has to quiet the lunatic. He moves in on Will, who, still cursing, is examining his leg.

"How about telling me what the hell this is all about," Justin suggests. "Are you crazy, or what?"

The steam has gone out of Will. He collapses onto Justin's sofa and pulls up his pant leg for a better look at the injury. It doesn't seem too bad, Justin notes, though Mac has broken the skin. A row of tooth marks the size of fork pricks are starting to bead up red, with blood. Justin finds some tissues, which Will uses to blot his ankle.

"What," Justin snaps, going for assertive.

"Toldja," Will mutters. "You're hangin' out with the snitch, and we wanna know why."

"What—or who—is a snitch?" Justin repeats, enunciating clearly. There must be some way to get through to this meatbrain.

"Dr. Martins," Will replies, just as testily. "Dr. Kisstheirass Martins, hired dick of the Revolution," he continues, rising slowly to his feet and looking like he might be getting ready to slam somebody against a wall any minute now.

Making the same assessment, Mac growls.

Justin steps directly in front of Will and goes for the eye contact. "I do not know Dr. Martins," he says slowly and clearly. "He came here today and paged my room. He is the SR of my boss. I never saw him before today and I hope never to see him again. He did not ask any questions about you. I don't know what the hell he wanted from me. I don't know about snitch, but he's a jerk," Justin concludes in his own natural voice, turning away. "I thought women were supposed to have better taste, these days," he adds in a mutter, to himself.

"Oh yeah?" Will asks suspiciously.

"Yeah." Justin nods. "Absolutely, yeah. And now get out of my face. I've had a long day."

Will studies him penetratingly for a moment. Apparently he is satisfied. He gets up to leave, not without a menacing mock-lunge in the direction of Mac, who growls but retreats a few strategic steps in the direction of the bedroom.

Is it possible that Will growls back? Justin thinks so. My God.

Closing the door, Justin collapses onto his futon and rests his head in his hands.

Immediately he jumps, startled. Something wet is nestling under his T-shirt sleeve. It's a nose, a small black nose, the nose of Mac. Justin extends a hand to pet him. He says, "Hey, big guy, you saved me, huh?" And Mac, hideous graceless Mac, wags a clumsy tail and squirms his ungainly canine rump as close as possible to Justin in a frenzy of pride and adoration.

The weeks pass, and Justin starts to relax about his counterrevolutionary cell membership. He's been to a dozen meetings, and nothing even remotely subversive has transpired. The meetings mostly consist of griping, talking, and blustering, which he's not always in the mood for, but which at times can feel amazingly good. It's hard to imagine that he could get into much trouble for this, even if they did catch him. Not that it's a favorite activity, and maybe someday he'll get up the gumption to say no to a husky Will knocking at the door to collect him. But not just yet, and in the meantime, it's bearable. Sometimes it's just the guys from his building; a few times they've been joined by representatives of other residences.

Yesterday, it was even kind of interesting. They got to talking about the future, when they'd have completed their evaluations and be able to move out. They'd live in much more comfortable housing, then. They'd have real jobs, paying real salaries. And that wasn't even, for most of them, the best part. The best part was that once you had your evaluations, you could try and find yourself a woman.

What kind of a woman might that be? Where would you find her? How would you get her interested? Was it true that, with so many men tied up in reeducation programs, sex-starved women would be throwing themselves at them the moment they were free?

A long and enjoyable hour was spent in related speculation. For the first time, Justin found himself totally absorbed, listening to the older, bolder men. Many of their suggested methods seemed unthinkably forward, but he took away one or two feasible ideas. For instance, Justin was fascinated to learn that walking your dog could be a good way to strike up conversations with women.

Will had been unusually quiet throughout that entire discussion, sitting in his usual place front and center of the circle with a smug look plastered all over his face. Then he had taken the floor, rising dramatically to his feet, and said that though it might be a little premature, he had something very interesting to tell them. Yeees, something very, very interesting, something that they would be totally blown away to hear. He had gone on in this fashion a bit longer, enjoying the attention and the growing suspense, and then he had revealed to them the amazing information that their movement included female members. Because, praise the Lord, the revo-goddamn-lution had not succeeded in turning all females into frigid ball-busting shrews, no, he was here to share with them the happy news that a few real women had survived, women who realized how stupid and ass-backward this whole New Order crap was, who didn't like it one damn bit, who still appreciated and were grateful for the chance to be with real men. Women that they, yes they, would be meeting, and socializing with, and etceteraetcetera! If they played their cards right. And these women could be very friendly and affectionate, if they got his drift! Will had paused meaningfully and granted them a jovial leer, just to make sure that his uncharacteristic restraint did not prevent them from understanding his meaning. Yes, women awaited them. These humble basement get-togethers were just the beginning, just the first tiny step, a chance for them to get their sorry asses to a better place. Step One, they needed to get to know each other, learn some basics about the movement—and pass muster. And they would, he said. They were coming along nicely, and in due course would be ready for initiation into the next of several levels. The one with the women in it.

The next day, reflecting on this meeting, Justin remembers the excited conversation that Will's announcement initiated. Women, in the counterrevolutionary movement! What sort of women can these be, Justin wonders. What kind of women would disdain the glory and distinction of their gender's new position in the world and prefer the old ways, which Justin has been brought up to believe were deeply degrading, intolerable, unnatural, and unfair? Under other circumstances, this would not worry him. But there is no way to dismiss the horrifying news that the basement meetings, in their reassuring triviality and harmlessness, are not the movement at all. That they are only the first innocent step onto the slippery slope of illegality and disaster. What to do? He has to get out of this somehow, the sooner the better. But how? He's really in a mess now.

Then it occurs to Justin that time is on his side. He might be younger than most of the other guys in the Residential Suites, but he's way ahead of them in the certification process. Stubborn, lazy, and resentful, most of them have had to repeat evaluations, or scored so low that remedial work was required. Justin, on the other hand, has been breezing right through. Let's say his luck holds, let's say he aces his fifth and final evaluation. He could be certified and done and out of his current residence in half a year. With luck, that'll be faster than this awful parallel vetting process he has unwittingly gotten himself involved in. How long does it take before you graduate to the next and more sinister level of basement sedition? He doesn't know, and Will didn't say, but with any luck, it will take a good long while. Don't they have to be careful, in underground organizations? They should want to watch you for a year, at least, before they trust you with any of the more secret stuff. Once he's out of the Residential Suites, and always provided things haven't gone too far and he hasn't gotten in too deep, it should be much easier to let his membership lapse. Once Will isn't living right next door to come and get him, Justin can gradually drift away, unnoticed.

Reassured by these calculations, Justin lets his thoughts return more pleasantly to the earlier portion of the evening, the part about meeting women. No woman will go out with him yet, but that doesn't mean he can't, you know, sort of start limbering up a bit. Just to be ready, when the time comes. That trick with the dog, for instance, there wouldn't be any harm whatsoever in testing the hypothesis that women feel compelled to strike up friendly conversations with a male person who is leading a furry mammal around. Are women attracted to men who have pets? It's almost related to his and Lisa's project, in a way; it's almost research.

Justin goes shopping. For his experiment, he needs a leash. The selection in the pet megastore is vast and confounding. There are geometric patterns and solids, of course, but there are also silver- and gold-colored leashes, neon ones, and ones patterned with lady-bugs or smiley faces, cartoon characters or tiny little bone shapes. And the accessories! He hesitates briefly over a selection of little dog-sized T-shirts with clever slogans. "I'm a lover, not a biter," one shirt reads. He decides against it, unsure of the aesthetics and not at all certain that Mac would hold still for one. Studying the leashes once more, he selects a green one with ladybugs, and a collar to match. It's pretty tacky, but maybe it will give Mac a more benign air; besides, close observation of the women in the office has taught him that, no matter what they may claim or even believe about themselves, most of them are still suckers for cute.

At home, though, outfitting Mac in his new purchase, he has a sudden empathetic flash wherein he sees Mac through the eyes of a hypothetical female pedestrian. Recoiling, he almost aborts the experiment. It's impossible to imagine a random female, one who has not had Justin's opportunity to get to know and appreciate this animal's fine character, getting garrulous and misty-eyed over Mac. And it's going to take a lot more than a sweetly decorated leash to endow him with the adjective "cute." If anything, Justin thinks, studying Mac dispassionately, the ladybugs are making things worse. Besides looking ugly, he now looks ridiculous as well. Damn. There must be some way to spruce the little guy up. Would it help to brush him? Might he benefit from a bath? Would one of those stupid T-shirts, by virtue of at least covering part of him up, have been a good idea after all? Justin decides he needs professional advice. He goes back to the pet store, taking Mac along this time.

Returning his earlier purchase, he seeks the counsel of the sales assistant, a fussy elderly man who shudders at the juxtaposition of Mac and ladybugs, pronounces him a "serious dog, a dog's dog," and produces his alternative suggestion, a thick band and matching collar, black leather with spiky metal studs. "Perfect," the salesman declares.

Justin isn't so sure. That's a pretty aggressive style. What will his intended female audience think? "There's no point going against type," the salesman advises. "That isn't just any old dog you've got there—you have a dog with character." And Justin has to admit that this outfit does enhance Mac's stubborn, piggish, ugly demeanor— if that's a good thing. "Very handsome," the salesman calls after them, as Justin authorizes the adjusted payment and goes home with the newly embellished Mac, who perhaps has understood the compliment, and walks with a jaunty new spring in his step.

"*Ohallgoddesses,* how totally adorable," the young woman shrieks, throwing herself on Mac. Well, okay, the *very* young woman. Lisa's niece, Cleo, to be precise. "He looks like a little baby *dino*saur or something!" she gushes. "Oh, just look at his collar! It really goes with him! What's your name, you cute little triceratops you!"

It's the annual Samhain office party, kids, pets, neighbors, seniors, everybody welcome, and Justin has decided to take Mac out for a test of his pet appeal. With glorious results, if Cleo is an indication. Amazingly, Mac submits to her tickling of his ears, the rubbing of his nose, even the lifting up of his stubby front legs in order to investigate whether he can walk on his two hind feet, all accompanied by a stream of high-pitched feminine chatter. Finally, the young assailant sits back on her heels and looks up at Justin.

"Is he yours?" she asks. "He is just *too much*! Lisa! Lisa, you've got to come over here and see this *puppy*! Doesn't he look exactly like a tiny little dinosaur?"

Justin develops new respect for the wisdom of older men this day. Not just Cleo, who after all is a child, but quite a few of the adult women seem to find Mac's ugliness unaccountably appealing. Incredibly, the word "cute" falls more than once, in reference to his ungainly body, his pugnacious face, and even the menacing metal knobs on his collar.

And Cleo, well, Cleo finally lets Justin take his pet back home, but not before extracting the solemn promise that he will bring Mac for a visit soon, very soon, the very next time she visits her aunt.

We've mentioned Cleo's mother already; if she has been generally absent from our story, that is because she is a very busy lady, with lots of important things to do, and not much spare time for her private life.

While growing up, Lisa and her sister enjoyed a typical sibling relationship. Little Lisa trotted worshipfully along behind her older sister, whenever she was graciously allowed to, and tried to get her in trouble by tattling, when she wasn't. Today she admires her, basks in the reflected glory of her fame and status, and, I suppose we could say, loves her.

Theresa is brilliant, has been since infancy; an impatient person with a quick mind and strong opinions. To no one's surprise, she has grown into a formidable woman with an impressive career in the natural sciences. She is a no-nonsense person, acerbic but not unkind, important but personable, a leader. Hearing her current views on men, we might wonder how she attained motherhood, and we might speculate that she probably chose to reproduce in the most cerebral way available, by letting genetic experts select the best paternal chromosomes from their DNA stockpile. But see, people are full of surprises, even people like Theresa, and that isn't how she did it, no, not at all.

Far from being the carefully plotted outcome of science and reason, Cleo is the souvenir of a passionate youthful liaison during

Theresa's research year abroad. It's a romantic story, the little bit of it that Lisa knows, the hazy bit that Theresa confided to her when she returned home, five months pregnant.

The lead researcher, the one with the glacier-blue eyes, the one who specialized in the political role of Middle and New Kingdom Egyptian women; Ivar, with a reputation of being standoffish and scratchy, impossibly conceited and so brutal that more than one research assistant had left the team meeting in tears. Ivar, whose ice-blue eyes turned warm the moment he saw Theresa, whose mouth lost its sardonic turn and softened into a real smile, as his team stared at Theresa in resentful amazement. He was never standoffish or scratchy with Theresa, but instead spoke to her entrancingly of life on the banks of the Nile, and personally designed a pleated gown for her to wear to the midsummer party, just like the one in the legendary *Papyrus of Ani*. He gave her a lapis lazuli amulet, apologizing for how dull its golden flecks were, compared to those in her eyes, and took her on lazy picnics by the riverbank, and there whispered fables about a magic cat and a charmed ibis into her ear. And one night he sneaked a priceless senet board out of the museum and showed her how to play that ancient Egyptian game, until that somehow segued into another two-player game of even greater antiquity . . . In Ivar, Theresa—a young, dreamy Theresa— felt she had met her romantic destiny.

It was the time factor, she had confided upon her return, to a Lisa who was much too young to be anything but smitten with such a grownup, spiritual, complex-sounding explanation. There was never any thought of living together, Theresa had explained with perhaps just a little too much vehemence, or even of trying to prolong their love affair. From the first moment it had felt like they were from different times, Theresa explained, like they were passing each other on trajectories that could bisect for no more than one ecstatic instant.

The spellbinding man with his stories of proud important ancient women, with his tales of pharaoh husbands and priestess wives holding earth and heaven up between them, men and women so cosmic, so incredible that they probably weren't earthlings at all but came perhaps from other planets, as witnessed by the pyramids, the fantastically harmonic alignments of which were still unexplained . . . though he perhaps might come closer to understanding them, one day, if he devoted his life to their study.

And the proud young woman at the very cusp of earth's bravest revolution, on the tremulous brink of an entirely new human future.

Ivar was thrilled when Theresa told him she was pregnant. He said it confirmed the uniqueness of their bond. He said that they were emissaries of two fabulous worlds, meeting to exchange a precious message. "A child," Theresa had whispered to her young sister, in the darkness of Lisa's bedroom, and Lisa had found it thrilling, spine-chillingly exciting beyond words.

A lot has changed since then. Along with the change from useless intangible studies like archaeology to solidly scientific ones like biochemistry, Theresa has also forsaken the romantic, Tarot-card-reading, reincarnation-believing feminism of those earlier years and is now part of the pragmatist backbone of the New Order. Geometry of the pyramids, indeed! And she doesn't need any more messages from men, either, thank you. It's been trouble enough, raising this one.

At times, the bitterness in her voice has inspired in Lisa the sacrilegious thought that, just possibly, there might have been more to Ivar's abrupt departure than the trajectory version alone can explain. On the other hand, it is hard to picture Theresa, even a younger Theresa, as seduced and abandoned. Or is it?

Be that as it may, the story of her daughter's acquisition has undergone heavy editing, in order to adapt itself better to Theresa's present persona and stature in society. Today, that pregnancy features in Theresa's biography as an early instance of reproductive radicalism combined with a generous dash of charming eccentricity. If you don't like the antiseptic path to modern fertility, your offspring brewed up in a lab and injected by a technician wearing gloves and a mask, if you prefer the human touch but you still don't want some guy thinking he can act important and throw his co-parental weight around for the next twenty years just because you needed an infinitesimal little microdroplet of his precious DNA, why, honey, you can just go and help yourself. It's not very difficult. It's like taking candy from a baby, Theresa usually jokes, at this point in her narrative. If you look even remotely female, then all you have to do is position yourself near your intended donor and he'll come trotting right up.

Just take a few simple precautions. Ensnare your genetic prey at a safe distance from home. Let the man think it's a casual affair and you're just playing. Keep your charts, review your temperature curves, and wait for a direct hit. As soon as the LDH reading confirms your success, turn shrewish, pick a fight, say you never want to see him again, and head home with your bounty; he'll never know.

In this version, Ivar figures as the duped collaborator in Theresa's first and most personal experiment in biological engineering, chosen for his incredible blue eyes, the longevity of his grandparents, and his IQ.

Even thus intellectualized, the episode remains something of a blot on Theresa's record. The ethics of sperm are murky. Is it still theft if the other person will never miss what you took, and has several billion more just like it? It's a confusing issue, always has been, and most New Order women agree that it's unwise to muddy the waters yet more through devious ploys like sperm abduction. Theresa's approach, while it continues to have its adherents, really is not the done thing. If you don't want a second parent, you're supposed to decide that ahead of time, and conceive your offspring through the good offices of voluntary anonymous donors who are reimbursed with a two-month reeducation credit. It's tidier that way.

In any case, Lisa remembers the original story and regrets the rewrite. She got a lot of vicarious pleasure out of the original. She can remember lying in bed at night, dreaming of cool riverbank embraces and monsoon winds, slender princesses in pleated linen lying down with their perfect twin-brother spirit-lovers, then coming home with serene smiles, hiding cherished secrets inside their gently curving bellies. She can remember waiting for this magic love-child niece to grow in incrementally increasing ellipses of her sister's silhouette and finally to emerge, noisy with life and damp and red and unbelievably wonderful.

Cleo, fond object of this auntly reverie, stretches lazily for another slice of ginger candy with all the regal grace of her namesake.

Meanwhile, in her laboratory at the Institute for the Guidance of Anatomic Destiny, with generous government funding and support, Theresa is hard at work studying the spotted hyena. Spotted hyenas are remarkable as a species in that the females are dominant. "And not in some half-assed way, either, where the females get to run their own harem while the big guy is off butting heads with the other alphas," as she explains. Oh no. Any way you look at it, the spotted hyena is one formidable gal. Hyenas live in packs of up to eighty, the leader is always female, and every last female down to the daintiest is dominant over every last male, even those twice her size. And the ladies are testy, too. They don't rely on charm, on goodwill, on batting their eyelashes. They maintain their ascendancy by biting and clawing fiercely at any male upstart who provokes them.

Theresa's project has discovered the secret behind this happy state of affairs: testosterone. In most species, the male gets the lion's share of testosterone, so he gets to be boss. The spotted hyena demonstrates an early anomaly. During gestation, all hyena fetuses, female and male, are bathed in the womb with very high doses, with identical doses, of testosterone.

"Male and female, they receive an equal dose and, with it, an equal shot at power," Theresa explains, in her project summary. Interestingly, that is enough to put the female life form into ascendancy. Given a level playing field, given simple chemical equality, the female leads.

Theresa likes that. The Ministry likes that. See: Mother Nature can be our friend, after all.

"But you aren't going to start shooting up our baby girls with testosterone, are you?" one squeamish reviewer blurts, upon hearing this conclusion.

Theresa is good with critics. "Laypersons tend to focus in on the word 'testosterone,'" she observes sympathetically. "We think of it as a male hormone, but that's really not correct. It's scientifically more accurate to think in terms of growth substances and supplements. The sun shines on us, and we grow straight, healthy bones. We add a tiny droplet of fluoride to a glass of sparkling mountain water, and our teeth stay nice and strong."

Lulled by the image of bubbling streams and of sunlight shining on happy little baby girls, the critic nods gently, votes for the budget increase, and fails to notice that she never actually got an answer to the testosterone question, or if she did, that answer wasn't "no."

On the main wall of the laboratory, in the place of honor, where in other ages and places you would have found a picture of a president, a king, a queen, a pope, where today you will usually find a picture of the Founding Mothers, Theresa has mounted a gigantic, framed portrait of a male dung fly. Her co-workers have named him Melvin. He certainly is unlovely, though, let's face it, that spot on the wall has never been assigned on the basis of looks.

But Melvin is not just hanging there to be irreverent, to amuse, or to startle. He is there for a much sterner purpose: to remind everyone, every day, that biology is war.

That sex is war. And that love is war.

That's a tough thing to conclude when at heart you are a romantic, as Theresa is, or at any rate once was. If there is any romance left in her today, then it belongs exclusively to Cleo, the love child engendered with that stranger so long ago. Nothing is going to stand in Cleo's way if Theresa can help it, certainly not biology.

You can't expect biologists to have many illusions, anyway. Dog eats dog, the fittest survive, the food chain chomps remorselessly away at the small and smaller, you eat or get eaten, spawn or go extinct, kill or get killed. If you hope for relief from these grim truths at least within your own species, within your family, or at the hands of your personal little love interest, forget it. "Biology is war," Theresa says, several times a week, and if anybody should ever forget it, they've got Melvin the Giant Dung Fly to remind them. Just as the spotted hyena shows you what splendid heights females can achieve, if chemistry but allows them, thus does Melvin show you to what vile depths males will stoop, in their selfish greed for stupid cellular immortality. In order to pass on its dirty dung-y little genes to glorious posterity, the male dung fly will grab himself a fertile female and mate. Even before he's all done, he gets kicked away by a bigger dung fly, who rinses away his rival's sperm and leaves his own behind, only to have it sluiced out by the next higher guy on the totem pole, until finally the poor exhausted girl fly has been worked over by the entire pecking order, and is groggily sloshing around in one disgusting cocktail of warring DNA. And even then there's no respite for her, because at that point, she dies. The winner's sperm contains a lethal ingredient to kill her, thus making sure that he will remain unsupplanted, the triumphant, the immortal progenitor of her litter of poor posthumous motherless dung babies.

What Theresa has taken away from this is the lesson that there is no surcease, not even in the brief embrace of reproduction, no respite, not even temporary, from the treachery of the male, no end to his dirty tricks, his lies, and the pain he inflicts. Relax for just an instant in the arms of your lover, and bam, he'll just as likely kill you with his poison sperm. If he's a dung fly.

And which one of them isn't.

There is a guest speaker tonight. Justin sees him entering the Residential Suites, an overweight jowly man with a net bag containing a copper pan and some cooking utensils, and takes him to be one of the domestic science instructors who frequently conduct tutorials for those in peril of failing their Self-Reliance Evaluation. But this, apparently, was only a disguise. A bit later, in the basement, minus the accessories, the same man strides to the front of the room to be introduced as one of the movement's prime thinkers, a beacon in the darkness, whom it will be an honor and a distinction for the privileged attendees to hear tonight.

The room is jammed with chairs: at least four cells have merged to hear today's lecture. Yes, today it's not just chat, today there is a real program. The guest will speak, then he will take questions, and apparently there will be a film, to judge by the equipment some of the men are noisily rolling into place. The lights dim, and we are ready for tonight's topic, "Heroes under Siege."

"Gentlemen," the speaker begins. "We are faced with a situation in which not just the social order, not just the continuation of the human race, but indeed the existence of history itself is in peril."

Justin is startled. History. He hasn't heard anyone use that archaic word for years.

The lights dim and the lecturer activates the screen, which shows, in rapid progression, a gigantic dam, a space station, some bridges, and a series of skyscrapers.

"History," the speaker is saying. "The record of man's accomplishments in the present, as well as a link to the great civilizations of our forefathers."

Onscreen, the temples at Karnak, the Roman Forum, and a pack of what appear to be Mongol riders on horseback flash by.

"The exploration of the wilderness! The conquest of space! Cure for diseases!" The speaker hurtles forward, straining to keep up with the rapidly changing images on his screen, as we see covered wagons rumble across a plain and astronauts float outside space stations, followed by men in white lab coats peering intently into test tubes.

"This is your heritage, men. The greatness of science and history! The march of time! The rise and fall of empires!"

Now some scenes of epic battles are unfolding, tanks rolling up muddy hills, some sort of Roman legion swarming across a plain, then back to modern times, men with agonized faces dragging wounded comrades through a jungle, some officers huddled before a collection of radar screens, and then the rush of jets thundering across a night sky.

"Gentlemen. The human race has always been a race of warriors, of inventors, of builders! With blood, sweat, dreams, and genius, we erect our worlds! Out of struggle, greatness is born! In conflict, the human drama finds its climax! We march forward, and great men lead us."

Behind him, faces fill the screen; for the benefit of the younger audience members, who may not recognize them any longer, captions show their names. Julius Caesar. Alexander the Great. General Rommel. Adolf Hitler. Winston Churchill. Genghis Khan. Napoleon Bonaparte. George Washington. Lenin. Mao Zedong.

Abruptly, the screen goes blank, and the speaker is silhouetted in stark drama before it.

"How many of you younger men," he asks, in a quiet, somber

voice, "even know these names anymore? Schools are forbidden to teach them, we are forbidden to speak them. Yes, men," he says, "we are supposed to forget all of that. History has become 'Chronics,' a bloodless, watered-down porridge of feel-good do-good bedtime stories. And we, we men, the former heroes of history, have been turned into tame, vegetable-eating, housebroken eunuchs."

He lifts up the bag that got him into the dorm, the bag filled with kitchen implements. "Swords into egg whisks, gentlemen, that is where we stand today. Heroes into mother's little helpers. And when that is accomplished, then history will truly be at an end. There will be nothing new, nothing great. Just a globe full of ladies' sewing circles, extending endlessly into a bland, castrated future."

There is silence while the audience contemplates this dark vision.

"And why?" the speaker asks, after holding the pause. "Why are they erasing history? Because they need to conceal the one essential truth that could bring down their pitiful sham of a New Order: the fact that all truly important accomplishments of civilization, art, and culture were, always have been, and always will be created by men—the gender of visionaries, inventors, artists . . . the gender of heroes."

There is sustained applause.

In the back row, Hugo belches.

The speaker remains in place for a long moment, allowing a solemn silence to fall over the gathering. At last, with a curt nod, he gathers up his bag of pans and gravy separators, taking on again the persona of the domestic arts tutor, and leaves.

And then, since Friday is traditionally Classics Night at the Club, everybody settles in to watch some pirate copies of that golden oldie *Baywatch*.

Except for Justin, who takes a handful of chips from the refreshment table and departs, unnoticed, for his rooms, to think about history.

Due to a scheduling foul-up, the quickrope team Lisa coaches has an away game on Tuesday, when she's supposed to watch Cleo. She needs a replacement babysitter. She remembers how well Justin and Cleo hit it off, and that Justin promised to let Cleo play with Mac. So doesn't Justin maybe want to get started on his credits?

Justin is marginally annoyed. Come on. The time when he might need someone to watch a child that he might one day father with a woman he might one day meet, if he passes his evaluation and is even allowed to begin trying for a relationship, seems as remote as the afterlife. He needs Nurturing Exchange Credits like he needs a hole in the head. But yes, okay, he'll do it. Really, he'll be glad to. It'll be fun to be with Cleo, in Lisa's comfortable apartment, and altogether it beats another boring evening in the Residential Suites.

Besides, he has some personal research to do.

They've had their snack; they've gone for a walk with Mac and tried to teach him tricks with no success that Justin can see, though Cleo insists that Mac is highly gifted and *obviously* just on the brink of getting it; they've reviewed her homework; and now Cleo has some sort of elaborate puzzle sheet spread out in front of her and is engrossed in trying to unlock its pattern. He studies her, planning his approach.

"Cleo," he asks her, "in school, do you have, you know, history?" He uses the expression timidly, worried that the archaic term may shock her, but she just looks puzzled and shakes her head.

"What about Chronics, do you have that?"

"Oh sure." Cleo nods. "We have Chronics four hours a week."

"Really!" her interviewer exclaims in that benevolent, too-interested voice many grownups, though she would have thought not Justin, use when they are conversing with younger persons. "What are you learning about in Chronics right now?"

"Well," she says, frowning slightly in response to his weird intonation—what's the matter with him today?—"we just started a segment on paid and unpaid work through the ages."

Justin nods and thinks about how to frame his next question. "So," he asks then, "do you learn about famous people, too?"

"Uh-huh," Cleo confirms, distractedly. She fears she has taken a wrong turn in her 3-D maze. Should she go back, or persist until she's sure she's on the wrong path? That's what she wants to think about, not Chronics. It's so boring, the way older people always feel they should talk to you about school.

"Do you learn about famous men, too?" Justin persists.

Aha! So that's what this is all about, Cleo thinks. He isn't just asking her questions to make conversation, he's having an identity crisis. Poor him! But no sweat. Cleo knows all about this, she's got it covered. The boys in the class had a similar complaint just a few weeks ago, and the teacher went over the matter at length, so Cleo knows just what to say.

"Of course there have been famous men, too, Justin!" she says, in a kindly voice copied from her teacher. "Men are not born bad. It was just the social conditions that kept them from contributing more to society and the family, depriving them of opportunities to be caring and making them act violent and destructive. But even so, even under those disadvantaged conditions, in every age, there were good and important men. In fact, I just did a report on one."

"You did?" Justin repeats, disarmed by her sweetness but a little dizzy from her rendition of his gender's role in world affairs.

"Yes!" she nods. "Do you know World War II? Well, my report was on this man called Simon Wiesenthal. All these countries suddenly went, like, completely crazy, and they locked up thousands and thousands of children and women and old people, and other people, too, in these camps, and they *murdered* them. And Simon Wiesenthal was locked up, too, and he was tortured and almost murdered, but then he was rescued, but the countries that rescued him, they weren't really very good either, because they should have rescued him much sooner, but, well, none of the countries were good in those days, they basically were all the same, just interested in making lots of money and fighting wars and oppressing others and having power, because of course that's just the way things were under the AR, and before our New Order. But anyway, after he was rescued he worked for justice, and the bad people were trying to hide, but he helped find them. But mostly he believed in justice and tolerance and he built a museum about it, so he was ahead of his time and that is why we like to remember him. And I did a poster to go with my report," Cleo finishes.

"That's nice," Justin says. "Very interesting. And probably the others in your class also did reports about World War II? About some other famous men in World War II?"

Cleo looks at him blankly.

"I'll bet there were some famous generals and political leaders, maybe a president or something, who helped end that war," Justin cues her.

Cleo smiles pityingly. "Justin, security is important and that's why we have civil defense, and even if we hate weapons, we do have to be prepared against attacks, but in those days it was different, those generals *loved* war, so they don't deserve to be honored for that. And the political leaders, well . . ." Cleo's shrug speaks volumes. It is obvious that she feels no need to go on, because everyone knows that all AR politicians were so contemptible that the decision to consign them to mnemonic oblivion needs no further explanation.

Justin finds himself in some sympathy with the idea that evil, self-aggrandizing behavior should not be rewarded with fame and immortality. Still, can the biggest names in history, the legendary, the epic, so easily be gone, gone, gone, erased from the slate of young brains just like that? Is that possible?

"Those countries that went crazy," he probes, trying to stay in her language, "the ones that murdered millions of innocent people, didn't they have a famous leader, who gave them those crazy ideas? You know who I mean," he continues deviously, "it's on the tip of my tongue, oh gosh . . . what was his name again? Something with an 'H' . . . Hit . . . Hit . . ."

Now he really has managed to shock Cleo.

"Hush, Justin!" she exclaims, appalled. "We don't remember the names of evil people!"

But, mindful of her responsibilities toward older, confused

individuals, she collects herself, pushes the maze away with a sigh, and gives her full attention to Justin.

"Under the AR," she reminds him, "you could become famous by doing terrible things. That was so sick! The more terrible the things you did, the more famous you would become! And in the really olden days there were like, kings and emperors and stuff, who killed thousands of people and piled up their skulls into huge towers," Cleo explains with grisly relish, "and they would be very famous and cities would be named after them and all that. And thousands of years later, people still knew their names. And some people would admire them and try to be like them and do more bad stuff. Well, don't you think that was wrong, Justin?" she asks didactically.

Hypnotized by her solemnity, he can but nod.

"And even crazy people, that murdered a lot of other people, they could get famous, too, and then other crazy people would get ideas from them and copy them. Or they would murder someone famous, and that would make *them* famous." Cleo winds down her lecture with satisfaction. "So now, if you do something terrible, you don't get to be famous. We don't want to remember you at all then! We don't want to see your face! We wish you had never been born! Your name gets erased forever, and nobody talks about you or what you did. Isn't that better, Justin?"

Sensing Cleo's agitation, Mac, curled up at her feet, lets out a hoarse bark. And, satisfied that she has spread enlightenment, Cleo returns to her puzzle.

Justin almost turns himself in. He considers that possibility very seriously. It's just that he's not sure what will happen to him then. Possibly, since he hasn't done anything really bad yet, he'll be able to strike some kind of deal and not be punished too severely. But he's sure to lose his evaluation credits, and be in for a lot more counseling. They'll let him leave the Residential Suites, but they'll move him into a different place very much like it, probably with less freedom. And if the underground is as pervasive as Will suggests, and if they find out he betrayed them, they'll come after him wherever he is.

Justin never used to spend much time thinking about politics. He didn't question the evaluations, any more than a young person questions his algebra exam, his biology term paper, or the need to sit down for four hours to an SAT test. These are the things you do to become an adult member of your society, so you do them. You can gripe about it if that makes you feel better, but you do them.

Nor did Justin previously spend much time thinking about the Revolution. It happened, it was a great thing, and everyone is much happier now; that's what he's always heard and he has no reason to doubt it. But now, unbidden, an option has been dangled in front of him, the option to take sides. To exercise this option, Justin first has to decide where he fits in. Is he a revolutionary or an antirevolutionary? It sounds simple, but Justin is not finding it so. The Revolution says it stands for fairness and equality; the counterrevolutionary movement makes the same claim. The Revolution says things used to be terrible; the antirevolutionaries claim they used to be great; Justin is too young to remember. The Revolution, that's Nadine, a curt, self-righteous woman who bosses him around, and a slew of counselors with syrupy voices, endless questionnaires, and annoying programs; the counterrevolution is Will, a growling klutz who pushes him around, and a basement full of dullards. Where does he fit? Justin suspects: nowhere.

When in doubt, people tend to go for the known quantity. The Revolution hasn't done anything bad to him. He's comfortable, or at least he expects to be just as soon as he moves out of the Residential Suites. Besides Nadine, the Revolution is also embodied by women like Lisa; she's nice and he likes her, and the other women in the office have made him welcome, too.

However—now that he's started to ask questions—he does wonder about the government's level of competence. Are they on top of things? At times they seem sort of bubble-headed. Do they have the slightest clue what is in the hearts of men? Beneath their smiling, optimistic, world-improving demeanor, do they have the tiniest inkling of what is happening in, for instance, re-ed basements all over town? Should he tell someone?

It's a sunny day. Justin and Lisa collect their lunch trays from the cafeteria and sit at one of the picnic tables that dot the rooftop garden.

"So!" Justin asks, casually. "Everybody's happy with the Certification Program? Going well, is it?"

"I guess." Lisa shrugs.

"So, after those five reeducation segments, the men pretty much fit into the New Order, do they?"

"Mmmmm," Lisa agrees uninterestedly, returning a stray slice of pickle to her sandwich.

"There sure are a lot of different sorts of men out there, to reach them with just one program," Justin persists.

Lisa looks up. "What are you getting at?" she asks.

He hesitates. "Nothing," he says. "Nothing at all! What could I be getting at? I was just, you know, thinking. Since I work here now, and all, I was just thinking about the different ministerial programs."

Lisa is perplexed. What is he carrying on about this for? "Thinking about the ministerial programs," like hell. Something is obviously bothering him. Astute questioning might get her somewhere, but she chooses to handle the situation instead of studying it. This probably has to do with the reeducation process, Lisa decides. Many men chafe at it, she knows that. Trying to recollect the substance of a recent Managing the Transgender Workplace seminar, and mindful of her responsibilities as a mentor, she goes for the empathy.

"You know, Justin," she explains kindly, "many men incorrectly think of reeducation as a punishment. But that's not what it is, not at all. It's just that we live in a time of transition. We *are* the transitional generation. We were born into the Old Order, and young as we were, it tried to put its stamp on us, and we need to get free of it. Many men wrongly believe that they are being discriminated against or even punished, and they find the evaluations insulting, but women get reeducated, too. I went through the exact same thing that you're doing now. We all need it. It's not fun, I know that. You have to question a lot of things, face up to a lot of things; it can be scary. I'm sure the process feels restrictive at times, and endless, but you're very close to being finished. You'll have learned a lot, you'll have a much better perspective, and you'll be ready to strike out on your own. And don't think for one moment that just because you're a man, you won't have good chances for advancement. There are so many opportunities for talented men! I mean, just look at Brett, for example."

Concluding her pep talk, Lisa smiles encouragingly at Justin.

"Gee, yeah, that's right," he agrees, in an ominously pleasant voice. "When I grow up, maybe I can be just like Brett."

With that he grabs his drink and the remainder of his sandwich and stalks off.

Well! "Touchy," Lisa exclaims. What's wrong with him, anyway!

Justin takes himself and his sandwich to a quiet bench on the lower level and sits there, in a funk. He's mad at Lisa, but he's mad at himself, too. What kind of a childish scene was that? Yes, Lisa in her didactic mode can be hard to take, but still, she's always been nice to him, and he didn't need to blow her off like that. He values their friendship a lot. She's like the sister he never had. Plus, she provides a little window into the thoughts of women.

Not that the view through that window is very reassuring. Even once you're certified for them, love affairs appear to be a mixed blessing, if Lisa is any indication. Some days she seems happy, but more often she doesn't, and while she doesn't confide in him, exactly, she does make the occasional wry remark from which he concludes that life with Brett is far from rosy.

As for Brett, Justin has developed a deep-seated, a really vivid dislike for him, made up of equal parts envy, brotherly solidarity with Lisa, and disdain for his position as one of the Revolution's pet males. How can Lisa like him? Worse still: love him? Can't she see what a fraud, what a smug conceited jerk he is? Or do women like that? Will he, too, have to become more Brett-like in order to attract a mate?

I see that people haven't gotten any less self-centered, despite all the sharing and caring opportunities the Revolution provides. Me, me, me, that's still what makes the world go round, I see. Justin's interest in politics and society lasted for what? About fifteen seconds. Now we're back to worrying about Justin. His ego. His masculinity. And above all, his future chances for a date.

But perhaps you, also, are wondering about the potential future of Justin's personal life. You're not alone in that. An entire bureaucracy, the Ministry of Cohabitation Sciences, is devoted to that very question. They're trying to find a family form that will work. They've mostly got anthropologists assigned to the effort; sociologists don't have a lot of credibility in that field, after announcing the "death of the family" for five or six decades in their professional publications without trying to resuscitate the patient.

Here's what the anthropologists have got, so far: the last time marriage worked, somewhere back in the Pleistocene, kids were raised by mom, grandma, and Uncle Charlie. "Bio-Dad" would breeze in and out for conjugal visits, bringing chunks of mammoth and other thoughtful gifts, but he wouldn't stay. Apparently, women do better at roping their brothers in than their lovers; also, brotherhood is a permanent assignment, while marriage, despite the best of intentions, often isn't.

But the Ministry plans to study the matter very carefully, considering many alternatives. There's no hurry, after all. During the final decades before the Revolution, moms and kids learned to go with the flow of joint-custodial-Wednesday-to-Saturday dad, visiting-weekend dad, said-he-was-coming-but-didn't-show-up dad, the-support-payment-check-is-in-the-mail dad, temporarily-living-with-mom-and-pretending-to-like-her-kids potential stepdad, actual stepdad, second stepdad—come to think of it, old reliable Uncle Charlie is starting to look pretty good.

And love, you want to know? What of love? Honey, when it comes to love you're on your own; you know that. Love is the wild card. Ain't no revolution gonna change that.

In one corner of a huge meeting room at the Ministry of Thought, several figures huddle in intent conference. Their body language speaks volumes. They are extremely worried about something important. And their meeting is conspiratorial.

"We're so close," Person Two breathes. "We have all the information. We're ready for them."

"They're bound to be jumpy, though," Person Three notes. "This is the big one. They know what's at stake. What if they back out at the last minute?"

"That worries me, too," Person Two admits. "This time, we're prepared. Next time, they may catch us by surprise."

The tension in this room is, I fear, beyond what can be handled by even the highest, most euphoric settings of the ergo-display. I mean, just put yourself in their place.

Imagine that you are a gifted, committed intelligence operative forced to work under a bunch of do-gooding superiors with saccharine views of the world, who won't listen to you or take proper precautions. Even after you alert them to the existence of an underground counterrevolutionary organization, they persist in viewing this as a minor affair. Never mind, it's just talk, they say, just a few disoriented men getting together in basements to ventilate. The reeducation process will take care of it. Even faced with the occasional act of terrorism, they instruct you not to overreact, not to "spoil the integrative process."

Exasperated at this attitude, you and a few like-minded colleagues make it your business to look into the counterrevolutionary underground, on your own time. What you find is disturbing, worse even than you had suspected. You discover that the counterrevolutionaries are better organized and more numerous than previously believed. United by your secret research effort and by your contempt for incompetent superiors, you find yourselves coalescing into a kind of rogue unit.

And then you learn that your opponents are preparing a definitive strike, aimed at a complete overthrow of your Revolution.

Now you have two things to worry about: one, the plot; and two, that if you tell your superiors about it, they will botch things. With enough advance notice, presumably they'll be able to stop this immediate plot, but will even that experience bring them to their senses? Or will they continue to give saboteurs and conspirators much too much leeway?

You sense an enormous though terrifying opportunity: say you don't tell them, say you let the plot go forward. Meanwhile, clandestinely, you take your own defensive measures against the conspiracy. If you succeed, you emerge triumphant. Your wimpy sellout superiors are discredited and the counterrevolutionary conspirators finally get the crackdown they deserve.

Of course, if you mess up and fail to stop them in time . . . But that doesn't even bear thinking about.

You take all possible precautions. Your network is expanding, you have supporters in all key facilities, your plan is in place. But your nerves are on edge. The stakes are enormous. The risk is high.

And there's another, more insidious kind of risk: that the plotters might back down. They've got to be even more nervous than you are. What if they get scared, and back out at the last minute? This time, you're ready for them. Next time, you might not be.

So here's what we've got: we've got the leaders of an elite rogue intelligence unit, in the grip of two anxieties. That a terrifying subversive plot might go forward. And that it might not.

Person One has risen to pace, and is thinking out loud. "They've got to be afraid of being caught," she observes. "So far, they haven't detected our surveillance, and they don't know who our agents are. That's good, because it's given them the confidence to move forward. But we're at a critical juncture. They know we have a significant security apparatus. If there's no sign of surveillance at all, they'll begin to find that suspicious. We've got to do a more amateurish infiltration job."

What?

Patiently, Person One explains. The conspirators know that Intel has to be aware of their existence. Therefore, you've got to lull them into a false sense of security. Throw them some agents they can catch.

Person One smiles tightly. "They think we're stupid, anyway. They think women are squeamish, full of scruples, easily frightened; they've been underestimating us for the last ten thousand years, and our current Directorate has given them every reason to continue doing so. We just have to conform to their expectations. Let's give them a spy, one who won't get any further than the margins of their organizations, one they can catch without too much trouble. That will reassure them that we don't have a clue."

The others mull this over; they nod. That's clever. Yes. Give them a decoy. A red herring.

They just have to find the right person for the job. Or maybe the right person will find them.

Lisa asks to see Nadine in private.

"I don't think I can complete my project," she says, coming right out with it. "I'm sorry. I guess I'm just the wrong person for it. I can't do it, and I don't feel right getting any more work-study credits for this."

Nadine is silent. She fiddles with something on her desk and does not even look at Lisa.

"I'm not doing this impulsively," Lisa adds, nervously. "I'm not a quitter. But this is too important, and I'm botching it." Nadine unnervingly still says nothing, so Lisa feels compelled to continue.

"I plowed through all the suggested materials," she explains. "I developed categories . . . and Justin worked very hard, it's definitely not his fault, he put in lots of extra hours, and he deserves to get credit. And of course I'm not just going to drop this, I'll put together everything we've got and leave behind an orderly file for my successor."

Finally, Nadine deigns to look up. "Vot you sink is making zis so hard for you, Lisa?" she asks softly, almost kindly.

It's a fair question, one that Lisa has asked herself many times over the past few days.

"I'm not passionate," she says, thinly.

Is that a quickly suppressed smile or just a facial tic jerking the corner of Nadine's mouth? It must be a tic, because already she is solemn again, and looking at the younger woman with great empathy.

"Tell me," she says, encouragingly.

Lisa hesitates for a moment, but then she speaks. "I don't have any problems with sex, I like sex, it's great. But my idea of sex is, I guess, kind of boring. I don't feel the things the people in those books feel. Most of the stuff they get all excited about, I just don't get it. Just thinking about it usually makes me laugh, or I get distracted imagining how that outfit must itch, or how uncomfortable that position would be, or how stupid you would feel. First I blamed the books, but really I guess it's me. I'm lacking in passion. I'm too boring for this assignment. Camille Paglia was right," she adds, in a brave little voice. "Not about feminists in general, but about me. I'm a prude."

Nadine gives Lisa a kindly look. "I sink about zis," she says. "It is good you come to me. I sink about it, den we spick again. Tomorrow, yes? Not here. You come to my house tomorrow, we spick."

Quickly she scrawls an address on a slip of paper. Then Lisa is dismissed and finds herself standing dizzily in the hallway. A private summons. To Nadine's home. This is weird.

Lisa has never been to Nadine's apartment before, no one in the office has. It's in the best section of Elizabeth Cady, a fashionable and exclusive neighborhood, that's the first surprise. Somehow, Lisa had pictured her boss as living somewhere more austere. Though come to think of it, you'd be hard pressed to find anything very austere, these days. This has been a very stylish revolution. You know women, they like to accessorize. In the past they had to content themselves with decorating their homes, their fingernails, and their hair—but those drab utilitarian days are over now, and the whole world is theirs to color-coordinate, to stencil and remodel. Gone are the parking lots and the parking garages, the warehouses, the depots, gone the ugly buildings. If some phallic monstrosity could not be torn down, then it has been repainted, outfitted with a veranda, decorated with murals, glued over with mosaics, and given a trellis.

Maybe it's a delusion, but many people swear that even the climate has improved. The air seems softer and warmer, as though a Mediterranean goddess, as a gift to her newly triumphant mortal sisters, were caressing the planet with mild and fragrant breezes.

And I'm sure it's just Lisa's imagination that makes the lobby of Nadine's building, a perfectly attractive space with planters and buffed hardwood floors and huge bowls of apples at the security desk, seem a few degrees chillier than the air outside.

The apartment Nadine admits her to is elegant, high-tech. She waves Lisa into the living room but stays in the entranceway herself, doing something elaborate to the control panel. Lisa strolls the room's circumference, stretching her neck, trying to see as much as possible of the rest of the apartment, but only a dim hallway is visible. The doors to the rooms leading off on either side of it are all closed. Probably some sort of constipated Germanic neatness habit, she supposes. Frustrated in her nosiness, she turns back to Nadine, who is now fiddling with the monitor and turning up the white-noise switch. "These new buildings," she murmurs. "Flimsy construction. At times I can hear the music they're playing next door. But now we should have complete privacy."

Complete privacy? What is Nadine planning—Gestalt therapy? Torture? Lisa looks around, wondering if Nadine lives alone. The sleekly spartan living room, mostly glass interspersed with a few pieces of warmer Euro-country pine, offers no clues to the existence of other occupants. She is starting to feel uncomfortable, even dizzy, but doesn't exactly know why.

"We need to have a very private conversation," Nadine explains, catching Lisa's doubtful look.

With that, she strides purposefully to a Bavarian hand-stenciled cabinet, pulls out two glasses and a bottle of liqueur, pours out generous amounts, takes a deep swallow, and hands Lisa the other glass.

"Try it," she orders. "Kräutergoldbecher. It's mostly herbs. A friend brings it for me from Bratislava. It's good for you. Burns life's little aggravations right out of you. Clears the brain."

Lisa takes a sip, and a taste first too sweet, then immediately too bitter rolls unpleasantly over her tongue before hitting the back of her throat with a fiery punch. The humming whirring noise of the machine turned up too high, the drink . . . She feels really dizzy. With a radiant smile that exposes a row of large carnivorous teeth, Nadine brings her arm forward to click glasses with Lisa; involuntarily, Lisa takes a step backward. Please, please, don't let this be some sort of a weird seduction effort. Don't let Nadine be thinking, just because Lisa has made the mistake of letting her guard down and being open with her, that they are some sort of soul mates.

"To the Revolution!" Nadine calls out, her arm advancing remorselessly in pursuit of Lisa's retreating glass.

Lisa freezes as the cause of her dizziness suddenly comes to her: no accent. Nadine has no accent. She is speaking the English of the Puritans, perfect and clear as a bell. Lisa shakes her head to reactivate her ears; that drink! it must be incredibly potent! But wait!

When was the accent lost? Did Nadine still have it when Lisa first arrived?

Nadine has stopped talking and is regarding Lisa impatiently. "Come on," she says, "snap out of it. A lot of things are not what they seem, don't wimp out on me this early in the game."

"You're talking funny," Lisa says stupidly. "I mean, you aren't. I mean, what happened to your accent?"

Nadine sighs. "It's just to distract attention from other things about me. And I see it's effective, at least with you, Lisa. Come on, pull yourself together!"

And that is how Lisa, too, ends up in a cell.

"I like you, Lisa," Nadine says, guiding her debilitated guest to an armchair. "You underrate yourself, you know. You're a valuable team member. Or you could be. You will be. These are not easy times for a young woman. Of course," she adds, "when have the times ever been easy for young women?"

Nadine shrugs philosophically and regards Lisa with a benign parental eye.

"We need you for a very important assignment. You have the stamina and you have the sort of mind that we are looking for."

Lisa does not know what is going on.

"Remember the little speech you gave in my office yesterday?"

Lisa nods, flushing.

"It was very sweet," Nadine says. "So sincere. So excessively humble. You didn't fail at your project. I've been impressed with your diligence and your determination. And I'm sure you have plenty of passion, too. Your resignation speech, though, was perfect, was wonderful. So wonderful that I need you to give it again, verbatim if possible. To Xenia."

Lisa stares. Nothing, nothing is making any sense.

Nadine laughs gently. "You think you are not good enough for your assignment, but I think you are capable of a far more difficult, more demanding—and yes, even dangerous one. One that your government urgently needs you for."

Dangerous? Government? Lisa is so captivated by the intensity of this bizarre moment that, though she hears and registers the words, she fails to challenge them.

"You should know, Lisa," Nadine continues, "that our struggle is far from over. The Revolution is not safe, not by any means. Not everyone wants to live in a fair and peaceful society. There are forces at work who want things to go back to the way they were before. I'm sure you've heard of the Restore Harmony Movement."

Lisa nods earnestly. She's heard of it, yes. An outlawed organization, fanatics.

"A restorationist group," Nadine recites in a mocking singsong. "Unhappy, frustrated individuals, getting together to moan about how great things used to be. Crazy misfits, malcontents, but basically harmless."

Lisa nods.

"Yes," Nadine snaps, "that is what most people believe, and that's what we want them to believe. A healthy society cannot grow in the shadow of fear. Therefore, the decision was made to downplay Harmony. A wise decision, on the whole. It's wrong to give fanatics too much publicity. But the truth is, Lisa, that Harmony is considerably more threatening than the public realizes."

She points to a thick file on the coffee table; it contains, she says, documented evidence of terrorist incidents, assassinations, hostage situations, and other subversive acts directly linked to Harmony. Lisa opens it. A few of the more spectacular news items catch her eye. She remembers some of those incidents; remembers, too, that they had been reported as accidents. Collisions. Gas leaks. Abandoned ammunition depots exploding.

"And, Lisa, I need to tell you something even more shocking," Nadine continues, gently taking the file away from an ashen Lisa. "We're not just dealing with counterrevolutionary men. There are women involved in this, too. Confused, unstable women. Collaborators. They join that movement because they are desperate for acceptance, they want to do something secret, something forbidden, to feel important. Then they are drawn into destructive, illegal activities. After that, there is no way out for them."

She pauses. "The things in that file are bad enough," she says. "But we have discovered that they are planning something bigger, something much worse. Unfortunately, we don't know exactly what it is. And that, Lisa, is where you come in."

Lisa peers covertly around the room. Maybe this is some kind of a new party game. Maybe the other women from the office will come leaping out from behind the furniture, laughing hysterically, as soon as she engages seriously in this insane discussion. Because it can't be true; Nadine can't really be trying to recruit her as a secret agent.

Guessing her thoughts, Nadine speaks softly. "It's not a joke, Lisa. It's quite, quite serious. Harmony is the deadliest threat our society faces today."

"But how could I possibly do anything about it?" Lisa mumbles.

Nadine smiles encouragingly. "All I'm asking you to do," she says, "is to meet with Xenia and repeat to her, as exactly as you can, your wonderful little speech about passion and prudery."

Lisa shakes her head. "How could that possibly help?"

Nadine walks to the window, plays with the screen, looks outside. "We have reason to believe that Xenia is part of the Harmony Movement," she says, finally. "We've been wondering for months how to approach her, how to get a mole into her group. We couldn't come up with a suitable plan. Everything we thought of seemed too transparent. But your speech, Lisa . . . well, it was brilliant. When I heard it, I thought: Yes! That is it. It wouldn't do for someone to come right up to her and ask to join, that would be far too obvious. They like to recruit their members themselves, especially the women members, we know that. But how to get her attention? And then, my dear, you come strolling into my office and you blurt out the perfect, the picture-perfect cover story. If you can just do it again, we're in! She'll think you came to her because of her performance about passion and freedom the other day. Believe me, Lisa: this can work. I want you to talk to her tomorrow."

"But the last time I saw her, in your office, I was rude to her. I told her off. She'll never believe that I'm coming to her for advice," Lisa protests.

Nadine disagrees. "Wrong. Actually, that makes you doubly credible. A real infiltrator would have tried to ingratiate herself, so by acting hostile, paradoxically you have created a setting of trust. You will tell her that the things she said that day, the stuff about freedom and dark eros and all that crap, were profoundly upsetting to you, *because* those are the things missing in your own life. And now you've realized that the reason you were so upset and so rude was because you envied her. She'll love that. I promise you. She'll eat it up. That's just the sort of twisted, sick thinking they like." Nadine nods, briskly. "It's perfect."

Amazingly, she's right. When Lisa timidly asks to speak to her alone, fully expecting to be sneered at and rebuffed, Xenia looks intrigued and agrees immediately. Lunch, today, she suggests. In the park.

Nearly choking on her egg salad with nervousness, Lisa squirms about on the bench and recites her spiel about inhibition and prudery. The effect on Xenia is amazing. Putting her own lunch down, Xenia reaches over to embrace Lisa. She grabs her hand and squeezes it. She swivels around to gaze somberly into Lisa's eyes—eyes which, at this moment, brim with tears from a celery chunk which, in all the excitement, has gotten stuck midway down her throat. Xenia takes this as a further sign of sincerity and profound emotion and wipes at her own eyes, which are filling with tears of empathy.

"You see?" she says to Lisa encouragingly. "You *are* a passionate woman. You are *full* of potential feeling, *stifled* by that awful frigid bunch of *nuns* who are running things. Lisa, you did the right thing today. You have embarked on an exciting journey, and I am going to help you."

And she promises to introduce Lisa to "a community of kindred spirits, a Family of Feeling." Can she really mean Harmony? Won't it, more likely, be some harmless collection of Xenia-like nuts? Can this flaky person really belong to a deadly organization?

Lisa is distracted from these ruminations by a sudden dismayed gasp from Xenia. There is a problem.

"We believe that men and women—well," Xenia stops herself. "Well, it's complicated, you'll hear about that later. At any rate, the thing with our group is, it's actually a men's group. The women who are there, they come with a man. I'm with . . . Marcus," she confides. "He's wonderful."

Lisa tries for an envious smile.

"A lot of people who join us come as couples," Xenia continues. "The way it works is, the men usually join first, and then they bring you along. That's how I got in, because of . . . Marcus."

Xenia has the habit of pausing dramatically before saying his name, which cues Lisa that a response is expected. She manages another smile.

"Very occasionally, a woman wants to join on her own. Then the District Commander finds a man for her. So don't worry, Lisa. It's really not a problem at all, when I think about it. There's a surplus of men in our group anyway, you'll be more than welcome. I'll prepare a profile of you, and they'll match you up. We'll include a picture. You'll want to make a bit more of an effort, I expect," she adds, studying Lisa with a thoughtful frown. "Wear something a little more flattering, and you'll want to do something about that sallow complexion . . . a lighter foundation, some concealer, a *lot* of blush . . ." With pursed lips, Xenia indicates the areas of Lisa's face where serious work will have to be done if she is to be made marketable to a lunatic man engaged in criminal anti-state pursuits.

There is a pause while Lisa struggles against the impulse to slap Xenia and Xenia continues her frowning appraisal of Lisa's features and ways to greatly improve them.

"And I'll compose a text about you, a bio," Xenia says next. "We'll stress the part about how you are looking for passion, and are interested in exploring new sexual frontiers, and how for *too* long you've been a victim of the anti-erotic, unnatural, forced Puritanism of the feminists, but *now* you want to learn how to be a real woman again. Oh! The guys will love that. You'll probably get to choose from several candidates."

Xenia's eyes are half-closed as she gives herself up to this delightful fantasy of Lisa's thrilling future, and it's a good thing, or she would see the look of high alarm on Lisa's face at the prospect of being handed over to an unknown restorationist man eager to experience borderline erotic activities with a repentant feminist.

No. She can't possibly go through with this. No one can expect it of her. On the other hand, look how far she's gotten. Xenia totally believes her. It seems like a shame to back out now. Think think think. Okay, the main thing is, she has to avoid coming into this group as an unattached female. Brett? Could Brett be persuaded to collaborate with her? Then they would have a mission, something really important to do together, just the way she always dreamed it . . . But no—reality quickly reasserts itself. Inform Brett that she is now a secret agent, infiltrating a Harmony cell? Even if he agreed to help her, he would never be able to act the part. First of all, he's too well known. They would not believe that he is a turncoat. Second, he's so . . . well, stuffy isn't a very friendly word, but he can be, let's say, very rigid in his behavior. This assignment calls for a person with a sense of humor, a person who is flexible, who is good-natured . . . let's face it, above all, this calls for a person she can totally control.

Frantically, Lisa's brain reviews all the men she knows who fit those criteria. The list is short.

There actually is only one name on it.

Justin.

But, no, that's impossible. Justin is a re-ed. She can't get him involved in something like this.

"Oh, Lisa, you won't regret this. You're doing the right thing, you'll see," Xenia enthuses, clutching again at her hand in girlish rapture and digging long fuchsia claws into the soft pad of flesh at the side of Lisa's palm. "I'll put down that you're looking for someone masterful, someone who will sweep you off your feet, for a man who—"

"Actually, I have someone," Lisa interrupts frantically. "A man! I've got a man! No need to match me up, thanks."

Xenia looks doubtful, but Lisa tells her decisively that she wishes to join as a couple. With a man who feels exactly the same way she does, who is just as—she grabs at their recent conversation for the appropriate phrase—just as stifled and in search of passion as she is. If Xenia could kindly arrange their invitation, please.

Already, Harmony is having a counterrevolutionary, detrimental impact on Lisa's state of mind. For the first time in her young life, she is agonizing over what to wear. Well, in her defense, this is hardly your standard social situation. What *do* you wear when telling your assistant that you wish him to pose as your aspiring demon lover and wild man, but only for the purposes of infiltrating an outlawed, violent right-wing restorationist group?

The chilliest model of female authority that comes to mind is Antonia Mazzini, so Lisa roots through her closet in search of something severe, intellectual, and forbidding.

Nadine wants all transactions related to Operation Harmony to be conducted off the premises of the Ministry, so Lisa asks Justin to come to her house. "Six o'clock tomorrow. A project discussion," she orders, standing by his desk, and then bustles importantly into her office and closes the door firmly to forestall any questions.

Justin arrives a few minutes early. He is clearly surprised to find Lisa so formally attired in tailored blue jersey. "Oh," he says, gesturing at his own casual outfit in confusion. "Is this some formal high-level thing? We're not doing a presentation, are we? Did I miss something? Will this be okay?"

"You're fine," Lisa snaps.

Looking into the apartment, and seeing no sign of other participants, no flipcharts, no screens, he asks, "Did I mishear the time? Where's everybody? It's a meeting, right?"

"Oh, Justin, stop fussing," Lisa says, unfairly. "Yes, it's a meeting. You and I are having a meeting."

Rebuked, Justin stands in silence, but you can see the thoughts floating through his mind. Why is she dressed up like this for a meeting just with him? Why is she so cranky? Maybe she has another appointment right afterward, and her mood has nothing to do with him at all. He waits.

"I have asked you here," Lisa announces pompously, "to discuss something very important."

Justin nods agreeably. They are still standing just inside the door, which seems a little odd, but hey, he's not asking any more questions. This woman is not having a good day, best not provoke her.

"You can come in," Lisa says, realizing belatedly that the foyer is not the usual spot for project discussions.

"Sit down," she says. Her words are clipped. She is in charge: here, now, and forever after.

Justin seats himself at the small breakfast table, with Lisa opposite him.

"What," she asks, "do you know about restorationist groups?"

Good thing Justin is sitting down. If standing, he would probably collapse. Even so, he feels his heart give a powerful thump and his head go dizzy as the blood rushes to his gut and feet. He is discovered! Lisa has discovered, somehow, that he attends those miserable basement meetings, and now he is exposed as a conspirator, an enemy of the state. Despairingly, he tries to remember what the punishment for that is. He's in his final evaluation, that will make things much worse. Having been almost completely reeducated, he won't be able to plead ignorance. He'll be judged incorrigible, constitutionally unfit for integration. He'll spend the rest of his life in a dormitory like the one he's in now, with only guys like Will for companionship and only Mac to love.

But why is Lisa confronting him with this in her home? Does that mean she's the only one who knows? Does it mean she might be willing to hear him out, to give him another chance? He is about to throw himself on her mercy, to blurt out the whole story about Mac and the dorm and Will and the basement meetings, and how it is his cowardice and not his political values that got him into this mess, but fortunately Lisa forestalls him.

Seeing his drained, shaken face, the tremor in his jaw, and the way his mouth is struggling to form a sentence, Lisa concludes that she has underestimated Justin's admirable commitment to the New Order. Just look how upsetting the thought of a counterrevolutionary movement is to him! See how easy it is to underestimate men! She is touched.

"I know," she says comfortingly, patting his hand in a comradely way. "It's terrible. Insane people, trying to destroy everything we are working for! It's very upsetting, I know. But we can help. We can do something, you and I, Justin. It might be dangerous, though," she cautions.

As Justin collects himself and looks at her intently, searching for a clue to whatthehell she is talking about, Lisa returns to her more formal demeanor, sits upright in her chair, and decides to just get it over with.

"Okay, here's the deal, Justin. We have been asked to infiltrate the Restore Harmony Movement. You and I. Posing as a couple. We will have to act like we believe in Restoration. Now, I have to warn you that Harmony is not just an ordinary opposition group. It is a very dangerous organization. They are terrorists! We will have to pretend to agree with them. We're supposed to find out exactly what they are planning and who they are. It's a very important assignment. And," she winds up, "during their meetings, we may have to pretend to share an interest in archaic and perverse sexual practices, because apparently they're into that. Now, Justin, I want to make it clear that you are under no obligation to do this," she adds. "This is not part of your Personal Development Profile. This would be strictly voluntary, and if you prefer to stay out of this, that will not affect your credits and there will be no hard feelings what-soever. But it's a very important assignment, and you could be a big help, so I hope you agree."

"I . . . so, we would basically attend some meetings?" Justin asks.

Lisa nods. Actually, she is far from sure what exactly they will be doing, but meetings seem like a safe bet.

"And we'll pretend to agree with them, and try to find things out?"

Lisa nods again.

"And some sex stuff might go on?"

Lisa agrees curtly that this is so.

Justin shrugs. "Okay."

"Don't you want to think it over?" Lisa asks.

"No," he says. "It sounds okay. I'll do it."

It sounds okay? Lisa is taken aback, but puts it down to idealism. "Well, if you're sure," she says, "then I'll tell—the person in charge. I'll keep you posted. And remember, not a word about this at work, not even when we're alone. Because they might have spies. We're to continue with our project. And, well, I guess you should know that we can trust Nadine completely. But Xenia, who I don't think you've met yet, watch out for her. Because she is one of Them, the one who will get us in."

This time, our rogue intel group is seated at the large round table in the Ministry of Thought's conference room. The walls, the floor, and the ceiling of the room are paneled in soundproof, microwave-proof material disguised, to prevent claustrophobia, as beige rattan wallpaper. The table bears the usual paraphernalia for a large meet-ing: pencils, notebooks, compu-plugs, crystals. In a large basket, opals, amethysts, and rose quartz are available for those who prefer not to expose their personal stones to the stress and bad energy of a potentially contentious larger gathering. There is obsidian, too, useful in overcoming blockages and obstructions, and splintered chunks of pink and green zoisite, which grants healthful sexual energy and strong nerves and is a favorite of many women. And there are polished disks of deep green chalcedony, in case someone gets overly excited. A calming pitcher of chilled barley water, surrounded by clay cups, stands to one side, beside a bowl of digestion-friendly ginger candy and anise biscuits.

But the individuals who have gathered in the room pay no heed to any of this spiritual and mental refreshment. Their heads are bent close together, we can't see their faces, so let's continue to refer to them by numbers.

Person Two appears agitated; chalcedony might help, but she clutches the edge of the table instead. "I'm having a big problem with this," she says. "It's not right, and it's not what we stand for. We're treating these two people as dispensable operatives, and I can't countenance that. We are lying to them about the purpose and the risks. That is immoral and it is wrong."

The anger level in the room rises; you're supposed to reach for the obsidian when you feel that way, but instead, fists clench and blood pressure counts go up.

"A revolution is not a dinner party," Person Three snaps angrily. "How dare you complain about my ethics! How dare you question my honor! We stand to lose everything if we start getting idiotically sentimental now! There's a lot more at stake here than two lives," Person Three continues, choking down a rising tide of emotion. "Maybe you've forgotten what this is all about, but I haven't! I'm not going back to a world where women died because they got no food, no medical care, and a lifetime of abuse. Just a little more than a hundred years ago, men weren't letting us vote, own property, go to school, or decide the fate of our lives and our bodies! Do you think we're safe? Do you think the Revolution's over? We're not safe. Yes, we can force men to sit through a few lectures. Does that mean they've changed? They haven't changed! Give them an inch, and they'll have things back the way they were, faster than you can say clitorectomy! They have to be completely and totally controlled with no chance whatsoever of wrecking what we've accomplished. How long did it take us to get this far? It took us more than two thousand years! I'm not putting that at risk!"

Her angry speech is instantly swallowed up by the carefully engineered acoustics of the room, but the group remains in the grip of her words. No, they don't want to return to a world that, for the majority of the planet's women, had been not merely somewhat annoying and slightly unfair but chillingly brutal and totally inhumane.

"Of course, what you say is entirely true," Person One says now, taking charge in a brisk voice. "And that is why we are here, because all of us share that commitment. Now, we have an issue before us, and I'm sure we can deal with it calmly. We are discussing the deployment of two individuals into a potentially hazardous situation, without their full knowledge of what is involved. My friends, let's address that.

"Let's start with the young man. We don't need to concern ourselves about him. He is a counterrevolutionary. An ungrateful and stupid young man who, after enjoying four segments of careful social education, intended to provide him with a good and happy life as an equal member of society, has gone slinking off to join a band of miscreants. He has sided with the enemy, and cannot expect any consideration or mercy.

"The young woman, now, she's a different story. She is one of us. Her commitment is beyond question. She is a fine, dedicated citizen who has placed herself and her skills at our disposal. So in ethical terms, our responsibility lies in making sure we optimally utilize her gifts. Where, we must ask ourselves, do her special strengths lie? Not, I think we will all agree, in the field of literary research or intellectual endeavor. I don't mean this disparagingly," Person One adds quickly. "That would be an elitist form of thinking, which we rightfully reject. From each according to her abilities! And what abilities does our young sister bring to the table? Loyalty, sincerity, and courage. Estimable qualities, all. Whereas the intellect is a cold tool," Person One ruminates, philosophically. "And greatly overvalued by patriarchy, an imbalance we must ever strive to correct."

Stung by the reprimand, Person Two, who had been about to protest Lisa's designation as not very bright and therefore dispensable, falls silent. And offers no argument when Person One concludes, very kindly, that while Lisa may very well—and every effort must and will be made to achieve this—survive her assignment, it would be equally compatible with this fine young woman's own innermost values if, regrettably, things took an unfortunate turn and her life had to be sacrificed for the Greater Good of Womankind.

And that is how Lisa and Justin end up as official cannon fodder for the Revolution.

The following days pass in a blur. I suppose life goes on, and I know work continues, but Lisa can think of nothing but her upcoming date with the dastardly. It's almost a relief when Xenia finally signals to her meaningfully in the hallway and whispers that the next group meeting, and with it her Harmony debut, is all set for tomorrow night.

That evening, consequently, is briefing hour at the Schneider residence. Three women are in attendance, besides Nadine, Lisa, and a fidgety Justin.

"He's really, really upset by Harmony," Lisa explains to them sotto voce, when he stumbles out of the room to get himself another cup of tea and Lisa intercepts their doubtful looks about this new candidate for the secret agent position. Her explanation is well received, and when he bumbles back in, smacking his arm on the doorway, hitting his ankle on the end table, and sloshing tea into the saucer as he goes, warm smiles accompany his awkward transit.

"Let's get this meeting under way, then," the slim woman, Sheila, suggests. "There's some information we want to share with you, but let's be clear, all of this is closely held. We are keeping these facts from the general public in order to avoid panic and discord. We don't want women to feel threatened, and we don't want our many right-minded male citizens to face distrust and discrimination, just because of the actions of a minority."

Justin nods vigorously.

"However, the safety of the community is our first responsibility." Sheila frowns. "Harmony has been linked to numerous acts of terrorism, some of which you know about. The explosion at Deecee University. The power failure at Channel Two. In both cases, it was pure coincidence that the explosive devices did not properly ignite, and there were no fatalities. What we managed to keep out of the news was a major case of drug tampering, poison in three kinds of medication taken only by women. They had infiltrated the packaging plant, but an alert quality control supervisor got suspicious and called for a check. Thousands of innocent women would have died otherwise. In these and in some other instances, we have smoking guns pointing to Harmony, but we have not caught the actual perpetrators and we do not have enough proof. We need two things. We need to know what they are planning next so we can stop them. So far we've been lucky, but eventually they will succeed and there will be deaths, possibly a large number of deaths. We need better intelligence. That is where you come in."

Lisa swallows. She was expecting to report back on some forbidden AR thinking, a bit of deviance, but this? Terrorism?

As for Justin, I leave it to you to imagine his thoughts.

"Yes, it's scary," Sheila says, noting their dismay. "We are asking you to expose yourself to real danger. Now, you can be sure that we will take all possible precautions. A security team will have no other assignment than to monitor your movements and keep you safe. We think the risk is containable, but there is a risk, and we want you to feel absolutely free to refuse."

"They tried to poison thousands of women?" Justin asks. "Poison them to death?" Shock appears to have put him in something of a time warp, so that he is many sentences behind the flow of the discussion.

Lisa, though, is in the moment. "If you all think we can do this, I'm prepared to try," she says. "Justin?"

And Justin hears himself pledging gladly to do his part.

The address for the Harmony meeting turns out to be a church. You enter a brightly lit vestibule that widens into a kind of reception area. Lisa, determined to be a good spy, tries to absorb as many details as possible. There is a table as you enter, behind which two greeters stand dispensing drinks and exchanging a few words with each new arrival. To Lisa and Justin, they say, "Oh, I'm afraid you must have the wrong address, this is a private party tonight." As they speak, their voices elevate slightly, and three burly men step forward to check out the intruders.

"We're new," Lisa tells them, tentatively.

The three men look them over unsmilingly, taking their measure.

"Xenia invited us," she adds uncertainly, looking around for a sign of her sponsor.

"You a potted plant, buddy, or you got a voice, too?" the tallest of the three men replies, at last, addressing Justin.

"I'm with her," Justin says, politely indicating Lisa.

"No you're not, buddy," the man corrects him. "She's with you."

There is silence while everybody ponders the deep meaning of this profound remark.

Then the man smiles, a cold assessing smile that fails to reach his eyes. "Xenia told us you were coming. We do welcome you both," he says. "You, sir, can take the lady's coat and hang it right over there, and there's a bar set up in the corner, make sure she gets a drink, and then just proceed on into the assembly room and make yourselves right at home. Enjoy your evening."

Mechanically, Lisa and Justin move as instructed. They feel deflated, both of them; already, the fun has completely gone out of this adventure. A new and uncomfortable thought makes its home in Lisa's head: the thought that she will have to be less forthright if she is to fit in here without attracting attention. Justin, she sees, is hovering beside her, unsure exactly how to implement his instructions concerning her coat, which she does not appear to be prepared to surrender.

"I'm cold," she tells him preemptively, to avoid participating in that archaic ritual at least. "And I'm not thirsty. Let's just go in."

The assembly room is not what Lisa expected. What she was hoping for: a businesslike lecture hall, with rows of seats and a podium where the speaker will stand and neatly outline the upcoming subversive plot for Lisa to commit to memory and report to Nadine. What she has been fearing: a cushion-lined dimly lit group-sized boudoir for the kind of weird, sick partner-swapping bacchanal Xenia has alluded to.

This room is neither. Our two secret agents enter a kind of auditorium, bare of furniture or decoration and not set up for a lecture. There is a small elevated stage. A few dozen people are milling about, conversing and laughing in small groups. No one is wearing a jacket and everyone is holding a glass, making Lisa feel unpleasantly conspicuous. She scans the room for Xenia, but doesn't see her. Well, that's just great.

She slips out of her jacket and hands it to Justin. "Whatever has the highest percentage of alcohol," she whispers. "In the largest glass you can find. Please."

Justin has just returned with their drinks when the talking quiets to a low expectant murmur and the formless milling crowd coalesces into an amoeba-shaped circle facing the stage. Looks like something is about to happen. Sure enough, a door opens and a tall man emerges and marches energetically up the few steps. He stands there for a moment, waiting for complete silence and looking penetratingly at the couples before him.

"Okay!" he announces at last, in a mellow voice. "No lectures tonight, folks. I hear that y'all worked real hard last time, so tonight it's time to play. I say we let the good times roll. And the first thing I'm going to need is a beautiful, sexy lady, because my own lady stood me up tonight. Can you believe that? Fortunately, however, as I can see when I gaze out into this room, we are just chock-full of sexy, beautiful ladies tonight! So the only remaining question is, which gentleman will loan me his partner for an hour or so? Don't worry, you'll get her back, almost as good as new."

A short monologue, but it has left Lisa gasping. The term "lady" in all its anachronistic dissonance would be shocking enough; never in her life has Lisa heard it paired with the term "sexy." And the notion that a man is able to make a disposition regarding his partner, loaning her out to another man, is nothing less than breathtaking; illegal, too, Lisa believes. The other occupants of the room do not share her dismay. Incredibly, many of the women are responding to this disgusting speech with shrill, delighted giggles—an archaic form of female laughter Lisa has read about but cannot recall actually having heard before.

The men seem less amused; several of them pull their partners possessively toward them by throwing beefy arms around their throats in a gesture somewhere between affection, pride of ownership, and strangulation. And this, Lisa notes with revulsion, makes the women giggle even more, and teeter on what Lisa now sees are oddly shaped, bent, partially elevated shoes, and lose their balance and mock-fall against their male companions' shoulders, all the while tossing their heads in a way calculated to throw a maximum of hair into the men's faces. Lisa looks around with anthropological fascination, until the voice of the man onstage recalls her to the present.

"Now, I warn you," he says, playfully, "if there are no volunteers, I get to pick! Come on, girls, be brave. I don't bite—very hard!" he chortles, pleased at his wit. Terrified that she might catch his eye, Lisa shuffles slowly to the left, taking shelter behind a tall couple. Finally, two women grab a third one, who shrieks and struggles and protests, and the crowd begins to push her forward. At the last moment, she reaches up for her abductor's hand and clambers onto the stage willingly enough. And just in time, too: Lisa was about to depress the alarm button on her HUE band to summon aid against the legendary, defunct crime of rape. As she stares in bafflement, the woman achieves the stage; abandoning any further pretense of reluctance, and preening a bit, she minces into the spotlight. The man embraces her; they kiss deeply, to further hooting, laughter, and applause.

"Okay, folks, I have my victim," he announces. "So let's do it!" He waves his hand; the lights dim. Lisa looks around desperately— what hideous perversion is next, and how will she get out of it? In her frantic survey, her eye falls on Justin, who does not appear worried in the least. He is sipping his drink, apparently quite at ease. Onstage, the man is still embracing the young woman, stroking her neck and arm as his sinuous voice whispers into the microphone. "Gentlemen," he says, "remember, it's up to you to take the initiative. Put your arms around your lady."

Couples come together, snapping into position in each other's arms like positively and negatively charged ions. Justin and Lisa alone remain frozen in place, a good foot apart and stunned. Neither one of them has ever witnessed such a display of public intimacy between men and women; with more, apparently, to come. Justin looks to Lisa, waiting for instructions.

Lisa has been afraid of something like this, had mentally resigned herself to various potential patriotic sacrifices, but she never dreamed they would be demanded so soon. Not during their very first session! She thought there would be some warning, some time to get guidance from Nadine. What now? They can't stay like this, they will be too conspicuous. But they can't join in, either. No matter how crucial their mission, she is just not ready to be part of an antediluvian orgy scene. Even if she were, Lisa virtuously reflects, she has no mandate to drag a re-ed, with his but incompletely shaped vulnerable young male sexuality, into such a sordid setting without adequate preparation.

Delay, she has to find a way to delay. And just then, in the deep night of her despair, there appears a beacon. Two beacons, to be precise: two small red lights in one corner indicating the rest rooms.

"Go stand on the side," Lisa whispers to Justin. "Keep looking for Xenia. I'll be right back."

With those words, Lisa strides purposefully into the crowd, an obstacle course of hugging, kissing, rubbing, smooching dyads that impedes her progress until, like a swimmer emerging from a tangle of seaweed, she reaches the other side, takes a deep gulp of air, and dashes directly into the women's sanitary facility.

Tiled in peach and cherry red, empty of other occupants and brightly lit, it offers splendid sanctuary. With a sigh of relief, Lisa selects the outermost cubicle, closes the door behind her, pulls down the quilted lid of the commode, and tries to come up with a plan.

What has she gotten herself into? How will she bluff her way through an orgy? How will she get herself and poor Justin safely out of here? And on the topic of Justin: it was shameful to abandon him like that, and she can't leave him alone out there for long, at the mercy of that voracious, licentious crowd. She feels sick, just thinking about it.

That's it! she thinks. Sick, that's it. She'll simply fall ill. She'll teeter out of here looking feeble, grab Justin, and get the hell away, and if anybody challenges them, she will say that she is coming down with the flu. Yes, she will say that she was feeling funny earlier today, but didn't want to miss the event, but now has taken a turn for the worse, is definitely contagious, and has to go home. Has to be *taken* home, by her partner, Justin, she revises, pleased with herself. Yes, that's clever. They'll like that formulation, and it'll keep Justin safe. Maybe she's better at this spy stuff than she is giving herself credit for.

With that bracing thought, Lisa lifts herself from the seat, steps boldly out of the cubicle, sends an encouraging smile to her reflection in the mosaic-set mirror, and marches to the door. Steeling herself for whatever depraved sight may await her, she resolutely swings it open and blinks into the gloom.

Everyone is still vertical, what a relief. The embraces have tightened into even closer clinches, but they're all still dressed. Onstage, the head honcho has huge meaty arms around his borrowed partner and is nuzzling her neck and mumbling something about getting ready into his collar-clip microphone. Ready. Lisa slinks along the dark wall, thinking that these couples look about as ready as you can get, when his murmured message changes. Muffled by the insulation of his partner's hair, it reaches the room as a blurry mumble, but Lisa finally makes it out. "Stepandstep," he instructs, "stepandstep, get ready, half turn, stepandstep . . ."

It's a dance, Lisa realizes, as the couples jolt into motion. Just a dance. They are merely doing one of those old hetero contact dances.

Annoyed with herself, Lisa spies Justin; he doesn't see her, his eyes are half-closed, and he is rocking, swaying, and taking little dance steps in obedience to the instructor's orders. His arms, Lisa notes with displeasure, are slightly extended and bent into a semicircle to harbor the imaginary giggling, tripping, stupidly dressed, and archaically shod traitorous Harmony female he is having a repulsive little fantasy about. Well, not on her watch! Not while she is responsible for his education! Zigzagging through the pulsating mass of clenched bodies, she reaches Justin, grabs him, grabs her drink, and makes for the sliding doors. She has seen one or two other couples vanish that way.

Lisa and Justin find themselves in a small garden; there are benches. In the moonlight, Lisa can make out the outline of one couple, apparently engaged in some advanced groping; a second couple has taken its dance effort to the farthest, darkest corner of the garden and stands there swaying in weak alibi while two sets of hands busily explore body parts not usually involved in the fox-trot. Lisa doesn't care what they do as long as she can retreat undisturbed and undetected to one of the cold stone benches to sit this one out, regroup, and think.

Lisa is prepared to hunker down here for the rest of the evening, but luck is with them. After one more touchy-clingy dance, the lights brighten, flushed couples disentangle, the beat picks up, and our two secret agents, alerted by the new rhythm, return to the auditorium for a lesson in line dancing. This proves a successful strategy: for most of the evening, they mime the eager participants; during the slow, clingy stuff, they retreat to the garden. And so it goes, until at last their host, with another slew of innuendo, formally ends the evening and takes his leave.

The crowd starts to break up, but Lisa is still hoping to find

Xenia. This can't have been everything. Merely a dance class? After which everyone goes home? She wants to hang around a bit longer.

"I need another drink," she tells Justin.

"You don't need any more drinks. I'm taking you home," Justin says in a firm voice. What? Perplexed, Lisa notes that besides having gone insubordinate and insane, Justin is doing something funny with his eyes. His eyeballs roll toward the right, and, following their weird course, Lisa sees one of the three men who had earlier intercepted them at the entrance. Seemingly, he is just staring off into space, but he is close enough to hear their every word. Justin winks. He jiggles his eyebrows. Any minute now, he'll break into pantomime.

"Well, if you think so," Lisa says quickly, to cut him short.

"I'll bet he was eavesdropping on our conversation," Justin says, the moment they are alone. "How do you think I did? Was I convincing?"

So now he's proud of his impromptu bit of paternalism, really! What an infant. Sarcastic retorts spring to Lisa's mind, but she suppresses them. Leave him be; he's being a good sport about this whole thing.

"You were fine," she says.

"I thought I'd better sound decisive. You know, not be a potted plant. That part about I'm taking you home? I got that from——" Justin stops. From *Baywatch,* he was about to say, remembering just in time that *Baywatch,* like the group he watches it with, is subversive and illegal. "From a show," he says, instead.

"It was inspired," Lisa says.

Nadine has advised that, after meetings, Lisa had best take Justin home with her. After all, they may be followed, and should appear to be a genuine couple. "They're likely to check you out, at least at first," Nadine warns. So Lisa and Justin pick up some food and plan to have dinner at her apartment before Justin heads back to the Residential Suites.

"That was one strange evening!" Lisa exclaims, as soon as the door closes behind them. "I don't think I'm cut out to be a spy."

She's right. Any self-respecting spy would notice immediately that the bedroom door is ajar, where earlier it had been closed; that the magazines are on the floor instead of the end table; that, in short, an intruder has been, and possibly still is, in her apartment.

Instead, totally oblivious, Lisa sets up for dinner. She takes plates out of her cupboard and fishes the silverware out of the drawer while Justin undoes the flaps on the steaming food containers.

"What do you mean, not cut out to be a spy?" a voice behind them asks, and a pert little face appears in the kitchen doorway.

"Cleo!" Lisa exclaims. "Sweetie! What are you doing here?"

"Well, Mother had to take over the Territorial Behavior class for somebody who's having a baby. It's a weekend class, so she thought I'd better spend the night with you. Is he spending the night, too?" she adds matter-of-factly, indicating Justin.

"No, he's just having dinner with me," Lisa replies tartly. "With us. Or did you eat already?"

Obviously not, given the enthusiasm with which her niece digs into the Panang curry. But she has not forgotten her earlier question.

"So what were you saying about spying?" she asks again, licking red sauce from her spoon.

"Spying?" Lisa repeats, to gain time. "Did I say something about spying?"

"Yeeeeeees," Cleo replies mockingly. "Yes, you did. You said, 'I'm not cut out to be a spy.'"

Lisa stuffs a large forkful of noodles and watercress into her mouth to gain a few more seconds.

"We were talking about computer games," Justin says, leaping into the breach. "We were talking about which ones we like. I like ones with a spying angle, what about you? Do you know Sorceress in the Castle? Or do you prefer Backlash?"

Cleo brightens. "Those are both great games. So you like them? Did Lisa tell you that we made up our own game, I Spy Cleo? We hide in the New Mudds and Lisa has to find me. I leave good clues."

"Exactly," Lisa says, grabbing the lifeline Justin has thrown her. "That's what Justin and I were talking about. I was telling him that I'm not as good at the game as you are, and that I guess I'm not cut out to be a spy."

In her youthful egotism, Cleo has no trouble believing that her aunt and Justin spent their evening conversing about her and her computer games. So she just tells Justin, benevolently, that her aunt is being much too modest, and is really quite good at tracking her in the Web, and he could play, too, sometime if he wants to. She launches into an elaborate explanation of how the game works and what some of her cleverest moves have been, so far, and Lisa signals that she will rescue him if he wishes, but he seems totally absorbed in the conversation and quite happy. In fact, Cleo and Justin are developing possible characters he could play if he joins, and the evening flies by until it is time for him to go home.

"He's ultranicer than Brett," Cleo comments, when Justin has left. "Brett is so boring and really phallo. Are you going to dump Brett and will Justin be your SR instead?" she asks hopefully.

"Really!" Lisa exclaims sternly. "One doesn't 'dump' another person. What kind of terminology is that? I'm sure they're not teaching you that in school. And Justin is merely a colleague, a friend. And it's very late and you need to go to sleep."

"My mother dumped Sandra," Cleo replies, unrepentant, referring to her mother's last relationship. "And Sandra said so herself, she said, 'I'm going to miss you, Cleo, but your mother is dumping me to go hetero.'"

"Bed!" Lisa repeats. "And brush your teeth!" she adds. She is definitely not going to get involved in a discussion of her sister's love life.

And Cleo kisses her good night and dashes into the bathroom with a parting shot of "Brett needs to be dumped, it would be really good for him. He needs some setbacks to develop his character. That's what Janine, our literature teacher says, she says setbacks are good for character development."

Lisa frowns, but at what? At the impertinence of her precocious niece, or at the thought of Brett's character? Or maybe just at the mess in the kitchen. At the sauce that has leaked from the container, forming a sticky puddle that turns into a smear when Lisa tries to wipe it away, and the oily squares on the counter where food has soaked through the cardboard containers. At the swimsuit and towel she meant to hang up this afternoon, but left on the floor instead. And she's so tired. With relief, Lisa remembers that tomorrow is housekeeping day. Vera will take care of it.

And so she does. Vera retrieves the swimsuit from the floor and rinses it in the sink. She hangs up Lisa's bathrobe and places a stack of T-shirts, neatly steamed and folded, on their shelf. She moves on to the kitchen. She squirts the sink and the counter with a dilution of green tea oil, to disinfect everything. She wipes the salad bin with water and vinegar. The workroom is next. She swishes the desk with a dust-attracting micro-fiber brush. She activates the compuscreen and types in a special code; while it reconfigures, she efficiently gives the screen a quick antibacterial swipe with a damp cloth. Lisa's mail comes up, and Vera scans it to check for unusual messages.

Well, well, well. I don't think Lisa realizes that snooping is part of Vera's housecleaning routine.

Pausing to read the notes from Brett in their entirety, especially the parts that allude to their last shared night, Vera wrinkles her nose. Great erotic literature this ain't.

Vera likes Lisa, but feels no compunction about reading her personal mail. Taking an interest in her subjects' sex lives does them no harm, and it keeps her alert and motivated, which makes her more efficient.

Vera knows what other women think of her. She knows they regard her with pity and contempt, but that's okay. She knows better. She's a soldier in an army, an army of scorned, discarded women whose vigilance keeps the motherland safe. And she's important, trusted with a special assignment.

Forget the man in the raincoat, trying to hide behind a newspaper; forget the intruders in stocking masks, breaking into buildings at great risk to photocopy one lousy document. Intel's radical wing has espionage down to an effortless art. Its agents swarm across town every morning, wearing flowered overalls and carrying mops. I mean, think about it. Isn't it a secret police dream come true? Older women, as invisible as furniture, dismissed by all as dull-witted fossil remnants of a quaint domestic past. What exquisite bloodlines, what centuries of experience they bring to this assignment! Here we have a population group practically bred to snoop, born to obsess over the minutiae of other people's lives, to rake through their underwear, read their diaries, check their jacket pockets for change and their shirt collars for lipstick stains. A group so skilled at interrogation they can conceal their questioning behind a naggy gabby smokescreen of intrusive chatter.

It's a match made in heaven. Displaced homemakers, recruited by a rogue elite wing of Intelligence and sent into the homes of those who matter, disguised as lowly housekeepers. "They're perfect," in the immortal words of the genius who came up with this plan. "If the subject should come home unexpectedly to find them rifling through their desk or their drawers, no problem. They'll just claim they were straightening up. And it's good for *them,* too. Instead of snooping through their family's stuff out of neurotic jealousy and an obsessive need for control, they can do it to strangers, for the good of their country."

Okay, let's see what we've got here. Lisa's love letters are boring. Her boyfriend's jerking her around. Her maid is spying on her. Her boss is sending her on a weird secret mission. Her sister is a snob, and her much loved niece recently appears to prefer the company of an ugly dog.

I think she at least deserves a breakthrough on her day job.

Rebecca waylays her after a meeting. "Lisa," she whispers to her, with some agitation, in the hallway. "Have you got a minute?"

Sure, Lisa has a minute. Rebecca pushes ahead of her into her office, wags her finger coyly at Justin to make sure he doesn't follow, and pulls the door shut. What is *this* all about?

"Lisa, it's about your project," she says, still speaking in a hush. "I know you're not getting anywhere with it. And I know why. Science is Truth. You can't find the Truth if you are hedged in by taboos. You must be bold!" she hisses. She looks anxiously to the left and to the right and steps still closer to Lisa. "You have to see beyond the taboos, and recognize the Truth. And the Truth is that men and women are different," she announces in a hoarse croak. Then she pauses for a moment, possibly waiting for Security to drag her away or for a lightning bolt to hit her. When nothing happens she continues, "We aren't supposed to believe it anymore, but it's still true: sex isn't the same for women as it is for men. Women are more profound about it. Sure, it's fun, and you can be casual about it, too, sometimes. But there's still a difference. Sex will never be just recreational for women, just a sport, like it is for men. Women are . . . different," Rebecca repeats, clutching both fists to her chest to illustrate the deep feelings that women, as opposed to men, are capable of.

"You're never going to get anywhere by looking at that porno stuff. Or that boring theory stuff either. The key thing for women is Feeling. The key thing is Passion, is Love. I'm going to trust you with a secret, Lisa," she whispers. "I belong to a group."

Lisa pales. Please, no! Not another secret Harmony member! Not Rebecca, whom she has always been fond of! But no, it turns out that Rebecca means something far more benign. She's talking about a book group. Nothing really illegal, though many would consider it subversive. Which is why Rebecca makes Lisa promise solemnly not to tell Nadine or anyone else from the office. She wouldn't lose her job, but it could spell the end of her career.

"We read special books," Rebecca confesses, lifting her chin defiantly but still whispering and eyeing the door. "Romantic books. Romance books. We circulate them secretly, because it's so hard to get hold of them, but believe me, Lisa, we're not nuts. We're not some tiny pathetic minority, and we're not backward or disloyal either. It's a groundswell. Millions of women love these books. It's like a whole underground. I'm totally committed to the Revolution, you know that. I wouldn't go back, never! But taboos are dangerous. You can't turn off your heart!"

Won't she get a throat cramp, with all of this laryngitic expostulating, Lisa worries. Worse, she finds herself whispering back. "I don't understand. What books are you talking about?"

Rebecca lifts up her satchel and rummages around, finally pulling out a small square package and unwrapping a printed cloth to reveal a tattered paperback. The edges are worn and the corners fuzzy, but the illustration on the cover remains intact. The picture shows a woman with a mass of billowing hair. She is dressed in an elaborately flowing, floor-length dress. She is kneeling before an implausibly large, muscular man, embracing his middle and looking up at him rapturously. He is naked to the waist. His hair is as long as hers, and some sort of archaic fighting implement is strapped to his belt. While permitting her embrace, he is staring astygmatically off into some heroic distance.

"Romance novels," Rebecca whispers, quickly whisking the book away and back into her bag. "This one isn't mine, I have to return it today. We circulate them. You can buy them, but that's risky. They say they don't ID your purchases, but they can't fool me, computers is what I do. It's okay for you, though, for you it's research. If you do any printouts," she hints, and a longing tone enters her voice, "if you order books . . ."

"I'll pass them on to you when I'm done," Lisa promises, and is rewarded with a radiantly grateful smile.

Lisa makes some inquiries. Rebecca has not exaggerated. Despite the stigma, and the difficulties in obtaining them, there is an enormous black market in these books. You can purchase them by responding to discreet advertisements that try to allay your fears about embarrassment. "Buy without bar code," the booksellers announce, promising that the titles will not show up on your consumer records, where they could reveal to any background investigator that you are a frilly-hearted sentimental AR moron. Like Rebecca, most women distrust these reassurances. They prefer to get an elderly female relative to order the books for them. If you don't have a career to worry about, it doesn't matter, and it's understandable for older women to lag behind the times, since their brains and hearts have been damaged by years in the AR.

Lisa is excited. Could this be her turning point? Is enlightenment waiting for her in the syrupy glop of nonrev women's dreams, like penicillin in a tin of mold?

Calling up Archives, Lisa asks them to look for Romance and send it up ASAP. It takes a while, but finally interoffice mail dumps a medium-sized envelope at her doorstep. There are only two books inside, fat paperbacks with their covers obscured by gray cello-wrap that bears the warning ARM, antirevolutionary material. With all the gravity of her office, Lisa peels off the sticker and the wrap and examines the cover. It seems innocuous enough. It resembles the one Rebecca showed her. You see a man and a woman. They are embracing. The woman is looking at the man, who is not looking back at her. A cherry tree stretches candy-colored pink blossoms over them as a full moon glows through its branches. The woman is wearing some sort of antiquated party dress, pastel blue and heavily ruffled. The lettering of the title is in metallic pink. It reads: *Captive Heart*.

Lisa unwraps the second book with a frown. Did Archives accidentally send two copies of the same book? But no, this woman's dress is pink and her partner, though he seems to be the twin of the man on the other cover, has slightly longer hair and, in a radical departure, is actually looking at his partner. And the title is different, too. This one is called *Silver Flame*. Lisa shrugs, then drops the second book into her bag. Her theater group is meeting tonight, and that's a half hour on Eco-Trans. She can start reading it on the way.

"Thanks for choosing Eco-Trans, your socially responsible ecology-friendly transportation system," the tinny female voice says as Lisa passes through the barrier, enters a car, and looks around for the light that indicates the nearest vacant seat. "Good evening, Lisa," the voice calls after her, responding to the chip she has waved at the sensor in passing. "We always have a seat just for you on our quick and reliable public transportation. This trip will earn you three dollars, reflected in the balance shown on your next statement."

Lisa stows her satchel and nods politely to her seat neighbors. She reaches for her book, freezing in mid-motion. Wait a sec. She can't just take it out, with its soppy cover and giddy title; everyone will stare, and she might even get a well-intentioned lecture. Lisa doesn't care to experience that kind of public disapprobation, nor does she wish to stand up and explain to the population at large that she is just doing research. Fumbling in the bag, she manages to fold the cover and the first few pages back and to lift the book out carefully. Settling into her seat, she begins to read at random where she has bent it open, which happens to be page 37. Braced for treacle, pining hearts, and lacy dresses, she is startled to find her characters stark naked and already in bed.

> She ached for him, heated, damp, and swollen, was ready for him. Nothing mattered to either of them now but putting out the fire. Stroking the softness of her inner thighs, he gently pushed them apart, settling his lean hips between her legs. Then his fingers slid lushly over her wetness. "Do that again," she breathed shakily. He did, and she thought she would die. "Can you die of pleasure?" she whispered with a sigh. His hands slid down her slender hips and under her silky bottom, and he pulled her meltingly into his next, slow deliberate downthrust.

Whoa! Reflexively, Lisa starts to clap the book shut, remembering just in time that this would reveal the cover. Instead, she frantically flips forward twenty or so pages, hoping to reach more neutral ground.

> With her breasts raised high and mounded in his hands, he touched the nipples teasingly with his mouth, little tugging bites, soft light sucks, brushing his cheeks against . . .

Don't these people ever do anything else? Lisa speeds forward in large chunks, arriving at the final chapter.

"Come here," he said in a brusque, raspy tone . . . Unmoving, she gazed at him with wild, tempestuous eyes. "If you don't care to obey here," Trey said, "you will in the prison I can arrange for you." . . .

He reclined, braced against the gilded wood, his splendid erection blatant. Fully clad with only his trousers unbuttoned, his clothing, opposed to her nudity, was a calculated conceit to underscore her servility . . . Their eyes were level as she knelt beside him, both her hands held prisoner by Trey, and for a long moment she resisted compliance. Then her eyes dutifully lowered . . . But for all his flaunted indifference, his hands closed on her hips as she began to lower herself onto him, and when she'd fully absorbed his hard length and he could feel her hot around him, his eyes shut briefly and he groaned deep in his throat . . .

Flushing, Lisa shoots a frantic glance at her neighbors to the right and left. Are they looking over her shoulder? Trying to appear casual, she folds the book inside out from its midway point. With a painful crack, its spine breaks; two of her seat neighbors look up, but Lisa is already sliding the book safely, anonymously into her bag.

Has she, at unfortunate random, picked out a totally weird book? Or is this what millions of sentimental women are secretly reading? For the remaining twenty minutes of the ride, she studies the passing scenery and wonders what Rebecca can possibly have meant about women's different hearts.

The following day, she still feels uneasy. Maybe she had better clear this with her project supervisor before delving any deeper.

"Romance novels?" Mazzini seems startled out of her usual contemplative torpor. Lisa is apprehensive about what her superior will say, reluctant to feel her scorn or ridicule, but on the whole she is less afraid of Mazzini than she used to be. What is the disapproval of one lofty Italian, after all, compared to joining a cell, going undercover, consorting with terrorists, and other of her recent pursuits? In any case, Mazzini does not disapprove; quite the opposite. She starts to nod ponderously.

"Romance novels. In essence, an emanation of contemporary folk culture. Yes. In these texts, perhaps you may find the naïve expression of archaic longings and deeply rooted impulses and associations."

She falls into an introspective silence, then startles Lisa by suddenly snapping, "Archetypes! Look for the archetypes!"

And, still muttering, she turns gruffly back to her compuscreen, and Lisa understands herself to be dismissed.

Lisa scrolls through the summaries. Her expression is scornful, but, just between you and me, I think she's getting hooked. Never has she read books, heard of plots like these. The novels Lisa usually reads at night and on longer Eco-Trans rides, the ones sanctioned, subsidized, and advertised by the New Order, are nothing like this. New Order novels feature upstanding heroines solving socially relevant and personally challenging problems in mature ways. Sometimes, but by no means always, their path crosses that of a politically committed man with whom they forge a meaningful but restrained bond, one that does not interfere with the more important things in their lives.

But this! The language alone makes her catch her breath. Lisa stares at the screen with fascinated incredulity as garish words in lurid combinations prance by. Captive heiress. Locked up by her cruel guardian. Ravished by marauding tribal lord. Slate-eyed barbarian. Savage duke. Forced marriage. Virile and magnificent. Overcome with intense desire. Pursuing his sensuous prize. Braving any peril. Conquering his destined bride. Men too dangerous to love. But women capture their hearts.

Lisa is blown away. What kinds of stories are these? Like the child of dogmatically nutrition-minded parents suddenly unleashed in a candy store, Lisa's sober system greedily absorbs the unfamiliar confections and nearly goes into sugar shock.

Time machines hurtle lovely young women into earlier centuries and onto other continents, where they find themselves half-naked in slave markets, about to be sold to ferocious barbarian lords. Whose harems they must enter so that they can save them from the assassins who are plotting to kill them, which they must prevent because these very men are destined to become their loving soul-mate husbands in a later reincarnation, if they can just get this earlier lifetime safely behind them. Or they are proud but impoverished orphans flung into Regency ballrooms by their cruel guardians, there to be waltzed into peril by handsome troublemakers referred to as "rogues." Or the lovely young woman has a name like Mist or Cloud or Shenelle or Amethyst and lives in an unspecified future on an astronomically and geologically unlikely planet that faces destruction unless she and the brawny space-traveling hero she detests but finds sexually irresistible can tear themselves away from their antagonistic but insatiable lovemaking long enough to save the galaxy.

Sexually irresistible! Insatiable lovemaking! Lisa, who has been brought up to regard sex as a pleasant, healthful pursuit, in a category with reflexology massages and really good pasta, and who saw nothing in the weird impersonal encounters of her earlier reading to make her challenge that definition, now sits in amazement before pages that describe passionate, violent, shattering, cataclysmic encounters between women and men who deceive each other, hate each other, fear each other, but burn for each other. And even as she frowns her disapproval of this kind of anarchic coupling, Lisa is confused by the realization that there is always a conciliatory end. Always the identical end, in fact. In the end, the ferocious, wild, rape-prone, scornful, arrogant man is brought to his knees by the woman, and they marry and resolve to form the kind of mutually caring bond that even the Domestic Shared Living Committee, Heterosexual Division, might grant approval and give a license to, though they would certainly find it too tempestuous to be healthy, and would require the parties involved to commit to extensive counseling to cool themselves down.

"Archetypes . . ." Lisa murmurs, baffled.

As leader of her people, it was time for the beautiful Nazleen to choose a mate and produce a daughter and heir. For generations, the women of her race had kept an uneasy truce with the warlike men around them. But Nazleen dreamed of a joining of spirits as well as bodies—and she dreamed of a lover with eyes the color of the sacred green fire.

Now where are the damn archetypes? Stumped, Lisa decides to fall back on adjectives. Exactly. She will make a list of the qualities possessed by the heroines and heroes. She taps the neon green underline function and highlights "beautiful." Hesitating briefly, she marks "warlike."

Shayna journeys back in time, only to fall for the passionate and powerful Mikal.

She highlights "passionate" and "powerful," then pauses. Better to do this systematically. Lisa draws two columns, then goes back through the earlier entries, highlighting all adjectives as applied to female and male characters. She starts two lists.

Under the heading MALE, she enters "warlike," "handsome," "passionate," "powerful," "dashing," "virile," "magnificent," "gallant," and "cynical."

Under the heading FEMALE, after a long, careful search, she writes "beautiful."

Hmmm. Well, hopefully, that list will get longer. She scrolls down.

In search of a true and gentle love, Ly-San-Ter flees the lust-ful advances of the blue-eyed barbarian who has been chosen as her life-mate, confused and frightened by the fevered yearnings the handsome brute has awakened in her innocent soul.

Mary Frances leaves the convent and falls for a millionaire well known for his sexual prowess. But is he responsible for her sister's death? And will she surrender her innocence to him?

Lisa enters "lustful" and "barbaric" into her male column. She starts to add "confused," "frightened," "fevered," and "innocent" to her FEMALE column, but decides against it. Instead she stands up, stretches, and sticks her head through the doorway to see how Justin is faring. They have divided the territory. She is doing Futuristic and Regency; he has taken on Gothic and American. Hearing her approach, he issues his interim report without even raising his head. "Dark, handsome, hostile neighbor's plans threaten beautiful rancher's daughter," he calls out. "Beautiful woman falls in love with dark, handsome man only to discover that he is a vampire."

Lisa nods grimly and returns to her desk and her excerpts.

Horrified when she is forced to marry Kenric of Montague in exchange for protecting her home, the beautiful Lady Tess resists her feelings for the fierce warrior, who harbors his own inner pain.

Lisa adds "fierce" to her male list. Thinking for a moment, she adds "in pain."

Ordered by the king to take an English bride, Scottish laird Alec Kincaid selects the feisty, violet-eyed Jamie, who brazenly swears to resist Alec until she realizes her feelings have changed.

Well, finally! Sighing with relief, Lisa notes down "feisty" and "brazen" on the women's chart.

Captured by and married to the savage-looking warrior leader Connor Mac Alister, the beautiful Lady Brenna never hopes for love from a husband who claims to want her only in order to acquire an heir, until she learns about his true feelings.

Directly underneath "handsome" on the men's list, Lisa adds "savage-looking." "Archetypes," she mutters. Why can't she find them? She has the sense that the air is thick with them, that they are biting her on the ankle, slapping her in the face, but she can't see them, she can't see them. It's like finding yourself covered in itchy welts, and you never saw a single mosquito.

Outside, Justin continues leafing listlessly through his own texts, absentmindedly tracing a pattern on the desk, using his finger and a drop of spilled coffee. He is pretending to be a vampire. He is pretending the spilled coffee is blood. The fantasy lacks enjoyment; Justin is not having a good time. He almost wishes for Mistress Lockley. This adjective list is really making him nervous.

As we already know, Justin is prone to devoting some thought to the question of what kind of man women like, the qualities they find attractive. So far, most of his pondering has centered on Brett. Only too obviously, Brett is a shallow, self-satisfied, arrogant jerk, but in spite of that, he has evidently won the heart of Lisa, an otherwise sensible and attractive young woman. Now, how did he do that? Justin would very much like to know.

Reading these books which claim to reveal women's deepest, most secret romantic desires is proving to be an upsetting experience. Forget the politics, let the Ministry lose sleep over that. No, Justin is disturbed on a far more personal level. The composite dream man emerging here, adjective by adjective, appears to bear little resemblance to the sort of new and improved, reeducated, renovated, and fine-tuned man who might emerge, say, from the Certification Program. The objects of all these women's erotic fantasies do not appear to be good with children, color-sort their laundry, feel deeply averse to violence, or listen empathetically. Actually, unbelievable though Justin finds this, they seem to resemble Will more than they resemble, let's say, himself.

Smearing make-believe blood across his desk with an errant finger, Justin finds himself grappling with a conundrum. Most of the heroes stacked neatly up before him would, if they were real and lived today, be stewing in Zone Six camps, never to be allowed within five hundred meters of a woman. Women created this current order and appear to be thriving in it. Yet these same women are, apparently, and if these books are to be believed, still dreaming about bad boys.

Now, this cannot be correct. The reeducation program is the work of women. Obviously, they wouldn't have set it up to design men they would then no longer find desirable.

Would they?

In the neighboring office, Lisa is asking herself more or less the same question. Forget the archetypes—Lisa is curious about the sex, the steamy, dizzying, phenomenal sex that makes these men and women lose their heads and risk their lives, sell their souls, and save their galaxies. After all, she reminds herself primly, sex is her real assignment.

Are these vapid-looking women and these muscle-bound male dullards really having that kind of incredible sex, Lisa wonders, surveying the book covers. The synopses can't answer that question. Maybe, Lisa decides with a pleasant frisson of anticipation, she was too hasty, that day on Eco-Trans. Maybe she'll have to read the actual books.

The second Harmony meeting, and Lisa is ready. It's going to take place in the same church, so she knows the terrain. Xenia already told her she wouldn't be there this time, so she won't waste time and nerves searching for her. ("Gosh, sweetie, don't tell me you were upset when you didn't find me! That's so sweet, but Marcus and I don't go to *those* meetings, honey, we're at a whole different *level.* I *almost* came, because I promised you, but Marcus and I were feeling so *cozy,* and I thought, no, she'll be okay, it's such a fun bunch, they'll make her feel right at home.")

And Lisa knows enough to take her jacket off outside the door. And she's been preemptively bossy with Justin for two days before the meeting, so in case his head swells from that AR stuff going down, it'll have plenty of room for expansion.

But she's not prepared to have Justin whisked away from her right in the vestibule. There's absolutely nothing she can do about it; a half-dozen men appear out of nowhere and hustle him away, while she herself is engulfed by a swarm of chattering women and swept upstairs.

An hour will pass before they are reunited—an endless, horrid hour, during which Lisa has to submit, in pretended good grace, to disgusting activities—and yes, I'm going to outline what they are, in just a moment. Photos are even taken, by some idiot intrusively prancing about, and there's nothing Lisa can do to stop it. Vainly she tries to at least get some spying done, by asking questions, but these airheads won't engage, and soon the excitement level has risen to such a hysterical pitch that conversation is unthinkable.

"Oh my God," they screech. "This is wild!"

And what have they done to Justin! He looks like he's been through some kind of wringer. Lisa spots him in the assembly room, where she is finally sent for "refreshments." He's standing there with three other men, one of whom keeps punching him on the arm. His hair is all messed up and his shirt is half in, half out. What have they done to him? As she gets closer, though, Lisa sees that he is smiling. His smile fades when he spots her, replaced by a look of surprise; by a stare of sheer shock, actually, almost as though he'd never seen her before. His neighbor stops punching him long enough to emit a low whistle.

"Is that babe yours?" he asks. "She is hot!"

"Excuse us," the hot babe snaps. "Justin, come with me. Dear," she adds, belatedly, remembering their cover.

Her dignified retreat is disturbed by a leeringly proclaimed "*I'd go with her,*" and a "Hey, me too, man," that follow her as she leads Justin to a deserted spot near the salad bar.

"Are you okay?" she whispers urgently, studying him with concern. His T-shirt is ripped at the neck and wet at the center of the chest, and he's bouncing restlessly on the balls of his feet, as though he is extremely nervous.

"I'm fine," he answers. "I'm good. We won," he says.

"The game," he explains. "My team won the game. The basketball game. We were just, you know, playing basketball. There's a court out back. I got fouled," he adds, fingering the ripped shirt. "But I made the free throw."

Still bouncing lightly, he fishes a broccoli stalk out of the salad bowl, bites off the head, and slam-dunks the stem into the trash bin. Then he squints at a speechless Lisa.

"You look—really different," he says at last, looking her over. "Were your nails always that long?" he adds, drawn by the shock of color to notice her sharp vermilion claws.

"Of course not," she hisses.

"But then how did they grow so fast?" he whispers.

"They're glued on," she snaps back.

"Wow," he says. His eyes move upward. Her hair has been shaped with hot curlers, and sprayed; it falls in sharp ripples to her chin. Her mouth has a sort of brown edge around it, and her lips look shiny, a little swollen, and very red. Her face, on the other hand, is pale, except for two orange-colored stripes that extend on the diagonal from the middle of her cheeks to the outside corner of her eyes. He nearly raises his hand to her face, to wipe away those smudges, but their symmetry implies that they are probably deliberate. Her eyes blink involuntarily at his gesture, and astonishing eyes they are, thickly outlined in black, the lids a sparkling, silvery purple, the lashes a lot longer and clumpier than he remembers— but maybe he'd better not ask any more dumb questions. They can't glue stuff to your eyes as well, can they?

"So, what were you all up to while we were playing basketball?" he asks, instead.

"We talked about our colors," Lisa says, in a harmless little singsong voice laced, to Justin's ear, with contempt and sarcasm. She lifts a large manila envelope in illustration. "Then we cut out swatches in our colors so that we'll always have them available for reference. Then we did makeovers."

Justin nods wisely. He has no clue what she's talking about. What's a swatch?

"I think that's the whole program for tonight," Lisa says. She tries to take a pimiento-spread toast triangle from the buffet, but her nails hit the table well in advance of her fingers, and she can't figure out how to get one without actually spearing it, which seems disgusting.

Never mind, the evening is winding down. A female voice comes booming through the speakers. "Everybody, girls, if you're going straight home by private vehicle or eco-cab, you can leave everything on, but if not, if you came by Eco-Trans, please don't forget to wash it all off. There's cold cream and tissue in the bathrooms."

Lisa hesitates. On the one hand, the thought of scraping off this layer of gooey gunk is very tempting. On the other hand, Lisa can only too readily visualize the scene in the ladies' bathroom. It'll be the whole makeover experience again, only in reverse: the measuring looks beneath the sugary compliments, the chemical smells of the products, the mirrors fogged over from all that condensed narcissism. She doesn't think she can stand any more giggling togetherness tonight.

"Let's go," Lisa says, and forges ahead, impatient for the comparative safety of their car. It takes her only a minute to realize that the routine tasks of driving—those familiar buttons and switches that she can manipulate in her sleep—are a whole new ball game when inch-long extensions of sharp plastic are attached to each of your fingers.

"Why don't you drive tonight," she says.

One useful thing about those nails: on a dashboard, they allow you to tap out an eloquent beat of annoyed impatience.

"You seem to have quite enjoyed yourself tonight," she says, accusingly.

"Oh!" Justin exclaims. "Well! I wouldn't put it that way. We didn't really *do* anything. It was just basketball. I play that a lot. But these guys were pretty good, so it was, you know, more of a challenge. *That* part was good."

Lisa sniffs.

"So, I guess you had a really bad time," he supposes, sympathetically, but is brushed off.

"It's not an issue of having a good time or a bad time," she replies huffily. "It was a waste of time, that's the point. I had a bunch of icky stuff slopped on me, half of it probably chemical carcinogens, but I didn't learn anything about their plans. Unless their plans are just to make everybody look like an AR prostitute."

"You don't look bad, you know," he offers, kindly.

"Yes I do," she says.

And that's pretty much the end of that conversation. Upon reaching her apartment, Lisa disappears immediately into the bathroom, from which sounds of vigorous rinsing and scrubbing can soon be heard. Most of everything comes off, except for the nails. Lisa tries soap, but that doesn't budge them. Justin suggests olive oil, and pours out a little dish of it for her to soak her hands in, but that doesn't work either, and then he thinks gasoline might do the trick, but Lisa decides not to try that. In the end, she has to sleep with the claws still attached, and visit the Ministry's health station in the morning, and wait forever while the nurse consults the engineering department and then brews up a smelly potion of solvents and cream. "It was for an assignment," Lisa proclaims defensively, even though no one has said anything. "It's part of my office project," she insists, as the nurse, one eyebrow eloquently raised, peels the bright chips from Lisa's fingers and refrains from comment.

The smell of olive oil and turpentine has barely worn off when Lisa confronts her next aggravations.

It is Thursday night. Brett was supposed to come over, but something came up at the last minute and he canceled. Never mind, he won't be missed. Lisa is in bed with someone else, preparing to give herself up to irresistible, cataclysmic sex. With Falon, who wears three thick golden belts, a torn shirt, and tight black leather pants, and looks angrily down at a slim blonde in shredded lavender gauze. Well, it doesn't look like they're much enjoying themselves, but they must be. Their author, who pouts glamorously from the back of the book, is described as one of the most successful authors of romance, each and every one of her many books a bestseller. Rebecca will be ecstatic when Lisa is through with Falon and passes him on. *Keeper of the Heart*—a classic. Lisa snuggles into her blankets, opens the book, and warms immediately to the heroine, Shanelle. Shanelle is the daughter of a "mixed marriage" between a member of a primitive warrior race, her father, and a member of a highly advanced technological race, her mother. She herself is away at college, learning to become a spaceship pilot. For her semester break, she plans to visit Dad, bringing along several girlfriends who are curious to see her remote, exotic birthplace. To top it off, it's carnival season on Dad's planet, and the girls are looking forward to a few weeks of partying with the reputedly good-looking natives before returning to their rigorous technical training. Lisa is pleased. A young, fun-loving pilot: now, there's an acceptable role model at last. She breezes happily along to page 20, and so far so good. But now trouble strikes. Shanelle learns that the carnival is in fact a joust intended to identify the strongest and boldest of the planet's warriors. Her father wants to find this man, because he plans to marry *her* off to him. Daddy, it seems, has had about enough of her mother's outlandishly emancipated thinking. Become a pilot, indeed! Instead, he plans to turn her into a nice, subservient warrior's wife. Infuriated, Shanelle throws herself into the carnival nightlife. Her plan is to find Mr. Right on her own and jump into bed with him. With her virtue compromised, her father won't be able to pressure her into an arranged marriage.

Lisa is so alarmed by this development that she spills her wine. What kind of a stupid plan is this? Shanelle should jump right back on her spaceship and race back to college, beyond the reach of her barbarian father!

Shanelle, unfortunately, is oblivious to good advice from a concerned reader. She goes out and picks up a guy. He's handsome, and charming in a rustic sort of way, but their tryst turns bad. Besides being bossy and possessive and talking in weird ungrammatical sentences, he gets so carried away in bed that she ends up with bruises, crushed ribs, and other injuries requiring medical care. He tries to keep her his prisoner, because he knows he's made a bad impression and wants a chance to redeem himself. She still feels some kind of chemistry, but after this experience, she's not planning to have sex with him again, thank you very much. She escapes. But the psychopath pursues her. He is convinced that he has found his soul mate and destined bride. He got crazy because she is his one true love! If he can only take her to bed again, and do a better job of it, she will love him back and go off with him to his remote backward fiefdom to live in primitive conditions as the disenfranchised wife of an impulsive muscle-bound lunatic.

Incredibly, the nut turns out to be a respected member of the warrior community, so he gains her father's support for this plan.

Daddy betroths Shanelle, in absentia, to the bad-in-bed crazy man. Shanelle escapes in a spaceship, but her fiancé sets forth to track her down. She flees to a nearby planet run by women, hoping for help, but they turn out to be an awful society practicing slavery and torture. Instead of helping Shanelle, they take all her clothes away and tie her up in a dungeon, and the bad terrible woman leader gets ready to beat her into submission. But Falon arrives. Finding Shanelle conveniently undressed, he engages in some serious foreplay, to see if he can't turn her on. And it works. It works so well that Shanelle is completely beside herself, and demands to have him right then and there in the dungeon with armed hordes of evil feminists pounding on the door, but he backs off, to impress her with the fact that he has himself under control now. He takes her home, marries her, and whisks her away to his redneck duchy, where he consummates their marriage (good sex this time), confesses his deep love for her, institutes all sorts of progressive social reforms to show how deeply she has influenced him, and then gives her a beating, to punish her for running away and make sure she doesn't try it again.

> He simply pulled her to the bed, sat on it, and down she went across his thighs.
>
> The first smack was merely a hot sting. Shanelle had time to wonder whether, if she screamed loud enough, he might at least cut her punishment short. Five more whacks and she had no control over her screams . . . Shanelle lost count of how many times Falon's hand descended. But there was no doubt about it. She'd definitely think twice before she ever disobeyed him again. But what was the most galling, perhaps even the most humiliating, was that when he was done, that beast lay back on the bed and held her in his arms until she stopped crying—and she let him.

Lisa drops the book, flicking it away from her like the nasty thing it is. She has had it! With this book, but even more so with Rebecca and the rest of the sorry members of that pathetic subterranean reading clique, who, it is clear, are one very disturbed bunch in need of ex- and intensive psychiatric treatment. And furthermore, Lisa is appalled at the permissiveness of her Ministry and plans to take this matter to the highest possible authority. How can this kind of trash be allowed! These books shouldn't just be frowned upon, they should be banned! Burned! Stomped to pulp. This is liberalism gone too far!

The morning after dawns dismally. Lisa awakens uncomfortably to find the recumbent form of Brett intruding heavily, sweatily on what is definitely her half of the bed. Right, she remembers him wandering in after midnight, trying to be quiet but waking her up anyway. She gives him an unfriendly shove, but he just grunts and turns over. Exasperated, she sits up, focuses groggily on the floor, and sees, as her first image, the slim figure of a woman kneeling beseechingly before a large male in shiny black pants. That damn book again! Lisa gives it a kick, but later she will retrieve it; she needs it as Exhibit A in her planned censorship campaign.

So this is not a propitious day for Rebecca to come before the eyes of Lisa. Innocent of the distressing night Lisa has spent in the service of Romance, she bustles cheerily into Lisa's office. "So," she says. "How is it coming? Are the books helping?"

Lisa glares at her in disgust. "Your books," she says, "are revolting. I promised you confidentiality, so I suppose I can't report you to Group Health, but as your colleague, I'm telling you that you need help."

"What are you talking about?" Rebecca asks, baffled.

"How can you like this stuff?" Lisa hisses. "Stupid women who flirt and simper and lie and manipulate, falling in love with stuck-up bossy muscle-bound morons, and they like getting raped, mauled, and, and, and beaten!" she sputters, in outrage. "I ask you! By their stupid Neanderthal gloomy broody so-called lovers, and—"

"Hey, whoa, slow down. What on earth have you been reading?"

Seeing that Rebecca looks genuinely befuddled, Lisa pulls last night's reading material from her bag, picking it up between thumb and index finger as though it were radioactive. "I have been reading this, this, this—muck of yours!" she says.

"Okay, okay," Rebecca replies, soothingly. "Let's just back up here for a minute, and let's look at what's upsetting you."

Disarmed by Rebecca's empathy, Lisa takes a few deep breaths. She brings out her adjective list.

"We've looked at the summaries of eighty-nine books," she tells her. "The plots are bad enough, but even leaving that aside! Just look at the attributes of the male and female main characters. We've made a list and it is pitiful. The women are beautiful, long on hair and legs and short on everything else, except, sometimes, temper. The men are"—she pauses to consult the list—"surly, snarling, warlike, passionate, cynical, savage . . . The women are simpering little damsels in distress, and the men are assholes, unless, of course, they're world conquerors committing massacres right and left and then hopping back into bed with our heroine, not before giving her a beating—"

Rebecca has been shaking her head with growing vehemence. "Lisa!" she interrupts now, in mild rebuke. "No wonder you're upset. You aren't reading the right books. Those aren't the ones I was talking about. *I* am going to select the books you should read. You and your cute little sidekick," she adds playfully, "are clearly amateurs at romance."

The very next day, a package arrives for Lisa, wrapped discreetly and marked top and bottom with the warning PERSONAL. Trailed by a curious Justin, she dumps out the lurid contents. There is a note inside, from Rebecca. "*This* is what you should be reading," it says. "No wimpy heroines here! Enjoy!"

Lisa picks up a volume at random. A banner across the front announces that here is a book about "a beautiful woman space warrior," surprisingly attired in some sort of ball gown, and "the slave of her desire," a stocky, muscular fellow with long, wavy blond hair and dressed in an extremely skimpy loincloth.

Lisa and Justin exchange glances; he shrugs, and Lisa turns the book over to read aloud from the back.

"'He is Wolf, one of the few survivors from the planet Trios, conquered by the mighty intergalactic Coalition. Magnificently hand-some and virile, he is a valuable sexual slave programmed to please a woman beyond her wildest dreams.'

"Well, okay!" Lisa exclaims, with a wide nasty smile, reading on with greater exuberance.

" 'She is Captain Shaylah Graymist, the Coalition's beautiful and fiery ace fighter pilot, with countless battles and victories to her credit. Medals are but a part of the reward for her heroism. Another is Wolf, offered to her as a special accolade. But Wolf, whose spirit stays free even as his flesh is pressed into service, stirs more than Shaylah's hunger. He melts her heart. And they join together as equals to battle against slavery and the evil Coalition . . . and they unite as man and woman in the forbidden feeling called love—causing a burst of passion to shake the stars and light the vastness of space . . .' Now, how about *that!*" Lisa cries.

Justin, listening with one eyebrow raised, has fanned the other volumes out, cover sides up, across the desk. There they lie, a welter of chests, breasts, loins, thighs, waists, and hips, all protruding from torn or inadequate amounts of clothing, all of mythic propor-tions.

"I think I deserve a night with Wolf, to make up for my abuse at the hand of Falon," Lisa announces, ostentatiously packing the vol-ume into her bag.

"I guess," Justin says, smiling tolerantly. He grabs a few of the remaining books, promising to have the adjective count by tomor-row.

"Enjoy!" he calls out in parting, nastily mimicking Rebecca's note.

Justin stands before the mirror and juts out his chin. He looks sternly into the glass. He tenses the muscles in his neck; gratify-ingly, there is some movement at either side of his throat, though he wouldn't say that his muscles are "forming ropes." Moving closer to the glass, he glares at his reflection, narrowing his eyes. He pulls his shoulders back and sets his mouth into a grim line. How does that look? Dangerous? Attractive? Sexy?

"You too?" a voice says, behind him. Justin jumps a little, startled, but the other man doesn't notice.

"I think it was that damn tofu salad," the man is saying. "I've had diarrhea ever since. Gonna kill us one of these days with that crap. Want one?" he asks, offering Justin a pastel-colored tablet.

Justin shakes his head. Great. Try to be a romantic hero, you end up looking like you have the runs.

L isa has lunch with Brett, during which he announces that he will come over to her place again today after work, probably, unless he gets tied up, but Lisa informs him that, alas, she has other plans. This is unprecedented, but he recovers quickly. "I'll come over later, then, and spend the night," he offers.

"Actually," she replies, "I'll be with someone else tonight. But," she adds kindly, "I'll call you tomorrow to see how your seminar went."

For just one little tiny fraction of a second, his eyes reflect astonishment, even shock, sending a warm thrill of pleasure through Lisa.

Which makes her realize that she really needs to see her Emotional Development counselor. You are not supposed to hope that your SR will feel pain and jealousy. You aren't supposed to spend your productive daytime hours, let alone your regenerative leisure time, wondering why your SR flinched at a broken date: because he loves you and feels jealous; because he thinks he owns you and feels angry; or because he thinks he is such a goddamn hotshot that you will just sit around forever waiting for His Majesty to make time for you in his busy schedule—no, no, no! Oh hell. She'll make an appointment for next week, she really will.

But first Lisa has a romantic assignation with Wolf. Yes, the virile Wolf, trained sex slave, awaits her pleasure.

He: a prisoner, taken captive in the war that destroyed his civilized, cultured home planet and now owned by the Coalition, a high-tech, low-sentiment sort of place with a labor force based on slavery. These slaves, including Wolf, are equipped with a collar that is linked to their neurological system and their brain waves. Through a kind of remote-control unit, the owner can exact obedience by inflicting pain or, less crassly, by altering the slave's moods and thoughts. Being recalcitrant and strong-willed, Wolf often incurs the wrath of his owners. He is also exceptionally attractive and well endowed, and so has been trained in the erotic arts and is deemed an appropriate reward for the fleet's star pilot when she touches down for some R and R.

> . . . The heavy decanter of brandy appeared on the table before her, placed there carefully by a strongly muscled arm that was nearly as golden as the liquid. Her gaze jerked upward. He was, without a doubt, the most incredible male she had ever seen . . . His shoulders were wide and strong, his naked chest was broad and smoothly hairless, giving emphasis to the scattering of fine golden hairs below his navel. That scattering of hair thickened as it trailed down below the edge of the trewscloth he wore. She felt an odd flush of heat as she looked at the full, masculine contours the brief garment hardly covered . . . He was staring at the floor as he stood quietly . . . as if awaiting orders.
>
> Orders. She sucked in her breath as the realization hit. Her gaze snapped to his neck . . . He was a slave . . . His wrists bore the mark of chains long worn. Her eyes flicked down the long, leanly muscled legs to his feet; the marks were there, too, around the ankles . . . She vaguely heard Califa giggle. "Like him? I thought you would."

Wolf is lent to her by Califa, Shaylah's college friend and his owner. But a quirk in the pilot's biography makes her unable to enjoy command-performance sex with a slave prostitute: she was raised by eccentrically monogamous, idealistic parents. She wants him, but not under these circumstances.

He extended one chained hand. She looked and saw the controller resting on his palm . . . All she had to do was take it, activate it with her systems card, and this magnificent creature would be hers to command. He would clean her flight boots, kiss her with machine-induced passion . . . and mate with her until she was limp with physical satiation . . . She could even use the brain-wave system to achieve the simulation of bonding if she wished. She could turn the man called Wolf into her dream lover . . . who would . . . declare himself hers forever out of love.

But that would be a lie based on coercion, so she sends him away. He leaves without comment, even though he knows the consequences of his dismissal and she doesn't. His owner will conclude that Wolf must have offended Shaylah, to have been rejected, and will order him severely punished. When Shaylah learns of this, she is horrified. Then she learns that if she rejects him again, he will be put to death. Once again he arrives at her door, this time battered and shaken from the torture he was subjected to.

Bracing his unsteady right arm with his half-functioning right hand, he once more held out the control unit. This time, though she had no intention of using it, she took it. A tiny breath, barely noticeable, escaped him.

He was standing beside the bed, his feet apart slightly as he braced himself against the tremors that still shook him. His unsteady fingers were plucking at the ties of his trews-cloth, and color rose in her cheeks as she realized he was about to take it off.

"Don't," she said quickly.

His head came up. He said nothing, but stopped. He lowered his hands to the traditional clasped, submissive position . . .

Shaylah swore, low and harsh. She looked at the controller . . . "I can't remember," she said. "Tell me."

His voice was flat when he answered. "The blue one."

. . . "Not that."

Bitterness flashed in his eyes again. "Then perhaps you want the yellow one."

. . . "Why in Hades would I want that?"

He just looked at her.

"Why would you think I want to cause you more pain?" she demanded.

"Because you asked for me this time. When I am . . . like this."

"You think I enjoy it? That seeing you like this excites me?"

"There are those to whom it brings pleasure."

Shaylah is appalled. She manages to figure out how the machine works and to get his shackles off. And then she tries to be nice to him, platonically, because she doesn't want to take advantage of him. Though he's a bristly sort of pet, because he resents her charity and doesn't like being beholden to a member of the oppressor class.

Just as they're starting to work this out and be friends, a military emergency calls Shaylah away. When she returns a few weeks later, she discovers that Wolf has gotten himself in trouble once again, and Califa has lost patience with this ornery plaything and has sent him to the quarries.

Rushing to his rescue, Shaylah finds him near death from hard labor, starvation, and beatings; she spirits him away, carries him off in her spaceship, and nurses him back to health. There, in deep space, they finally give in to their mutual attraction. But Wolf just can't believe that his intense feelings for Shaylah could truly be real, so he suspects that she is using the little button on his remote control to artificially induce them by messing with his brain waves. She despairs of ever gaining his trust and love, he despairs of ever regaining his freedom, and both of them wallow in a stew of misery, pausing occasionally for a bout in bed.

Whew! Lisa takes a break.

Well! So much emotion, the pages feel heavy with it. Talk about lurid! She's realizing one thing, though: it's always about power, one way or another. There must be a stray sexual nerve ending somewhere in the power zone of the mind, causing crossed signals. Or do power and attraction amalgamate? A sexy, great-looking man, equipped with a control device that can bring him to his knees with pain or make him do and think and feel whatever you wish . . . Lisa puts the book aside and roams around her apartment for a few minutes, pulling stray leaves off her houseplants.

Does she still think Rebecca needs to see a counselor? Would it be somehow exciting, to have power over a lover, but you were too decent to use it, but he couldn't be entirely sure of that—would this give your time together some extra edge? And what if you weren't quite as high-minded? What if she could administer the occasional judicious jolt of well-deserved punishment to Brett?

Carrying a plate of cookies, fuzzy slippers on her feet, Lisa returns to Wolf, uppity slave stud, to ponder her sadistic potential.

So, after her impulsive rescue of the runaway Coalition slave, Shaylah parks her spaceship in a dark corner of the galaxy. One day, chatting with Wolf, she accidentally blurts out a military secret: that his home planet has not, contrary to official statements, been entirely destroyed. A small, ragtag band of survivors remains, still offering resistance to Coalition forces. Wolf is electrified by this news. Wresting control of the ship from Shaylah, he sets course for Trios. Upon landing, they are immediately surrounded by the natives, who recognize Wolf: as their long-lost prince and heir! As for our star-crossed lovers, the tables are turned now. While Wolf is borne away for a delirious homecoming, Shaylah is thrown into a dungeon and threatened with gang rape and execution. She thinks that a vengeful Wolf has ordered this, but he had nothing to do with it. He finds and frees her and, together, they liberate his planet. With her inside knowledge of military technology and his valor, they repel the Coalition forces, get married, and are crowned king and queen. Happy end.

Lisa finishes her cookies and collects some fallen sesame seeds thoughtfully. Glancing at her pad, she finds that she has scribbled down "enslaved, distrustful, in pain, fearful, humiliated, and misunderstood" as the key erotic words. Tomorrow she will add them to her list. Will that list, when complete, provide enlightenment? Lisa cannot imagine how, but at least she has been entertained.

"So," Brett says, on the phone the next morning. "You had a pleasant evening, I trust?"

His tone is light, his words are measured, but Lisa knows him well enough to catch the undertone of nervousness and displeasure. She had planned to come clean this morning, let him in on the joke, but now she finds she can't.

"Oh, it was . . . exceptional," she replies.

"Anyone I know?" Brett asks, casually.

"Oh, you wouldn't know this guy," she says. "He's a, a, well, actually he's a sex slave."

Silence ensues while Brett digests this unthinkably tasteless, inappropriate, sexist statement and Lisa breathes a deep sigh of evil emotional fulfillment.

What's this?" Lisa asks, of the envelope that Justin has just unceremoniously dumped on her desk.

"A disk," he says.

Well, she can see that.

"And may I learn what kind of a disk it is, and why you are placing it before me?" she intones carefully.

"It's labeled," he says.

Aren't we testy today. Well, fine. She slides the disk out of the envelope and sees that it bears the markings of the Ministry of Reeducation. "Interim Report Form 501/M," it says. Lisa is not enlightened.

"And this would be . . . ?" she asks.

"I've been here for three months. So 'this would be' the first report you have to file about me," he says. "You know, about whether you're satisfied," he adds, "that I'm going to fit into the modern world. Whether you think I'm acceptable. '501,' for first-trimester report on the fifth evaluation. 'M' for male."

Justin holds the ensuing awkward silence for a long moment, then leaves.

"It's due by the end of next week," he adds in parting.

Well, good, that gives her plenty of time. Lisa starts to put the disk away, thinking to return to it tomorrow, but then she changes her mind and slides it into the drive. It's not that long and not that different from the other personnel reports that workers are constantly filling out about each other. It's not so awful. Sure, the Ministry of Reeducation is notoriously short on tact. None of that democratic "how are we all doing and how do we feel about each other" stuff that other offices engage in. They like to make it clear that you have to satisfy certain conditions before you are a citizen, and that men, given their past record, have to fulfill a few more than everybody else. And that women have to sign off on them. Frankly, that's fair, and Lisa isn't going to apologize for it.

In that mood, she swiftly ticks off Justin's standing on a variety of qualities and on scales of one to ten. She writes a brief paragraph summarizing his particular strengths and then pauses over the section where she is supposed to describe what he needs to work on. This one's the killer, she knows that. You can't leave it blank, and you can't say somebody's perfect, but if you like them, you have to be very careful about what you write. It has to sound like a criticism but actually be a sort of ass-backward compliment. You know, you can say that they work too hard, that they're too meticulous, things like that. Justin really has been great, and she wants to do right by him. She'd like to consult him, but given his present mood, perhaps she'd better not. Fortunately, she still has a week, so she decides to leave that final section blank for now. She pops out to see if Justin has calmed down and wants to go to lunch with her, but he's left already. Still in a snit, evidently; well, he'll get over it.

By afternoon, Lisa has completely and totally forgotten about the form. Which means that Justin is obliged, on Day Six, to nudge her about it.

"Oh!" she says. "I've almost finished it. Thanks for reminding me."

Then Nadine calls a meeting, and Cleo phones to say that she has sprained her ankle in gym, and Lizzie asks her to review some reports, and, well, you get the idea. Lisa forgets once again.

On Day Seven, Justin will once again need to bring the matter up. But he doesn't. Because the evening of Day Six, coincidentally, there was a basement meeting, and during the ritual go-around, where everyone aired their griefs and grievances, Justin had shared his feeling of humiliation at having to be evaluated and, worse, at having to plead to be evaluated.

"She wants you to sit up and beg," Will had opined bitterly. And Karl had added sagely that the intent was obvious, they were trying to cut his balls off.

So Day Seven passes with Justin's disk gently collecting dust on Lisa's side table.

And Day Eight begins with Justin filling out a resignation form and transmitting it to Lisa's screen, where she finds it in her morning mail.

It's so unexpected, such overkill, that she doesn't make the connection to her delinquent evaluation form at all. She is merely thunderstruck.

She almost lets him go. He hates her, evidently. Hates this office and hates her. So much so that he is ready to lose three months of his life and start all over somewhere else, from zero, on his final accreditation.

Maybe she remembers her team-building lessons, or maybe she's just panicked at the thought of going to the next Harmony meeting by herself. At any rate, instead of impulsively approving his request for a transfer, she asks him to please step into her office, and closes the door behind them for privacy.

She is hurt and annoyed, so she plans to be formal. Instead, she hears herself asking softly, "What's up, Justin?"

"Well, it's really quite simple," he replies, coldly. "Obviously, my performance has not been satisfactory, since you find yourself unable to complete my review on schedule. So it will be best if I take my talents, such as they are, elsewhere."

"Oh shit," Lisa curses. "So that's what you're all bent out of shape about. But hey, I wouldn't have missed the deadline, I didn't forget, I put it in my automatic pop-up for 1 p.m. today. And besides, if you thought I forgot, why didn't you just remind me?"

"I am not 'bent out of shape,'" Justin replies with dignity. "And furthermore, this whole evaluation thing is *your* horse and pony show, not mine, and I'll be damned if, on top of everything else, I'm going to *beg* Your Ladyship to sign off on me so I can be issued my dog tags and allowed to roam the streets."

Well, Justin certainly must be very upset, or he would never mix his metaphors like that.

"So," he winds up, "in case you *forget,* allow me to *remind* you that my resignation is on your screen, and I will be leaving now, *goodbye.*"

With that, he strides toward the door.

Lisa steps in front of him, blocking his exit with her body, an action that is explicitly, absolutely, totally, and completely forbidden by Workplace Regulations and could get her in serious trouble.

She says, "I've made you feel bad. I'm so sorry. I didn't mean to. It's got nothing to do with you, it's just that I'm a lousy administrator. You're great to work with, and you're doing a wonderful job. Please don't go."

He is looking off to the side, more uncertain now, which makes Lisa feel that perhaps she still can sway him.

"Come on, Justin, please don't do this," she adds. "I'll never survive this project without you. And who will I go to the meetings with?"

"Well," he says, grudgingly. Lisa gives him an exaggeratedly contrite smile. Justin frowns. "Well, okay," he allows, finally. "Maybe it *was* a misunderstanding."

And then Lisa, and I don't even want to think about what the Contemporary Interaction Department would do if they ever, ever found out about it, impulsively leans forward and kisses him on the cheek. "Friends?" she says, and he throws his hands up in exasperation and replies, "Yeah, I guess, sure. Friends."

Lisa is tired, bored, and lonely and can't go to sleep. Should she e-shop for her sister's birthday gift? Review her accounts? She decides to listen to the radio instead. ". . . and a heartfelt GOOD RIDDANCE." The scrappy voice of 103.3, Kiss-Off Radio host Melanie Diss is just yelling out her signature phrase. "Danny, you double-crossing hyena, with the wish that you may never darken her door again, this song is for *you*!" Lisa taps her fingers and her feet to the beat of the country song "My SR Was an SOB." Next we hear from Jeanne, who wants an oldie played for Christopher, because that's where he belongs, way, way back in the AR! "Jeanne hopes never, ever to see you again, Christopher," Melanie summarizes jauntily, "she expects you to have all your stuff out of her apartment by noon tomorrow, and here's a golden oldie to speed you on your way," and then Lisa nods her head to the beat of Nancy Sinatra, walking her boots all over the dastardly Christopher. There are some who feel that Melanie Diss should be banned for promoting unconstructive, vindictive feelings between unlucky-in-love women and their mostly male partners. Others think it's purely a recreational thing, and you shouldn't be dogmatic. Still others actively champion it. The goal, they feel, is to wean women gradually away from their stupid feelings for men altogether, and this show can help.

"Oh, Thoooooomaaaaaaas!" Melanie calls, seductively. "Yes, you! Got a message for you, Tommy boy! From Susan. Remember Susan? She's the brown-haired one? The tall one? The one whose name is on that lease next to yours? The one you have a six-month-old baby with? Is it slowly coming back to you? Now, don't get nervous. We all know that when you took your lying stinking self on over to Tanya's place for the weekend, it was just simply because you had forgotten all about Susan. It can happen! Hey, we all forget things! And you know what? Susan is planning to forget all about you. She's packed up your things and left them with your buddy Jeff! And as for you, Tanya: he's all yours. Good luck and Gooooood Riddance! Here's a little ditty for the both of you," Melanie promises, as the radio launches into "Nothing but Lies."

Lisa doesn't know about the social merits of it, but there's something deeply satisfying about Kiss-Off 103.3.

Justin is tired, bored, and lonely and can't go to sleep. Shall he read? Catch a film? Lounging on his futon, he decides to listen to the radio. 103.3, that's his favorite program. From walking down the halls at night, he happens to know that others in his building like it, too, though of course they would never admit it. Justin considers it a very romantic program; listening to it always puts him into a sad, sentimental state of reverie. True, the callers are all angry, filled with rage at their deceitful, unworthy former lovers, and use the glib hostess to send messages of loathing and defiance. But, reading between the lines, Justin finds that he can home in on what must have come before. You don't feel that much anger unless you loved the person once. You aren't that defiant unless you used to be vulnerable. Closing his eyes, Justin listens to the rude brush-offs and conjures up the sweet intimacies that must have preceded them. He sees Jeanne, content in the arms of Christopher, Thomas and Susan conceiving their child in blissful entanglement on a bed with crisp white sheets, before that idiot ruined everything by messing around with Tanya. From the contempt and rage in these women's voices, Justin distills an essence of passion and longing. Will anyone ever feel this way about him?

I know what you're thinking. You're thinking these two are going to fall in love. Lisa will overcome her character flaws—ambitiousness and insecurity—she'll dump that prestige-bringing pain-in-the-ass Brett, and then she'll realize that there's this nice, good-looking, funny, and charming guy right behind the next desk. And Justin, instead of just using Lisa as a template for some hypothetical future fantasy female love object, will see her as a real and attainable woman.

Well, that might happen. Or maybe an attractive young woman and a handsome young man can actually have a friendship because they like each other. Maybe they can look at each other, and feel something other than sexual attraction or indifference. I'd call that a revolution!

Today, it seems, will not be a routine sort of meeting. There is a palpable air of expectation in the room, Brett can feel it the instant he walks through the door. He can also tell, instantly, that his arriving last is not a coincidence. Everyone else, it's clear from their posture, has been here for a long time, not just a few minutes.

"Did I get the time wrong?" he asks.

The General is far too smart to lie to him. "Dr. Martins!" he greets him, cordially. "No, not at all. The rest of us convened a bit earlier, we had some technical matters to discuss, didn't want to make you sit through that. Nothing substantive without our quorum, that goes without saying."

Brett is still suspicious, but he nods and takes his seat. The air is charged. Henry, the most volatile member of the group, is practically vibrating with excitement, but even the others betray clear signs of it.

The plan. Can they possibly have finalized the plan? They've been speaking about it for so long that Brett had nearly assigned it to the realm of fiction and fantasy, but as he notes the palpable tension in this room, it is once again a very real presence. And, he finds to his surprise, one that frightens him.

"The plan is ready," he says, in a flat voice of certainty.

Henry smacks his palm against the table and whoops. "Way to go, Doc! Nobody keeps secrets from our own Dr. Strangelove!"

"There can be no question of keeping secrets from each other," the General reprimands him prissily. He is standing in his customary place, at the head of the table. His control, as always, is total, except for a very slight tic in his left cheek.

"But you are correct, Doctor. Our plan is indeed ready to be submitted to the quorum. Uwe and Robert have gone over everything one final time, that's why we met early. The plan is ready, and can go into effect as soon as the orders are given. For that, of course, our Council's unanimous vote is required, as per Article VII of the Civil-Military Relations Code, Restoration of Order Plan."

Brett nods. The Code, sure. Drafting that and a whole slew of other declarations and regulations made up the bulk of Harmony's activities in the first years. Brett, bored senseless by the nitpicking debates over first and second and third drafts, tried to stay as uninvolved as humanly possible and can now barely remember any of the products. Most of the others, though, seem to thrive on this stuff. He does remember, of course, the heated arguments over civilian-military relations, culminating in the decision that the civilian-dominated Council had to approve all military action by a unanimous vote.

"So," he says. "The computer assault team came through, then? They're ready?"

The General pulls himself up even straighter. "What do you think the assault team's mission will be?" he asks, looking directly at Brett.

What is this, a quiz show? Brett sighs. "We're going to incapacitate the computers, make basic services malfunction, show this regime up as inept and amateurish. Undermine their legitimacy, their client base, their support. Demonstrate the need for a stronger representation of male technical expertise," he recites, not bothering to mask his irritation. But the General is undisturbed.

"Yes, that was our original plan," he agrees. "So I am pleased to tell you today that Computer Assault, under Robert's first-rate leadership, has truly exceeded our finest expectations. I've known what they were working on, but I didn't want to get anyone's hopes up. Today we have final confirmation and it is an excellent, an excellent plan."

"Happy Valentine's Day!" Henry whoops.

Valentine's Day? What's with all the bizarre friskiness?

"The virus. It activates on February 14," the General is explaining. Even he is far more animated than usual. His generally stoic, expressionless face is aglow with energy and enthusiasm.

"Kiss the girls!" Henry chortles. The others exchange tolerant glances. Obviously, they all know what Henry is talking about.

"Why doesn't somebody just tell me what the hell is going on," Brett snaps, truly annoyed now.

The General nods briskly. "That's why we're here," he agrees. He pauses. "Without exaggeration, I can say that we have finalized a truly impressive plan. We're not talking about trains running late or bank transactions going haywire. No, sir. When this virus activates, the entire domestic and civil defense structure will shut down. Communications will be impossible. Police and military systems and barriers will become inactive. There will be no defense. The security system will, to all intents and purposes, be totally incapacitated."

Brett nods. Well, that should cause some confusion among the leadership, but it's not like there's a war. It's not like enemy armies are poised on the borders. There isn't even any crime to speak of. You could shut down security for forty-eight hours and no one would even know the difference, probably. And by that time, surely the regime will have regrouped. Why are they so thrilled about this plan? A breakdown in banking or in public transportation would impact far more people.

But the General is still speaking. "Some days earlier," he is saying, "peripheral surveillance will have been inactivated. Of course, we have our cells in every internment and reeducation facility, so those populations will be ready to march as soon as that happens. They will overrun seven major cities. In the smaller towns and cities, the members of our local chapters will be ready as well, and we expect them to be joined by many dissenting elements. Even if it were fully functional, the security infrastructure would have trouble dealing with a mob of that size. And, of course, it won't be functioning at all."

Dimly, Brett begins to understand the magnitude of what the General is saying. Everything is electronic, controlled by computer security systems. The locks on apartment doors and on shopping complexes, on campus dormitories, banks, private houses. Video surveillance, alarm systems—everything runs through computer programs. If you shut those down, there won't be a locked door in the country. That wouldn't matter much, given the general placidity of civil society under the New Order, but if you simultaneously unleash the criminal elements and the dissenting male supremacists . . .

"Of course, the security forces won't just go home and hide under their beds," the General is continuing, with an effort at humor. "We do expect some resistance. They won't have effective leadership or communication, but individual units will probably try to act on their own. Their first dilemma will be deciding where to concentrate their forces. Possibly they can guard the leadership, because they can collect them in a government building and mass their forces around it."

Brett thinks of the team of three that guards Lisa's huge apartment complex by keeping a casual eye on the control panel and the surveillance screens. Are they even armed, or are they simply instructed to call Central Security in the Highly Unlikely Event of any sort of dangerous incident? What will they do if a mob overruns their complex?

"There will be some armed confrontations," the General says, as though reading his mind, "but they won't lead to a resolution either way. The regime forces will be in too much disarray, and they don't have any real weapons anyway, just a bunch of nonlethal stuff. The rebels don't have the matériel or the discipline. It will be a standoff, chaos. That's the beauty of this plan." The General nods, permitting himself the tightest of smiles. "It allows our own forces to remain almost completely uninvolved, while being preordained for victory. We pull the plug on security, pit them against the mob, and then, after a judicious amount of time, step in. We're the heroes, we save the day. We round up the miscreants, we restore order. And we'll seem very moderate, after everything that's just happened."

Brett tries to visualize events during this "judicious amount of time." A horde of infuriated men, deemed intransigent, uneducatable even by the pie-eyed optimists who run the reeducation campaign, having been locked up for years in remote settlements with only each other for company, steaming with rage and testosterone, unleashed on unguarded cities full of women they regard as uppity.

Brett feels the blood drain out of his head and his fingertips tingle; shock always wreaks havoc with his circulation. He opens his mouth a few times to protest, but nothing comes out.

"Yes, it's a bold campaign." The General nods with satisfaction, mistaking his dismay for speechless enthusiasm.

No one else seems to have a problem with this plan. Brett realizes that he will have to tread carefully, so he searches for the neutral phrase.

"There'll be a lot of societal disruption," he manages to say, finally. "I think we should reconsider whether this is really wise. I think we should consider going back to our original plan. I mean," he says, losing his moderation, "just imagine what those guys are going to do! If you let them run loose like that! Isn't this a little too . . . vicious? Aren't we unleashing too much . . ." With an effort, he collects himself again and gropes for a professional, a clinical term. The word "evil" comes to his mind, but that sounds antiquated. "Too much hostile affect?" he finishes instead.

The General regards him with displeasure. "A revolution is not a dinner party," he snaps. "And anyway, this government has been amply warned. They had every opportunity to work with us. We begged them, we pleaded with them, to at least restore the military establishment. But no, they think they can do it all by themselves, their own way. They want to play hardball with the big boys. Fine. Let's see how they like it."

Brett still isn't looking too convinced, I guess, because Henry smirks.

"Hey, the *dottore* is a lover, not a fighter. Right, Doc?"

Well, *il dottore*'s got more spunk than I would have credited him with, because he chooses again to blurt out his lone protest.

"I'm really not persuaded that this is a good idea," he says. "In my professional opinion, I think it's overkill. This will create an enormous level of trauma. We don't want a civil war; civil wars leave scars that last for generations. Besides," he continues, thinking how to appeal to the General, "this is an unfair fight. It's dishonorable to pitch criminal elements against, ummm"—he fishes for the proper military term and finds it—"against female noncombatants. That violates the military ethos—"

"You are overstepping your bounds, Doctor," the General interrupts, sternly. "This is really not your field. Besides, you are exaggerating the impact. Yes, there will be a few weeks of chaos, but we don't forecast an excess of actual bloodshed. I anticipate mostly looting, possibly some significant property damage, and of course a considerable amount of rape. The Zonies will run wild; then we'll move in to restore order. We'll be the good guys. We'll come down hard on the marauders. We'll impose martial law, execute the ringleaders, put down the uprising. Everyone will realize that we are essential to national and civil security. Everybody will have learned a valuable lesson: that the world is not a goody-goody place that you run by putting a bunch of female civilians in charge and having them send each other Hallmark cards and flowers."

The General has worked himself into a lather; he takes a moment to compose himself.

"We need to follow the chain of command," he says, "and stick with our respective duties. How women feel"—he waves vaguely—"it's your job to think about things like that. *My* job is keeping sight of the big picture. No room for sentiment there. I don't like making war on women. I don't countenance rape any more than you do. But in the end, this will save lives, reduce violence, and shore up our homeland against much worse peril. If we don't put a serious, viable national defense system back in place, there'll only be worse catastrophes later. You call what they've put together a defense system? It's a joke. Relying on nonlethal weapons only. Reeducating dissenters. I'm just waiting for them to appoint the tooth fairy as SecDef! These girls need a wakeup call. And the country needs order, defense, and structure. We'll move in, we'll round up the UEs, then we'll set up a normal government again. Heck, we'll include a bunch of the gals. That'll be your job. You'll pick them up, you'll dust them off," he says. "Counseling, trauma centers, whatever. You'll fix 'em up good as new, I'm sure. We're not throwing the women out of government, they'll have their say. We'll even put them on the Council, they can run health care, transport, geriatric affairs, things like that. We're not talking about going back to the Middle Ages here. We just want a more realistic balance. By the way," he adds benignly to Brett, "if there are any women you particularly care about, I recommend you relocate them out of the major urban areas for the duration. Each of us is entitled to five slots at Main Base. Just evacuate your dependents to that location by February 10. And now, gentlemen, if there are no further questions, there remains but one formality, our vote. Shall this plan go forth, yea or nay. Mr. McAllen?" he calls, pointing to his adjutant.

"Aye," the man says.

They move around the table, and the chorus of ayes meets no opposition, until finally it is Brett's turn.

"Last but certainly not least, our good doctor," Henry announces archly. Twelve pairs of eyes regard Brett cordially, without suspense, none of them reflecting any anxiety that he might dissent.

And correctly so.

"Aye," Brett says.

Brett goes home. His fingertips are still numb, especially the ring finger; Brett tries to remember whether, in neurological terms, that makes sense or not.

He massages the lifeless tip of this finger. He rubs his wrists to stimulate circulation.

He will be Minister of Social Health, once the Council is established. Well, that will be very gratifying. He will be one of the seven most powerful people in the country.

Still, he hadn't visualized anything like this. He had been thinking of a simple computer virus, something to cause power outages, mess up credit card reports, shut down offices, confuse telescreen broadcasts, bring down the bureaucracy.

He reviews the meeting in his mind. Everyone was so determined. What could he have said or done to force them into some more civilized, less horrible variant? Nothing. They had it all worked out, didn't bring him in until the very last second. They knew he was the squeamish one. And they knew he'd go along in the end.

He decides to think this through dispassionately. The General's arrogant assertion that he and he alone is capable of seeing the "big picture" still irks him. Taking the long view, Brett reflects that indeed mankind's history is violent. Battles, massacres, civil wars—it's true, change is always bought with blood and pain.

And Brett agrees with the General's critique of the current government's military planning. With their high principles and their pacifism, the ruling women have embarked on a perilous experiment. Can you have a purely defensive military, based only on non-lethal weapons systems? Won't some aggressor eventually make easy pickings of you? Won't there be far more rape, pillage, and death then, maybe even followed by foreign domination? Whereas their coup will be almost like preventive medicine, a quick surgical intervention; you have to cause the patient a little bit of pain, but only in the interest of health.

Brett feels better.

He'll have to figure out a way to protect the women he cares about. He starts preparing a mental list. Five of them can be sent to absolute safety at Main Base. Let's see. That will be, of course, his mother. His two sisters. His sister-in-law. His four adorable nieces. His favorite aunt, Irene. Lisa, certainly. As he adds up this first, minimalist, tip-of-the-iceberg list, and realizes that five slots will never do, Brett's fingers once again begin to tingle, worse than before.

———————

So disaster is looming, but our friends the government ladies don't know that. It's business as usual, so far as they know. They work, they meet, they organize. They team-build. They even, goddess bless them, have office parties. Alicia, for example, is leaving to take part in an exchange program, so her workmates arrange the obligatory farewell luncheon to send her off in style. She will be spending a year in Spain. She's a graduate of the Metropolitan Institute of Dance, and she's been assigned to take part in a project to redesign the flamenco—you know, to come up with a version that doesn't feature all of that obnoxious rooster-like male strutting. Then, if that goes well, they might think about rehabilitating the tango, which for now, of course, has been banned.

So where shall they take her? The Full Moon Teahouse is nice and serene, what about that? Or the cafeteria of the Botanical Museum, that's a festive and elegant setting.

"Boring," Tamara protests. "That's where we *always* go."

"Okay, then let's take her to Balls," Rebecca suggests mischievously.

Yes, at this point in my story, I'm going to invent a theme restaurant named after a colloquial term for two round, gender-specific body parts. You're right to balk at this. It's in such bad taste, a preposterous notion, something that could never actually exist, let alone develop a clientele, or forheavenssake become a *franchise,* in a civilized modern society. But this is a science fiction novel, so I'm allowed to come up with totally outlandish stuff like this.

Eva giggles as the others exchange uncertain looks. Well, that would be different. True, the popular chain restaurant is despised by some. And they, after all, are from the Ministry. Is it even okay for them to patronize such an establishment? On the other hand, the theme restaurant is a frequent venue for office parties, conference breaks, and the like, offering a slightly risqué experience, good for bonding.

Nadine is in an expansive mood. "Vai not?" she booms.

Lisa is put off by the idea. To take Alicia to Balls, really! What an adolescent notion. Although Lisa has never been there, and okay, she is a little curious. And the only way a self-respecting person can go there *is* in the context of an office party, where it's just a humorous, quasi-sociological outing. Otherwise, it would be sort of pathetic to go to a restaurant just to stare at . . . but let's not make an issue out of it. Let's just follow them, Lisa and her officemates, nine women and one re-ed who set off in good spirits to give Alicia a fun send-off.

The group takes the citibus. The usual complicated negotiations delay their boarding, as people who have no imminent travel plans requiring air or private cars are lobbied by those who do, and end up ceding them their ecocredits, which of course requires the other person to key you in with their code so they can collect your fare. The dollar you earn for a citibus ride hardly seems worth all this maneuvering, but when you're saving up for a trip, every little bit counts.

After just a few minutes' ride, they can see the restaurant's logo: a medieval juggler tossing two striped balls into the air for ambiguity's sake while the restaurant's actual namesake inspirations bulge the front of his checkered spandex tights.

"We make a reservation, from M.O.T.," Nadine informs the maîtresse d', who consults her list and nods.

"Party of ten," she affirms, then peers more closely at her screen. "I don't see a room preference noted here . . . but that's no problem. We can accommodate you in any of the three chambers this afternoon. Which one would you like?" she inquires. "The Renaissance Room? Stone Age? Or Balls and Bats?"

"First visit for everybody," she deduces, when they fail to respond. "Then let me run it by you. We have the Renaissance Room, our logo is derived from it. Medieval dress, jugglers, fire-swallowers, and of course your waitpersons, in tights." She grants them a complicitous smile, eyebrows arched meaningfully. "Or," she goes on, "you might prefer our Stone Age Room. A Neolithic

setting, caveperson paintings, and your waitpersons in loincloths."
She winks.

Eva giggles.

"Or thirdly," the maîtresse d' concludes, "perhaps you would
prefer to be seated in our popular Balls and Bats chamber. It has a
sports theme, replicating a locker room, and your waitpersons will
serve you attired in towels, jockstraps, and jerseys."

She beams at them expectantly as the group exchanges undecided glances. "I suggest the Renaissance," she advises. "Especially
on a first visit. Though you really can't go wrong. All of our boys are
out to show you a good time. And that's what it's about," she adds
primly to Nadine, whom she has easily identified as the leader, "a
good time. I'm sure I don't have to remind you ladies of our house
rules," she says. "No touching, no grabbing our young gentlemen.
We're all just here to have fun."

The Renaissance Room it is, and soon they find themselves
seated around a massive oak table, being offered a choice between
mead, nonalcoholic mead, ale, ale lite, or diet ale by their waitperson, who introduces himself as "Alaric."

Like the strolling bards who pass between the tables, tinkling
away on oddly shaped string instruments, Alaric is outfitted in a colorful vest that ends well short of his waist, and is sheathed from the
waist down in flesh-colored tights that warp out around his thigh
muscles, form the fatty tissue at his rear into perfect globes parted
by a crooked nylon seam, and prominently display a lumpy bulge of
compressed genitalia in the front. But I see that my purely factual
anatomical description is inadequate, and is not taking into account
the distinctly mood-enhancing effect of his mode of dress on the
female patrons of the establishment—if their shrill voices, loud
laughter, crass vocabulary, flirtatious glances at passing staff members, and flushed faces are any indication.

"More buns, ladies?" Alaric hovers over the neighboring table,
indicating the emptied bread basket. "Sure, bring 'em on," a tidy
brunette replies. "I'm partial to buns," she goes on. Raucous laughter greets this bit of wit; Alaric, who is hearing this joke not for the
first time, smiles patiently.

But at Lisa's table, Helen, who has been surveying the hired help, is displeased. "Some of them are wearing codpieces!" she complains.

"Maybe they have something to hide," Edith supposes.

"Or maybe they *don't* have much to hide!" Helen shrieks, hilariously.

Lisa looks to Nadine, expecting her to put the brakes on this unbefitting banter. But her boss appears amused.

"Maybe ve introduce dis style for de office," she even suggests, archly. The Germanic atmosphere seems to suit her: she is well into her second tankard of ale and in better spirits than anyone can recall. Lisa glances at Justin, to see if he is minding any of this, but he is sipping steadily at his drink with a noncommittal smile. Well, if nobody else objects, why should she?

To hell with the nonalcoholic mead. For her next round, Lisa orders up some of the real thing.

By the time the party breaks up, she's feeling the effects. That's not good; she's supposed to stay with Cleo tonight. She splashes cold water on her face in the rest room, rinses her mouth, and thinks about chewing on some mints, but mead and mints, uck, she'll get sick. She hasn't really had that much to drink; the fresh air will sober her up. At her sister's place, Lisa keys herself in and calls out to Cleo, but there is no response. She checks the time, it's seven, Cleo should be back from archery practice by now. Dropping her bag on the sofa, she hears a sound from the back of the apartment, an unhappy muffled sound. It's Cleo, facedown on her bed and sobbing.

"Cleo! Sweetie! What happened? What's wrong?" Alarmed, Lisa rushes to her niece and embraces her.

Filtered through a damp pillow, all she can make out is something about terrible day, teacher, and hate. Relieved that no physical injury or other tangible disaster is involved, she sits on the bed and gently massages the child's quaking back. Finding the relevant accupressure points on Cleo's wrist and lower calf, she pushes against them firmly, with her thumbs, to a count of seven, and makes Cleo rub her breastbone with her index finger, to center herself. Only then does she attempt to elicit her story.

There was an unannounced school inspection. By the Ministry of Education. They marched into Cleo's class and made Anne follow them out into the hallway. The children could hear them arguing. After a few minutes, everybody came back inside. Anne was smiling "but she didn't look like she meant it, it looked really fake, like she was upset and just pretending to be happy." In a fake-happy voice, she announced that, as a special treat, they would be having a guest teacher today, Ms. Evans, who would be introducing a very interesting new subject. Then this Ms. Evans walked up to the board and wrote today's date. She said it was Revolution Appreciation Day, a brand-new holiday. But it wasn't the kind of holiday where you don't go to school. It was the kind of holiday where you do special projects and think about important things. And today they were going to study life in the past.

Then she started to unpack a large box. She unloaded thick packs of folded paper, and said they were newspapers, exact replicas of newspapers, which was how people used to find out about the news before they had good compuscreen systems. Then they got put in groups of four, Cleo relates, and each group got one of those newspaper thingies. They were already marked up in bright orange, but Ms. Evans told them to browse through the entire newspaper first and then to carefully read the highlighted parts, which would tell them about the life of women and girls in the olden days. And to remember that these weren't just stories, they were the actual things that had really happened on that day, a day exactly like today, to girls and women exactly like themselves, only before the Revolution.

Although they were a little worried about Anne, who was still acting weird, the class was initially glad for the interruption, and those newspapers were interesting. You saw ads for the movies people used to watch, and pictures of the clothes you could buy, and there were cartoons. Then Ms. Evans announced that it was time now to read the articles. Cleo's face puffs up in ominous prediction of further tears.

"Honey!" Lisa exclaims. "Sweetie, don't get upset again. Just tell me what happened. Talk it out."

Okay, Cleo says. At first it wasn't that bad. But then they got to the first highlighted story, on page 5, and it was about a girl, she was eleven, and she was riding her bicycle that she just got for her birthday. But somebody went after her, a grownup, a man. And he smashed the back of her head in with a rock. Until she was practically dead. Then that person tore her clothes off. And then, well— Cleo grapples with the unfamiliar concept, for which she lacks a term—well, then he had a sort of sex with her, even though she was practically dead, and only eleven years old, and afterward— Cleo blinks through swollen eyes and gulps down a throatful of tears—afterward he suffocated her. And then she was dead and then he dumped her in a ditch.

And the other story was, there was this boy in Florida, and he killed the girl next door and hid her body in the frame of his water bed, and when they arrested him he said he did it because he wanted to be close to her, because he loved her.

And Ms. Evans said that was what they used to mean by love.

If they had lived back then, Ms. Evans said, terrible things exactly like these might have happened to any one of them. Cleo starts sobbing again, quietly. She grabs her pillow and hugs it hard, crying into its wet patch, and Lisa makes no attempt to stop her. She is nearly as upset as her niece. Her mouth still thick from the mead, she gropes for words of comfort.

"Well," she says, inadequately, "they weren't as good at finding out who the really sick people were, in those days, sweetie. And they couldn't reeducate them or relocate them the way we can today. They were much more backward. They didn't have good security. So once in a while, a crazy person could get loose. But," she concludes, "I'm sure it was rare even then. It's not like it happened every day."

Her statement, intended to calm, has the opposite effect.

"Ms. Evans said it *did* happen every day," Cleo wails. "She said we could pick any day of any year we wanted, and we would find stories like these. After she left," she adds, "we asked Anne if it was true, that men hate women and that they always will. That the

Revolution is never safe, because men will always try to go back to the way things used to be, because they hate us. We thought she would explain it and tell us that it wasn't true, but she didn't. She said she doesn't know."

But Cleo still hasn't finished.

"At lunch," she mumbles, "I asked Matthew what he thought about it. And he didn't answer, but Isaac said that Ms. Evans was just jealous because no man would ever love anybody as ugly as her. And Matthew laughed, and then they went and sat at a different table."

Lisa puts Cleo's pillow back in its place, turns it dry side up, smooths it. She knows that Matthew is, or until today was, one of Cleo's very best friends at school. She supposes that youthful bravado, and maybe embarrassment, prompted the behavior of the two boys, nothing more evil than that. More than anything else, she wants to comfort Cleo. She wants to assure her that the Ms. Evans version of things is not true, that those newspaper reports related to rare and freakish incidents, that men never hated women, and that girls are safe forever. That's what Lisa wants to say, but she finds that the words won't come.

Lisa is experiencing something that happens to many parents, and surrogate parents—the child grows up, and the pains and dangers it faces grow larger, too. With nostalgia, she remembers the days when her biggest dilemma concerned the matter of dolls.

It seemed like a big deal at the time. Cleo was part of the first postrevolutionary batch of girls to reach doll age, and they caused quite an uproar. Should dolls be banished altogether, or only the ones that sent wrong messages? The panels and commissions that were established to set new doll guidelines! No more crying, peeing baby dolls, to indoctrinate little girls into motherly self-sacrifice. No expensive breakable ones, to impede the natural boisterousness of girls. And definitely no vacuous sexy ones. Until from the fray and the assorted marketing disasters there emerged the new kid hit, Sylvana the Witch. Immediately inspiring a new wave of controversy.

Parents complained that she was suspiciously similar, indeed nearly identical, to an infamous predecessor. Some doubted whether the factory had even changed its molds. Where was the progress, they asked, if you were going to crank out the same old blank-faced, narrow-waisted, big-boobed, long-haired plastic dimwit and merely give her a new name and fake pagan bloodlines? By the time Cleo reached that point, the small consumers had spoken, the Ministry had approved, and there was no turning back. Sylvana took the Revolution's girls by storm. Every girl had to own at least a dozen, and Cleo wanted to play Witches and Spells and Coven Party until Lisa thought she would lose her mind. Then there was Sylvana's best friend, the Evil Witch Gisela, her little sister, Teen Witch Tamara, and the less popular Warlock Gregg. And of course all the accessories, the little books of incantations and tiny bottles of invisible ink and eentsy flasks of good- and bad-smelling potions, the cauldrons, the glow-in-the-dark wands, the black cats, the spiders, the toads . . . And don't forget the scads and scads of glittery sorceress clothing, the capes and veils and pointed hats and masks. All of this *stuff* has, thankfully, been relegated to the floor of the closet, Cleo now judging herself too grownup to play with dolls.

Then came 3-D mazes, and twice a week Cleo was glued to the screen for the cult serial *Adventures of Lillian, Marine Psychologist* and her assortment of depressed dolphins, heartsick whales, and jittery reef corals. It's a cute show, Lisa guesses, though its theme song could drive you crazy.

> *Everything has feelings, feelings, even the algae in the sea,*
> *our underwater friends have feelings,*
> *yes, ocean dwellers are just like you and me,*
> *protozoa, protozoa in the sea.*

Sometimes it took the rest of the evening to get that silly jingle out of her head. Not to mention—Lisa shudders to remember— the phase when Cleo and her friends insisted on communicating only through echosound, in weird, piping grunts . . .

But today Lisa finds herself wishing she could have those harmless little annoyances back. Cleo's still a child—she shouldn't be sobbing over the grim realities of the world yet, or feeling a pain that Lisa can't make better.

In the days that follow, Lisa will come to think of her stupid office party as a kind of watershed, a weird beery marker between past lightheartedness and approaching menace. It's not just Cleo, it's not just school. Things are starting to feel different altogether, more serious. Where did those Mediterranean breezes go? There's a nip in the air.

And there's definitely a chill in the office. The higher-ups stop mingling with the masses the way they used to; at lunchtime they cluster together, talking in low voices. They're in meetings all the time, and when they're not, they're downstairs in Holistic Health, swallowing vitamin megadoses and having their chakras aligned. Tech support is constantly being called in to check the diffusers, and one day Lisa hears the restrained, glacial Mazzini actually yelling in the hallway when the technician insists there is nothing wrong with the aroma-ergonomics system. Nadine, too, is acting stressed. For one thing, her accent has become erratic, taking on a heavy Prussian inflection at times, only to disappear altogether for the space of a few sentences. Preoccupied with their own thoughts, no one seems to notice.

Lisa is restless; it's claustrophobic, to sit there behind her desk in the middle of this buzz of nervous energy. Distractions are welcome. Urban Creativity, formerly City Planning, is inviting them all to a presentation? Excellent! Presentations by other offices are usually pretty boring, but everyone reacts to this one eagerly, like schoolgirls looking forward to a field trip. A chance to get out of the building—yes! Besides, after their last presentation, Lisa struck up a sort of friendship with one of the landscape experts, an herbal sculpture artist, and she looks forward to seeing her again. Maybe they can chat over lunch.

However, entering their seminar room, Lisa notes that this looks like an entirely new team; she doesn't recognize any of them. That's odd; it's unusual to have such a complete reshuffle of a staff. Also, she can't help but notice that this group seems less friendly than the last bunch; they're clustered around one corner of the table looking important, with not a smile or a nod for their arriving guests.

They've got a re-ed with them. Well, that's nice, a friend for Justin! Lisa looks around to see if he has noticed his counterpart. Yes, there's Justin, just across the table from the Urban Creativity guy, they're exchanging a curt look and now seem to be studiously ignoring each other.

Well, it's none of her business. It's not like she's Justin's mother and has to arrange play dates for him.

Suddenly, wind chimes clank over the speakers and an acrid burst of citrus and something else puffs from the vents, making everyone blink. Grapefruit and lily of the valley, Lisa decides, sniffing. Rather bitter, and an unusual, aggressive choice for a meeting. The lights dim, and a huge map of the inner districts appears on the screen; a stern young woman with a cursor wand steps up beside it, ready to highlight the individual features of her office's new plan for the city.

"We have a lot of ground to cover today," she begins briskly, "so let's dispense with the intros. I'm sure you recall the original design," she says, turning to the map. "The Elizabeth Cady Stanton Fountain was going to go here in the center, with the Lucretia Mott Rose Garden around it, Clara Barton and Margaret Sanger in front of the hospital, then the interactive Rosa Parks Bus Monument was going to go right here, in the middle of the playground, well, I won't run through the whole thing, you've all seen it, and the virtual is in the appendix of your folders. Anyway, we've scrapped that plan," she announces briskly. "The concept was unoriginal and sentimental."

A flutter of surprise goes through the meeting.

"I expect you all agree," the young speaker adds. "Nothing against these women. I'm sure they made fine contributions, though frankly, I'm also sure we're all sick of hearing about them."

This time the gasp is audible, but the young woman continues undeterred.

"The real problem with the original concept," she explains, "is that it only tells part of the story. The sugar-coated part."

Slashing her cursor wand through the air like a rapier, she clicks up the new display. She certainly has everyone's attention.

"As a working title, we're calling it Martyrs' Mall," the presenter says. "But that's not set in stone. Another idea is Museum of Misogyny; personally, I like Female Genocide Park.

"Here's the basic concept. We plan to place statues of individual heroic and martyred women in these circles here, so that, as you can see, whatever street you take will pull you into the theme and then lead you over here, to the central mall, where we will have a series of monuments dedicated to collective martyrs. Let me walk you through one example. Let's take Founding Mothers' Avenue. We have Sophonisba, here at grid 1. That, of course, is the neighborhood where most of the embassies are located, so as a martyr to diplomacy, she is a very appropriate choice. Grid 2, right in front of the Museum of Science, we've got Hypatia."

Shooting a stealthy look at the others, to see if they are smarter than she is, Lisa discreetly consults her folder. Sophonisba, she reads. Died 205 B.C. A politician's daughter, she agreed to marry the Numidian king, Masinissa, for reasons of state, to save her city. But he deceived her. After having the bad taste to actually consummate their marriage, her treacherous new husband delivered her to the camp of her Roman enemies, where she was made to drink poison. Hypatia. C. 370–415. A brilliant mathematician as well as a great beauty, she was the head of Alexandria's Neo-Platonist school and a revered teacher with a large following. Until the Christian patriarch had her kidnapped by his monks, who dragged her to a church, stripped her, tortured her, dismembered her, and finally torched what was left of her shredded body.

Gulping down a too-hot swallow of fennel tea from the thermocup before her, Lisa gulps again when she hears a familiar voice.

"Will there by any monuments to men martyrs?" an unusually assertive Justin wants to know.

"Whom did you have in mind?" the presenter asks, nicely.

Lisa cringes, but Justin takes the question at face value and reflects for a moment. They don't seem to like the obvious choices, given how they've dealt with Parks and Mott and Stanton. Of course, it can't be anyone military. And with his Biographic Enrichment segment still fresh in his memory, he recalls how most of his former idols were thoroughly debunked in that class, shown to have been cruel to their wives, indifferent to their children, promiscuous, dishonest, egotistical, and perverse. For no particular reason, he finds himself thinking of Albert Einstein, who stole several of his epoch-making ideas from his brilliant first wife before unceremoniously abandoning her, and dumped their handicapped child in a home and never visited him again, for which reasons he ended up completely estranged from his gifted second son.

"Maybe Thomas More?" he suggests. "When he stood up for religious freedom, the king had him beheaded."

"Ah yes." The woman nods. "The good Sir Thomas More. A great humanist, when it came to the rights of the Carthusian monks. Less enlightened on the subject of innocent, learned, and wise women, who could be slaughtered with impunity, as far as he was concerned. A firm supporter of the persecution of witches, your fine Sir Thomas. Not unlike that other great thinker Martin Luther, who also will not be receiving any future monuments, I don't think. 'I have no compassion for witches. I would burn them all,'" she quotes that leader, as Justin ducks down in his seat and busies himself with his folder while his fellow re-ed smirks.

"But your question brings us directly to the first circle," she transitions smoothly, "where we have our first group monument, to the martyrs of the witch-hunts in Europe, the estimated two million women who were burned at the stake. We envision a sixteen-foot hologram, showing victims being tortured on the rack"—click goes the pointer—"then bound to stakes and set on fire." Click. "The fire theme will blend into the next space, our memorial to Indian widows burnt alive on their husbands' funeral pyres, right over here, and young Indian brides who had their saris soaked with kerosene and set on fire over dowry disputes, at grid 4." Click,

click. "Victims of honor crimes, to the left. For that section we envision a dense circle of barbed wire, shaped into shrubs, representing AR, opening up onto a sunny meadow, representing the Revolution. As you can see, that brings us to the other side of the mall," she continues.

"Over here, the Sisters of Mercy Hospital Center—which needs to be renamed, so if you have any ideas for that, please take part in our competition, entry forms are in your folder, and there are some nice prizes! And over here we have begun to fix up the Botanical Gardens, as you can see."

On the screen, a choppy expanse of raw bare earth appears, remnants of flower beds and elaborate manicured hedges in the process of being plowed under by heavy machinery. "We are converting this space into a field of rock salt and thorns, dedicated to the estimated fifteen million girl babies martyred through female infanticide and selective abortion in Arabia, China, and India during the last century. Many were suffocated by having their little faces pressed into loose salt," she adds, helpfully. "That's what inspired the idea for a field of rock salt."

She pauses, ready for questions.

"So the playground idea has basically been scrapped?" Eva asks, in a squeaky falsetto.

"If you feel this material lends itself to a playground, we certainly invite you to submit your designs," the presenter replies coldly. Eva falls silent. There are no further comments, just an extended, awkward period while everyone's head bends over a folder and people appear to be intently studying the sketches.

Nadine breaks the silence. "But you are moving me," she says. "Ze emotion in ze work, ze honesty of ze message—you give an example to all of us. Excellent. Excellent." She clutches her hands to her heart and sits nodding for several moments in quiet introspection before she finally rises, and everyone can consider themselves dismissed.

As the participants file out, Lisa finds herself walking out the door next to Rebecca. "Well, well," her colleague mutters, "interesting, don't you think? Hold on to your hats, girls—the times they are a-changin'!"

As for Justin, he has barely recovered from his public rebuke when he again finds himself singled out for attention.

"Jostin, please," Nadine calls out, at the conclusion of the morning meeting. "I get a memo to remind you, you alvays must vear de HUE band. If you don't vear de HUE band, you lose three monts' reedukayshin credits."

Everyone stares at his wrist. It's there, it's always there, everybody's HUE band is always there. Why is Nadine picking on Justin?

"He's wearing it," Rebecca points out.

"I tell you I get a memo," Nadine says, holding up her compupad to justify herself. "Please inform male co-vorkers of new safety regulayshun. I know Jostin wear it, Jostin is a smart boy."

Justin's band, a nearly weightless semitransparent tan-colored strap tastefully embossed in a Navajo pattern, has never bothered him before. It is carefully designed for ultimate comfort and non-obtrusiveness; you are supposed to forget you have it on, and most people do. Hypoallergenic, rubbery, and flexible, it adjusts to your body temperature and molds itself to the contours of your wrist, never too tight, never too loose. You can wear it in the water, the sun, the sauna, it isn't bothered by soap, lotions, heat, or cold. A great deal of care has gone into making sure there is nothing uncomfortable about it.

But after that morning meeting, Justin's band unaccountably starts to turn into a major encumbrance. It feels much heavier. It gets in his way. It itches.

"This thing is a real pain," he mutters. Lisa looks at him oddly.

"And anyway, what happens to you if you don't wear yours? What's the penalty for that?" he asks.

Lisa doesn't know. She's worn hers since they were first devised and distributed, when she was fourteen or fifteen, twice upgrading it for a new model. It would never occur to her not to wear it.

"And how come the men's bands look different from the women's?" Justin demands.

"Well, that's obvious," Lisa says. "Because women and men prefer different colors and patterns. So ours are neutral, to match any style of outfit, and yours are also very neutral, but with a small masculine sort of ornamentation."

"Oh? And since when does the Revolution encourage that kind of thinking?"

Lisa looks down at her own band, a thin, almost transparent strip of soft iridescent plastic with a discreet, only slightly elevated, lozenge-shaped lid protecting the buttons you can push in the event of an emergency and a barely detectable seam forming the clasp where, should you need to, you can unfasten it. No, they don't usually care much for stereotypes like that. Justin has a point.

Nor are his HUE aggravations over. Indeed, they have just begun.

"Jostin," Nadine booms, at a meeting some days later, singling him out once more for her unwelcome attention. "Venever you can, you go downstairs. The Human Resources Office likes to see you betveen eleven and three today."

Justin thinks nothing of it, it will be just one more of their innumerable forms and applications and feedback questionnaires. He allows himself to be ushered into an antechamber where a good dozen other male employees are already waiting. One by one they are summoned into an inner office, which apparently exits into the hallway, because they don't return. Whatever is being done to them, at least it's quick, and Justin is kept waiting for no more than half an hour until his turn comes.

"We're issuing improved HUE bands today," a middle-aged woman announces in a bored Southern drawl, probably for the nth time that day, as he enters. "So if you'll just remove your old band for me, honey, I'll give you your very beautiful, highly fashionable brand-spankin'-new one."

Justin takes his band off and drops it into a large box with the other discards. He expects to be handed a new one, but instead the woman gestures impatiently for him to extend his arm. She loops the new band around his wrist. Then she threads the ends into some sort of a clamping device and pushes a button. With a soft hiss and a puff of heatless smoke, the ends of the band meld together, forming a bracelet around Justin's wrist.

It's different from his old one, narrower but slightly heavier. Even the material is different, opaque rather than transparent, a metal rather than a plastic compound. Sliding the lid aside, he sees the two familiar oval buttons, but he can't find anything resembling a clasp.

"How do I take this off?" Justin asks.

"Oh, you don't want to take this one off, honey," the woman says. "It's meant to stay on. It'll short-circuit if you try to force it, and give you a nasty shock. Plus you'll have a rescue team on top of you in nothing flat, and if there's no emergency, you'll have a lot of explaining to do."

Justin nods. He is halfway out the door when a rising wave of anger, like a sudden unexpected attack of nausea, overwhelms him and stops him in his tracks.

"Why are we getting bands that can't be taken off?" he asks.

"Well now, honey," the woman replies, conspiratorially, "I can tell you the reason for that. It's that macho thing. We found out that a lot of you fellas are just not wearing your HUE bands. That's not safe—what if something happens to you? How are you going to get help? So we looked into it, and it turns out that there's been a lot of pressure on guys, from other guys, not to wear them. Apparently, it's not macho. Because if you wear it, you're implying that you might need help? That you're scared? That you can't handle every possible thing that might come at you all by your big strong clever self? So we thought, this way, if you can't take them off, then not only is your safety enhanced, but you can't give each other any flak about it either, right?"

She gives him a friendly, maternal smile.

Justin thinks about it. Maybe he's overreacting. It's true that Will, for one, never wears his band and has expressed the opinion that it's for sissies. He won't be able to do that with the new one, it'll be soldered on. He won't like that much.

"Are the women getting new bands, too?" Justin asks. "Are they getting this same kind that you can't take off?"

"In all honesty, honey," the woman says, impatience tingeing her voice as her finger moves to the buzzer that will summon the next man, "I can't answer that. I work with the Men's Program, I wouldn't be able to tell you about the women. They have periodic upgrades, I do know that. Maybe they'll get the same thing as you, and maybe they won't. However, I don't think a lot of women refuse to wear their bands just to show everybody how tough they are. It's for your own good, honey," she reiterates, in dismissal. "We don't want y'all to get yourself hurt, just because you're trying to act macho."

Justin slouches on up to his office, still not happy. He wishes he had worn a shirt with long sleeves so he could hide the new band under the cuff. Immediately, he runs into Helen, who would certainly not look at his wrist and not notice his armband if he were not so clumsily seeking to conceal it.

"Hi, Justin," she says. "Whatcha got there? Oh, you have a new HUE band. It looks different. Skinnier."

Justin murmurs something noncommittal as she peers at it.

"How do you open it?" she asks.

"It doesn't open," he mumbles.

"Oh," she says. "I didn't know they made that kind. Were you worried about losing it?"

And Justin, who has never thought of himself as macho, finds himself on the horns of a dilemma. He can go along with her assumption that he had a choice, and freely chose to be permanently shackled—because he is such a chicken that, in perpetual terror for his personal safety, he feared losing the normal removable band.

Or he can admit that he meekly held his arm out to Miss Louisiana and allowed her to handcuff him.

"Well, I'm sure it's practical," Helen says, seeing as she isn't getting an answer, and not really caring much either way.

Lisa makes no comment at all, but later that day, she spends about three seconds pondering Justin's situation. Why *are* the men's bands visibly different from the women's? Why are they being issued a new style that can't be removed? It's odd, yes, but Lisa is not a conspiracy theorist, so she soon forgets all about this minor mystery.

The young officer dashes into her superior's office in great haste, nearly knocking down a departing visitor and a rubber plant. "There's been a breach of Zone Six security," she reports, breathlessly. "We feel just terrible that this happened, but we're fixing it. We've set it as our goal to have the system up again within seventy-two hours, at most. In the interim, as a backup, we plan to—"

"No," her boss interrupts. "Don't fix it."

The young woman swallows hard. Excuse me? Don't fix a breach in Zone Six security? She has been expecting a sharp rebuke, maybe some panic, anything but this.

"We know all about it, dear," her commander says. "It's part of a plan, a plan I can't share with you. National security, gamma clearance only," she adds kindly. "Don't worry about it, it's under control."

"But almost one third of the perimeter of Zone Six—" is unsecured, she wants to say, but is interrupted.

"We know," her superior snaps. "Leave it alone. That's an executive order," she adds, sternly.

The young officer flinches as though she had been slapped, then puts her palms together in salute, and leaves.

Aₙd the temperature keeps dropping.

Ms. Evans is back. This time, she arrives during EASY class, the weekly Early Adolescence Sex and Youth class. Girls and boys are separated for this hour, and Ms. Evans is there to speak to the girls. For most of them, it's one of their favorite classes. It meets in a special room, not a regular classroom. There are no desks, no swivel chairs, no compuscreens; instead, the room is divided into several intimate, inviting nooks supplied with futons, sofas, and mats. The three mottoes of EASY, which are recited in unison at the beginning of each hour, are also proclaimed on large posters on the walls: "My Body Is Beautiful," they announce in bold fuchsia letters. "Sex Is Fun." And "Growing Up Is E-A-S-Y."

Today's topic, had there not been this unscheduled visitor, was to have been "Our Sensational Sensations"—though if you are a reader from an earlier century, you may need to translate "sensations" back into the arcane term "cramps." An array of warming capsicum-and-mint lotions, tranquilizing herbs, and other sources of luxury and succor to the female body in some of its less comfortable hours waits in readiness on the teacher's table in a corner.

The girls are ready, too, sprawled comfortably into beanbags and cushions, with trays of cookies and stylish teacups on low tables before them, prepared to unwind, bond, and learn how to deal with any little tweaks or twinges anatomy might have in store for them, when Ms. Evans walks in.

Score a home run for Pavlovian responses. The girls go rigid, instantly associating her face with bad news, terror, and shock. But she smiles, seemingly oblivious to their reaction.

"Hello, girls!" she says cheerily. "What a lovely room! Oatmeal cookies—my favorites! May I try one?" She has no newspapers with her, either. Tentatively, the girls start to relax.

"I won't keep you long," she says. "Just have a quick little question for you. But first"—and her face goes serious again—"first I'd like you to tell me: how many of you want to help the Revolution?"

Help the Revolution! Everyone sits up straighter at the importance of that thought, and every hand goes up.

"That's wonderful," Ms. Evans says. "Now: how many of you want to have a happy and a peaceful classroom?"

All hands go up.

"You know, girls, I felt so good about your group when I visited you last time," Ms. Evans says, clasping her hands tightly with the intensity of pleasure and warmth they make her feel. "I could tell that you care about each other, that you care about every member of your classroom community and want the best for them. For the boys as well as for the girls," she adds.

She pauses for a moment to let this thought sink in.

"And because I know that you care about the boys in your classroom, I am going to ask you to help them with something. Our newspaper exercise the other day was hurtful to you, I know. It hurt me! I hate to tell you these sad and frightening things, to put you on your guard. I wish you could grow up careless and free, taking your safety for granted, but—"

She stops herself. She is not here to deliver another lecture. "It has come to our attention," she says instead, and her voice goes all soft and sweet, "that as hard as our lesson was for you girls, it was equally as painful for the boys, and some of them are still really . . . struggling . . . with it. And because we care about them, and want them to grow into wonderful young men, we have to help them, isn't that right? Some boys were so upset by what we studied that they reacted by laughing about it, by teasing the girls, or even by denying that any of it was true. This may seem like an odd way to act, but as a scientist I know that boys can be a little different from us sometimes in the way they show their feelings, and that this behavior was just a way of letting us know that they are upset and need our help. Now, I have some slips of paper here, which I am going to hand out, and I want each of you to write down the names of the boys in your class that are having this problem. So we can get them a little extra help and make everybody feel happy again."

Cleo takes the paper and thinks immediately of Matthew and Isaac. "Odd way to act" is right! Ever since that stupid ridiculous tantrum at lunchtime, Matthew has ignored her. Didn't show up, just left her partnerless, at the Jump-Rope Jump-off, at which they were practically guaranteed to win first place. Got himself assigned to a different team in spinball, moved to a different table in art class, and has been demonstratively sitting with Isaac, Cardiff, and Jakey at lunch and snack. The hurt around her heart from all these rejections eases somewhat at the thought that he just needs help.

She starts to write his name down, and to put down Isaac and Cardiff and Jakey, too, when something stops her. A bad feeling. The kind of feeling that their teacher, Anne, has told them they should always, always listen to.

With a frown, she tries to explore that feeling, to trace it back to its wispy origins. Is it coming from Ms. Evans? She studies the woman, summoning up everything she has learned about auras and subconscious messages, but her readout detects no malignant emanations, just sincere resolve.

She puts her pencil to the paper once again, but another wave of ill feeling washes over her. Clenching the pencil hard in her fist, she looks around angrily for its source, but it seems to be coming from inside herself. It has to do with Matthew. She's angry with him, very angry. She wants things to be okay between them again, and it's his fault that they're not. She wants to help him, and Ms. Evans says that reporting him will do that, but she wants to hurt him, too. And somehow, every time her pencil gets close to the paper, the hurting-him part feels a lot stronger than the helping-him part. And Anne has told them that it's bad, oh, very bad karma to act with malice. "Don't incur karmic debt," she often pleads. "Children, be strong and resist acting on bad intentions, because it will poison your lives and injure your souls." Cleo drops the pencil and hands the slip of paper in, still blank.

On Monday, two boys from Cleo's class, and forty-nine from the school as a whole, are gone. Their applications to attend a school with a wonderful specialized arts program have been accepted, which is why, although they will be missed, each and every member of the school community should feel very happy for them. If it occurs to anyone to wonder why only boys, and such a large number of them, most without any prior discernible artistic gift, applied for a special program, in midyear, without mentioning it to any of their friends, the cheerfully blank expression on the face of assembly leader Ms. Gant deters any questions.

On Wednesday, in her lunch box, Cleo finds a pack of yogurt-covered raisins that she did not put there that morning. As her friends know, yogurt-covered raisins are her absolute favorite thing. Looking up, she finds Matthew watching her, but when she sees him, he turns and runs after Isaac.

Ms. Evans has joined the permanent roster of teachers now and is scheduled to conduct class, so Lisa decides to pick Cleo up from school. She wants to be there for her niece. And she'd like to figure out what's behind the universal chill.

It's strange to be in a school building again. Lisa arrives a few minutes early and wanders down the hallway. She passes an empty classroom and peeks in. The chairs look a lot more comfortable than she remembers, fancy ergonomic numbers that swivel and adjust in height and let you lean back or kneel forward, as you choose. Other than that, it resembles the classrooms of her own schooldays. The back wall is decorated by a gigantic and apparently ongoing collage showing the major food groups. A row of lockers lines the inside wall, each one bearing the name of a pupil; some compartments are open, revealing the owners' sneakers and towels and art supplies. There is a wide bank of windows on the left wall, with neatly framed samples of quilting between them. And the front wall is of course dominated by a large portrait of the Founding Mothers; Lavinia Tree and her predecessors Gisele Delacroix and Inge Fried smile down benignly at the empty room. Then the bell rings, and Lisa hurries outside to find her niece.

Cleo looks okay today, not upset. They stop for a muffin and some verbena tea, and Lisa makes sure to keep the conversation light, and not mention Cleo's school day until they are at home.

Yes, they had Ms. Evans again. They're going to have her every week now. For a new class called RAH. Revolution Appreciation Hour.

Cleo seems composed, no tears, but Lisa doesn't like the expression on her niece's face. There's a pinched look about the eyes, and a defiant tilt to the chin.

"Are you okay with that?" Lisa asks. "I know that she made you feel really upset last time."

In a throwaway tone of voice, Cleo informs Lisa that this had been an immature reaction, which she is now well over. Only a baby would get upset over realities. Facts are facts, you have to face up to them like a woman! Together with Ms. Evans, they are going to work with newspapers and other authentic documents, because they need to be exposed to reality. Her tone is dismissive as she turns back to her screen game, Fly the Bird.

As a responsible mentor, Lisa feels she must persist. Soooo, she asks brightly, that's nice, and what did Ms. Evans teach them about today?

"We just read stuff about Africa," Cleo mumbles, eyes firmly fixed on the fluttering parrots of her game.

About how in a bunch of countries in Africa and North Africa, if you were a girl, they would saw off most of your genital region with a broken piece of glass, and then they would kind of staple you shut with thorns. And it hurt like crazy, or you could get an infection and die. And when you got married, they had to cut you open down there with a knife, so you could have sex. Which would always hurt you, and you would always hate it. As Cleo speaks, she is very busy with a fast-moving mynah bird. And they called it klitter-something, she mumbles into the screen.

Lisa doesn't know what to do. It was wrenching the last time, when Cleo was so upset and cried so much, but her sullen composure now is almost worse. She hates the controlled look on her niece's face. There is a hardness that wasn't there before.

She hates Ms. Evans for putting it there.

Absorbed in this resentful thought, she doesn't immediately realize that Cleo has shoved the game control away, releasing the buttons and allowing all her birds to flutter away into the ecological disaster zones she had so studiously been guarding them against, and is looking at Lisa.

"Some of us were talking after class," she confides, in a lowered voice. "That can't really be true. People wouldn't do something that neuro! It was probably, like, just a rumor or something. That ended up in the newspaper. I mean, that's like totally sick! Don't you think? I'm not saying Ms. Evans is purposely lying to us or anything, she probably believes it, but it must be just a whatdoyoucallit? A legend. Like . . ." She searches for an analogy. "Like vampires! Something a lot of people believe was true, but it wasn't. It *isn't* really true, right?"

Cleo's face is like before again, open and trusting, the kind of face you have when you believe that no, of course not, hundreds of thousands of little girls certainly did not have the softest parts of their bodies crudely sawed off and sewn shut like an old gym bag. In confident expectation of a denial, Cleo looks at her aunt.

Lisa feels sick to her stomach. She wishes she hadn't eaten the muffin, which is now lodged in her stomach like a lump of cement.

"It's true," she says.

Lisa is on the fourth floor, Office of Growth and Development, taking a test. Sometimes Lisa thinks of the Revolution as a kind of giant Red Cross truck, incessantly demanding a donation, not of your blood, but of your thoughts and feelings. Sucking them out of you, leaving you limp and debilitated, then reviving you with a mug of hot chocolate and sending you home.

Lisa sits before her umpteenth test battery, listlessly twirling a strand of her hair with the pencil and studying her effort thus far. It's the kind of test Lisa hates the most, the kind that calls on you to be creative. Good thing it's anonymous, Lisa thinks. Asked to do a symbolic representation of her feelings about work, she has drawn herself as a flattened figure crushed under a mountain of books, but somehow they have come out looking more like a malformed stack of pancakes. What will the psychologists make of that? In hopeful revision, she adds feet and hair to the bottom pancake, takes a look at the result, and shudders. Now it looks like the Breakfast of Cannibals.

Well, never mind. Making sense of these questionnaires is somebody else's job. Finish the statistical section, and she'll be done. Age Group: 18–25. Personal Lifestyle Preference: Single. Spiritual Affiliation: None.

There. Lisa lays aside her pencil, hands her form in to Astrid from Human Resources, and has already taken three brisk steps toward the door when Astrid calls her back. "Wait up," she warbles. "There's a randomized follow-up session, and we need you for it! Room 307, please."

Lisa is annoyed. No more drawings, please! Besides, she had plans for the afternoon; hopefully, this won't take too long.

Her interlocutor is a slim woman in a loose beige cashmere sweater and tan leggings. A thin strand of coral decorates her neck. Her hair is chopped into sleek black layers. She has a discreet black geometric tattoo on the back of her left hand. A small lacquered name plaque cuddled into the luxurious fur of her sweater announces that she is Riva, and that she is a belief counselor for the Office of Growth and Development.

"We're conducting a segment on holistic balance," she announces. Her tone is indifferent, but Lisa feels uncomfortably transfixed by her oblique gaze. "You are . . ." She looks down to consult a list, but Lisa has the strange feeling that this woman knows exactly who she is. "Lisa!" she announces. "Random samplee 14069! And thank you *so* much for your time." She smiles a thin aggressive little smile and waves Lisa into a stuffed chair. She herself is sitting on something imposing and artistic made out of wood and Lucite that is definitely not standard issue from Ergonomics, but must be something experimental that OGD has dreamed up.

"Well," she drones impersonally, and again Lisa feels that the bored monotone is in conflict with the intense, stealthy look she is receiving from the other woman, "as I mentioned, we're working on a research segment concerning holistic balance. We are interested in emerging patterns of symmetry between the objective and the subjective, the interior and the exterior, the Kopf and the Bauch. Why don't we start with, ummmm"—she appears to be consulting a printout sheet and then to be selecting a topic quite coincidentally— "yes, why don't we chat a bit about spiritual affiliation. Now, how would you best describe your personal spiritual affiliation, Lisa?"

"I don't have one, and I don't want one," Lisa says firmly. Belief counselor indeed. When she wants help with her belief system, she'll ask for it, thank you very much.

"Mhhmmmm," Riva responds, checking something off on her paper. "I see. And which of these statements would you say best reflects your motivation for this—I'll give you four choices: (a) religion has been a patriarchal tool and I consider it irredeemably contaminated; (b) as an activist I have neglected my spiritual dimension in order to focus on the here and now; (c) I feel a deep spiritual need and am hoping that a religion compatible with our Revolution will soon emerge; or (d) I am still considering my options and expect to select my affiliation in the near future."

Riva looks up, pencil hovering impatiently over the answer sheet.

Lisa is stumped. "None of these really—" she starts to explain, but her interviewer is not amenable to prevarication.

"Not sure? Then let's come back to that one a little later," the woman suggests briskly. "Now, for our next question, I'll need you to summarize for me your definition of a meaningful life."

While Riva's pencil taps rhythmically against the Lucite armrest of her fabulous chair like some sort of horrible metronome, Lisa hears herself stammering out a collection of trite sentences about being a useful member of her community, enjoying her friends and family, and setting goals for herself, before petering out into a humiliated silence.

Riva makes an extensive notation on her sheet, scratch scratch scratch, while Lisa still cringes under the weight of her banal utterances. A lengthy silence falls.

Finally, her tormentor addresses her in a calm, kind voice.

"Our project is called Reclaiming Religion, and we designed it because we discovered that many intelligent women are in a bind," she says. "To be effective and lead fulfilled lives, we all need to link ourselves to a higher plane. We need to find the meaning, the divinity within ourselves. However, women have been burned by religion. Literally!" Riva says, with emphasis. "Witch-hunts. Sanctimonious male priests, condemning women to lives of cowlike fecundity, no matter what the cost to their health and their spirit! Declaring them not in the image of God! Not worthy of the priesthood. Second-rate for all eternity——" Riva pulls herself short with an effort and nods to Lisa.

"It's totally understandable that smart, committed women like you are leery of religion. But don't throw out the goddess with the bathwater! You need a spiritual hold to claim your full power and balance. Given your profile," she says, scooping a file from her desk, and abandoning any pretense that Lisa is really just a random pick, "I would say, let's rule out the Cult of Mary. Weeping statues, bleeding hearts, fingers rheumatic from embroidering altar cloths, knees scabby from sliding around on wooden benches sobbing at the feet of impaled male deities?" She looks inquiringly at Lisa; the younger woman shudders, and Riva nods. "My sentiments exactly. Not that I agree with those who think the Mary Cult should be outlawed; that would only feed their masochistic martyr complex, and demographic projections clearly show that it will fade away within an estimated twelve years."

Despite herself, Lisa is beginning to take an interest in this strange conversation.

"So let's look at our next possibility." Riva says. "The Cult of Astarte. I don't know . . ." she muses, studying Lisa as though fitting her for new eyeglass frames. "I don't really see you as the licentious sort. Bacchanals, lunar eclipses, getting drunk and writhing about on freshly harvested wheat fields with men in ivy circlets?"

Riva regards her client doubtfully as Lisa faces the grim fact that, once again, a perfect stranger has spotted her for a prude. Scratching herself involuntarily against the image of itchy wheat stubble, she resentfully shrugs her agreement that yeah, okay, she's probably not the orgiastic kind.

"I'm not sure I see you as a witch, either . . ." Riva muses. "They're a good group, I often place clients there. But for you . . . you really need to have some occult, fringe qualities for that, which I don't see in your charts . . ."

She studies Lisa for a further moment and then leans forward. "Maybe I shouldn't get so personal, but for me, the only true choice is Pele," she confides in a harshly intense whisper. She fingers the coral beads around her throat significantly, and Lisa realizes that they have some kind of religious meaning.

"Let's face it," Riva says. "What is Mary? A whimpering, tragic puffball of hand-wringing and tears. Dolorosa, dolorosa! Astarte has a kind of cachet, but basically she's just a slut."

Riva turns pensive. "I think divinity presupposes an element of fear, don't you?" she asks. "You can't be scared of Mary. Astarte, okay, she has to be reckoned with. If she gets carried away, that can be bad news for her little boy toys, who can find themselves suddenly missing a few essential parts, but that's just craziness and alcohol. If you want a powerful goddess, somebody who always got respect, even in patriarchy's darkest days, someone with clout and fire, it really comes down to Pele."

For an instant, she stares at Lisa so intensely that the flames of that ancient goddess seem to spark from her eyes. But quickly she leans back again, assuming her former aura of professional reserve. She ruffles her papers studiously, hands Lisa a pamphlet and a calling card, thanks her for her cooperation in a cool voice, and dismisses her without another glance.

"Human Resources sent a missionary after me today," Lisa reports wryly to her sister, later that day. "They want me to join the Cult of Pele."

But she gets little sympathy.

"Maybe it's something you should think about," her sister reflects. "Because really, where *is* your spiritual dimension? Desk jobs like ours are too cerebral."

"I wish!" Lisa retorts. "Lately, mine has been positively abdominal. Gonadal!"

"Well," her sister replies, "I'm sure HR has nothing but your welfare in mind."

Loyally, Lisa agrees.

Fortunately, she is not inclined to conspiracy theories. Fortunately, she believes that her government is good, and benign, and would never overstep its democratic boundaries. Because if she were less trusting, she might start asking uncomfortable questions. How does she feel about Big Sister watching—even with the best of intentions? Watching *her*? How come Human Resources knows so much about her? How does she feel about having Riva assigned to worry about her soul?

By odd coincidence, our maverick intel group is discussing just this very matter.

"Civil rights have to remain our preeminent focus," Person Two says. But her voice sounds more timid than insistent.

"Well, of course civil rights are important," the much more forceful voice of Person One asserts impatiently. By now we have all guessed who this Person is, so we might as well call her by her name. "But our *preeminent focus,*" Nadine says, emphasizing the phrase with nasty mimicry, "is to make sure we continue to even *have* a society, the civil rights of which we can then proceed to worry about. Need I remind you, we are dealing with opponents who have none of our scruples." Person Three nods.

Nothing new here. It's the age-old dilemma of the Righteous who, having come to power, find themselves obliged to start slicing away little bits of their righteousness in order to stay there. You need information, because bad people are trying to do bad things to you. You need to watch some of the people, some of the time. From there, it's really just a small step to watching all of the people, all of the time.

Given the strain Cleo is under, Lisa is very glad that she has a pet, something to love and fuss over. Well, it's Justin's pet, theoretically, if you want to use the word "pet" for something as uncuddly as Mac, if you think you can apply the concept of ownership to the imperiousness with which Mac gives his particular brand of affection to members of a larger species who have unaccountably taken it into their heads to feed and stroke and keep him.

Theoretically, yes, he belongs to Justin, but de facto he spends most of his crabby little life with Cleo these days, and Lisa is glad of it.

Cleo loves Mac. "Oooooooooh," she says to him, in gurgly bubbly baby talk, "ooooooh, Mackiepoozie, you are soooooooo ugly! You are the ugliest mugliest most horrible thing I've ever seen, come here and give Mama a kissy kisskiss!" And her feelings, apparently, are returned. Mac, turned into a mushy mass of loving delirium by these words, wiggles his hideous self over to Cleo and digs his wet nose ecstatically into her ankle, and licks her toes and signals with every verb and adjective of body language available to him that he is ready to obliterate and pulverize and atomize himself, if that will please her.

"I think Pele's dog looks like Mac," Cleo muses, in an aside to her aunt. "Her dog is little and white, too, just like my sweet little Mackiewackie."

"Who?" Lisa asks, abstractedly.

"Pele. The goddess. We're learning about her in EASY. Don't you remember? *You* set Riva up as guest speaker for us."

"Oh, that's right, yes. So that worked out okay?" Lisa asks.

"In red!" Cleo enthuses. "Riva is great. And she's really important! Well, she doesn't brag about it or anything, but she knows everybody in the government, and her best friend is, like, the personal bodyguard of Lavinia Tree! And she lives in this beautiful place! We all went over to her house to see her meditation altar. And she gave each of us a real lava bead necklace," Cleo relates happily, pulling hers out from under her shirt to show to Lisa.

"Pele's sister is the spirit of dance," Cleo continues, jiggling her head playfully and doing a few hula movements. Lisa has to smile; even when she is trying to be funny, Cleo's slender limbs are full of grace.

"When she appears in human form, her little white dog is always with her. But she herself might decide to look like an old woman, or a young girl. She pretends to need help, to test people. If you help her, she will rescue you someday when you are in trouble. After she tests you, she disappears into thin air," Cleo narrates excitedly.

With a gleeful expression, she remembers more. "Pele has lots of lovers. But she always makes them live on the other half of the island so they won't get in her space. She has terrible tantrums with fire and lightning, and when she gets mad the whole earth shakes. I feel that way, too," Cleo confides, darkly. "When I'm upset, really upset, I feel like the sky should go all black and everything should just explode and get smashed into a million bits! I get so angry! So I don't think Pele's that scary at all. Not scarier than me."

And on that theological note, Cleo grabs Mac and dashes out with him for a run along the lake.

Yes, as far as the guidance counselors are concerned, Mac is still Justin's nurturing object, and he still has a doggie bed and a bag of dog food in Justin's apartment, but to all intents and purposes, he's switched allegiances.

The Revolution has worked its magic on one male, anyway. Mac is a whole new dog. "Dog" may not even be the right term to use, anymore; he has metamorphosed into something closer to an accessory. Or, if you prefer, a witches' familiar, a soul mate. Cleo and her friends go nowhere without him. If he never wanted to walk again, he wouldn't have to. A host of preteen girls is prepared to carry him everywhere, like some Oriental despot borne on a litter by slaves. Mac is transported tucked under their arms, bulging out of their backpacks, comfortably ensconced in their picnic baskets. He is splendidly groomed, brushed within an inch of his life, and decorated with collars that are lovingly crafted just for him in art class. He is the mascot of the jumpball team, overseeing all games from a special stool placed courtside, rewarded by strips of Tofupet ("the healthy snack for your dog") when the game goes well, consoled with the same treat when they play badly.

Sometimes his new friends overshoot the mark. They tried to clip something onto his ear once, and on one incredible occasion sought to paint his nails in the team colors, but such presumptions are easily thwarted by a growl and a judicious nip at their girly little fingers. Then they shriek, "Oh, Mackiewackie, *I'm* sorry. Did you not like that, you little Mackiewackie, you?"

At first he thought their voices were too high, but he's gotten used to it. Asked for an endorsement of female government, Mac would have this to say: It's like you died and went to heaven.

Well, good. At least somebody's happy.

Not Lisa, though. Okay, so the books she's reading now are not too terribly offensive, and people are having actual sex instead of just handcuffing and flogging and doing medieval things to each other. But the story lines remain quite weird, and Lisa is almost as confused as ever.

She needs to approach this in a more scientific way. She tries to think of the most scientific person she knows. Well, that would be Theresa. Not that her sister has much respect for the project Lisa is working on. As far as Theresa is concerned, there is nothing about love or sex that requires further exploration, nothing that a good hard look at Melvin the Dung Fly will not explain.

But okay, she is willing to consider her younger sister's problem from a purely methodological standpoint. Let's transpose it to her own area of expertise. If an animal proves elusive, if you have trouble with its categorization, one useful thing to look at is its ecosystem. This may work for archetypes, too, Theresa suggests offhandedly.

"Look at the ecosystem," she repeats. "What environment is your subject operating within?"

Lisa stares at her, hope warring with incomprehension.

"Just choose a unique, an apparently paradoxical feature," Theresa adds, impatiently.

Lisa remains completely at a loss. Theresa sighs.

"The setting, Lisa," she explains. "Find some element, some *place,* where those lovelorn characters of yours like to hang out. I don't know. Where do you typically find them? Don't say 'bedroom,' that's too general, and you need specificity. Find a locale that you think is unique to your species, I mean, to your characters. Then see what correlations you come up with. Try that, and if you're *still* having trouble, give me a call."

Lisa returns home on Eco-Trans, jotting down as many words from this conversation as she can remember. "Specificity. Species. Unique ecosystem features. Correlations." Yeah, that's good, that's very good. These will sound great in her final report.

The next day, Lisa embarks on this new approach. Squeezing her eyes shut, she tries to remember the prime locales of her heroes and heroines. Let's see. They are often in ballrooms. On ranches. In elegant salons. On horseback. No, that's no good, those locations are too commonplace. She needs something less ordinary, something unique. Slave markets show up with some frequency, Lisa recalls, she could try that. She'd prefer something a little more contemporary, though. Some place a little less socially appalling. "Quarries," Justin suggests.

Lisa shrugs and cues in this romantic locale: quarry.

The screen fills.

Bingo.

Just to make sure it's not a fluke, she types in "cave," "ditch," and "salt mine." No dice on those; romance writers have shunned them. Lips pursed, Lisa stares at her screen. What could possibly be erotic about a quarry but not about a cave, a ditch, and a salt mine? She orders printouts.

By midmorning, Lisa is slaving away in the quarries. So to speak. She has a whole pile of them, of scenes set in quarries, printed out before her, highlighted and underlined. In these quarries, the male heroes toil. An evil spell has placed them here. They are noble convicts, wrongly accused by an evil enemy, innocently imprisoned. Though superior in every way to their vile owners, they are slaves.

Lisa is bent over the printouts, her grimace implying that the dust of shattered granite fills her nostrils, that the staccato sound of powerful tools is pounding in her ears. Quarries. Think about quarries. Why why why is a quarry romantic?

Okay. So a quarry is a very physical sort of place. The workers are young, brawny, and covered with sweat. They grunt under the burden of heavy weights, grimace at the relentless sun, and flinch under the overseer's whip.

And don't forget the power thing, Lisa instructs herself, gnawing on her cuticles. All these guys are slaves or something very like slaves. They are on a chain gang, or they are intergalactic war prisoners, or captives of an Oriental despot. Wearing little or no clothing, they are conveniently exposed to the heroine's gaze while engaged in muscle-flexing activities.

One of her printouts, she notes from the addendum, identifies its text as not just any old book but a famed classic of AR literature.

A weighty work, not some piece of romantic fluff. A book that spawned a whole school of philosophy, acquired a cult following, was the topic of university seminars, sabbaticals, thesis papers. By a female author. Impressed, Lisa plucks *The Fountainhead* from the stack.

Meet Dominique, a neurotic but beautiful rich girl/design journalist/ice maiden, who is killing time at one of her father's estates, which happens to border on a quarry also owned by Dad. One boring day, she strolls on over for a look.

> . . . She felt as if she were thrust into an execution chamber filled with scalding steam . . . The air shimmered below, sparks of fire shot through the granite; she thought the stone was stirring, melting, running in white trickles of lava. Drills and hammers cracked the still weight of the air. It was obscene to see men on the shelves of the furnace. They did not look like workers, they looked like a chain gang serving an unspeakable penance for some unspeakable crime . . .
>
> She looked down. Her eyes stopped on the orange hair of a man who raised his head and looked at her.
>
> She stood very still, because her first perception was not of sight, but of touch: the consciousness, not of a visual presence, but of a slap in the face. She held one hand awkwardly away from her body, the fingers spread wide on the air, as against a wall. She knew that she could not move until he permitted her to.

"Heroine immobilized by spell," Lisa writes in the margin. She gets up, stretches, walks to the window, back to the desk, then suddenly freezes. Frozen like a mannequin, she stares at her desk lamp, imagining it to be a person with orange hair.

> She saw his mouth and the silent contempt in the shape of his mouth; the planes of his gaunt, hollow cheeks; the cold,

pure brilliance of the eyes that had no trace of pity . . . She felt a convulsion of anger, of protest, of resistance—and of pleasure. He stood looking up at her; it was not a glance, but an act of ownership. She thought she must let her face give him the answer he deserved. But she was looking, instead, at the stone dust on his burned arms, the wet shirt clinging to his ribs, the lines of his long legs . . . she was wondering what he would look like naked . . .

She thought suddenly that the man below was only a common worker, owned by the owner of this place, and she was almost the owner of this place . . . She hoped he had a jail record. She wondered whether they whipped convicts nowadays. She hoped they did. At the thought of it, she felt a sinking gasp such as she had felt in childhood, in dreams of falling down a long stairway; but she felt the sinking in her stomach.

O-kay! Lisa thinks. Whatever! She turns the book over; Ayn Rand regards her sternly, pointed features in a frame of dark hair so choppy that she must have cut it herself, or perhaps had it cut with a power saw by a man who worked in a mine. A headmistress face, a masculine, no-frills no-nonsense face. Someone who could perhaps be friends with Mazzini. Does Mazzini dream of angry men with hypnotic gazes, getting whipped on dusty ledges? Would that be an archetype? Lisa decides to read this book very, very carefully.

What follows is a busy week for everybody.

Lisa attends a graduation party for Rebecca's friend who has completed her degree in Quartz Studies and is leaving town to work in the Mineral Healing Department of a hospital in Iowa.

Dominique summons Roark, the sexy sadomasochist of the quarries, to her house on the pretext of needing a piece of granite replaced.

Vera leaves a chocolate cream pie, and it is eaten in its entirety by Justin, Cleo, and Mac, obviating the need for any further deceptions.

Roark doesn't show up for his second appointment at Dominique's home, so she saddles up a horse and goes looking for him.

She finds him in the woods. He speaks to her insolently. She slashes him across the face with a horsewhip.

Cleo has to prepare a term paper for psychology, and for her topic proposes "Insecurity about Chronics in Older Men. Justin: A Case Study." The teacher is dead impressed.

Dominique leaves the patio doors of her house unlocked accidentally-on-purpose and Roark comes in that night and rapes her.

Nadine is out of the office for two days. Everyone amuses themselves by walking around speaking in heavy German accents.

Dominique discovers that Roark is actually a gifted architect who was only working in the quarry on a whim. She dedicates herself to destroying his career—not, as you might think, out of revenge, but as some weird sort of aphrodisiac. Whenever she manages to screw up another major contract that he really, really wanted, she shows up at his office for some punitive sex.

Lisa asks Brett about his vacation plans. He tells her he will be conducting a Men and Intimacy Retreat in Nevada to help participants enhance their partnership skills, and she should go ahead and make her plans without him.

Dominique and Roark get married. He builds fabulous skyscrapers. She rides up and down elevators admiring them.

Lisa props the book up on her desk so that Ayn Rand's face will be the first thing she sees when she comes in tomorrow. She's going to deal with this woman and with Miss Dominique, too, but not right now. Right now she's had it with both of them and could not be objective.

"Oooh," Justin says, popping into her office to say good night. "I don't know about the red-haired dude in the quarry, but that lady there could freeze you in your tracks with one look!" He leaves the office backward, making a hex sign.

Lisa remains at her desk. She's tired, and the late afternoon go-home-and-unwind mood-inducers, patchouli and orange blossom, are having an effect. Under the enigmatic gaze of Ayn Rand, she drifts into a daydream.

In her daydream, she is standing on a hill. She is looking down into a quarry, from which a lot of noise and little bursts of dust puff up toward her. In the quarry, men are hard at work, hauling huge blocks of stone with ropes and pulleys and drilling with heavy machines. One of the men is Brett. He is wearing a small ragged garment around his hips, and his body is straining against the weight of an enormous chunk of stone. Behind him, an overseer approaches on horseback, snapping a whip. The overseer yells something in a blunt, angry voice, and Brett strains even harder. Then he looks up and sees Lisa on her lofty perch, surveying the prisoners. His eyes blaze up at her.

Lisa freeze-frames the moment and steps back to look at it. Brett in a quarry, suffering a little and, for once, in no position to lecture anyone. This is not without its appeal. But will she able to sell Gender Amity on it? Lisa shakes her head and goes home.

All she wants to do is relax, but this is not fated to be. Vera's jacket is still hanging neatly by the entrance, and her large Ecuadorian woven bag stands beside the sofa, revealing that she is still in Lisa's apartment and will have to be empathetically interacted with, oh shit. Where is she anyway? The apartment is silent, bereft of the clattering and singing and mumbling that usually signal her presence. She's not in the living room, not in the kitchen; the bedroom is where Lisa finally locates her. There she is on Lisa's bed, in peach-colored work overalls and stocking feet, snuggled up against the quilted headboard and so engrossed in *Love's Burning Flame* that Lisa has to call her name three times before she responds. She jumps half a foot into the air then and turns bright pink in embarrassment, but she makes a good recovery, and quickly begins to berate Lisa for her choice in literature.

Soooo, is she still going to insist that everything is going so great in her life and she doesn't have any problems? Is she finally going to face facts and listen to Vera, who means well, who wants only the best for her, who wasn't born yesterday, who has been around and knows what's what? Or does she expect Vera to stand idly by, watching a pretty and intelligent young woman like Lisa, who should be enjoying life, throw herself away on a cold-hearted, stuck-up jerk-who-thinks-he's-such-a-big-shot, while filling the resulting empti-ness in her heart with trashy novels? Not that Vera snoops, she holds her clients' privacy in the highest regard, but Lisa after all has been leaving these books, these sad testimonials to her impoverished per-sonal life, lying about in plain view! She paid no attention at first, but as the weeks passed and Lisa kept reading the same sort of mis-guided and, if Vera is not mistaken, practically illegal publications, Vera began to see that she had an obligation to act. Leaving these books out, Vera believes, was a cry for help! "I told you that man's no good for you," she says, winding down with the sentence that concludes most of the one-sided conversations she has with her young employer.

Lisa is exasperated. "This is work," she explains to Vera. "It's my job. I'm working on sex and love. I'm not reading this stuff for fun. Not that it's helping . . . but I don't want you to worry about that. I'm sure I'll have a breakthrough soon. Especially with all the help you're giving me, freeing me from drudgery and domestic worries! Doing all of these nice caring things for me. Thank you, Vera," she adds, responsibly.

Vera sniffs, and straightens the criticized literature into a neat pile, and fusses around the apartment for a while longer. "A package came for you," she says, on her way out. "I put it on the table. It's from your sister. It rattles a little, I think it might be jewelry."

Lisa sighs. Well, at least she didn't open it.

A package from Lisa's sister—I interpret that as a peace offer-ing. Theresa must have realized that she was a bit abrupt when Lisa came to her for guidance. I'm glad she retains enough human rela-tions skills to recognize how rude her behavior was. Smiling to imagine nosy Vera shaking the package, Lisa cuts open the tape. There are three items inside, two from Cleo, one from Theresa. Cleo has sent a drawing and a necklace. The drawing shows a vol-cano with red lava flowing down the side; a woman who rather resembles a Klimt heroine stands beside it, raising her overlong arms skyward. The necklace is a string of beads, glass interspersed with coral, chunky and uneven but pretty. "I made these for you in our new Spiritual Guidance class," Cleo's note says. "We all think you're double-ex for sending us Riva. Her class is really fun. XOX-OXOXO, Cleo!"

Lisa smiles. She thought Cleo and her classmates would like the self-possessed, elegant Riva, and she knew Riva's office would welcome the opportunity to send her as guest proselytizer to a school.

From her sister, under the Institute's logo, there is an envelope containing a scanned page. It has a faint line down the middle and is darker in some spots than in others, revealing it to be the unenhanced copy of an old text.

She intends to read it, but not right now, so Lisa sticks it on the refrigerator, alongside the picture of the volcano.

Later that evening, she wanders into the kitchen for a snack. Waiting for the leftover pad thai noodles to warm up in the thermocube, she plucks her sister's missive from the refrigerator. It's an excerpt from some treatise by an apparently very famous founding father of reproductive biology, way back from the year 1886.

> A few days since, I brought a male of mantis carolina to a friend who had been keeping a solitary female as a pet. Placing them in the same jar, the male, in alarm, endeavored to escape.

Lisa pulls a glass of chopped peanuts from the shelf and a container of sliced pickled radishes from the refrigerator and shakes some of each into a bowl, pulling out a few slices of the radish to chew on as she reads.

> In a few minutes, the female succeeded in grasping him. She first bit off his left front tarsus, and consumed the tibia and femur. Next she gnawed out his left eye. At this the male seemed to realize his proximity to one of the opposite sex, and began to make vain endeavors to mate. The female next ate up his right front leg, and then entirely decapitated him, devouring his head and gnawing into his thorax. Not until she had eaten all of his thorax except 3 millimeters did she stop to rest.

Still reading, Lisa wanders over to the drawer and fishes out a pair of chopsticks.

> All this while the male had continued his vain attempts to obtain entrance at the valvules, and he now succeeded, as she voluntarily spread the parts open, and union took place. She remained quiet for 4 hours, and the remnant of the male gave occasional signs of life by a movement of one of the remaining tarsi for 3 hours. The next morning she had entirely rid herself of her spouse, and nothing but his wings remained.

That's the end of the text. Lisa discovers that her sister has added a personal message after all, scrawled in such small angular writing that she had initially taken it for part of the printed page.

"Hope he had some great fantasies!" Theresa has written.

The thermocube beeps. What is Theresa trying to tell her? Lisa isn't sure, but when she sits down at the table and lifts the noodles to her mouth, she discovers that somehow her appetite is gone, and she isn't hungry at all anymore.

Brett is in his home office, working. Trying to work. Next to his keypad he has placed a notebook, because he keeps remembering additional women who will somehow have to be accommodated at Main Base. He is not happy, and he is not feeling good. It might be nice to have Lisa's company; she always shows gratifying reverence for his intelligence, and her efforts to conceal her hopes and feelings are amusingly transparent. It's clear that she still loves him, despite her recent weird behavior and her halfhearted attempts to disengage. Actually, it would be fun and challenging to see if he can't reel her back in, get her to be as trusting and sweetly open as before. Several strategies for achieving that come to mind . . . but the experiment will have to wait, because she's out of town for her semiannual two-day Awareness Renewal Retreat. While he is here, stuck with a horribly mushrooming list of salvation-worthy women.

See, there's one peril of promiscuity right there. Even if you're not the most reliable relationship material, even if you're an egotistical, narcissistic liar and cheat, still you risk growing fond of your playmates. You might not want them thrown to a brutish, sex-starved, woman-hating mob. Brett, I agree, is an immature cad, an emotionally underdeveloped selfish spoiled bratty jerk, but he's not entirely heartless and he's not a monster. Consequently, his list is growing to nightmarish lengths.

There's the Teen Softball League team he coaches, twelve delightful young ladies on the poignant brink of womanhood. Though charmingly nubile, at fifteen they are still children in his eyes, but those undiscriminating animals loosed from UE camps may not share his scruples. Then there's his Fostering Transgenerational Understanding project, the ten adorable grannies from the retirement home who, with his encouragement, have formed a Hawaiian traditional hula troupe called the Lei Ladies. Uneducatables might prey even upon them.

Plus, of course, we have the myriad women who touch and improve his life. There's Cynthia, his astrologer, and that cute little nutrition counselor Marietta, to whose devoted interest he owes his spectacular cholesterol count. LeslieAnn, his first love, almost first wife, and still good friend. Oh God, he almost forgot Helena, the physical therapist who lives on the third floor. The one that takes such an interest in his meniscus. Not everybody, Brett has learned from sad experience, cares about your meniscus. There are those, he reflects darkly, who remain unmoved even when unbearable knee pain forces you into an anguished limp, and even call you a hypochondriac. But not the lovely, kind-hearted Helena, Helena of the menthol rubs and heating pads. She doesn't deserve to be fallen upon by barbarians. The provisional passenger list of Brett's ark is up to eighty-seven.

His face grim, Brett opens the door to put out his recycling bin and bumps right into Irma, the chaotic red-haired mother of twins who lives down the hall from him. And adorable twins they are, so like their charming, bubbly mother. Dropping tennis balls and laughing as she goes, her firm tanned limbs protruding from tight gym shorts, Irma races down the corridor in pursuit of her lively daughters as Brett looks benignly on. Can't throw those three to the wolves, either, can he? Clearly, he's going to have to start another whole section of his list for women he isn't related to, doesn't mentor, and hasn't slept with. And how, please, is he going to convince all of these women to leave town and go to the country?

All the stress is making him hungry and thirsty. Brett fills a bowl with tortilla chips and pours himself a shot glass of tequila.

He's supposed to be calculating a budget for his post-counter-revolutionary office, but he can't concentrate. Names and faces keep popping into his head: women, delightful women, entertaining women, women worth saving—they are multiplying in his notebook like bacteria in a petri dish. Soon Brett is up to 149 rescue candidates. If he organized a really intriguing retreat, could he get most of them to sign up? No, of course not, that's ridiculous. What if he said he had a premonition of disaster and begged them to take shelter for a few days? No, that won't work. A few of them, the holistic ones, the ones who read Tarot cards, might be susceptible to that kind of a scare, but not the majority.

He goes back to the kitchen for a tequila refill and comes back with the entire bottle.

Besides his good heart and his conscience, one or two other little things are also tweaking Brett to reconsider the coming counter-revolution. For example, there's that nagging sense that the other members of the Council take him just a little less seriously than they take each other. They've always made jokes about his profession, about his seminars, even about the way he dresses and acts. Does this bode well for his future? It irks him that he wasn't included in the planning of V-Day. Because he's not a military man, and it's not his field, like they said? Or because, fundamentally, they don't respect him?

Frankly, he also has to wonder whether a counterrevolution is even a good career move. To be a Council member, to be Minister, that will be terrific, of course. But you have to put it in context. It's not just the Council. Men will be running the whole world again. And it has begun to occur to Brett, dimly, belatedly, that this may be less than wonderful for him. Actually, women seem to like him a lot better than men do. Most women have a soft spot for him; the same cannot be said of most men. The world he is about to help re-create suddenly strikes him as a hard and bristly place, as opposed to the soft, fluffy cushion of a world he has been flourishing in for lo these many happy years.

He's a founding member of Harmony; his loyalty, and his right to a place on the Council, are beyond question. But haven't things gotten wildly out of hand? All he wanted was a slight shift in the power balance, something to put men back on top. Not a real upheaval, just their birthright back: the slightly bigger slice of the pie. Valentine's Day will be more, much more than that. There won't be any going back, after V-Day.

Things won't be the same with women, either. After Valentine's Day, no self-respecting woman will come within ten feet of him. They will shun him. His name will be mud. He'll be important, he'll have power, but so what! He's important now.

Angrily tossing back another shot glass of tequila—how many does this make?—he realizes that the only women who will like him anymore will be the Harmony crowd and their ilk. And he doesn't much like those women. Doesn't like the way they look, the way they dress, the things they do to their faces and their hair; he doesn't like their smiles, so bright and bubbly but with a cold, sly undertone. Their brand of femininity strikes him as false and almost creepy. Sometimes you feel that they have only taken on the outward appearance of women, and at any moment they might suddenly shed their fake eyelashes, hair extensions, glued-on fingernails, and silica gel implants to rise up from this pile of scales and plastic all huge and menacing to reveal the perilous Gorgon-like man-eating monster that lurks beneath . . .

Brett shudders. These fears came up years ago, in analysis, but his therapist said they were normal, a normal combination of womb envy and the transference process. He can still remember that session, remember confiding these thoughts to Dr. Geiger, Anneliese Geiger, or, rather, to her hovering presence in the Thonet chair behind the couch where, Freudian eclectic that she was, she liked to place her patients. And she had murmured comfortingly that it was important to address such fears and projections thoroughly, in a safe environment and with an expert. Then, before you could say "countertransference," there she was, flopped across him on the couch with her shirt unbuttoned and her breasts billowing forth, gasping something about how none of it was silicone, it was real, all real, and don't be scared of Mama.

Shit, Anneliese. He's nearly forgotten Anneliese. What ever happened to her, anyway? Is she still practicing?

Wherever she is, she's not going on his list. No way. Anneliese doesn't need his help. With her deep understanding of the male psyche, she should be able to handle a few rampaging UEs.

Ooooh, are we feeling a little hostile? If he were sober, Brett might want to explore that, but instead he bows elaborately to the sofa and drinks a gleeful toast to his vision of a beleaguered Anneliese, backed up against a wall but still lecturing a horde of rabid attackers on male anxiety and the vagina dentata. And good luck!

The image cheers him for only a moment. Brett is beginning to see his situation with the crystalline clarity of much alcohol. He has made a mistake, an awful mistake. Is he not a tragic hero on the Shakespearean scale—brilliant, a prince, envied by men, adored by women, yet driven by the tragic flaw of ambition to cast aside what fate has showered on him. What has he done? Far better to be a prince, a prince in paradise, than to be king of a bleak, cruel, stony desert! Unsteadily, Brett stumbles over to open a window. He needs air.

Pushing them wildly aside, he remembers that Lisa helped him choose these curtains. A nice girl, Lisa; too earnest and too vulnerable, and no match for him, of course, but sweet. Just look at how solemnly she pursues her assignment, her ridiculous assignment. Ridiculous, yes, the whole current order is ridiculous, just as the General said, in its missionary approach to human nature, its belief that you can make everybody act nice and everything be fair. On Valentine's Day, the whole illusion will blow up in their faces, and the people who take over will not be ridiculous, nor will they be nice.

Brett staggers over to the mirror and looks at himself, seeking in his florid countenance some sort of enlightenment. I would put him at philosophical drunk, not falling-down drunk, not yet.

Not liking his reflection in the mirror, Brett starts to pace. It's why he helped found Harmony, because it was clear that a bunch of naïve, pie-eyed, do-gooding women should not be exclusively in charge of anything as serious as a planet, but just now Brett cannot remember why that seemed so self-evident. Is clever-but-ruthless better than nice-but-naïve? Didn't clever-but-ruthless rule the planet for centuries, with uniformly displeasing results?

Even assuming that he could build a kind of Noah's ark and float his 149 nearest and dearest women to safety, what about the rest? It makes Brett sick to his stomach to think about Valentine's Day. Exhausted by this insight, Brett collapses back into his chair, in front of his computer. Almost of their own volition, his fingers begin typing up a report about the General, the Council, and the Valentine's Day plan, flagging it urgent and tinkering around within the frame until the message seems to come from elsewhere, from the anonymity of deep cyberspace. The touch of a button sends it to Lisa.

Lisa, after all, sits right in the heart of Command Central. When she reads this, she'll know where to take the information.

Brett wakes up late, mouth dry, head throbbing, pajamas askew, to realize the unutterable stupidity of what he has done. The point of no return was crossed long ago—there's no way back. If the counterrevolution fails, his goose is cooked. If anyone finds that message, he and his fellow conspirators will be found, tracked down, tried, convicted, and jailed. Though there is no death sentence, this, after all, is high treason, and the penalty will be extremely severe. No one involved in this scheme will ever be a part of respectable human society again. An anonymous warning—my God, how much tequila did he drink? If he was going to betray the plan, at least he ought to take credit for it. In the cold light of day, a thoughtful evaluation of the facts leads inescapably to only one possible conclusion: he's screwed.

And there's only one way to shovel himself out of the muck: he has to send the message again. With his name on it, so at least his belated remorse will count in his favor. Presumably, in exchange for his turning informer, they'll pardon him. He'll go from being a well-paid, much-admired star to being a remorseful conspirator, with humble pie as the new main staple of his diet.

Then he remembers that Lisa won't be back until tomorrow. He can go to her apartment and erase the message.

And after that he can conquer his silly jitters, take his rightful place as a leader of the counterrevolution, and be a man!

Every nerve in his body screams at him to race immediately to her apartment and take care of his problem. However, his scheduled all-day seminar starts in thirty-five minutes—and if he hustles like mad, he may just barely make it. Conceivably, he could call in sick, or cancel—hell, he can simply fail to show up. The world is about to explode; people will soon have a lot more to worry about than whether or not he's reliable.

On the other hand, the General has stated forcefully that they are not, under any circumstances, to attract notice. They might find it difficult, he had warned them, to carry on with their daily affairs, but that was precisely what they must do. They must not arouse suspicion, not at this critical juncture. They should not vary, not one iota, from their usual habits. They could not know who was watching them; they could not know which small signal might put their opponents on the alert. "Intuition . . ." the General had grumbled dimly, and Brett had been momentarily dismayed to sense in their leader a narrow vein of vulnerability, a wispy shadow of fear. While their opponents, these women, were in every way his tactical and strategic inferiors, still they might have some incalculable, formless, murky female resources that a man could not anticipate and perhaps had better not call forth . . .

Brett does not share these fears. Women hold no mystery to him—or so he believes, and Anneliese isn't here to tell us otherwise. But he will allow that the General's instructions make sense. So close to V-Day, it's essential to avoid anything that might arouse suspicion. People betray themselves not because they *are* guilty but because they *feel* guilty. He needs to go about his business; he does *not* need people wondering where he is, and asking questions.

Besides, he tells himself, the risk is minimal. It's not Vera's day to clean, and even if it were, that bad-tempered old broad has just barely enough brains to run a vacuum cleaner, and surely won't go near the compuscreen. He can go to Lisa's apartment after the seminar and still erase the files in plenty of time. Plus, Security will find his visit a lot less surprising in the evening than in the morning, right in the middle of the working day.

He takes a deep breath. He needs to take control, that's all. And he needs to get moving. Resolutely, Brett dispenses himself two droppers of Detox, dribbling the bitter fluid under his tongue to combat his hangover. He assembles the visuals for his seminar, then stands himself under the hot spray of the shower. It was perfectly normal to get the jitters, but he's over it now. Everything will be fine. He will learn to like counterrevolutionary women. So they're superficial—what's wrong with that? Superficial can be fun. With the sheer numbers of gorgeous females who will be throwing themselves at him once he's on the Council, why would he want permanence, anyway? Superficial relationships will be all he has time for. And as for the other women, what was he thinking about? They won't cut him, and they won't scorn him. Beggars can't be choosers. Compared to their highly limited new alternatives, he'll still look pretty good.

He's not ashamed of his little crisis. Crises are good. They make you stronger. They make you face your demons.

Unfortunately for him, Brett hasn't thought of everything, not quite. Brett thought of his past, and his future. He thought of his erotic preferences, and he thought of Lisa. He thought about the Revolution and the counterrevolution. He thought of Vera, though in dismissing her so cavalierly, his thinking was flawed. And as to Cleo, he failed to think of her at all.

Cleo is bright enough to run any machine or gadget in existence. Cleo has very little respect for other people's privacy. And Cleo loves to spend time in Lisa's apartment when no one else is there. A whole afternoon at her aunt's place, with Lisa away, that's almost too good to be true. I'm fairly certain that, the minute school is out, Cleo will be on her way.

Brett nearly has a seizure later that evening when, having dashed to her apartment the instant his seminar ended, he can't find his message on Lisa's screen. He spends the better part of an hour checking, rechecking, searching; it's not there. Lisa must have come back early—that's his first thought. She came back, read her messages, and even now is attending the emergency meeting at the Ministry. Then he notices other messages, also from yesterday, still unread.

Is there a chance that his message never arrived? No use trying to reconstruct the previous evening, it's just a headachy haze. Maybe he never even sent the message. Can he remember actually pushing the button? No, he cannot. Maybe the whole thing was just a stupid drunken idea, and he never acted on it. Maybe his subconscious had the intelligence and foresight to push DELETE instead of SEND; that's possible. The subconscious is a wondrous thing.

There are other possibilities—intercepts, wrong addresses, security agents monitoring Lisa's messages—but they don't bear thinking about, and there's nothing he can do about them. Any of those, and he's dead meat.

As he leaves, it occurs to Brett that, no matter how things turn out, this is likely to be his last visit to Lisa's apartment. Given his sensitive nature, he had better stay away from her, lest she disturb his fragile equilibrium even further. He pauses at the door and looks back. What do their respective futures hold? In the bigger scheme of things, it's really better if he comes out of this on top. Lisa's not important enough to suffer any real retaliation from the new leadership; not brilliant enough to have more than a mediocre career in the Revolution; and young enough to tolerate change. It really doesn't make all that much difference to her destiny who runs the world. She'll adapt.

Brett goes home. Oddly, he's feeling better, as the calm of resignation settles over him. There's nothing he can do now but hope. The die is cast, the bridge is burned, the river is crossed, and his ambivalence is resolved. Either they'll start rounding up the conspirators, and come get him, in which case life as he knew it will be over. Or, if Luck is a lady, his message will have been lost or never sent, the counterrevolution will proceed, and he will be powerful and important.

As for that list of his, he's ditching it. He can't save 149 women. It's best not to take anyone to Main Base at all, best to make a clean break of it. On the new Council, womanhood will have a friend in him; he'll speak up for them, make sure the backlash isn't too severe, and keep their well-being in mind.

I'm tempted to leave Brett's fate undecided just a little while longer; I'm savoring the thought of him dangling over the precipice. That image is so satisfying that I'm reluctant to let it go. But the clock is ticking, Valentine's Day is approaching, it's the end of January, so we'd better find out what happens next.

So here's Cleo, released from school, and on her way to Lisa's apartment.

In luxurious delinquency, she drops her jacket right in the middle of the hall, steps out of her chunky shoes, and wiggles her toes on the heated tile floor for a moment, enjoying the sensation of its warmth creeping up through her soft cotton socks. She takes a deep, pleasurable breath and pretends this is her own apartment. She pretends that she is Lisa, returning from an important day at the Ministry to this lovely, comfortable apartment, of which she is the sole mistress, and where she can eat what she wants, wear what she wants, and do what she wants with no well-meaning adults intruding. Kicking her book bag into the corner, she decides that her homework can easily be completed in fifteen minutes tops, so there is really no sensible reason to abandon this pleasant fantasy and bother with composition just yet. Instead, she drifts into the meditation corner of the living room. She lights a smudge stick "to clear her head," a chic phrase she often hears her mother and other adult women use. The pungent smell of sage surrounds her, and Cleo begins to feel very sophisticated, but also a mite bored.

Considering herself to now be sufficiently centered, she wanders into the next room and plops down in front of the main screen, intending to check in with her friend Francie. But what's this? A flag icon in the left corner, its neon stripes waving in an imaginary breeze, signals an urgent message. Well, maybe it's for her! Maybe Lisa left her a note. Or maybe it's an important message for Lisa, in which case she ought to try to reach her!

Her snooping thus amply justified, Cleo activates the flag. She reads through the text once, quickly, and then again, more carefully. As she reads this terse summary of a horrendous plot about to shatter her world, Cleo's little face begins to cloud over in disastrous realization of what this means. Betrayal!

Betrayal, alas, as filtered through the egotistical lens of a child. Cleo starts to sniffle, a little sniffle of pain. Justin and Lisa, she thinks, angrily. They are playing without her. She was the one who invited Justin to play, out of the kindness of her heart, and now he's edged her out and is playing I Spy Cleo with Lisa but without her! Betrayal!

Cleo rereads the text of the message scornfully. A massive computer virus, a Security breakdown, dangerous UEs on the loose, an evil General, rape and mayhem, yeah, right! They're trying to be such big shots about this, turning it into a whole political adventure story! And they think she's not smart enough to follow their oh-so-grownup new plot, so they're playing without her. They probably think she's a baby.

In a fit of narcissistic fury, Cleo slams her fist down on the table, but that just adds a pain in her hand to the pain in her heart. Well, they're not going to get away with this! She'll show them!

With a single angry slash of her highlighter and a vicious stab of an index finger on the pad, Cleo takes their whole stupid game and blasts it into cyber-oblivion, gone, erased, finished! So there! They may not want to play with her, but they're not going to play without her either.

"You seem to be acting on impulse," the computer's mellifluous voice whispers. "Want to reconsider that delete?"

Cleo pulls herself together. It's no good banging on the keypad like that. That just activates the computer's socio-sensors. She jiggles her fingers to loosen them, summons up a feeling of serenity, and taps the CONFIRM key with just the right amount of mature, restrained control. The computer, falsely reassured as to her emotional state, obeys.

It's no fun being in Lisa's apartment anymore. Cleo grabs her books and her jacket, stomps her feet violently into her bucket-like shoes, and marches off to Francie's house, leaving no visible sign that she has ever been here at all, except for the fact that she has just erased the warning that could have saved civilization as she knows it.

And Brett—well, the phrase "lucky bastard" comes to mind. At least he doesn't know it yet, and sleeps badly, waiting for the knock on his door, expecting to be hauled away at any moment.

How annoying. There's so much going on *already,* what with the project and the extracurricular espionage. Justin really does not need to be whisked away for a four-day intensive re-ed seminar. Nadine isn't pleased either; she frowns as she reads the directive, and mutters something about excessive coddling and Club Med revolutionaries. It's unfair of her to blame Justin, it's not like he asked to go. Nor does it strike him as especially pressing to learn about Gender Aspects of Sibling Rivalry, when he has neither siblings nor offspring. Still, it's only four days, and four days in Florida at that.

As he packs, Justin feels his annoyance diminishing, his excitement growing. Four days of sunshine! A trip! A stay at a resort, instead of the Residential Suites!

The flight is uneventful. The seminar hostel, when he arrives there in the early evening, seems pleasant. The man at the desk is cordial, but has startling news. Justin would like a schedule for tomorrow morning? The seminar doesn't start tomorrow morning. Tomorrow is Sunday. Sessions always begin on Mondays. No, there's no mistake. He's a day early, though his reservation indeed has been made for today. It's hardly a problem, in any case. Why doesn't he relax, and enjoy himself at leisure? Justin realizes how stupid it would be to complain. Complain about a day at liberty in the Florida sunshine, all expenses paid?

"There's a private beach right behind the meditation grove," the receptionist points out. "It's perfect during the early morning, before it gets too hot and the bugs come out. It's an experience not to be missed, take my word for it. You can even have your breakfast there, right on our pier. I'll put you down for a wake-up call."

Well, he had intended to sleep in, but the man is right. A morning on the beach, that's appealing. All right. The clerk shows him to a comfortable room decorated in a marine motif. This reeducation process is starting to look better and better.

Eight o'clock on Sunday morning finds Justin already up and feeling decadent, sprawled in an Adirondack chair with a bloody Henry and a heaping buffet plate on a low wooden table beside him, alternating bites of blueberry muffin with sips of the peppery drink, watching the birds, watching the waves, lazily studying the sinuous coastline for the perfect spot to enter the water a little bit later. Though if he's going to swim, maybe he shouldn't be having this drink, he thinks. It tastes very strong, not that he's any judge. Beer is pretty much the only alcohol he ever gets, the only intoxicating beverage broadly condoned for re-eds. But the waitperson offered him this glamorous drink, and as it sits there on the side table in its elegant crystal glass, gathering beads of moisture in the morning air, it almost seems a necessary part of the tropical experience. Anyway, he's a good swimmer. A little vodka won't change that. Sighing with pleasure, Justin permits himself another contented spicy sip.

Yes, this is paradise, and it's his, all his, his alone. Aimlessly sketching a zigzag pattern in the sand with his bare toes, Justin slants his face to the morning sun and enjoys his solitary realm, feeling like Robinson Crusoe before Friday, like Adam before Eve. Whoever made that mistake in the booking did him a giant favor, landing him here in the blissful interlude between two sessions. Tomorrow the seminar will start, and in the breaks the beach will be crowded with noisy men, an outdoor version of the Residential Suites. But for now all this splendor is his.

When the little triangular shape first appears on the horizon, it is merely a colorful dot, one of several that sprinkle the shimmering water like confetti. Boats and buoys. But the other dots stay distant, and this one is coming closer. Justin keeps a casual eye on it as it approaches, noting that it has a green-and-red hull and is piloted by a lone figure.

It comes closer still, and closer, until to Justin's displeasure it clanks right up against the dock, and a large man leaps from it, ties it up with a casually economical motion, and yells something. Unable to make it out, Justin shades his face and peers frowningly toward the man.

"You Justin?" the sailor asks.

Startled, Justin nods.

"Well, hop aboard, we're going to the Island."

"Me?" Justin asks. "Island? Why?" he stutters.

"Dunno, pal," the man says. "They just told me to come get you. And bring you back later," he adds, reassuringly. "You *are* Justin, right?" he confirms, as the younger man still makes no move to join him. "Come on, down the hatch with your drink, bottoms up, and let's go."

"Is this to do with the seminar?" Justin asks. Damn, and damn. His beautiful day, all shot to hell.

"Sure, buddy," the man says. "The seminar. Let's get moving, come on."

Well, it was too good to be true. Overcome with disappointment and annoyance, Justin rises to his feet, finds his sandals, and reluctantly shuffles off behind his guide, who waves him impatiently on board and into a seat, and immediately roars away.

If he weren't so angry at the interruption, a boat ride could be fun. Far from enjoying himself, though, Justin is starting to feel sick. Waves of nausea sweep over him as the boat picks up speed and swings into its choppy amphibious gait, swooping into the air for a few meters before crashing back onto the surface of the water, lifting off, slapping down. Justin clings to the rail, takes deep breaths of salty air, and prays to not throw up. Also, a nagging thought is tunneling its way through his brain. Where the hell does this jerk get off, bossing him away from his wonderful beach and into the boat like that without so much as a decent explanation. The seminar doesn't even start until tomorrow, they can't command his time today. In the back of his mind he can hear Will, grumbling his customary refrain during the basement meetings. They're turning us into eunuchs. Snap their fingers, we jump through hoops.

Justin decides that he has a right to know where they are going, and why. Swallowing hard against his nausea, he yells his question through a cloud of salty spray. The man ignores him. The dismissive wave of his hand indicates that he's heard Justin's question, all right, but is choosing not to answer.

Justin gets angry. At himself, mostly, for timidly submitting to authority like a frightened little mouse. And at this arrogant jerk. Also, Justin is a little nervous. Does this thug really look like a reeducation counselor? Or doesn't he seem a lot more like those thugs who guard the Harmony meetings? It makes no sense that he, and he alone, is being whisked to an early seminar session. It occurs to Justin that he is being kidnapped.

"Take me back!" he yells.

The man turns around and gives him an annoyed look. Noticing that his passenger is distinctly green around the gills, he attributes his agitation to seasickness. And to the effects of whatever they decided to drug him up with. If you ask him, it's pretty stupid, to drug somebody just as they're about to get on a boat. But do they ever ask him? Oh no. Their High and Mightinesses know everything better.

"We're almost there," he yells back to his green passenger, a little more kindly. He points to a stripe of land, the shoreline of an island, which indeed is coming closer. "If you're gonna upchuck, bend over the railing," he advises.

Justin is alarmed to hear that they are approaching their destination. "I want to be taken back right now!" he shouts, forcefully. In Violence Aversion he learned how important it is to state resistance and objections clearly. They spent an entire week on techniques for saying an unambiguous no, and were promised that this would make most aggressors back off.

"Turn the boat around right now," Justin orders, in his firmest voice. "I do not wish to continue on. Take me back."

"Yeah? Or else you'll turn yourself into a pelican and fly back?" this aggressor taunts, amused.

A wave of rage and nausea propels Justin forward. He lunges at the man, aiming for the arm that grips the boat's controls. The man jumps up in surprise, releasing the controls for a moment; the boat rocks wildly, and banks steeply to the left. Its startled captain aims one fist at Justin, delivering a glancing blow, reclaiming the controls with the other hand. Justin staggers backward, then again launches himself at his bulky adversary. The man punches him again, harder. The boat tips. Justin throws himself furiously forward. His head is throbbing, his aim is none too good, the boat is rocking wildly, the man is smacking him with one deliberate arm. Slipping on the wet deck, Justin slides against the side of the boat, grabs for the railing, misses, slips. And tumbles overboard, banging his head against the side as he goes.

The man brings the boat to a stop. His broad-spectrum curses include just about everybody, from the idiots who employ him to the young imbecile who has just landed himself in the water. The imbecile who, he sees, is floating facedown and seems to be unconscious. With renewed curses, the man jumps into the water after him; luckily, it is shallow and goes no higher than his chest. He yanks his passenger's head up before the moron can drown. He slaps him on the back, and a little water coughs out. Is he breathing? Yes. Good.

Now what? Drag and lift this limp sack of deadweight back on board? Holding his charge's head lovelessly above the water by the hair, the man thinks for a moment. It would be a lot easier to just haul him to shore. Those aren't his orders, but to hell with it.

Pushing and pulling, the man maneuvers Justin through the shallows toward the beach, dragging him unceremoniously by his waist and arm the last few yards before dumping him on a stretch of sand. Still breathing, so that's okay. He arranges him facedown, head sideways, so he won't choke, and gives him a final hard pounding between the shoulder blades, half resuscitation effort, half punishment for causing so much trouble. Then he wades and swims back out to the boat to contact his employers. Not very respectfully.

"Whose goddamn stupid idea was it to drug that guy before you put him on my boat," he begins. "Well, now you can go fish him off the goddamn beach." In this tenor, he completes his story, and listens grumpily to the replies.

At the other end, the Operations Team hears his story with composure. They wanted a mildly sedated Justin; they got an unconscious one. They wanted him to disembark at the pier in a compliant mood; instead, he's sprawled facedown on the beach, totally helpless. Never mind. To an experienced Psych Ops team, wrinkles like these are but creative opportunities. In no time at all, there is a Plan B.

"It's almost better this way," the team leader reflects. "The bonding should be accomplished more easily, and if he's a little incapacitated at first, it doesn't matter."

To accurately visualize our next scene, we will have to draw on Greek mythology. I ask you to imagine a Greek hero, perhaps Odysseus. His ship has foundered, and now he has washed up, unconscious, on a deserted beach. As he lies there, a beautiful maiden, possibly a stray Siren or other such female mythological creature, drifts gorgeously across the sand. She discovers this bit of male flotsam littering her perfect shoreline, and wanders over to investigate. She bends over him in kindly concern.

This is what happens next, sort of, to Justin. Okay, he's not Odysseus. And his discovery is not an accident. But yes, he is unconscious, and yes, a highly attractive female person has found him and is leaning over his prone form with a look of worry on her face. We couldn't classify her as a maiden, technically speaking, but she does have her CPR certification, which in this situation, I think you will agree, is distinctly more useful. Competently taking his pulse and positioning his head for better breathing, she next presses a button on her HUE band, and very shortly a response team arrives, and Justin is trundled onto a porta-stretcher and removed to the nearest station, which, since this beach belongs to the Committee, is the weekend resort of no less than the Founding Mothers Their Illustrious Selves.

So that, when Justin awakens, he finds himself looking directly into the flinty gray eyes of Lavinia Tree. This, his battered brain concludes, obviously cannot be correct, so he shuts his eyes once more very tightly, blinks three times, and shakes his head hard. The latter measure is a mistake, as urgent messages of pain begin reaching him from various parts of his body, but this massive response does cause him to conclude that he must be awake and alive, so he opens his eyes once more, cautiously.

Lavinia Tree is still there.

"Young man," she says in a deep, gravelly voice. "How are you feeling?"

No. It can't really be Lavinia Tree, inquiring about his welfare. Cautiously he moves his eyes a bit to the right, a bit to the left. Maybe he is dead after all. Dead, and attended by a celestial group of women. To Lavinia's right, we have a violet-eyed young woman, his rescuer, standing next to two young members of the response team. To her left, several medical women hover in their therapeutically beneficial, reassuringly nonmedical flower-patterned garments. Two other members of the Governing Body flank Lavinia. They have come directly from the beach and are wearing muumuus. Security, standing all the way at the back of the room, is in maroon jumpsuits, but to Justin's unfocused eye they appear merely as disembodied faces floating in some sort of purple haze.

I dwell on the superficial issue of everyone's dress to explain how Justin, whose vision is still blurry, might perceive his visitors as an otherworldly host of female faces and forms. They look like cherubs.

Well, not Lavinia. She looks more like a very businesslike sort of archangel.

"I don't think he should try to speak yet," the violet-eyed one says softly, studying him with a sweet frown.

Yes indeed, Justin concludes, he is clearly in the hands of angels.

"Nonsense, Violet," says the sturdy archangel with the amazing resemblance to Lavinia Tree. "Our med team assures me that he is fine, all readings normal, he's just a little shaken. Young man, try to sit up. We're very eager to hear your report."

It is a voice accustomed to obedience. Still trying to blink away his confusion, Justin makes an effort to comply, and the violet-eyed woman rushes over and gently grasps his shoulder to support him.

"Be careful, Justin, you mustn't hurt yourself," she instructs, as a strand of her soft hair falls across Justin's neck.

Three things strike him.

She's so nice.

Her hair smells like lavender.

She knows who he is.

She knows who he is?

Well, if this is a dream, or if he's in some paradisal hereafter, that makes sense. And that's what his best guess is, right now. Where else but in a dream do heads of state compete for your attention with lovely women whose names match their eye color?

"You know who I am?" he asks hazily.

But it is Lavinia who answers. "Well, certainly we know who you are, son," she replies, acerbically. "Why else do you suppose we're all standing here waiting to talk to you?"

But the tender vision with the violet eyes and the perfect name has something to say, too. "We've been expecting you, but we didn't expect you to be hurt by that bully," she says. "You got away from him, though. That was so brave!"

It's a subject worth pursuing, in Justin's view, but Lavinia butts in again. "Come now, young man. Get that blood circulating. On your feet, take a few steps."

And then she actually stretches out her very own exalted presidential hand to steady him, which so overwhelms Justin that he leaps to his feet to grasp it, takes a teetering step forward, and falls into a dead faint.

Could the medical team have been expecting it? Two of them catch him competently before he hits the floor. He is placed on a cot, irradiated, given a sublingual, then plied with barley broth every half hour, stimulated with a cone of lemon grass, and finally brought to with the Spectrum, a graded diffusion of light that moves from calming blue to invigorating orange. Three hours after his collapse, Justin is awake and feeling much better.

He goes to the bathroom—and no wonder, after all that barley broth. I mention this prosaic fact only because the men's room, as is often the case, abuts the similar facility for women. And since this is a lodge, built in a purposely rustic style out of planks, the intervening wall is so flimsy that, if you are standing near the sink, you can hear the voices of those on the other side. As Justin studies his bleary red eyes in the mirror and pats cold water onto his cheeks, the sound of two female voices penetrates the thin wall and captures his attention, because one of the voices sounds like Violet's.

"Wasn't your performance a little thick?" the first voice is asking.

"I was worried about that, too," the second voice replies. Yes, Justin decides, it's Violet speaking.

"When I first reviewed this behavioral application, I didn't think it would work. It seems so fake. Especially with the improvising we had to do. But my impression is, it went over. Perfectly," she continues.

"I'll say," the unknown other voice agrees. "He was lapping it up."

"You know," the Violet voice muses, "I've been in Special Operations, Manipulative Gender Psychology, for almost two years now, and I'm still amazed at how classic the responses are. Long hair, short skirts, flattery, an admiring look through tinted contact lenses—that's all it takes and you've got them eating out of your hand."

Justin would love to believe that someone else, someone other than himself, is the subject of this discussion.

"I might make some minor modifications, but on the whole, I think Justin is responding just as planned," Violet muses, cutting short that hope.

Her friend laughs.

Sight unseen, Justin hates the friend. But his primary emotion is a desire to flee, to get out of the bathroom before the two women emerge. Bumping into them, having to face them now, that would be the ultimate humiliation.

In his embarrassed retreat, Justin almost fails to hear what Violet says next. But his blind flight takes him in the wrong direction. He yanks open what he thinks is the exit and rushes into what in fact is a large supplies closet lined with shelves full of cleaning utensils and other sanitary articles. As a result of this delay, he hears the next portion of the conversation.

"You know," he hears Violet say to her friend, "I feel kind of bad running the protocol on him. He's really nice. Attractive, too. I like him."

And right there, amid rolls of toilet paper, spray cans of disinfectant, and boxes of tampons, Justin falls in love.

The next interview session, an hour later, is more conventional. Justin is fully conscious, for one thing, and in an upright position. They're in a small office. There's just Violet, and a second young woman in some kind of uniform, and a video camera trained directly on his face.

"We didn't want to make you nervous again, with a whole big crowd," Violet says. "But we're recording the session, because everyone's really anxious to hear what you'll be able to tell us."

"And you'd better have a damn good explanation, or——" the second one starts in, but Violet places a hand on her arm to stop her.

"Anita, please," she says. "We agreed that I would handle this."

"Well, get started, then," the other woman mutters aggressively. "But cut the coddling. He's not a celebrity guest, he's a suspected anti-rev."

Violet shakes her head sadly at her partner. "He is not a suspect," she protests. "He is a witness who is helping us. Justin, I'm counting on you to try very hard to answer our questions just as completely as you can, because we very badly need this information." She smiles at him warmly.

The interview gets off to a really good start, with Violet gratifyingly responsive to his story. Recruited as a secret agent, how exciting! And he agreed to do it right away, how brave! And she's really impressed with his recall. The way he can remember the layout of Nadine's apartment, and the names of the other participants in that meeting! Violet is so pleased with him, and Anita is so hateful, with that sarcastic smirk on her face, that the import of their line of questioning does not sink in. If he were not thus incapacitated by the powerful twin sentiments of lust and animosity, alarm bells would be ringing in Justin's head and he would have some questions of his own. Such as this one: If Nadine is such a big shot in the Ministry, entrusted with running a top-secret counterespionage project, then surely the government must know all about it. So why would they need him, a lowly re-ed, to fill them in on the details of the mission?

Before he can collect himself enough to wonder about this, the questioning has moved to shakier ground. Violet wants to hear about Harmony. He's actually infiltrated Harmony—how thrilling! And been to meetings. Lips eagerly parted, intelligent eyes focused completely on Justin, Violet leans forward to learn the deeply political, highly clandestine, explosively seditious information he will impart to her.

Well, he tries to embellish it, to make them understand how inappropriate and subversive the whole atmosphere of the gatherings is, but ultimately it boils down to this: Justin has played basketball and attended a dance class. A small tremor of disappointment passes across Violet's lovely face.

"Do you think maybe those dance meets could be a cover while something more secret is going on in other rooms?" she wonders hopefully.

"Why ask him?" Anita interjects, contemptuously. "He wouldn't know a secret if it kicked him in the balls."

"If you can't be more professional than that," Violet exclaims, with a furious look at her colleague, "you had better leave."

"Gladly!" the other woman retorts. "Talking to this loser is a total waste of time, anyway."

"I'm sorry," Violet tells him, as Anita stomps out. Where earlier she had been so enthusiastic, now she seems deflated and a little sad. And it's his fault. Justin feels lousy. She has put her faith in him, she had high expectations, and he didn't deliver.

"I'm sorry I can't tell you more," he says.

Sweetly, she demurs. "It's not your fault. You've been great. It's them," she confides, in a lowered voice. "My supervisors," she whispers. "They're too impatient. I'm sure you're on the right track. Infiltration is a tricky, arduous business. What do they know, they've never been in the field. You have to establish trust, get people used to you, pass subtle little tests. You were just getting started! I'm sure that if you persevered, you would deliver some really valuable information. Because you're obviously very smart, and you have a gift for making people confide in you. Just look at me." She laughs girlishly. "I feel like I could just sit down and tell you my whole life story. Which I won't do, don't worry. So listen, Justin," she finishes briskly. "I'll stay in touch. We'll get together. Just keep doing what you're doing, and we'll show them! I'm in this with you, Justin. I'll contact you, maybe you would be willing to come over, we'll talk and make plans." She steps up very close to him, so close that he can smell something heady and sweet, her perfume. Roses. "Please be careful," she whispers, as he inhales the delicious feminine aroma. "Those people are dangerous. If something were to happen to you, just because you're trying to help us . . ."

It's a profound moment. Her feelings have overwhelmed her, Justin can see that. She really cares. He returns her gaze for a long, deep instant; then there's a knock on the door, and the security crew arrives to take him back.

Reluctantly, Justin and Violet step away from each other. She waves after him.

Violet waits to be sure they have cleared the hallway, then calls out a brisk "All clear!" in the direction of the adjoining room. Her partner pops back in.

"That went well, I think," Anita says. "Ready for lunch?"

"If you can give me twenty minutes," Violet agrees. "I want to run upstairs and pop out these contact lenses. Let me take a quick shower, too, to get this rose gunk off, it's giving me a headache."

"Roses are red, and Justin loves *you*!" her friend taunts. Violet laughs.

"Your summary, please," Lavinia Tree snaps, to the four women standing in front of her desk. "In your view, what did we learn?"

The highest-ranking officer replies first. "The Radicals have recruited two operatives to infiltrate Harmony. Our informant believes himself to be on an official spying mission for the government, and as far as he knows, his female partner believes the same. Neither of these operatives was given any covert training whatsoever, and they are patently unsuited for a mission of this sort."

"Do we believe him?" Lavinia wants to know. "Can he have been putting on an act?"

"Sensor monitoring was highly successful during his testimony," the Tech person, Ruby, replies. "He took no evasive measures and, as far as we could tell, seemed oblivious to our monitoring altogether. Most interrogation subjects will either try to avoid the contact points or clutch them too tightly; at a minimum, they glance at them involuntarily once in a while. He did none of that. Involuntary focusing and dilation measures were likewise all negative. His reading fluctuations correlated only with the affective coordinates set by Special Operations," she adds, with a slight smirk.

Lavinia Tree looks uncertain.

"His pulse sped up whenever Violet came near," Anita translates.

"Which is good, because it tells us that he had no inhibitors," Ruby adds. "You can inhibit someone's responses altogether, but you can't select out the sexual stimuli. A subject either responds or does not respond."

Lavinia Tree nods. "So the Radicals are sending amateurs to spy on Harmony," she repeats. "That's not like them. There must be some reason why they're doing that. I'm afraid those two young people are in danger . . . but that's not our only worry. Why have they been sent on this strange mission at all—that's the big question here. Very well, thank you all, and let's hope we have more information soon."

Anita and Violet never look at each other when the word "Radicals" is spoken. Their eyes don't flicker, no muscle clenches, their pulse is steady. They're not being monitored, probably not, but if they were, it would take some very sophisticated instrumentation to find anything awry.

Justin is determined not to let Violet down. He's got to give her more than a few lousy dance sessions. He has to penetrate the depths of Harmony—and soon, before she loses faith in him.

He broaches the subject carefully with Lisa. Obliquely, since his encounter with headquarters is top-secret. He's got to stick to the seminar story, must not on any account tell anyone about his visit to the Island. Violet warned him about that, and Security spent an additional hour with him, making sure he understood and rehearsing his answers to questions he might be asked about the nonexistent seminar. No one is to find out that he has been questioned. Not even Lisa. Definitely not Nadine. No one.

So all he can do is express his general concern that they are not discovering anything worthwhile, that they are no closer to Harmony's secrets than when they started. But Lisa doesn't bite. Things are going exactly the way they should be, she says. Nadine has warned her that espionage is nine-tenths tedium. You have to wait, blend in, go with the flow. You have to be patient.

This viewpoint exasperates Justin, until it occurs to him that he has other resources. If he wants to advance in Harmony, Lisa isn't his best bet anyway. Nor Nadine, nor even Xenia. It's a men's organization, and any female route into it is bound to be a detour. But he's a man, and so has other, better avenues.

It's not that hard to get chummy with Will. A few good hard slaps on the back, a few anecdotes about Nadine, a few sessions working out together at the gym, and they're not just neighbors anymore, not just fellow cell members, they're best buddies. A few beers, and Will is ready to nod sagely while Justin vents about how he is itching for action, revved up for serious subversion, going nuts over the tame basement stuff. As evidence of his commitment, and to cover his rear end, he tells Will about Lisa. That he's sought out a second avenue of activism, and recruited a woman, and attended co-ed Harmony social events, but that he feels just as stymied there. Action, he needs some action.

"Let me think about it, good buddy," Will says. "See what I can do. Maybe I can help ya out."

And Will delivers. "My man," he drawls, soon thereafter, throwing a sweaty beefy arm around Justin as they leave the gym. "You are one lucky dude. I took your matter to the higher-ups, and it just so happens there's a special event coming up, and you're invited. The when, the where, the how, I'll get back to you on that, but I'm telling you buddy, this is big. Now, we won't be electing you president just yet, pal. But this'll be a giant jump forward. Some guys wait years for an opportunity like this. Some guys never make it. But thanks to Uncle Will, *you* are going places! You and the lady friend."

That's all he'll say.

Justin wishes he could call Violet, posthaste, to inform her of his impending intelligence triumph. But there's no way to reach her; he's supposed to wait for her to contact him. Which is probably a good thing, when he thinks about it. What exactly has he got to tell her, anyway? That he's invited somewhere, but he doesn't know where? Soon, but he doesn't know when? To do something special, but he doesn't know what? No. Then she'll get that look on her face again, that sweet, brave, disappointed look. He'll wait until he has a proper bombshell.

Justin spends a pleasant half hour visualizing the pleased look on Violet's face when he returns as a hero, when he delivers information that prevents a terrorist attack and saves hundreds of lives, when Lavinia Tree expresses the gratitude of the Founding Mothers for his act of courage while Violet looks proudly on . . .

At this point, it might be worth our while to glance at the calendar. How time flies! February already. Spring is around the corner. Birds are looking around for nesting spots, bulbs are gathering their strength, preparing to surge up through the dank winter soil, and into sun and color. And Valentine's Day is coming up, awaited eagerly by flower-growers, romantics, lovers, and of course counterrevolutionary woman-hating terrorist conspirators.

Justin's sense of urgency is very appropriate. Never mind impressing Violet—if his and Lisa's spying mission is to meet with any success at all, they'll have to hustle.

Still, when Will finally gives him the nod, instructs him to be ready that evening, Justin's impatience is replaced by high anxiety. Truth be told, he feels like maybe he could have waited a while longer, perhaps indefinitely. Too late to get the jitters. Next thing you know, he and Lisa are being bundled unceremoniously into a bus.

They can't really talk, with other people around them, but Justin can feel Lisa shivering in the seat beside him; the night air is chilly. Is she still miffed? She hasn't entirely gotten over the fact that it was Justin who came up with this potential breakthrough, he knows. Good thing the last two Harmony meetings were segregated—that gave him a plausible story for how this came about, since he could tell her that the invitation was issued when he was alone with the rest of the men.

The trip will take about five hours, their taciturn driver remarks. He doesn't look like he would be inclined to answer many further questions, and nobody poses any. Seven people, three couples and one lone man, jolt along in the bus, then disembark on a small airfield, then board a plane, then fly through darkness for an hour, then land on another small airstrip, then go by delivery van to a darkened station, get on a train, pass through a long dark tunnel, get on another van, drive for another hour or so, and are finally unloaded, jolted and shaken from the journey and feeling as dumb as luggage, in front of a large building.

"Shangri-la!" the guide announces, with a barking laugh. And waves his bedraggled group inside.

They find themselves in a large lobby, with a reception desk. As they are given their room assignments, issued directions to the restaurant, and told to assemble there for dinner at eight-thirty, it's reassuringly like a hotel, or the first day at college. A new guide appears, and leads them down a hallway, up a flight of stairs, and along a corridor, where he points them, one by one, to their quarters. He lets the men deposit the bags inside the doors, then summons them back to follow him.

"We're going to let the ladies settle in," he announces, "while you gentlemen come along with me."

Justin and Lisa exchange a quick nervous look, and then she is alone. She takes a deep breath and looks the room over. The suite, actually. It's not bad. The furnishings are rustic, but everything looks clean. There's no compuscreen, and no connector that she can see. She checks out the bathroom and washes her hands. She's back in the bedroom investigating the contents of the minibar when she hears the door open behind her.

"Justin?" she calls.

"No, I'm Carl," an unknown voice says. A husky man strolls into the room. "Your boyfriend'll be right back. But while we're waiting for him, why don't we just take care of a little administrative matter."

Administrative matter? He's not carrying a compu-pad, papers, or any other accoutrements of administration. Granting Lisa a vulpine smile, Carl extends one hand, closed into a fist, and advances on his guest.

"Now, honey, if you put your mind to it I'm sure you can get your boyfriend to buy you some prettier jewelry than this," he remarks jovially, reaching for her hand. Before Lisa can react, he has taken hold of her wrist and, with the slash of a razor, sliced off her HUE band. It falls to the ground; he bends quickly to retrieve it and stuffs it into his pocket. "I'll just get rid of that for you," he says. His words are ostensibly friendly, but the accompanying smile is feral. And the message isn't lost on Lisa. He could have asked her to remove the HUE band; even leaving aside the fact that he has taken it without her permission, there was no need to cut it, no need to approach her wrist with a steel blade. Still smiling broadly, the man reaches out and pats her cheek paternally before he leaves the room. Lisa stares after him. Her arm feels naked and vulnerable without the plastic bracelet. A shiver runs down her spine as the ancient intelligence of her body starts kicking out adrenaline in recognition of a fact that is just beginning to make its longer, slower way to Lisa's brain.

She's among enemies.

This is dangerous.

It's show time.

When Justin comes back, Lisa isn't over the shock yet. "They took away my HUE band," she informs him in an urgent whisper as soon as he walks through the door. "This gorilla with a razor came in here, he cut it right off my arm with a razor." She looks at Justin's wrist, expecting to find it equally bare, but his band is still in place. "He'll be coming back for yours," she warns.

But Justin shakes his head. They won't, actually. That was one of the things they talked about just now. They said they were working on a way to remove the men's bands, but hadn't figured it out yet. You couldn't just cut them with a blade, because they had a steel core. You could maybe slice through them with a power saw, but the technicians thought it best not to tamper with the core, or it would deliver an electrical shock, they weren't sure how severe. They even suspected that the bands were designed so that serious damage would make them explode. They were working on a way around that, but until then, the men would have to keep their bands.

Which is a monumental bit of good luck for them, he adds. At least they still have a way to summon help, in an emergency.

Where did they take Justin, anyway, Lisa wants to know. "It was just the orientation session," he explains. Everybody was taken to this large room. They gave them a rundown on the facilities, stuff like that. Nothing really dramatic.

Lisa is annoyed. "I wouldn't say that everybody was there," she observes tartly.

Justin stares at her. "Oh," he says, at last. "Well, I mean all the men were there. The women were in their rooms. Like you," he adds, helpfully.

He seems insufficiently contrite over his inappropriate use of language, Lisa notes, but perhaps she'll address that issue at another time.

"If it was an orientation," she wonders instead, "how come it wasn't for all the guests?"

Because this is a men's antirevolutionary movement, Justin could answer. That's why we're here, spying on it, he could say. But Lisa knows that. So he just reaches for her hand and gives it a reassuring squeeze. "I'm sorry about the HUE band thing and the razor. I would have been very scared if that happened to me."

"It's okay," Lisa says, "I guess I'm just nervous."

Well, on the subject of nervous, there's something else Justin thinks she should know.

"When they were telling us about the facility," he says, trying hard to sound casual, "well, somebody asked about the location, you know, I mean where exactly we are . . ."

He never finishes the sentence. Because Lisa, as she discovers, has guessed the answer already, guessed it probably the moment Carl made free with her wrist, or maybe even earlier, when they were in the tunnel.

"Zone Six," she says, and they look at each other in dismay.

Maybe some food will make them feel better. Or maybe it won't.

The dining room, when they enter as scheduled at eight-thirty, is set up like a restaurant. Couples are seated at small tables for two, while groups of men gather at tables for four or six. Will Lisa and Justin enjoy their meal, as enjoined by the host who seats them? It appears doubtful. They are too anxious to be hungry, too jittery to engage in small talk, too concerned about being overheard to discuss matters of substance.

Plates are put before them, two scoops of vegetables surrounding a thick brown slice of something rubbery that Lisa, probing it cautiously with her fork, cannot identify. "Beef, I think," Justin whispers. "Meat."

Meat! Simultaneously with the word, the sickening smell of dead animal reaches Lisa's awareness. She drops her fork in disgust and presses the napkin to her mouth to suppress a wave of nausea. "Try to eat just a little," Justin advises sotto voce, looking nervously around him to see if anyone has noticed this display. Lisa shakes her head. Impossible. In fact, watching the meat's juices ooze toward the carrots and the potatoes, she knows she won't be able to eat those, either.

What are the other guests doing? Animal meat hasn't been considered an edible substance for years, surely everybody else must be just as revolted as she is! Well, men are known to be less fastidious, and are probably getting off on the fantasy of being hunters and carnivores, but what about the women? Lisa looks around, but the adjacent tables are occupied by groups of men, and the other couples are too far away for her to see what the women are putting in their mouths. Watching everybody manipulate their utensils, she can see one thing, though. None of the women has a band on her wrist, while all the men do. Why does she feel envious? It's not like the men want the damn HUE bands, they just can't get them off without being electrocuted. There's no logical reason for envy, but Lisa feels it anyway.

Envy, and annoyance at Justin. Look at him, supposedly just forcing down a few bites of the meat to avoid being conspicuous, but in actuality shoveling it down with undeniable gusto, his high-and-mighty HUE band flashing in the light each time he raises a putrid forkful of dead flesh to his mouth. He has already downed more than half of the revolting slab; in quick sleight of hand, he now switches their plates and starts in on her portion. It's a good idea, Lisa can't fault him. A totally untouched meal might attract notice. Only, since when does Justin have the good ideas around here? Since when does he simply make decisions without her prior approval? Lisa stares down at the cooling, congealing, half-chewed chunk of meat on what is now her plate and tells herself that she is being stupid.

And things are about to get much worse.

Following dinner, the host announces, there will be a "social evening." But first the men will gather in the lobby for the next day's group assignment, while the "ladies" proceed to the gathering room, where a special treat awaits them. One of the movement's stars will favor them with his celebrated talk on The Art and Craft of Loving Your Man.

Justin shoots Lisa a worried look, but he needn't be concerned. She has taken herself to task and is on top of things again.

For about three minutes. Until she strolls into the gathering room, takes a seat, glances to the front where a group of handlers is swishing respectfully around a man in a gray jacket, and sees that the man, the movement's star, is someone she knows. Someone she has, with art and craft, loved.

Is Brett.

Brett.

Her Brett.

Pinned to her chair by the shock of it, Lisa finds thoughts racing through her mind. Is he a spy, like her? But wouldn't they have told her? It would have been much easier to send her out with Brett, then, instead of involving Justin. Could Brett actually belong to Harmony? It's confusing, and she needs to think it through.

In the meantime, he mustn't see her.

She has to get out of here.

To a quiet place, where she can think.

And she has to find Justin, to discuss this turn of events with her partner.

Lisa rushes for the door, which fortunately is right behind her, which, unfortunately, is guarded by a thug. "Hey there, miss. Where's the fire?" he asks, barring her way.

"I'm, I, we . . ." Lisa flounders. "I have to . . . I forgot . . . The dining room. I left my, my lipstick, on the table in the dining room. I'll just run and get it," she says, giving the thug what she hopes is a disarming smile.

He just stands there.

"It's my most flattering color," she blathers. "Sunset Scarlet. I'd better run, or I won't be back for the start of the talk. Loving Your Man!" she says. "Can't miss that!"

The thug steps aside.

It's a big building. Lisa heads toward the dining room, in case the thug is watching, then she veers off to the right. Down the hallway, turn left, the sound of voices, yes, she remembered correctly, there it is, there's the reception desk, she's in the lobby. And there's Justin. She wants to run over, grab him, blurt out her terrifying news, and run away. With enormous restraint, she strolls slowly over to him, instead.

"SOS," she whispers urgently, all the while struggling to keep a relaxed smile on her face. "You won't believe who I just—" She stops. A large man has just come out of the office, spotted them, done a double take, and headed directly toward them. Did the thug send a goon?

"And then I noticed that I had lost my lipstick!" she announces loudly, just in case, to reiterate her cover story. It seems flimsy, but it got her this far. The man has reached them, and his initial look of beefy determination turns into a wide smile. He looks her up and down with warm anticipation, as though she were his favorite snack food, then he steps closer and says, "Well now, a pretty thing like you doesn't need to worry about that. Your lips look just great to me, sugar. Now, who are you, and where have you been all my life?"

His face is so close to hers that Lisa can smell the meat on his breath; the decomposing meat, and a yeasty whiff of beer. For an instant, a weird kind of anthropological elation overcomes her, as though she were an explorer, on an expedition, and had suddenly stumbled across a legendary long-lost tribe. He called her a "thing." This beer-guzzling, carrion-eating individual has referred to her as an inanimate object. Women as sexual objects in prerevolutionary linguistic usage—she once wrote a term paper about that!

The man moves his face even closer, startling her out of her academic reverie. She jumps. What to do? Stay with the anthropologist mind-set, definitely.

"I'm here with him," she says, primly, and points to Justin.

It works. The man backs off.

"Well, well, well!" he exclaims. "Justin, my man! That's quite some little lady you've found yourself there, you lucky dog."

His voice is jovial, his message stupidly benign. Why is Justin turning as pale as a sheet?

"It's getting late. We'd better get to the gathering room," he squeaks, barely in command of his voice.

"Oh, what's the hurry?" the other man disagrees. "I thought you'd had enough of meetings! Isn't that why you're here?"

He flings his arm around Justin, who for some reason is squirming and avoiding her eyes, and turns again to Lisa.

"This is a great guy you've got here," he tells her. "He's gonna go far. We live together, didja know that? Yep, that's where I first spotted him, at the good old Residential Suites. Works in the revo-fuckin'-lutionary Ministry, but I guess you know that. We sure love the stories he tells, about that Nadine and the rest of 'em!" He chuckles, gestures expansively, then brings his alcohol-reddened face up close to Lisa's again. "I went out on a limb for this guy," he confides. "Ordinarily, you folks wouldn't be invited to the Center just yet. I vet my guys very, very carefully, but when Justin said he was sick of just sitting around talking, that he was ready to get involved in the real thing, well, I said, Justin, let me see what I can do for you."

Lisa's world goes dark and cold. Her eyes turn to her own personal Pontius Pilate, but he is studiously avoiding her. She notices that it hurts a little to breathe, as though she were suddenly on a cold dark mountaintop, as though a cruel altitude were squeezing her lungs. At the same time, she feels weirdly alert. She feels like a different person, a shrewd person with sharp thoughts.

"That's wonderful," she hears this shrewd person murmur cannily. "Justin is lucky to have a . . . a sponsor like you."

Hope against hope, she waits, to see if maybe she has gotten it all wrong, and his reply will provide some explanation other than Justin's evil, complete, premeditated betrayal.

But the man—who, as you have guessed, is Will—nods solemnly. Lisa feels an icy calm come over her. One last question, and Justin's guilt will be clear beyond a reasonable doubt.

"It must be so difficult to make a decision like that! How long does it usually take you," she asks casually, forcing herself to give Will an admiring look, "before you vet somebody?"

Will puffs up with pleasure, delighted to explain the important process and his important role in it. "It usually takes half a year at least, because I have to look the guys over very carefully. They have a lot of faith in my personal judgment, so what I say goes. But I vouched for Justin here, even though he's only been with our group for what? Four months?"

He turns to Justin for confirmation, but his protégé is oblivious. Frozen with shock, he is trying to send a nonverbal message to Lisa. Unsuccessfully, and who can blame him. "I can explain," he wants to say—try pantomiming that!

"And," Will continues generously, in the absence of a reply, "I'm not the only one who spotted this young talent! Brett Martins picked him out of the crowd, too! I didn't even know until a few days ago that Doc Martins was one of us, but him and your fella were already pals months ago. They hang out together," he relates, with paternal pride, remembering and exaggerating Brett's lone visit to the Residential Suites.

Lisa flinches as though struck, but forces herself to answer normally. "I'm sure your confidence in Justin is well placed," she says brightly, ignoring her former partner's frantic efforts to catch her eye. "Well, if you'll both excuse me for just a teeny little sec, I really do want to find that lipstick. No, Justin, don't come with me; instead, why don't you tell your handsome friend here how we met! That was *so* funny, he'll enjoy the story. See you in a bit!"

That should keep Justin, the Betrayer, the Traitor, busy for a while. Let's see him manufacture a story, Lisa thinks with malice. As soon as she has turned the corner, she starts to run. She has to get out of here. Immediately. It would be better to have a plan, better to have some sort of an idea of where she is and where she's going, better to be able to have it out with Justin, to try and find out just what his intentions were and what his orders are, but it's too risky. Her life, most probably, is at stake. She's in the snake pit, the lion's den. "Gotta get out of here," she murmurs to herself, "have to get out." Repeating this in the rhythm of her running steps, her beating heart, she races down the darkened hallway. She remembers having passed sliding doors and a terrace on the way to dinner—shouldn't they be somewhere in this direction? And this perpendicular hallway, it should lead to the stairs going up to their room. Dare she stop for a moment, to pick up a few things, a bottle of water, a blanket, a jacket, maybe a knife from the kitchenette? No, every second matters. If they catch her, she thinks, bitterly counting Justin among the "they," they'll probably kill her.

With absolutely nothing except the clothes on her back, Lisa finds the sliding doors and plunges into the darkness.

He knows all the sounds of the night. The animals that thrive in the darkness, mating and hunting and prowling while most living things sleep—he knows the hisses of their fighting, the howling of packs preparing for a sortie, the caterwaul of copulation, the warning hoots, and the batting of powerful wings. They have all become smooth sounds to him by now, sinuous sounds, sounds that blend into the familiar night. Not like these awkward, violent calls and crashes that rouse him from his sleep. Even before the human posse comes lumbering through the underwood near his cabin, when they are still a distant noise of twigs snapping and sharply barked commands, he is on full alert.

He doesn't like this, doesn't like unfamiliar incursions into what he has come to consider, over the years, his little kingdom, his private domain. He knows about the Center, of course. He was a little worried when they first constructed it, but it worked out all right. They don't bother him. Don't even seem to know he's there. None of them ever venture this far. They go to the stream to swim, and follow the deer run, to hunt. They never come his way, and they certainly don't rush about in noisy groups in the middle of the night. Something highly unusual must have happened. Pulling on a dark sweater and his shoes, he goes out to investigate.

Panting, frightened, kneeling on a soft bed of pine needles, shivering with cold, Lisa takes a break. She's out of breath, out of ideas, out of her league. She doesn't know which way to go. To survive, she needs to get to the border of Zone Six. That border will definitely be well monitored, and if she can only get near enough to it, Security will see her and come to rescue her. Only she hasn't got the vaguest idea where she is, in relation to that border. That should worry her a lot, but at the moment her time frame is more modest. Right now she just hopes to survive this night without being caught. Daylight may provide some sort of guidance.

Pine is good for the limbic system, she remembers. Crushing a handful of the smooth long needles to her face, she tries to breathe deeply and calmly while she listens for the sounds of her pursuers. She can still hear the posse, but at least they don't seem to be getting any closer. It almost sounds as though their shouts and crashes came from a slightly greater distance, over to the left. Of course, daylight will help them, too, maybe more than it helps her. Should she try to put more distance between herself and her pursuers, or should she try to find some kind of hiding place, maybe a cave or some dense growth?

If only she weren't so exhausted, so frightened, and so lost. Lisa's thoughts stray involuntarily to people in her past. She thinks of Mother McNeill, whose constant odes to the HUE band she took so lightly. How truly the woman spoke, and what a precious thing a HUE band would be, if she could only have hers back on her arm right now.

She thinks of Theresa. Lately, she had started to think that her sister was turning into a fanatic, an embittered woman, much too dogmatic on the subject of men. But Theresa was right. Look where Lisa's own naïve belief in the basically redeemable nature of men has gotten her. Betrayed by the two men she trusted most, by her lover and her best friend, hunted by a murderous posse, she may not live to regret her terrible error.

Finally, Lisa's thoughts turn to Riva. Riva's advice was valuable, too, and again Lisa was too stupid to listen. It would be so comforting, so good right now to have someone to pray to, to feel that some benign superior female force was looking after her. Who was that goddess Riva was recommending? Pele. Shivering, Lisa tries to warm herself with thoughts of Pele, to conjure up the flame-haired goddess of fire and volcanoes.

And behold, a gentle footfall heralds her presence. It's the goddess, responding to this humble supplicant!

Actually, it's not. Twigs snap heavily, and Lisa realizes that this is a mortal, not a divine, presence. Before she can run, her arm is seized, and a gruff voice orders, "Get up!" Not waiting for her to obey, her captor hauls her to her feet, propels her stumblingly forward through the darkness for a considerable distance, drags her to what she can make out as a kind of cottage, and shoves her through the open door. The push lands her up against an interior wall, where she grabs on to a coarsely hewn plank for a moment to regain her balance before whirling breathlessly around to face this new catastrophe.

There stands a stranger, a man, a large, bulky man dressed in black. Through predatory black eyes he regards her impassively.

It has been civilization's gift to Lisa that she has never, in all the years of her existence, been obliged to assess her personal value in terms of her body's combat potential compared to that of a male. But that happy period is over. Studying herself and her opponent through the cold pragmatic lens of the wilderness, Lisa finds herself woefully lacking.

In one corner, ladies and gentlemen, we have an unarmed, untrained, 113-pound individual in a female body with good tone but no real muscle to speak of. Nor is she in possession of any of the compensations a modern world offers to the weak. Missing her HUE band and having recklessly chosen Win-Win Negotiating instead of Wilderness Survival and Small Arms as her fifth and final reeducation subject, she brings pretty much nothing to the table. Well, she has her wits, her verbal skills, and possibly some vestigial feminine wiles. Let's see how far that gets her.

In the other corner we have Him, weighing in at 200 bearded, weather-beaten pounds of male flesh, broad-shouldered, solid, and at home in the wild. A hunter, Lisa grimly concludes, someone geared to strangling, skinning, and then devouring any cute little living thing that blunders into his territory. Such as a rabbit. A doe. Or a startled urban girl.

He resides in Zone Six, which means he has been judged highly and irredeemably perilous to female human beings. He lives alone, probably because he is too fierce and too mean for even the other Zone Six psychopaths to befriend.

Even with the deck stacked this massively against her, Lisa is not ready to give up. She has not been raised to capitulate to brawn. Her wits can yet get her out of this, she believes; her wits, and her social skills. She just has to center herself. She has to blank out the paralyzing terror and free up her brain for some strategic planning.

Lisa struggles to recall the central points of her Win-Win Negotiating course. She remembers that it is essential for her to make the first move, to proactively define their relationship and signal that she is self-confident and stands firm, but is willing to compromise. This leads with dreadful inevitability to the question of what, under the given circumstances, she might be obliged to compromise about: a complicated and uncomfortable question that sidetracks her for essential moments, so that it is not Lisa at all, but her predator, who seizes the initiative.

And elegantly, too. In one smooth, sudden motion he lunges, whirls her around, yanks her arms behind her back, and holds her in a vicious parody of an embrace, both of her wrists twisted together in his left hand and his knee pressed against her to keep her immobilized against the wall while his right hand roams systematically over her body. Through a haze of anger and fear, Lisa is just beginning to register that his touch seems professional rather than aggressive, that he is groping her thoroughly but is not lingering over any of the traditional hot spots, when the inspection ceases.

"Don't move," he orders, still holding her wrists but removing his knee and his right hand. Not applying his order to include her head, she twists her neck enough to see what he might be up to. He is fumbling for something in a drawer behind him, then he pulls it out, a small square box the size of a compu-pad. What can it be but a weapon? What can he be planning to do with it but to hurt her? Lisa decides to go down in glory, fighting. She summons up all her energy for a final burst of resistance, but again he is faster. Propelling her by her wrists and one shoulder, he spins her around to face him, pressing her hard against the wall.

"Don't move," he says again, enforcing his command by pressing the edge of his palm firmly, effectively against her throat. He runs the box down the length of her body, head to toe, left side, right side, and, yanking her forward a few inches, all the way down her back. Then he throws the box down and steps back, releasing her.

"No arms, no surveillance devices," he says, stating the conclusions of his research. "And we're in Zone Six. So you must be an invited visitor, not a Security official or a spy. So you're a Restoration lady. But you're the object of a manhunt. Very interesting. Very, very interesting. Okay, I'm ready. Let's hear your story."

He takes a step back and looks at her commandingly.

It has often been said that our lives are a preparation for the one moment when we will be called upon to show our grit. Are we a man, or a mouse? A woman, or a weevil?

Lisa's contemplation of this philosophical issue is making her captor impatient. He wants the truth, not some story she is concocting at her leisure. His large hand reaches out and knocks her, firmly though not too hard, against the rough paneling.

"Yes?" he says.

Lisa knows how Harmony women comport themselves. How they act. She could do a fair impersonation. She just needs to come up with a quick story about why she's on the lam in Zone Six. A quarrel with her Harmony lover? A jealous triangle?

But these are my thoughts, not hers. Lisa disdains to save herself by such an ignominious charade.

With the planks of the cabin's paneling digging splinters into her back, bankrupt of any personal resources against this superior enemy, Lisa faces her moment of truth.

"I'm not with Harmony," she says, drawing herself up to face the barbarian. "I infiltrated it. I'm a spy. I'm here to fight for the Revolution."

Okay, it sounds a little pompous, but under the circumstances, I think we'll let it pass. Situations like these seem to call forth the melodrama. Give me liberty or give me death.

"The Revolution?" her captor repeats.

"Yes," Lisa affirms with defiance. "In fact, I am an official representative of the Revolutionary Government. Ministry of Thought," she adds. And then she squints her eyes half-shut against whatever may happen next, and awaits her fate.

The predator's hand draws back from her throat. "Really!" he exclaims. "Well, no wonder they've got the dogs out after you!"

Their eyes lock.

Ha, got you! Of course their eyes don't lock. What do you think I'm writing here, a romance novel? No, their eyes don't lock.

Well, maybe they snag a little, like the sleeve of your mohair sweater brushing against the Velcro tab of your running shoe when you bend over to tighten it, leaving a wisp of yellow wool behind as it pulls free.

Maybe he thinks she's brave, all 113 unsubstantiated bluff-and-bluster pounds of her. Maybe she thinks he is beautiful, the hunter's body temporarily in repose, the hunter himself willing, apparently, to engage in conversation, thereby making the playing field substantially more level than it was two minutes ago. We don't need to explore the intricacies of sexual attraction—that's Lisa's assignment, not ours, and even Lisa has other things on her mind right now.

"So," the man says. "You split up to confuse them. How many of you are there?"

How many? Split up? If only, Lisa thinks with a pang. There used to be two, but one of them was a traitor. "There's just me," she says, as the pain and sadness of that thought washes over her.

"They've called out the Marines after just little bitty you?" he inquires, incredulous. "What did you do, bomb something? Kill somebody?"

So Lisa tells him the whole sad story about Brett and Justin, and Harmony and Nadine, and about Cleo and the happy peaceful future now jeopardized by terrorism and subversion. It's a very complicated story, especially for someone who has been minding his own business and living the life of a recluse. He wants to hear it all, so he offers her tea and gives her breakfast. By the time her story is finished, the young woman is pale and fading, and in all decency should be offered a hot bath and a bed, and before you can say "chivalry," she has subtly metamorphosed from a prisoner being held into a fugitive being harbored. A fugitive whose host now knows quite a bit about her, while her information level extends only as far as his name. Alex, he's told her it is, and that's all he's told her. And right now she's too tired to feel much more curiosity than that.

The bathroom is tiled in red clay. There is a wooden tub; containers along its edge hold bundles of pine needles and sprigs of rosemary. This Alex guy, even without the benefit of any reeducational sensitivity courses, evidently has an intuitive gift for aromatherapy and seems to be much in tune with nature. It's still scary, being alone with this total stranger, but so far he's acting civilized. Lisa turns off the water and inserts a cautious hand. Hot, it's fabulously hot. Her silk dress, suitable for the Harmony dinner party but less appropriate for the flight that followed, is ripped in a few places and very dirty, but the slip is fine and she can sleep in it. Worry about mending the dress tomorrow . . . The futon in the adjoining guest room is clean, and the linen sheet is soft, and by the time her host comes along to check on her, his fugitive is asleep. Almost.

Standing in the doorway, Alex studies the apparently sleeping woman. She's very attractive, with her tangled dark hair spread like brambles across the white pillow, her cheeks flushed, and her entire self trustingly unconscious before him. In her stubborn uppityness, she reminds him of his mother, but that thought causes pain and he pushes it away. It feels strange to have a woman in his house; in his house, in his bed, and, the thought fleetingly crosses his mind, in his power. He walks over and squats down beside her. With careful fingertips he touches her hair, which is still damp from her bath. He lifts the blanket to get a better look at her, and a scent of warm skin and rosemary puffs toward him. Her eyelids tighten at the intrusion, but he isn't looking at that part of her body, so he doesn't notice. She is wearing some kind of short, thin shift, an undergarment, and her body is curled in preparation for sleep, but he can see the slight swell of her breasts. Without much thought, he reaches for them. He only intends a gingerly, exploratory touch, but his hand shoots forward on its own and curves to feel the convex shape of her left breast. Immediately, a wave of desire washes over him. Without any involvement from his mind, he can feel his body straining toward the woman, clamoring to fit itself against her contours the way his hand is curled around her breast. He registers this inner mutiny with interest, but doesn't give in to it. He drops the blanket back over her. She shifts and turns away from him.

The man watches her for a few more moments, then he goes downstairs, to his office. He accesses his compucontrol, the one that manages his small but technically sophisticated home, and keys in the command that will electronically lock her room; though he can't hear it from downstairs, he knows that at the touch of the button the bolt on the guest room door will click into place, and the metal jalousies on the windows will lower and lock into their slots, as effectively as bars. Just to be on the safe side, he deactivates all power sources within her room so she won't have anything to tamper with. And with that, though truly asleep now and oblivious to the change in her status, Lisa goes from being a harbored fugitive back to being a prisoner.

Alex thinks about that for a moment, then gets up. You don't survive in the wilderness by being stupid, by being trusting, by believing that an attractive young woman has stumbled into your home by random accident. She told him a story, but that's all it is, an unverified story. He shrugs out of his black outfit, goes to his closet, and studies his other garments carefully. When he emerges from his room, he is a new and completely different kind of man.

Three guys sit on a low wall at the edge of the rifle range, waiting their turn. A fourth one saunters up and drops onto the wall beside them.

"Hey!" he grunts. "Howsit goin'?"

They mumble something.

"Just got here, but I heard about last night. Man, that must have been something. Can't believe they didn't catch that bitch."

The others grunt affirmatively.

"So many guys out looking, and she gets away!" he says in contemputuous wonderment, and finally has goaded them into answering.

"We weren't looking for her that hard," the burly one in the plaid shirt protests. "They said it doesn't really matter where she goes, so long as she doesn't get near the station. And even if she does, they said it won't bother things any, because they're almost positive she doesn't know anything. And neither did the goddamn son of a bitch that got her in here. Now, he's the one I'd like to get my hands on!"

"Oh yeah?" the newcomer interjects, encouragingly.

"Hell, yes." The other man nods, and his friends grunt vigorous agreement. They pass Alex a beer, and soon he knows as much about the two spies, about Valentine's Day and Harmony and the happy days of vengeance to come, as his new pals can tell him.

Lisa wakes up, and instantly the reality of her dilemma floods over her. Escape, capture, reprieve, a stealthy visit from a horny but—so far—restrained host, these things she remembers, but a groggy smog of disorientation remains. What time is it? It's pitch-dark in the room, it must be night. She makes her way to the window, planning to push aside the curtains, but her groping hands encounter something ribbed and hard. That's funny, she doesn't remember anything like that. Where's the control button? On the left? On the right? She can't find it, the window coverings must be centrally controlled from some other switch. Lisa taps her way over to the door, careful not to bump into anything. She thought the door had been left open, but now it's shut.

And jammed, somehow. She pushes it. Looks for a different handle, a latch, a release. Rattles it, but not too loudly. If it's the middle of the night, then perhaps all the rooms are locked, maybe they self-lock, and rattling around on them will needlessly awaken her host. Lisa taps her way back to the window; the darkness is making her feel claustrophobic, maybe there's a way to let in some light. The jalousies are metal, but slightly flexible. She finds that with pressure, they bend just a little. Through a tiny crack, she peers out. Into the bright light of day. The sun is shining.

"Alex?" Lisa calls. She finds her way back to the door, puts her face right up to it, and shouts. "Are you there, Alex? Can you help me? I can't get the door open." She repeats this refrain, louder. She bangs on the door with her fists. There is no reply. Lisa returns to the futon, crawls under the sheets, and pulls the blanket over her head. He's locked her in, and left her here in total darkness. She had thought Alex was nice. She had thought she could trust him. And she had thought Brett was nice, and had loved him. Had believed that Justin was nice, and was her friend. So it doesn't matter what happens to her, not really. Clearly, she's just too stupid to live in a two-gender world.

Lisa lies in the dark for a while. She cries a little. Those reports from Cleo's newspaper-reading sessions roll through her mind in vivid grisly detail. She imagines all the things that might soon happen to her, none of them good. Maybe Alex is planning to turn her in, to return her to Harmony headquarters. Or he might be a psychopathic loner, just as she had initially suspected, who will keep her as his prisoner and do terrible things to her before dismembering her and burying her in the woods. Worse, maybe he's not a loner at all, but intends to share her with his psychopath friends, and has gone to invite them to the torture party. Alternatively, maybe he has simply left. Maybe he doesn't even live here; maybe he has abandoned her here, and this room will become her tomb, and she is doomed to starve to death here slowly in the darkness.

Lisa thinks about her friends. She imagines them eventually learning of her fate, and mourning her. She thinks about her office-mates, and the women who sent her on this mission. They can't be blamed; they warned her that it was dangerous. Maybe she will become a heroine, a martyr. If her end is grim enough, maybe she'll get a little plaque on the mall, somewhere between the suffocated newborn babies and the burnt witches.

Lisa thinks about Cleo. She'll probably never see Cleo again. Besides making her sad, this thought also makes her angry. She can't just lie here sniffling into a futon and waiting for disaster to overtake her. She has more grit than that. There must be something she can do.

Her thoughts stray to Cleo's most recent homework assignment, in Spiritual Guidance class. It was about inner resources in times of tribulation. First the children were supposed to imagine one of three situations: (a) a bad dream, (b) something that frightened them, like heights or dark spaces, or (c) a task they thought was too hard for them. Then they were to choose one of four spiritual weapons from the pagan arsenal: (a) the athame, the magic witches' knife, (b) the elder-wood wand, (c) the cup, or (d) the pentacle. They were to cast a circle, image their chosen weapon, and feel its strength flow into them.

Lisa had refrained from comment, but privately she had thought the exercise a little silly. When you're frightened and in trouble, and facing a task you aren't up to, you need concrete, material help, not magic mumbo jumbo.

So Lisa starts a systematic tactile search of the dark room. She lifts up the futon and feels beneath it, but no one has helpfully forgotten any dynamite there, or a spare HUE band, or a key. She spends at least twenty minutes on the windows, systematically pressing each part of every louver in case there's a concealed button. By the time she reaches the final slat, her fingers are so sore that she can barely pry it aside for a tiny sliver of a look outside.

It's still daylight, that's all she can tell.

Next, she scrabbles around the edges of the room, systematically groping the floor and the walls for objects, switches, or buttons. If she could at least find something to stick between the slats, to hold them pried apart and bring a little light in! On her hands and knees, she works her way toward the middle of the room in careful concentric circles, not missing a single square inch, finding nothing. She moves very slowly, but eventually she arrives at the center.

Well, this is it. This is the end. She has nothing, not a stick, not a pin, not a needle. Just dust, in a dry powdery layer over her fingertips.

Dust, she thinks. When Cleo cast her circle, the first thing she needed was a bit of dirt, to call forth the earth element. Almost of their own volition, her fingers trace a quarter circle around herself. Raising her hand a few inches from the floor, she traces another quarter circle in the air, for the second of the elements. She keeps going, thinking of the sun shining outside, for fire and the third quarter. Water? Ironically touching a fingertip to her wet eyelashes, she completes the circle.

On that homework occasion, Cleo had chosen the pentacle as her weapon. She had closed her eyes, and imagined herself holding it in both hands. Following the instructions on the sheet, Lisa had prompted her niece's imaging effort by asking questions. What color was the pentacle? Was it heavy or light? Was it warm or cold? Cleo had knelt before her on the fuzzy white rug and had reported, with sweetly earnest concentration, that the pentacle was heavy, and cool in her hands. That it gave off sparks, and felt fizzy. That she could feel the sparks like tiny vibrations all the way up her arms. Her shoulders had dropped back as she spoke, her posture had straightened, and a surprised smile had crept onto her face. "I feel it! I really feel something!" she had exclaimed, opening her eyes in delight. "It works!"

"You're not supposed to break out of the image like that," Lisa had reprimanded her, studying the checklist and deflating her niece's enthusiasm with what now, as she recollects the incident, seems an embarrassingly pedantic bit of prissiness. She hopes that Cleo will not remember her that way, as a humorless tedious schoolmarmy nag. This thought makes her eyes tear up again, and to distract herself she decides to finish the exercise, and try the imaginary pentacle for herself. What does she have to lose? It will help pass the time.

I have no comment on pagan rituals. Pentacles, witches' knives, people sharing cups of grape juice and Styrofoam-flavored crackers while imagining it to be the blood and the flesh of the sacrificed son of their god—I have no opinion on any of this, so let me just stick to the facts. One such fact is that Alex has learned quite a lot on his little information-gathering expedition. He has learned that something very major, a cataclysmic event based on a breakdown of the security hardware, severe enough to blunt the power and maybe even end the rule of the current women's regime, is expected to happen on Valentine's Day, a holiday he has not had occasion to remember for many years now. He has learned that after the events of this day, men will again be on the upswing— himself, by extension, included. He has learned that what Lisa told him is true. She is indeed alone, a solitary spy. Also, the day has passed without any sign of a rescue effort on her behalf. As far as anyone can tell, nobody knows where she is, and nobody much cares.

Thus enlightened, Alex returns home to his cabin.

And another fact is that Lisa, who a short while ago was huddled miserably on the bed leaking sad little tears into her pillow and trembling as she envisioned the various ways in which she might soon be martyred, murdered, and abused, now imagines that her arms are tingling with mystical power, that the strong trunk of an elder tree supports her spine, that the energy of nature suffuses her, and that the energetic young goddess Eostar herself is filling her with courage and fortitude.

And finally the profane fact is that, men being what they are, a helpless sobbing terrified victim inspires one set of ideas, about what you might and could do to her. While an equally helpless but composed individual, facing you with dry eyes and her wits about her, is a whole other ball game.

Alex unlocks the door to the guest room, expecting hysteria, remonstrations, and distress. Instead he finds his prisoner seated calmly at the center of the room in what seems to be a posture of thoughtful meditation. She blinks at the sudden brightness, but otherwise appears entirely centered.

"I left for a while," Alex says. "I wanted to check your story out. I locked you in."

Lisa sits inside her circle, hearing his speech without comment.

"But I'm sure you know that," he adds, thrown off balance by her aura of enclosure. "You can come downstairs now," he says, "if you wish."

In one fluid motion, Lisa unfolds her legs and rises to her feet. She looks quite small and bare in her skimpy little shift. Standing opposite her like that, he feels huge, mean, heavy, a bully, a giant ridiculously overequipped for his battle with a wood sprite.

"We could see if any of my clothes fit you," he hears himself offer. Lisa inclines her head. Her demeanor remains cool; is she angry? Alex finds, to his surprise, that he would mind that.

"I hope I didn't scare you. Maybe I should have warned you," he allows.

"Well," Lisa remarks, still aloof, "it was not pleasant. And, of course, I couldn't be sure that you were coming back."

Now he really feels guilty. "You weren't in any danger," he assures her. "There's a fail-safe. Even if something had happened to me, you would have been okay. The door unlocks automatically after forty-eight hours."

A bit later, outfitted in a large sweatshirt and a pair of the thermal underpants he wears in the winter, she is seated in his kitchen and he is sharing the results of his reconnaissance mission.

Lisa relaxes a bit, with her liberty restored and her captor once again benign, but only until she takes in the full measure of his information.

The Harmony men aren't looking for her very hard. That's good news. But her compatriots don't seem to be looking for her at all. That's very bad.

Alex seems inclined to trust her now, to harbor no immediate intention of harming her. That's good. There's about to be a massive counterrevolutionary strike. That's terrible.

She finally has solid information about the plot, including a date, Valentine's Day. Good. Today is the thirteenth, V-Day minus one. Apocalypse now.

And she might be the only one who knows about this imminent disaster. She has to convey a warning, but she doesn't know how. She doesn't even know exactly where she is.

"Are we very far from the border?" she asks.

Alex looks at her thoughtfully and doesn't answer.

There's no way around it. She has to persuade this guy to help her. He has to take her to the border, within hailing distance of Security. And there's no time to lose.

"I'd like to make a deal with you," she says. "As I told you, I work for the government. I'm an official of the Ministry, and I must get to the border. If you help me, I can promise you a significant reward. Whatever kind of reward you want. Money," she suggests, realizing immediately how stupid that is. What would he do with money, out here in the Zone Six wilderness? But maybe he's ready to return to civilization. "If you wanted to come back with me, I could guarantee you a job placement, and an apartment," she promises. "In the light of your service to the nation, I'm sure I can get them to waive the evaluations."

He seems skeptical, but at least he hasn't refused, or laughed. That inspires Lisa to elaborate on her offer.

"You're probably thinking you might not get a very friendly reception. After all, you must be in Zone Six for a reason. You're not here with Harmony, so I guess you were banished. But if you're ready to assimilate, I'm sure I can resolve that. Whatever it was that you did, the Ministry can get you a pardon. I mean, within reason, of course. Unless it was something *too* awful . . ."

Her sentence peters out, the recklessly blurted conclusion hanging in the air. Unless you're a killer. A rapist. Alex has raised one quizzical eyebrow; there is a tiny, sardonic smile on his face.

What did he do, to get himself banished? What should he tell her? Several scary scenarios, with which he could suitably appall her, playfully suggest themselves. Shall he play with her a little? No, nor engage in revelations, either. He has no intention of blabbing out his autobiography.

Go back? Sure. Lately, he's been thinking about that possibility pretty much every day—trying to remember how things had been, trying to imagine how they might be now. Though he had not pictured his return as a Hollywood drama, a political thriller, blazing guns, midnight ride on horseback, with a rescued princess clinging to his back.

The princess, sitting at his table in his underwear, is getting fidgety.

"The border's a good solid hike," he drawls, leaving her other question unanswered. "And getting there won't do you any good. They've obviously found a way to tamper with border security, since they seem to come and go as they please. Those guys I spoke to? The Harmony guys, at the firing range? They definitely weren't worried about border security, or about your reaching the border."

There goes her one and only plan.

"Now, I've got some things to take care of," Alex says, rising from the table. "So I'll have to ask you to stay in your room again. But this time I'll leave the power on and the shades up. And I'll give you something to read. Sorry, but I shouldn't be gone for more than an hour."

Lisa feels her face flush as she realizes his meaning. So much for her status as government representative, Ministry official, and nego-

tiator of deals with Zone Six outlaws; so much for the burgeoning
civility of their interaction. The bottom line is, she can be sent to her
room and locked up at his whim. Lisa nearly loses her temper, but a
fruitless display of anger will only erode her position further. Better
to accede to her incarceration with dignity, pretending not to mind.

Her face carefully neutral, she waits in the doorway while he
retrieves the promised reading material from a shelf in his bedroom. The room is very neat, she notices; he wouldn't have any
trouble passing his Self-Reliance segment. The nightstand and
dresser are clutter-free, and in the adjacent bath, towels can be seen
rolled neatly on wooden racks. Unlike Brett, who leaves the sheets
twirled, the pillows crushed, and the blankets tangled, this man
makes a perfect bed, and an elaborate one, too, with precisely
aligned pillows and a crisply tucked duvet . . .

"Come here," Alex says, not sure which book to offer her, and
turns to find her staring at his bed. She frowns and takes a step backward, then looks angry and walks forward, into his room and right
up to him, and says, "What?" in a combative tone. And Alex looks
angry, too, and gestures impatiently toward the books. He might as
well have made the selection for her, because all she does is snatch
one at random.

Well, it's just a room, isn't it? Just four walls and some furniture. And yet bedrooms can make people nervous. Alex and Lisa,
for example, seem quite tense at each other's proximity, when they
have been just as close in the dining room, and closer on the stairs.

Which is good in a way, because it means that Lisa is actually
glad to retreat alone to her chamber, even if she's locked in with
only an ill-chosen volume of Darwin for company. And Alex is glad
for the fresh air as he sets forth on his errand.

He's a calm, centered person usually, but now he's agitated. A
curious mix of excitement and tension adds a spring to his step. He
even catches himself humming. He makes himself stop, only to find
himself doing it again, a few moments later. It's that song his mother
used to sing, he realizes, the blackbird song. That was so long ago; he
hasn't thought about it for a long time, why is it running through his

mind so persistently now? It must be the woman; she reminds him of his mother, we've already established that. And their situation is primal, just like in the song. How did the words go, again? Something about Eden. Actually, the analogy of Eden has come to him repeatedly over the years—though Eden is a place you're supposed to get banished from, not exiled to. Still, on crisp winter mornings, or sultry summer days, with nothing around him but the humming and buzzing of animals, and the flap of their wings, he has felt like the world's first and only man, inhabiting a pristine, lonely Eden.

Now there's a woman in it.

A woman who interests him a lot.

Her probable thoughts, her origins, her opinion of him, and the kind of world she has come from—all these matters excite his curiosity. He thinks of her as a stranger worthy of much thought, and certainly as a distinct person with her own weight and her own story.

I call that progress. In the Original Eden, face-to-face with a newly arrived female stranger, Original Man breezily assumed that she existed just for him, had been given her life solely for his comfort and convenience.

Because he held a presocial, egocentric view of the world—that's how Alex's father would have explained Adam. Because he was a coward and a manipulator, treating Eve as his inferior when it suited him, but pushing her forward to take the blame when the shit hit the fan—his mother would have added.

He tries not to think about his parents, and the way they used to interpret the world for him from their respective eccentric perspectives, because that makes him sad. But I'm going to tell you about them, while we're waiting for Alex to make his way to his nearest wilderness neighbor. Because, like Lisa, you're probably wondering just how this Alex fellow ended up in Zone Six, anyway.

Alex's father was an anthropologist. Men of that profession can make great fathers, by the way, because they never have any opinions. They just find everything really interesting. His mother made up for that—there was little ambiguity in her moral universe. She had studied theology, and led a congregation for a while, but the endless doctrinal disputes with superiors made her tired, and by the time Alex was born, she was running half a dozen charity programs instead.

Would his parents have weathered the Revolution? Oh, surely. His father would have been in anthropology heaven, buzzing about with his notepad and his recorder, figuring out why who was doing what, and pestering them for their "lineages." And his mother could have had her own church—heck, she could have started her own religion if she wanted to. Though she wasn't really interested in power; she was more the lyrical type, comfortable with solitude. Reading, and counseling troubled souls, and roaming around their backyard or their cabin planting things and singing her blackbird song. Well, we'll never know how they would have liked the Revolution; they missed it, by a hair. By a hair trigger.

There may have been a warning; if so, his mother would probably have chosen to ignore it. Threatening letters, menacing calls, these things were common in her line of work. The stream of battered wives, abandoned pregnant girls, incest victims, and in their wake the comet tail of angry men, men who wanted to kill them, or terrorize them into silence, or scare them into coming back. Those men used to make his mother so sad. She would pray for them, and meditate on them, and search the Scriptures for a way to reach them. Eventually, she would try to discuss them with his father, who would listen gravely, clucking and nodding, and then go off to find a relevant passage in his own scriptures, the works of Richard Leakey or Margaret Mead or Marvin Harris. He would pull out his well-thumbed copy of *Cows, Pigs, War, and Witches* and read:

> If I had knowledge only of the anatomy and cultural capacities of men and women, I would predict that if one sex were going to subordinate the other, it would be female over male. I would expect that the males would be shy, obedient, hardworking, and grateful for sexual favors. I would predict

that women would monopolize the headship of local groups, that they would be responsible for shamanistic relations with the supernatural, and that God would be called SHE.

I don't see how that was very helpful—though it was certainly prescient. But it seemed to cheer Alex's mother up. She would smile, and sigh, and make a few more calls to arrange another job placement and nail down one more donation, and then she would go to bed, and the next day she would wake up in good spirits, filled with hope and energy. As though the world were new again, and this day everyone would be happy and everything would be good. Just like in her song.

Alex wasn't home when the man came. He was out with friends, having a slushee. His father was home, upstairs in his office. When Alex got back, the sidewalk was cordoned off and there were lots of flashing lights, and his father was standing on the pavement looking bewildered, and a large policeman was standing in the hallway of Alex's house, and just behind him there were three lumps on the floor, covered by sheets. His mother, the young woman she had been helping, and the boyfriend who, as his grand finale, had stuck the pistol in his mouth and blown himself away right along with them.

The bewildered look never left his father's face; killing a woman because you wanted her back was, apparently, one tribal custom that he could not get any analytic distance to, not with his own wife standing in the crossfire. He had retreated to their high-tech cabin for a few weeks, to regain his balance; it was almost summer break, so Alex went with him. Then his father decided to stay longer, might as well, nothing to go back to, and work on his book. By then it was time for Alex to get back to his classes, though he couldn't imagine leaving his father alone in the state he was in. Conveniently, the Revolution made that moot. Everything was shut down for nearly three semesters while departments got reshuffled and books reprinted and pedagogy realigned. Rousing himself briefly from slumberous grief, Alex's father asked him to wait that process out, and not be hasty about going back. News of reeducation programs and rehabilitation camps served only to reinforce his view. "Let the dust settle," his father advised, abstractedly.

Contrary to what you might think, it wasn't boring, and his education certainly didn't suffer. There was a lively community out in those hills, in the early years: stranded cityfolk like themselves, sitting things out for a few weeks or months in their vacation homes; some monks; a group of high-level managers who had been in retreat at the lodge of said monks; a few hunters; some reclusive artists; many rednecks. At first, it was actually quite genteel, with a sort of colonial mood to it. You dressed nicely and visited your neighbors, drank tea and cocktails, exchanged rumors and suppositions, and talked about literature and art; it was terribly civilized and educated, as on a tea plantation in Ceylon. And the whole odd-ball assortment came together to clutch the tragically widowed anthropologist and his loyal, loving son to its collective bosom. Alex was missing out on his planned college education? Never mind, it was replaced by a set of eccentric tutorials. He learned how to brew berries into potent alcoholic digestives from the monks, how to quilt from Lucinda Franklin, a querulous eighty-year-old textile artist, and everything about the Punic Wars from her famous historian husband. He learned shooting and fishing and trapping, and trailer repair and satellite adjustment and welding, and how to teach a dog to catch a Frisbee, from the rednecks; and how to make out, from their daughters. The managers left early on, but not without showing him how to better invest his father's portfolio.

As time went by, though, more and more of the folks went back. Groups that included women went first, figuring they'd be okay. Most of the white-collar remainder eventually followed, deciding to take their chances with the new regime in order to get their lives back. The nature of the community changed substantially once all the women were gone. And it was a little eerie, because when people left, they basically disappeared, as if they had died; the consensus was that it was just too risky to exchange messages. Were they okay? Were they able to reclaim their homes, their property, and their jobs? If they had to "complete the reeducation process," as bulletins announced, what exactly did that mean? Then the Zone Six security perimeter went up, and the shopkeepers and grocers closed down and moved out, because they couldn't get their supplies in anymore, and the convicts started arriving. As they came, the community drew back ever farther into the remote uncharted wilds.

The good news is Alex's father, who seems abruptly to have rounded a corner. One day, a few months ago, he announced that this community of theirs was really quite fascinating. Interesting and unique. And if he didn't document it, who would? He'd gotten all excited, and then he'd raced over to their historian neighbor's place, and they had spent the afternoon refining his hypotheses. Then, two weeks ago, he'd packed his bags and off he'd gone to do "fieldwork." It should take about six weeks of good solid research, he had announced jauntily. He needed to catalogue all the inhabitants of their rural outback and get their stories. When he got back, he had announced a little tremulously, with his field notes complete, maybe they should talk about the future.

The historian neighbor, that's who Alex has gone to see. Because things have abruptly become unpredictable, and just in case something happens to him or he has to leave, someone needs to keep an eye out for his father.

Relations between Lisa and Alex remain uneasy after he has freed her once again. In silence, they pursue their own thoughts. Lisa's focus exclusively, and with increasing despair, on her dilemma. She can't just sit here while her world blows up. She has to act—but how?

If only they hadn't taken away her HUE band, she thinks, miserably. Serendipitously. Because with that thought a new plan pops into her head. Harmony men all wear HUE bands, which they have not been able to deactivate. If you could get close enough to one of them, you could push *his* panic button. That ought to be doable! She knows, thanks to Alex's foray, that there are outdoor locations where you can find a Harmony guy. Like the firing range. You don't necessarily have to enter their headquarters, which would require you to pass vigilant doorway guards.

Taking another stab at her negotiating effort, she shares this plan with Alex. He really should go for this new and improved offer, she thinks. He doesn't even have to *do* anything except point her in the direction of the Harmony shooting range. But no, Alex doesn't like this plan, either. A lot can go wrong, he believes. The men might recognize her; after all, they've been looking for her. And as she describes it, that HUE band thing isn't just a simple matter of pushing a button; you have to slide back a lid, then depress the button for three full seconds. They might realize what she's doing, and push her away before the alarm goes through. At the very least, they'll notice once she's done it. That will make them very angry, and if they get angry enough, they'll kill her. Maybe they won't want to compound their offense by committing a murder, but maybe they'll be too furious to care.

Lisa agrees that there are risks. But the bottom line is, she's willing to try it.

And the bottom line is, he won't allow it.

Won't allow it? Excuse me?

"You're on my territory," he says, stubbornly. "I'm not letting you go charging off into an entire campful of men with a half-baked plan like that. And don't try to sneak out of here during the night," he adds. "I won't lock you in your room, but when I go to sleep I *will* lock the perimeter."

What he doesn't say is, her plan has given him a stomachache, a deeply horrible déjà vu pain in his gut. Is he supposed to stand by and watch yet another good-doing woman get herself shot?

Lisa is silent, rage building inside her. He "won't let her"—well, that's just unbelievable. So now, along with being her jailer, he's appointed himself her guardian as well? What's next?

"Look," he says. "I'm not saying I won't allow you to get help. I tell you what—I'll think about it."

His statement entirely fails to improve Lisa's mood. On the contrary, cold resolve grows inside her as she feels her birthright slipping away. Isn't that part of why they had a Revolution? So that no adult woman's considered will could ever again be brushed away with a casual "I'll think about it"?

Steadily, she takes his measure. He looks pleased with himself, thinks he's being reasonable. If she's going to assert herself, stronger medicine is called for. What is she going to do?

Well, she could seduce him. Like those women in the books she's been reading. Given the fact that he's apparently been all alone here for a long time, deprived of female companionship, and judging from the way he's been looking at her, and groping her when he thought she was asleep, and getting all hot and bothered when she's in his bedroom, that might not be too hard. How do those Romance heroines go about it? They flutter, they're weak, they're confused, they're distracted, they're shallow, and then they strike. If Amber and Shanelle and Garnet and Flusilla and Glamorella and whatever-thehell they're all called can do it, she can, too.

"I guess you're right," she says nicely. "I do tend to be impetuous. And these last few days have been so crazy, I'm probably not thinking straight. If it's okay with you, I think I'll go to bed now. Tomorrow morning, after you've thought about it, we can talk again. Good night, Alex," she says, touching his arm lightly in parting, before stumbling over the leg of the table, and having to steady herself by grasping his thigh, which tenses gratifyingly under her touch, electrified. "Oh!" she exclaims, pulling her hand back quickly as though she, too, had felt a charge. "Sorry," she whispers, with a flustered smile that turns into a self-congratulatory smirk as soon as she turns her back on him. So far, so good. This is easy.

In the bathroom mirror, she tries to remember her long-ago conversation with Xenia. It seems like a hundred years have passed since she sat on the park bench with that traitor. What was it that Xenia had said, about her face? Sallow. Lisa fluffs her hair and rubs her cheeks. She rinses her mouth with a drop of cinnamon oil. She takes off the borrowed clothes and slips back into her little shift.

In the bedroom, she adjusts the shades to let in a sliver of moonlight. She thinks about other romantic accessories, all unavailable here: candles, fragrance, music, atmosphere. Well, judging from the way his muscles twitched and his face flushed when she touched him, Alex won't require such frills.

She stands at the window for a moment, looking out. It feels strange, to anticipate sex like this, so deliberately, with a near stranger. It feels like some weird kind of honeymoon from an era long and thankfully past. It feels primitive, a little scary, surprisingly exciting.

Unbidden, the murderous mirror images of dung fly Melvin and the female mantis pop into her head. One could hang their twin portraits above the bed, Lisa thinks, a grim His and Hers of love.

Alex is in his bedroom now, almost directly below hers; she can hear him walking around, opening and closing drawers. She waits. She can hear water running: he's taking a shower. The insulation is bad in this house; she hears the water, the clanking pipes. More footsteps. Finally, there is silence. She makes herself wait for another half hour. Then she screams.

Not too loudly. A soft scream, and she has to repeat it three times before she hears her housemate come lumbering up the stairs and along the hallway, hurrying at first, slowing down as he approaches her door, which she has left ajar, not closed.

"Lisa?" he calls. "Are you okay? Lisa?"

She moans again, twists into scrambled sheets as though just emerging from sleep, and struggles to a sitting position.

"Is something wrong?" he repeats, concerned, in a whisper.

"Alex," she says, putting relief into her voice. "It's you! I must have been dreaming."

Collapsing against her pillow with a shudder, she stretches one hand weakly toward him; thus encouraged, he comes closer and sits on the edge of her futon.

"Isn't that silly?" she says, smiling bravely. "I dreamed that I was locked into a tiny, tiny room. Bricked in! In total darkness, and running out of air. I couldn't breathe!" she waits a judicious moment, in case he is slow on the uptake, so that he can make the necessary association between this nightmare and her earlier experience of imprisonment, and feel guilty for the trauma he has inflicted.

"Feel my heart," she says then, pulling his hand to her chest with a self-disparaging little laugh, and silly her! getting anatomically confused and not finding the right spot, and having to use his hand to pad searchingly *all* across her left breast before finally locating her perfectly normal heartbeat right there just below its soft swell. He's into breasts, she knows that much from his earlier transgression. Still, is this maneuver too transparent? Is she overshooting the mark? Apparently not; Alex appears paralyzed, his limp hand obedient to her guidance.

"I woke you!" Lisa now exclaims. "I'm so sorry."

Alex mumbles something. She has withdrawn her own hand, but he continues to monitor her heartbeat for a few unnecessary moments before realizing where his hand is, and pulling it back.

"It was such a terrible dream . . ." Lisa murmurs. "And I just can't seem to shake it. I know this is silly, but . . . do you think you could hold me, just for a moment, until I collect myself?"

It's not entirely a lie. It's surprisingly comforting, to have his bulkier weight depress the mattress, a hard arm encircle her, a deep voice mumble reassuringly into her ear before her mouth, turning to find his, distracts him and his words fade away into a kiss. A halting, tentative kiss, before it heats up and his weight shifts on top of her, and their limbs entangle, and they are grabbing each other in hot and heavy preliminaries, and her shift and his shirt are being pushed this way and that to allow more skin to touch other skin. But then all of a sudden he breaks away and rolls over, to the far edge of the mattress, and looks grim, and smacks himself on the head with the heel of his palm.

"I'm sorry," he says. "I didn't mean to grab you like that. First I scare you and make you have nightmares, then I attack you—I'm really sorry. I don't know what's gotten into me."

Isn't that sweet? Lisa sits up, smiles at him kindly, then slithers over to embrace him, coming to rest with half of herself on top of him.

"Don't apologize," she says. "I liked it." She kisses him, an aggressive kiss, and lets her knee slide down between his legs.

"I don't know about this," he mutters. "Are you sure?"

They kiss some more, and after a while he is on top, and then she is on top, and then it starts to get hard to know who is where, and at some point his mumbled ethical reservations cease, and he no longer offers to stop, and Lisa might kill him if he did. She hasn't felt quite like this for a long time, maybe ever. For one regretful instant, she thinks of all the time she has wasted on Brett, when obviously *this* is the way it's supposed to feel.

With the man's breath uneven against her neck, and their bodies in a fluent agitated hostile starting-to-be-exhilarating exchange, she is distracted by one last thought. Weirdly enough, she thinks of the mantis. If you were an insect, could you lose some limbs and parts of your head, and not realize right away that your partner was not just sort of violently blurring with your body, but actually consuming pieces of it? Because just right now, even she with all her human neurons and brain lobes really isn't entirely sure where exactly she begins and ends.

But then she lets herself slip into the vortex, and for a blissful few moments her whole body locks into place around her partner's, and she doesn't think at all. And we'll observe a moment of discretion and silence, after all the ordeals this poor woman has recently been through, to let her enjoy her insect animal moment of pleasure and catch her breath.

All too soon, our heroine must disengage, reluctantly regain her contours and collapse onto the blanket beside her partner still damp and breathing fast, and still not thinking, while he turns his head drowsily toward her and kisses her shoulder, and finds her hand and interlaces their fingers and mutters something friendly.

It's not so bad, this espionage and seduction thing. She wouldn't mind staying right here, and doing this again tomorrow.

"I feel so warm," Lisa says, after a while. "Are you thirsty? I'll bring us a drink. I'll be right back," she says. He makes to sit up, but she rubs his hair affectionately, pushing him down into the pillow, and he drops back. Barefoot, pulling her shift around her, Lisa scampers out the door, so ebulliently that it just happens to click shut behind her.

Instead of going to the kitchen, Lisa pads into Alex's office. She moves with confidence. How hard can it be for someone from a high-tech security-obsessed civilization to figure out the serviceable but hardly cutting-edge electronics of someone who's been stuck out here in the boonies? Not very hard. And there's little risk. If it doesn't work, Lisa can always go upstairs and slip back into bed.

But it does work. Two and a half minutes later, if one were listening very carefully, and not drowsily floating in a tangle of sheets and pillows and satiation like Alex, one could make out a soft clicking sound at the windows and another at the door, as the bars slide into place, the louvers lock, and the power supply shuts down.

And Lisa really does feel hot, from sex or from sabotage, so after locking Alex into his guest room, and commandeering the rest of his security system and ha! defeating his much-vaunted perimeter defense with ease, she finally does proceed to the kitchen for a large, cold drink.

She feels bad, a little. It's a considerable modification of the accepted seduction scenario to jump right up, rush downstairs, and put your lover behind bars. It's not a very nice thing to do.

And if she was going to do it, then probably she shouldn't have let things go so far. She could have gotten thirsty earlier on. It was enough to lure him into her bedroom, it wasn't necessary to actually sleep with the poor guy. But he might have been more suspicious then, he might have insisted on accompanying her to the kitchen, really the success of the mission required her to follow through. She chokes on her last sip of water, which serves her right for being such a liar. Admit it, she orders herself. You slept with him because you wanted to. It was self-indulgence, pure and simple. Because things have been so scary, and it felt wonderful to let yourself go for a little while, in that archaic safe proximity of a man. She holds the cool glass against her cheek for a moment and wishes things were different, that she could just go back upstairs, snuggle up against that man, and sleep.

Or she wishes it would suffice to have seduced him, and that they could now be soul mates and set forth together to save civilization. The way it happens in those books. In the books, the earth moves, the skies open, and the lovers are permanently transformed, especially the men. In the books, sex with the heroine is so cataclysmic that the man's very personality melts down, and he rises from the bed utterly reconstructed. If before he was evil, promiscuous, and cruel, he will henceforth be devoted, faithful, and kind. One orgasm, and the guy is putty.

Lisa is reluctant to stake her life, not to mention the survival of her society, on her ability to duplicate this effect. The sex was good, but in the intervening five minutes she's got her brain back again, and there's no reason to suppose he hasn't.

Leaving the kitchen, she walks through his recently abandoned bedroom into the bath, which is still steamy from his earlier use, and drops her shift. Should she take a shower? The plumbing is noisy, as she remembers, and the sounds will rouse him; it seems better to let sleeping lovers lie. True, he's locked in, but still she would rather think of him drowsily waiting for her in bed than hear him pounding on doors and walls in premature awareness of her perfidy. She turns on the faucet instead and wipes herself with a damp towel. It's perfunctory, but that's okay. In some odd superstitious way, it makes her feel stronger to keep a little bit of his smell on her. It feels like a charm, like a totem. Not to overdo it: he has a bottle of lime water and witch hazel; she splashes that on the towel and rubs it all over herself.

She knows where he keeps his gear. She assembles an outfit, long black underwear as leggings and a cashmere sweater on top. If she rolls up the pants at the waist, it looks almost like a dance outfit, and the loose top covers the slight bulge of elastic at her midriff. The gray sweater comes down nearly to her knees, like a tunic, but the thin soft wool makes it easy to push the sleeves up to a comfortable length. The V neck dips rather too low between her breasts, but that's fine for this purpose. It's good. She looks good.

She brushes her hair, ties it back, then changes her mind and leaves it loose, to skim her shoulders. Remembering her makeover session with grim irony, she rummages around his cabinets for further embellishment. He has some medicinal kohl; she smudges it carefully around her eyes and into the crease. He has a vial of bayberry antiseptic; mixed with a dab of Vaseline, it serves to stain her lips a brownish carmine red. There. Standing before the mirror, she pronounces her effort a success. To the unschooled male eye, she will look like a fashionable woman, newly arrived from the city, who could not possibly be that evil Lisa, the target of their womanhunt, a fugitive who has been hiding in shrubs and bushes and must by now be scruffy and ungroomed.

Alex half wakes from his semi-sleep and reaches groggily for the woman, who isn't there. Tap tap, his hand blindly searches for her, but no, she's nowhere in this bed. Then she's probably gone to the bathroom, though there's no light on and he doesn't hear her; well, she'll be back. Sleep has almost reclaimed him when a sudden nasty thought jolts him awake. Could he have been wrong? Did he misread her signals? Well, he couldn't have misunderstood her in the beginning, she was an eager participant and no doubt about it, but events did overtake him rather quickly after that. After all that abstinence, and with the undeniable exceptional attraction he feels for her, it's possible that he got carried away and missed something crucial. Did she change her mind somewhere along the way, and he failed to notice? That would be terrible, to have abused someone who essentially is his prisoner. Is she huddled downstairs in some lonely corner, feeling angry, put upon, and upset? He'd better go see. Raising himself to his elbows, he taps the light, which fails to go on. Proceeding to the entrance in darkness, he calls her name, pushing confidently against the door and finding it to be very locked and very unyielding.

He comes to rest with his back against the wall and recognition dawning. She's gone. And she is conversant with electronic security, or she couldn't have imprisoned him, so the perimeter lock will be no challenge for her, either. She's halfway to wherever she wants to be, and this is what she thinks of his condescending promise to "think it over" . . . He almost gets very angry, but instead he laughs. He underestimated her; he shouldn't have.

Having strapped together a compact but comprehensive back-pack—thermal blanket, nutritabs, hygiene kit, filtration bottle, luminator, insect repellent—Lisa sets out into the night. Alex's description of high-tech target ranges gives her hope that a few men might be out rehearsing their infrared skills even at this late hour. If not, she plans to camp out near the firing range, dozing propped up in a seated position to preserve her grooming effort, until dawn, when the first eager beavers are sure to appear.

On her way out, she touches the doorjamb to thank the house for its hospitality, and gives a brief thought to its owner. Hopefully, he is fast asleep upstairs, and will not wake before the morning. Hopefully, he will summon up the inner resources, and probably the rage and hate, to carry him through the forty-eight hours of his confinement, until the system auto-releases him.

Alex, as we already know, is not asleep. The dim outline of his home is just vanishing into the darkness behind Lisa when he rouses himself and discovers his situation. She has just stopped for the first time, to shift the weight of her backpack, when he recovers from his first surprise and swings into action.

When Lisa found herself imprisoned for the first time, earlier on, and knelt at the center of the room drawing enchanted circles and holding imaginary pentacles, we might have taken her for a witch. Alex, now, acts the wizard. With dark deliberation, he paces the room, coming to stand in one particular spot. He raises his right hand, and his left, as though feeling for invisible currents. Then he chants. His performance is interspersed with claps and some stomping, and requires two changes of direction. It is chilling. It would be hard to duplicate, even after you heard it once or twice. Is it an invocation to some pagan god? A curse, called down on the perfidious woman who bedded him with deceptive intent and then abandoned him to darkness?

Actually, it's a Navajo dance.

You don't want to fall victim to your own gadgets; you don't want to get yourself locked in, not even for forty-eight hours, and you certainly don't want your absentminded, grieving father to accidentally imprison himself when you're not home. What code can Dad easily remember that will be difficult for anyone else to crack? A segment from one of his early field studies.

Tribal societies are responsive to ritual; appropriately programmed security systems are, too. Alex claps, stomps, turns, and chants, and bars rise, louvers loosen, locks draw back.

He goes downstairs. His formerly pristine bedroom suite looks as if a marauding tribe has passed through. It's a mess. Someone has used his kohl, and a trail of the sparkling black powder spills across the bathroom counter. Someone has plundered his aftershave, spilled his bayberry, stolen his aconitum, and rummaged through his wardrobe and other possessions, discarding what they could not use. Seduced, abandoned, and robbed, Alex has every right to be angry. As Lisa's lover—technically speaking—I suppose he also has a right to worry about her. He feels all of that, but mostly he finds himself suffused with a weirdly elating buoyancy and excitement. After all these quiet years, life is about to take an exciting turn. And he has options, important options.

He can pursue the woman and stop her. That will increase the likelihood that the plot will go forward and the Old Order be restored. Then he can return to a world much like the one he left so many years ago, a world friendly to men, and sympathetic to a returning diehard male exile and his father.

Or he can do nothing and let the chips fall where they may. Maybe the girl will succeed in warning her cohorts, maybe she won't. Maybe it'll make a difference, maybe it won't.

Then there's his third option. He can go after her, and help her.

That option is the haziest. After all, he knows what the old world was like. And he knows what it's like to stay out here in the wilderness. But when he tries to picture the Revolution, his imagination can only populate it with a series of Lisas—a bunch of idealistic, slightly pompous, rather tentative, highly entertaining young women. And apparently, when they want something from you, they seduce you.

Cheryl Benard

While the Harmony men, in their efforts to persuade, are just as likely to shoot you dead.

He walks into his closet to dress.

While he's doing that, suppose we go and see what's been happening with Justin.

When we left Justin, as you will remember, he was in what Lisa supposed and hoped would be a very embarrassing position, obliged to fabricate an amusing story about how they met, but he extricated himself with no trouble at all. What has he been doing for the past weeks but reading books about women meeting men in romantic, unlikely, often comical ways? Unlike Lisa, who skimmed them quickly in search of the pruriently pertinent paragraphs, Justin always lingered, enjoying the sentimental parts. His mind is absolutely loaded with fluffy, frothy, frilly stuff. A love scene? He can pull one out with the ease of plucking a tissue from its box.

And Will is hardly a discriminating audience.

So Justin rattles off a scenario, then excuses himself. He puts a lot of effort into seeming relaxed, but inside he is combusting with panic. He needs to catch up with Lisa, ASAP. As fast as he dares, he makes his way to their room, hoping to find his partner, but she isn't there. Now what? He can't search the entire building. She'll come back to the room eventually. She has to, all her things are here. And where else can she go? So the thing to do is to wait.

Justin is still pacing restlessly around their room when the first alarm goes off. Within minutes, the building is a beehive of activity. A woman is "missing," according to the loudspeakers; some girl made a run for it, is the hallway version. Security has set out after her, and the rest of the men are forming teams to help.

He can't stay in his room. If they know who the missing woman is, they'll know she came with him. This room is the first place they'll look . . . but halt. I'm getting the order wrong and being unfair to Justin. Let the record show that before he started worrying about his own neck, he fretted extensively over the safety and well-being of Lisa. Why did she have to run off like that! Why didn't she give him a chance to explain! What will happen to her now! Etc., etc. Just imagine another half page of worrying, interspersed with exclamation marks, and you will possess insight into Justin's thoughts. He would help her, if he could. Since he can't, it's really only human to worry about his own survival.

He decides to try and blend into the crowd. Probably it would be best if he joined a search party, but he doesn't have the heart to do that. Instead he rushes busily up and down the hallway for a few minutes, seemingly about to join up with this or that group.

Then he ducks into a dark corner. He knows what he has to do. It's obvious, really. If ever there was an emergency that called for HUE, this is definitely it. On the other hand, if Security comes, this will turn into a battleground. Won't he get shot? His finger hovers over the band. Another group goes thudding by. Justin sees that they are armed.

The buttons are protected by a cover. He slides it back. He takes a deep breath. He pushes the red alert button good and hard, too hard, the way civilians unaccustomed to guns will pump the entire cartridge into their opponent and go on shooting, long after he has fallen. Finally he removes his finger, and the spring on the lid slides it shut.

It is an enormous letdown when nothing happens, even though Justin had to know that nothing would. It will take hours for a response team to arrive, though presumably they will react top priority, and massively, when they see the location of the call.

Justin hears another group approaching. This one moves more slowly, men fanning out to shine the bright beam of their flashlights into corners and crannies. Justin can see streaks of light illuminating the hall a hundred yards away; then he hears the familiar voice of Will, calling his name. "Justin, hey guy, where areya, I needya!"

That sounds friendly enough. Maybe they won't hold him responsible for Lisa. Besides, they're going to find him anyway, in another few moments they will be passing his niche, and he won't be able to elude them.

So he replies. "Over here," he shouts, as jovially as he can manage. Will approaches with a smile, extending an arm for his signature backslap, but suddenly he lunges, and several of the other men do, too, and Justin finds himself pinned to the floor in a death grip. It goes so smoothly that they must have choreographed it. One man sits on his chest and leans a heavy arm against his throat. Another has his legs captive under 230 pounds of body weight. His hands—they are, in addition, the subject of much excited yelling, and loudly barked orders. "Get the hands!"

What's the big deal with his hands? Face contorted with pain as the boots grind his fingers against the floor, Justin groans in understanding. The HUE band. They're trying to prevent him from activating his panic button, not knowing that he has done so already.

As he feels his skin scraping off the bone, Justin tries to figure out if their error is a good thing or a bad thing. Before he can decide, he is being grabbed under the armpits and lifted to his feet; his wrists and fingers remain held in a relentless grip. Justin tries to think. What would he do now, if he were innocent? He would get angry.

"What the fuck are you doing?" he yells.

Well, that was the wrong thing to say.

"We know all about your goddamn so-called girlfriend," one of the men yells back with equal ire, a chorus of furious voices joining his. As they speak, they are pulling him forward, awkwardly, to maintain their hold, and an uneven mobile sort of dialogue ensues, with Justin issuing denials and everyone else barking accusations, and the whole group lumbering along the corridor crabwise, until one of the voices takes things up a notch.

"Let's kill the back-stabbing son of a bitch," the voice proposes.

Assenting murmurs deem this a good idea.

"At least let's hack off his goddamn band and see what happens," another suggests.

"Innocent until proven guilty," Will growls.

They have arrived at their destination, where more men are busy rigging up some kind of a contraption. Mittens are pulled over

Justin's hands and fastened tight around each wrist with a strip of Velcro. Next he is fitted with two pairs of handcuffs, one for each wrist. The second ring of each pair is attached to the contraption, until Justin finds himself crucified, arms stretched wide. With the backs of his hands bleeding into the mittens, he hangs there, stigmata and all. Bringing to mind Jesus, or, if you prefer, his much older historical predecessor, the young harvest god who was sacrificed every fall and rose up again in the spring—an outcome Justin is unlikely to share.

Will steps up to him.

"I don't want to think I was wrong about you, buddy," he says. He looks at Justin for a long moment, until the younger man, surprised to find himself overcome by shame, averts his eyes.

"Okay, guys, here's the deal," Will now announces, to the assembled men. "If he's got anything to say, he's not gonna say it voluntarily. We can pound it out of him, but I'm not doing that unless I'm very damn sure he deserves it. So here's how it's gonna be. He's gonna stay right here, where he can't do any damage. Nobody touches him. It's only a matter of time before we catch the government girl, and when we do, we'll know a lot more. Maybe she tricked him," Will suggests, and the men nod. Sure. That's true. Women trick you. Everybody knows that.

The group breaks up. Will leaves last. Before he goes, he walks over to Justin. "Hey, J.," he says. "Buck up, guy. I don't think you double-crossed us. I believe in you, buddy." He pats him gently on the arm, then he leaves. And only Justin remains, feeling so lousy inside and out that he expects he might die of it.

Several hours pass. There is no sign of rescue. Justin is beyond miserable. The backs of his hands hurt a lot. He can feel shredded, ripped pieces of skin hanging over raw bands of flesh. Blood has seeped into the fiber of the mittens, forming a gluey bond that tears open his wounds with each involuntary microscopic twitch, sending waves of agony through him. And that's just the pain; what about death? If the search party finds Lisa before the response team arrives, and if they force her to talk by whatever horrible means they have been alluding to, the details of which he would rather not contemplate, then they'll interrogate him next, and after that they'll probably kill both of them.

How did he get himself into this? Actually he didn't, Justin reflects with much self-pity and some justice. Lisa got him into it. But not really. That superficial involvement would have been survivable, had not Violet, the lovely enchanting seductive Violet, lured him deeper. Violet, the thought of whom fills him with tender longing even now, while another part of him reflects that, had he never met her, he wouldn't be hanging here.

What's up with Violet, anyway? Well, as a matter of fact she's thinking about Justin at this very moment. She feels a little bit of residual guilt for manipulating him into his espionage role, for goading him into the lion's den. Is he managing okay? But at least he's on the right side, and if he gets in trouble, well, he's got his HUE band. All he has to do is push a button.

And when he does?

"Your guy just put out an SOS," Gemma reports to her commanding officer. "You know, Justin. Your spy guy."

"That's fine," Nadine says.

"So what do you want us to do?"

"No action is required," Nadine says.

"But wasn't there a female operative with him, too?" Gemma asks. "Do you think she might be in trouble as well?"

"It's all under control, thank you," Nadine says.

Gemma shrugs. Fine. She's got enough other stuff to worry about.

That brings us up to date on Justin. On Violet. And on Nadine, Person One in the triumvirate—no, I guess you can't have a triumvirate if you're three women, not if you've learned your Latin.

Meanwhile, back in Zone Six, Lisa approaches the target range in a crouch. It's just after midnight. An adrenaline surge, tinged with apprehension, rushes through her as the movement of distant shadowy figures indicates that at least a few men are still out there, taking night-vision potshots at dim targets. Lisa is totally psyched. Fear has turned her entire self into a high-strung monitoring device. All her senses are raw, and she is agonizingly aware of every sound and every motion around her. Alex, intent on following her trail of occasional footprints and broken twigs, overshoots his mark before he knows it, and feels his own stolen handgun at his neck.

"Hey!" he protests. "Put that away. I came to help you."

She hesitates.

"If you want," he adds. "If not, I'll leave. But I'd rather stay." He raises his hands cautiously in the universal gesture of harmless intent.

She decides to trust him. In fact, to be honest, she's relieved that he's here.

"Still the same plan?" he asks.

That's right. She plans to walk up to the men, engage them in conversation, pick out one of them to flirt with, move in closer, and make a grab for his wrist.

Alex nods judiciously, in order not to set her off again, but he still thinks it's risky. The men might recognize her. Even if they don't, she will need to get really close to one of them. She'll have to work the situation so it will seem natural for her to touch his arm. Then she has to find the cover, slide it away, push the button, and hold it down for three seconds without having the guy realize what she's up to. That's only possible if things are getting pretty hot and heavy between them. And what about afterward? At some point he'll realize what she's done, and he'll be irate.

It seems she's thought about that part, at least, since their last conversation.

"They'll know Security is coming," she argues. "They'll know that they're about to be arrested for sedition. They won't want to compound it by making it murder."

Yes, it could work. But he doesn't like it. It's dangerous. "I have a better idea," he whispers. "It looks like there's only three of them. I can take them out before they even realize what hit them. Then it'll be safe to move in and use the alarm on their HUE bands. After that we can go back to my house and wait for the response team to show up."

It takes a moment for Lisa to translate the euphemism. Take them out? Out where?

"You can't just kill innocent people!" she protests in horror when she figures it out. His face is close enough that she can see his eyebrow do a sardonic rise at the word "innocent."

"No!" she orders, as emphatically as she can.

He gets mad. "Look," he drawls. "I respect your sensibilities and all that. So why don't we say you tried to talk me out of it, and I didn't listen. I'll try not to kill them," he lies. "I'll just injure them a little, so they can't run away."

Actually, he plans to sharpshoot, onetwothree, before they can return his fire or call for help.

And he is starting to get mad. This is ridiculous. What are they doing here, squatting behind some bushes, having an ethical debate?

"How many scruples do you think these guys have about what they're planning to do to *you*?" he hisses, harshly. "You want to run the world?" he adds. "That takes guts. If you can't stand the heat, get back in the kitchen. And what kind of revolution was that anyway, if whenever you've got a problem with a guy, your first idea is to throw a little sex at him? Do you still have a term for that, or is it just your standard operating procedure?"

Okay, that's not nice, and Lisa gets angry back. "Yeah, and what about your idea? Someone's in your way, so you kill them? Yeah, that's brilliant, and so original. The world was a great place when you guys were running it on that principle."

She doesn't even know how below the belt that one is.

You know the joke about the rabbi and the quarreling couple? First the rabbi listens to the man, and tells him he's right. Then he hears the woman's side, and he tells *her* that she's right. And when a bystander protests that this can't be, they can't *both* be right, he agrees with the bystander, too.

Alex is right, I think. It's a little sleazy, and not really very honorable, to solve your problems by offering, or seeming to offer, sex. And Lisa is definitely right: it's quite horrible, and really very barbaric, to solve things by extinguishing your opponent's sad, brief, mortal life.

So we've got two time-tested recipes here, courtesy of Gender One and Gender Two, and frankly, neither is very appealing.

How incredibly lucky that at that very instant, that historic instant when our two templates of humanity take a good hard look at their respective problem-solving strategies and rear back in horror, fate should step in.

There is a hissing noise, followed by three dull pops. One by one, the men on the shooting range tumble to the ground.

Alex drops flat to the ground, aghast, unceremoniously yanking Lisa down beside him. Where is the assassin? He waits, he listens, but there is nothing; no footstep, no rustle, no motion. He taps Lisa to get her attention, and she lifts her head. With a supplicating gesture that sues for a truce and begs her cooperation, he signals her to be silent and remain exactly where she is.

He creeps into the arena and over to the recumbent men. Still there is nothing, no sound from anywhere around him.

Placing his hand cautiously on the back of the first one, he detects movement, the rise and fall of his chest. He checks the others. They're alive. There's no blood on them. He can't see any injuries.

"Lisa," he calls. "Please. Quickly. I don't know what's going on, but we'd better get that alert out. You do it. I'll keep us covered."

Lisa comes at a run. Choosing an inert male at random, she pushes up the sleeve of his sweatshirt.

A little cry escapes her. The HUE band seems to have come alive, and is glowing and blinking with electronic activity.

Alex takes a careful look. Interesting! So the bracelets have a stun function. So that's why these men collapsed. Well, all right!

This is an impressive display of nonlethal weapons technology. Obviously, this Revolution is not as fastidious as he has feared. The New Order goes up in his estimation; it has some muscle after all, he's glad to see.

He can spot the cover Lisa was describing, on the band on the man's arm, and is about to reach for it when she restrains him.

"Don't," she cautions. "We don't know how this thing works. I'm not even sure it still has a warning function, or ever did."

Now what? Who ordered the stun, and why? Did somebody back home find out about Valentine's Day, even without her warning? Or has a war started? Are they fighting in the city streets even now?

"I have to get back," Lisa states, categorically. "I have to find out what's going on."

"We'll take my Allterrain," Alex agrees. "It's in the shed. We can get a good start before daybreak."

"But I can't leave Justin behind," Lisa says. "I never even gave him a chance to explain. And we were friends. I came into Zone Six with him, I can't leave him here. He's my partner."

She thinks for a minute.

"Let's assume the men are all knocked out. I guess there were, probably, fifteen women at the lodge, all in all. Some of them are probably asleep and won't know what happened until morning. We'll have to watch out for them, but I think it's safe to go in."

And yes, it's safe; safe in an eerie, ghostly, horrible, dreamlike way. It feels like yet another version of the Sleeping Beauty story, after the Brothers Grimm, after Anne Rice. The guards at the entrance and behind the reception desk are unconscious, gently collapsed in their seats as though merely asleep. Some men were caught in the lobby, having a late-night drink; they are slumped over the bar, and one man reclines across the pool table, knocked out just as he was about to sink his shot. By the weird glow of the safety lights, Lisa and Alex make their way through all of this unnatural somnolence, searching for Justin. From behind one of the office doors, they hear female voices, conferring excitedly about what to do, but Alex and Lisa don't pause to discover what that might be. Making sure to glance at each and every collapsed form in the hallways, Lisa hurries to check the room she and Justin had been assigned, but it's unoccupied. Cautiously they survey the common areas, the dining room, the other hallways. It takes them nearly an hour to find Justin.

Lisa gasps and Alex frowns when they finally come across him, sagging unconscious against his restraints, his weight dragging against his shoulders.

"Good thing we came for him," Alex remarks. "Looks like your pal wasn't with the bad guys after all."

Racked with guilt, Lisa helps Alex free her unfortunate assistant; then Alex slings him over his shoulder and carries him to a couch in the lobby. He can stay there for now; even if the Harmony women come out of their conference, they'll never notice that one unconscious man has changed his location. Alex will bring the All-terrain as quickly as he can. And he'll leave a message for his father, telling him that he's gone off to do a bit of fieldwork of his own, and will return as soon as possible. Lisa will wait with Justin, ducked behind the reception desk in case someone comes. Then Alex lopes off into the darkness.

It's nearly dawn when our little expeditionary force gets under way. How idyllic; they look just like a 1960s family going on a trip. The man is driving. The woman sits beside him. Justin is in the back, belted in for safety and covered with a blanket like their napping child. Are we there yet?

Their prospects are poor, by the way. The border station they are aiming for had its surveillance disrupted long ago, just as Alex suspected. It's the main crossing point for Harmony, and Zonies are massing there, as yet unaware that most of their leaders are unconscious, that the buses that are supposed to take them to the nearest urban center are not coming, and that their plan is up in the air. Assuming our three friends make it to the border, they will run smack into a restless, leaderless, itching-for-action Zonie mob.

When you're in this kind of a bind, only a deus ex machina will do—well, a dea ex machina, in our case. Two of them.

Violet and Anita are on their way to the dorm. Tomorrow's a big day; no one's going home. They'll just catch some sleep in the office dormitory. But first, as every night, they detour past the screening room. Violet wants to say good night to Justin-the-blip; to see the signal from Justin's armband displayed on the monitor and calm her conscience that, despite the situation she's gotten him into, he's fine. The ritual seems more urgent tonight. Tomorrow is V-Day, and while Violet isn't high-ranking enough inside the Radical wing to know all the details, she knows it will be a big deal.

Violet stands before the wall-sized HUE screen. She's found the appropriate grid, located his ID number, and there's Justin, clearly displayed as a blue light. She frowns.

"Why is his light blinking tonight?" she wonders. Usually it's just a steady blue dot.

"Oh, that's the alarm signal," the woman at the monitor says, sipping her iced mint tea. "He pushed the SOS button about two hours ago."

Violet's breath catches. Something's gone wrong after all. "Will they be able to get him out?" she worries.

"No, they're not going to do that. We reported it," the woman, Gemma, offers. "They said not to worry about it. Anyway," she adds, "whatever his problem was, it's academic now."

"What are you talking about?" Violet asks, in growing agitation. "Academic?"

"I guess I can tell you," Gemma says, self-importantly. "It's not that you aren't cleared for it. It was purely a need-to-know restriction. I mean, it wasn't related to your part of the mission, but you'll find out, anyway, in a little while. The men's new HUE bands have a stun function," she informs Violet. "And some other functions, too. Just the men's bands. That's why we switched them. Those are *our* bands," she adds proudly. Technology right out of the Radical laboratory. Technological innovation right under the noses of the incompetent Directorate. They authorized the new bands, and paid for them, with no clue about their nifty added functions.

"So whatever his problem was"—Gemma looks at the time display—"by now he should be out like a light and feeling no pain. And in no danger," she adds kindly, "because all of his buddies are out, too."

"When are they waking up again?" Violet asks.

Gemma purses her lips; she's said enough.

"They *are* waking up again?" Violet pursues, getting suspicious.

Gemma takes the high ground. "Really," she says angrily. "I should think you'd have other worries. Like our entire future, for example? Like everything we've been working for? What's with this obsession over some guy? As soon as things settle down again, you'd better see your supervisor, something obviously needs to be adjusted in your protocol, it's getting to you."

They glare at each other. Violet backs off.

She stomps over to Anita, grabs her by the elbow, and hauls her roughly into the hallway.

"She's right, you *are* obsessed," Anita notes, allowing herself to be pulled out of hearing range.

"It's not right to do this to Justin," Violet argues. "He was on our side. And he called for help, fully trusting that we would bail him out."

Anita rolls her eyes.

"I got him into this," Violet says. "He believed me."

Anita gives her a dark look, but Violet can tell she is making some headway.

"He's part of our team. Well, he *is,* sort of. I would get *you* out, if you were in trouble," Violet goes on.

Anita is wavering.

"If he gets killed because of me, I won't have any peace," Violet persists. "It'll be terribly, terribly bad karma."

"What are you proposing to do?" Anita asks, against her better judgment.

Violet rewards her with a radiant smile.

"We can get him out," she says. "It'll be easy. When this all starts to go down, any minute now, there will be total chaos. Nobody will even notice if we just take one little helicopter and do one little search-and-rescue flight."

"I can't believe I'm even considering this," Anita growls.

"I would help *you* if you asked me," Violet reminds her.

By the time Lavinia Tree's Presidential Guard Unit arrives to take over Headquarters Security, with orders to put as many people as possible in temporary custody until the renegades can be sorted out from the loyalists, and people start resisting this order on the grounds that it's arbitrary and not backed by any sort of democratic decision, and reports of computer breakdowns start pouring in, causing panicked officers to stop worrying about loyal or disloyal and use every available staffer to try and get the systems up again, by the time the chaos Violet alluded to starts unfolding, a few hours sooner than expected, she and her cursing, complaining, whining pilot are out on the airfield and nearly ready to take off.

Alex, Lisa, and Justin are driving along, toward the border, toward the mob. From a few miles away, and from well above them, not just one but two deas in a machina are approaching.

Violet is at the GPS screen. "I don't understand this," she cries out, alarmed. "He's moving! Look at this, he's moving! How can he be moving?"

"I don't understand any of this," Anita grumbles. She's still extremely pissed. "Above all, I don't understand why I let you talk me into this." Cursing and fuming, she guides the helicopter toward the choppy terrain of Zone Six.

Violet ignores her. "Are any of the others moving, too?" she mutters to herself in alarm. "Are they regaining consciousness already? Are the bands malfunctioning? Better check. Let me randomize." She punches her gadget to make it scan 150 random band-wearers, then sighs, relieved but still puzzled. "No, everybody's still out. At least, they're all perfectly stationary. But then how can Justin be moving around?"

"You'll have your answer in about seven minutes," her friend tells her. Then she gets back on line with Air Defense, to discuss the mass of guys she has spotted just below them, collecting at the checkpoint.

Back at headquarters, Nadine and a handful of other conspirators have been admitted into the presence of Lavinia. She greets them coldly. Her guards surround her. In her hands she holds a substantial dossier, of which the lost-then-found Valentine's Day report, the one that Brett filed and Cleo deleted and Security restored, is only the latest and most damning entry.

"Why are you trying to destroy us?" Lavinia asks.

Nadine steps assertively forward. "We are trying to save you," she says. "Not just from these fascists in Harmony but from running our New Order into the ground with your excessive liberalism and indulgence. *You* have put us in jeopardy. Maybe you can accuse us of not sharing our information with you. But if it had been up to you, there wouldn't have *been* any information. And you can say we let the Valentine's Day plot go too far, but if we had told you about it sooner, you would have slapped a few wrists and ordered a few remedial reeducation sessions, and that would have been it. In a short time, the counterrevolutionaries would have regrouped. That won't happen now, thanks to us. There's no whitewashing this. There's no glossing over this. No fancy consultants are going to handle this one by handing out pet gerbils to men. This is treason, high treason, and thanks to us, the traitors are signedsealeddelivered. We gave them enough rope to hang themselves with."

Lavinia freezes her with a level look. There is truth to these accusations. Official security *was* a total failure.

"That's not the only reason you let Valentine's Day go forward," she says, finally. "You also wanted to discredit the government. Discredit me. This was an attempted coup d'etat."

She lifts the dossier meaningfully. The evidence is inside. Maybe. Or maybe she's bluffing. Maybe this is merely her best guess. Nadine can deny it, and see what happens.

"That's true," Nadine says, instead. "But plans can change. Right now, you are planning to prosecute us. Once you have studied the situation, and seen how many of us there are, in what key functions, how valuable we are, how *right* we are, and how incredibly shoddy your own security has been, that plan might change as well."

Lavinia's guards, offended by this blanket insult, move angrily forward, but Lavinia waves them back. "It might," Lavinia says.

She allows Nadine and a few of her associates to advance to the conference table. The parties sit down. All around them, the room begins to fill as more and more advisers, cabinet members, heads of divisions arrive in response to summonses and rumors. As they enter, they gravitate to one side of the table or the other. Lavinia must be shocked to see how many of them gravitate to Nadine's side, but she doesn't show it.

Alex, Lisa, and the inert Justin go bumping down the road, making good time, moving quickly toward—though they don't know it—trouble. I wouldn't want to be Lisa when they run into that mob. I wouldn't want to be Alex if he decides to help her, and I think he would. Justin might be okay, an unconscious lump under a blanket on the backseat.

Chop, chop, chop, what is that? A helicopter hovers over them, swoops forward a bit, comes up, lurches to the side, in the awkward movements of that vehicle's flight. Lisa peers up, trying to identify it, to see if she can distinguish friend from foe. It has markings, but they are those of the elite security force, and Lisa does not recognize them. Alex steps on the gas, reflexively.

"Why do people always do that?" Anita muses, easily keeping

pace with him from above. "They always speed up when they realize I'm on top of them. Like, right, they're going to outrun me!"

Lisa is still peering up, Violet is peering down, but what with the motion and the jolts and the angles, neither of them can see very much.

"It looks like more than one person in the car," Violet reports, before scrutinizing her GPS screen one last time. "One of them has got to be Justin, his signal is coming in from right under us. That explains the movement. Someone's packed him into the car, and they're driving. If it's a man, and he's conscious, then he hasn't got a HUE band, so he's got to be a Zonie. So we need to intercept before he gets much closer to all his friends at the border."

"Let's do it," Anita decides, quickly calculating her velocities.

Then she swoops the helicopter forward, brings it down, and bumps it onto the road neatly just in front of our group, blocking the road but allowing them enough space to come to a screeching halt. Well done!

Everyone leaps out of their respective vehicle. Everyone has a weapon.

"Security!" Violet yells. "Put your weapons down! Identify yourselves! Hand over the hostage!"

"Ministry of Thought!" Lisa shouts back with equal authority. "This is an official mission! This is my deputized associate and his requisitioned vehicle. I have my partner in the backseat."

And the next sound after that is Alex laughing. He can't help it. Three days ago, he was a hermit, and now he's apparently a deputy sheriff in a women's Wild West extravaganza. Requisitioned, indeed!

The women look at each other. Why is this man laughing? The excitement and the stress must be too much for him.

Alex is ordered to surrender his weapon and stand against the car with his hands on its roof, and he obeys with good grace. Violet throws open the back door and checks Justin's vital signs. Anita interrogates Lisa. Headquarters is called for verification and a decision, but no one of any importance can be reached, as they are attending to far more essential matters, such as trying to overthrow each other. Warily, Violet and Anita make their own judgment call. They load their passengers into the helicopter, put the seat belts on lock-restraint mode, keep Violet's weapon trained on them just in case, and fly them out.

As he boards the helicopter, just before he is put in the seat farthest from Lisa's and strapped in, Alex whispers something to her. "I want you to know I'm not a one-night-requisition sort of guy," is what he says. "So I hope we can deputize again real soon."

Really. The things men think about when they've just been saved from a counterrevolutionary mob and are about to fly into a coup attempt.

And before we move on, and in case you missed it, I want to point out that Justin's HUE band, intended to put men out of commission, combined with Violet's unanticipated affection for the object of her gender manipulation exercise, ends up saving Lisa. See how interrelated survival is? What an uplifting message. The Gender Amity Review Board would be so pleased, except it won't have that opportunity, since it will soon be judged frivolous and disbanded.

And why is that? Time to see what's been happening in the civilized world.

We need to back up a bit. It starts two days before the helicopter mission. It starts with an argument between Cleo and her mom.

"We can't constantly impose on your aunt," Theresa says, facing her daughter down sternly via telescreen. "Lisa is working on an important project, she can't be babysitting you all the time. Besides, I haven't been able to reach her. I really think you should go and stay at the hostel, I'll call them and arrange it."

"Mo-o-om," Cleo whines, "I'm not a baby. I don't *need* a babysitter, that's *so* before! And I hate the hostel, I won't go there. I can be by myself for a couple of days, honest! What can happen? And anyway, I don't bother Lisa. I don't stop her from working. She always says I'm no trouble and I can come any time I want! I got sick the last time I stayed at the hostel. And some of the girls sneak out at night and meet re-eds!" she adds piously. That should scare her mother! She has to avoid the hostel at all costs. It's a terrible, noisy place, full of wet smelly babies and screamy little kids, and if you try to complain because you need to have some peace and quiet, the extra-cheerful supervisors give you a lecture about nurturing.

"Cleo, please. I don't have time to argue. And I cannot concentrate on my presentation if I'm worrying about you," Theresa snaps. "The hostel is perfectly all right, thousands of children stay there every year. I'm sorry, sweetheart," she adds, in a more conciliatory vein. "How could I know our presentation would go over so well that they'd insist on adding an expert workshop? It's a big honor, and very important, or I would have come back today like I promised. You'll be fine at the hostel, and anyway, I cannot have you staying at home alone."

"I can get somebody to stay with me," Cleo offers eagerly, sensing weakness. "Mackenzie," she says. "Mackenzie is very mature."

In the background, she can hear loudspeakers announcing the end of the break.

"Oh, all right," Theresa says, exasperated. "Have your friend stay over, and I'll check with you tomorrow. And try to get hold of Lisa, but don't bother her if she says she's busy!"

Yes! Cleo dances up and down in excitement. Freedom! Three whole entire days of freedom! She plants an exuberant kiss between the ears of Mac. Well, it wasn't a lie. He *is* staying over, he *is* a friend, and for all she knows, Mac *could* be short for Mackenzie.

Freedom is wonderful, but can get boring after two hours or so. Tomorrow looms yet more boringly ahead. Of course, her mom forgot that it's their Directional Assessment break, and no classes all week. All of her friends have gone to visit grandparents or fathers or to camp. The more alert parents, which as far as Cleo can tell is just about everybody but Theresa, made their break arrangements long ago.

Lisa's not home yet when Cleo calls her at five-thirty, or at six, or at seven. Maybe she has a sports meet, or went out to dinner. At seven-thirty Cleo decides to go to her aunt's apartment and wait for her there.

When she arrives at eight-fifteen, no one is home. At nine she calls Brett, but he isn't home either. She resolves to wait patiently and not fret, and that plan lasts until 9:03, when she phones Justin at the Residential Suites to ask him when Lisa left work today and whether she said anything about her evening plans, but Justin isn't there. She decides to wait up for Lisa, and since it is already too late to go back home, she settles in for the night. She folds up a nice fluffy bath towel and places it in a corner for Mac. Then she borrows pajamas, washes her face, brushes her teeth, and curls up in her aunt's bed with some magazines.

When she wakes up eight hours later, she is still in Lisa's room, sprawled diagonally across the bed, magazines scattered around her. She and Mac are alone.

Cleo fixes them breakfast. Then she decides to check Lisa's mail—maybe there will be a reference to something that explains her absence. Maybe she has a new SR, Cleo reflects gleefully. Maybe he sent her a mushy love letter! Maybe she spent the night with him.

Her mood turns from romance to worry as the screen brings up several messages from Lisa's office. There is a series of courtesy forwards of messages from Security, noting with increasing ire that Justin has failed to check in, has still failed to check in, has not called in sick, is now seriously delinquent. There is a message from someone named Rebecca, regretting that Lisa missed their meeting, hoping she isn't ill, and relating that Nadine has been acting even more strangely than usual today. Why would Justin be AWOL? Where is Lisa? Cleo decides to take Mac for a walk. Then she goes to the Sports Center and swims. She stops by the Craft Center to see if they've got the new glazes yet. They do, so she tries them out on a jar. Time for another walk with Mac.

When she gets back it's six o'clock, and Vera is in the apartment. "Sweetheart," the older woman exclaims, dropping everything to enfold Cleo in a warm, vanilla-scented hug. "You're not getting too grownup to kiss your Auntie Vera, are you?" she asks, snuggling the girl against her bosom. It's what she always says, and Cleo permits this affection with all the sovereign generosity of youth. Anyway, she likes Vera, though she's been warned that you have to be careful around her. Cleo knows that you have to be kind to women like Vera, because they have a sickness, which makes them love to spend all of their time inside of houses cleaning away dirt, and they're not contagious or anything, but you still have to be kind of watchful, because they have a hard time respecting emotional boundaries, and can get way too involved in you if you let them, but it's not their fault and you have to be patient and nice.

"What are you doing here, honey?" Vera asks. So Cleo explains, and midway through it occurs to her to ask Vera the same question. Because, come to think of it, this is an unusual time for Vera to be cleaning. The latest Cleo has ever seen her here was five, and even then she was already done with her work and just hanging around to chat with Lisa.

"I'm running late," Vera explains. "I wasn't feeling good this morning, so I shifted things around. And now I'm glad I did. Imagine you, here all by yourself!" And she declares that she will stay, and fix dinner for Cleo, and keep her company. If Lisa doesn't return, she offers warmly, she will gladly spend the night. They can have hot chocolate with marshmallows, and Vera can show Cleo a new way to braid her hair, and for breakfast she will bake muffins. "Of *course* you didn't want to stay at that awful hostel," she agrees sympathetically, giving Cleo another hug.

There have been times when Cleo has wondered what it would be like to have someone like Vera as a mother, instead of someone like Theresa. Actually, she pretty much has this thought every time Vera gives her a hug, or brings her a piece of cake, or insists that she leave those dirty plates and those scattered art supplies right where they are and go out and play, because Aunt Vera will have those few little things cleared away in a minute, it's not even worth talking about.

Vera bustles into the kitchen to start dinner, while Cleo withdraws to the living room for a while to listen to music. Then she decides to finish her acronym list, to give herself a step up on the English homework, and after that she watches a disk she recorded last time she was here. Then they have supper, and then she takes the dog out for his final walk of the day. She tells herself that Lisa will be back when she returns from the walk, but she's not, so she checks the compuscreen for a message, but there's no message. Vera is in the kitchen again, cleaning up from their dinner. Cleo considers trying to call her mother for advice, but that will open up the whole hostel discussion again, so she consults Vera instead.

"Vera," she says. "I don't know what to do. It's not normal for Lisa to be just all mysteriously gone like this. I know she had plans for the weekend, but she said she'd definitely be back Sunday night. She said she had really important meetings on Monday and Tuesday, and they're looking for her."

"Don't worry, everything will be okay in the end," Vera replies quickly, deepening the weirdness of that non sequitur by flushing. Cleo's friend Ginny looks like that when you catch her cheating at Medusa or she doesn't want to give you her last stick of gum. When she feels guilty.

Before Cleo can ponder the significance of that, Vera rushes forward and folds her into a crushing embrace. "It will be fine," she insists. "For all of you young girls, things will be fine. That's who we're doing this for, just remember that. It's for you, sweetheart. Whatever happens, promise me that you'll remember that."

Whatever happens? "Okay," Cleo says, more confused than ever and trying to squirm out of Vera's bear hold. "I will, Aunt Vera."

But Vera doesn't release her. She keeps her enfolded in a warm, soft embrace, murmuring about how everything will be all right, and after a little while Cleo stops resisting and relaxes into it, starting to find it soothing, and before she knows it she is sobbing, and Vera is murmuring reassuring, loving little words into her ear and patting her hair and cushioning her in a generous body that is softer than Theresa's, softer than Lisa's, softer than any of the athletic female forms that Cleo usually derives her low-fat 2 percent version of maternal comfort from.

"What's the matter, honey," Vera murmurs, and Cleo sobs it all out, the whole story of the compumessage that she erased because she was so sure it was just a game, but now it's the day before Valentine's Day and Lisa is missing, and Justin is missing, too, and all the adults seem much more nervous and jumpy than they normally are, and things have been weird for weeks now, and it just feels like something is *wrong,* and Cleo is terrified that the message may have been true. And she ought to report it, and turn herself in, but she's scared of getting in bad trouble! But Vera has made her feel calmer, and stronger, and now she knows what to do. She has to go and report the message right now.

There must be plenty of ways in which a grown woman like Vera could outsmart a ten-year-old, and in a few moments she would probably start thinking of them. But before that can happen, an enraged "No!" escapes her, and a startled Cleo sees a hideous grimace contort the older woman's face and jumps back in alarm. And Vera, who is definitely suffering from a clinical disorder, though probably not one as benign as Domestic Obsession Disorder; Vera, who under calmer circumstances nonetheless might get a grip and develop a plan, instead sees her illness mirrored in Cleo's terrified eyes and spirals off into madness. She starts gesticulating. "It's all for the best," she yells. "We're going to build you a safe world. You have to break a few eggs, you can't make an omelette without breaking a few eggs! I'm doing this for you, sweetheart," she cries, advancing on Cleo with her arms spread wide. Cleo shrieks and makes to run out of the kitchen; Vera blocks her.

Cleo, too, could think this through and come up with a plan, a way to soothe Vera, to talk her down, and then, ever so gradually, ease herself out of the apartment and get help. But Cleo, though smart, is nonetheless a child, and panics at the sight of a grownup melting down.

"Let me out," she shrieks. "I'm telling! I'm telling!"

That's a mistake. But Vera makes a mistake, too. She seizes a weapon. An impressive weapon. She grabs it out of the sink, and it's pretty scary.

There are a lot of scary things in kitchens, you know. Women in all their apparent harmlessness have actually been heavily armed for centuries, without even realizing it. Traditional weaponry, chemical warfare, it's all there in your average woman's average pantry. All those years, instead of sobbing into their dish towels, women could have been defending themselves, but somehow they just didn't see it.

It's amazing really. I mean, think about the lives of women, say, a century before the Revolution. When your average man was already a highly sedentary, fastidious being who worked in an office with paper, women were still in the kitchen, practicing the savage arts on mammals and on fish: cutting off heads, slicing out intestines, severing limbs, then cleaning the bloody implements with toxic chemicals. They had the skills, they had the wherewithal, but they lacked the paradigm. That happens more often than you might think. Take the Chinese, enjoying their ornamental fireworks and never realizing they had invented gunpowder, until the white dudes started blowing them up with it. That's how it is with women. Put four men in a kitchen, and they could have a war, bombs and all. Put a thousand women in a kitchen, and all you'll get is a bake sale . . . but that's a different subject.

Vera, in any case, is a martial woman and wastes no time seizing her implement. It's a frightening weapon with clearly lethal power. It looks like something out of a medieval armory. It's a cruel metal device, an oval rim bristling with long sharp prongs. What is this terrible thing? Well, technically, it's a baked-potato holder. You can spear a half-dozen raw potatoes on it, to hold them upright in the oven. Or, should that be your inclination, you could use it to gouge out someone's eyes, pierce their skin, and rip the flesh from their bones.

Vera grasps it by its rim, giving herself a deadly, many-fanged claw. The sight would send me cowering into a corner, but as regards Cleo, escalating the confrontation to this level is a mistake on Vera's part.

Getting attacked doesn't scare Cleo. In obedience to New Order pediatric guidelines, she's been taught self-defense ever since she was big enough to toddle into a karate studio. Caring loving teachers dressed as large scary assailants have been attacking her practically since birth, to give her a chance to steel her nerves and practice her parries. She can go through her black-belt forms the way kids used to rattle off multiplication tables. At the sight of a weapon, her fear completely evaporates and she clicks into gear like a well-programmed little fighter—"android," I want to say, but we can't call her that, not if we've learned our Greek, and "gynoid" sounds strange, so we'll say "robot."

Vera has no comparable background, but insanity is a great equalizer. A terrible ballet ensues, feint and parry, lunge and duck. There's not enough room for proper kicking, or Cleo might be able to knock the weapon from Vera's hand. Even so, once or twice Cleo almost finds enough of an opening to get by her, but Vera tires of the game and throws herself at the girl in a sudden manic rush, catching Cleo off guard. The prongs are only a few inches from the girl's face when Vera screams and stumbles backward, her arm's vicious trajectory interrupted. She catches her balance, still screaming, still holding the pronged device, and now she slashes downward with it, and the kitchen echoes with an agonized yelp, and she slashes again, reducing the second sound to a haunting whimper, followed by Cleo's scream.

The yelp, the whimper, that's Mac. He has dug his teeth into Vera's calf. He has hung on heroically through her first slashing; his lacerated back is bloody, and shreds of fur hang raw from his body, but he is trying to hold on. His teeth are still sunk into her flesh, though his voice is down to an anguished moan, when Vera gives out a barking cough and sinks to the floor. Cleo drops the cast-iron griddle and stands there trembling at the sight of Mac, her little Mackiewackie, her faithful friend and ally, near dead on the floor.

"It's okay, Mackie," she promises, tears streaming down her face, shaking with fear for him. "I'll get help," she says, and rushes to the alarm button to call Security.

And the line is dead.

It's 11:11. At eleven o'clock, the Valentine's Day preliminaries started to go into effect, and local security is disabled.

Ohallgoddesses. A doctor. She needs a doctor fast, judging from the limp mangled form of Mac, whose jaw has gone slack and who lies on the kitchen floor, his body jerking mechanically, his blood trickling across the tiles.

Riva lives close by. Riva loves dogs. Riva's deity Pele is the patron of small white dogs. Best of all, Riva is important, and can mobilize VIP help. Cleo dumps out Lisa's large fruit basket, spilling papayas, bananas, and loose grapes. She layers some terry-cloth dish towels into the basket, then lays it on its side next to Mac and, with a soft wail of empathetic pain, rolls him into it as gently as she can. Then she lifts her burden by the handle and scoots out into the night. With her mother's oversized white T-shirt flapping around her loosely from shoulders to mid-thigh, hair flying behind her, body akilter from the weight of Mac in the basket, she runs out into the perilous, security-disarmed, almost-Valentine's-Day darkness.

There's a full moon tonight. Riva is standing on her balcony, looking out at the vanilla-yellow orb presiding over a perfect sky. You can't feel a wind, but there must be one at higher altitudes, because gauzy wisps of clouds are flitting by with some speed. Riva is just giving herself up to the wonderful somnolent mood of nearly midnight when she spies a figure running awkwardly down the middle of the street.

It's a girl, pale in a flowing garment. She runs, accompanied by an eerie sound like the whimper of an animal in terrible pain. As she comes closer, Riva sees that she is carrying a basket containing a small white dog. The girl's face looks anguished. Pele has taken on human form, and come to test her.

Did I mention that Riva has been smoking her favorite evening sedative-euphoric, a mixture of *Artemisia* and *Nepeta cataria*? Better known as cronewort and catnip and easy to grow, in case you are for any reason interested in information about cultivating legal narcotic plants.

Anyway, the effects of this combination are mild, and Riva is an intelligent and rational woman, so her semi-hallucination lasts only for an instant. Of course she doesn't really believe in visitations by goddesses. I shouldn't even have mentioned it.

The girl comes closer, and Riva realizes that she has seen her before, though she can't immediately recall the occasion. The child looks very upset, Riva can see that now. Her body language spells trouble.

The girl has reached the enclosing shrubbery. "It's me," she gasps. "Cleo. Remember? Lisa's niece. And you're our teacher in Spiritual Guidance class? And you had us over to see your altar, and you gave us those beads? Something terrible is happening. You have to help me. I need help for Mackie right away, or he's going to die. And also there's a plot."

"I'll be right down, honey," Riva replies. "I'll turn off the perimeter, just wait thirty seconds and you can come through to the door. I'm on my way."

Cleo steps through the hedge. She doesn't need to wait any thirty seconds. As she already knows, and as Riva is discovering right about now, there *is* no more perimeter. As she will learn in a moment, when she rings Security to alert them to this glitch, there is no connection to Security. By the time she reaches the door, she is concerned enough to be receptive to Cleo's outlandish story.

Cleo is disciplined. She keeps her narrative down to the bare essential minimum. A plot. To destroy the Revolution. And Lisa was warned about it, but Cleo erased the message, because she thought it was a game. And she can't remember the details, or the people that were named, but Riva could hypnotize her, or put her in a trance, to bring it back. And Lisa and Justin are missing. And security is disabled. And Vera is part of the plot. And she tried to kill her, but Mac saved her life, and now look at him. And he needs a doctor right away, right away, she won't be able to bear it if he dies, and after they save him, then maybe somebody can hypnotize her, because it's nearly Valentine's Day, and they're all going to be murdered and everything destroyed, because she is a stupid, stupid, jealous girl. "I know I'm in trouble," she concludes.

Riva takes charge. The dog is in bad shape, but he comes first only in Cleo's sweet cosmology. Assume there's something to this story. You won't need a trance or hypnosis to find out, just a few key words and an approximate date, to retrieve Lisa's data. Big Sister is always watching, fortunately, and has endless megabytes of memory.

"Let's go," she says.

And that is how the information about the coming cataclysm reaches the New Order government: via ecologically correct electroscooter, driven by a slightly high belief counselor, accompanied by a girl in a floppy white shirt and an almost dead dog.

Except they already know. Not everything, but part of it. Enough for officials to have been woken up and summoned to headquarters, for the governmental district to be a frenzied hive of activity, for defense teams to be assembling, and panicking when they find most of their systems incapacitated, for roadblocks to be going up haphazardly and reserves wandering about the streets looking for other members of their units.

Riva and Cleo arrive at the doors of the Interior Ministry. Riva identifies herself, rattling off the names of a good dozen very important officials who are her friends. They're in.

Some med-techs, clucking, take charge of Mac and whisk him away.

Riva's friends turn up. They call in technicians to quiz Cleo about the deleted message, then they hurry away, presumably to retrieve it. It's the middle of the night, but you wouldn't know it. The building is alive with people, humming with activity. There's an atmosphere of high tension. More people keep arriving. Some wear uniforms and run down corridors in small groups, looking determined; others consult in small huddles and then hurry away, their faces grim. Cleo wants to be with Mac, but Riva tells her that it's time to be strong now, that Mac did his duty bravely and that the best way for her to honor him is to do the same. They wait for some time in the office of one of the friends, then someone comes to get

Riva, and by extension Cleo, who is sticking like Velcro to the only adult she knows here, and eventually they are ushered into a large, busy room abuzz with what appears to be a war council.

In this war council, Nadine is implementing Plan B. Not gladly; she liked Plan A a lot better. Under Plan A, the Zonies would have started reaching major urban centers around noon on Valentine's Day. Civilians, becoming aware of this threat and calling for security only to find it disabled, would have panicked. But Radical units would have been ready. Security, frantically trying to regroup with all their systems down, would have gratefully fallen into line behind the Radicals. The government would have been theirs for the taking.

Intelligent people know that things can always go wrong, so there's a Plan B. If the government discovers the plot too soon, and takes its own measures against it, and might be able to deal with the Zonies on its own, and would certainly hold the Radicals accountable for whatever terrible things happened to large numbers of civilians if it didn't, then it's time for Plan B. The government knows more than the Radicals hoped it would. And any moment now, it will know even more. One of the Radicals' operatives, reporting in from the floor of Lisa's kitchen in a semicoherent, severely concussed voice, nevertheless manages to reach Person Two, Xenia—her Radical contact as well as a highly successful mole inside Harmony—and report that she failed to stop a messenger who has the full details of their plot, who consequently is now on her way to turn them in.

Riva and Cleo are just in time for the big showdown. Nadine's heart might be pounding, but her tone is accusatory and her supporters, massed around her, look determined. Lavinia, she states, should be grateful that loyal and dedicated members of Intel, and their talented and devoted allies in Security, had the courage of their convictions. Call them a rogue unit if you like, the fact is that without them, without the Radicals, the government would now be helpless in the face of the Valentine's Day conspiracy. Or do they suppose that, with such short notice, when they discovered security to be breaking down at 11:45 p.m., they could have put together an effective defense? And please remember, were it not for the HUE stun bands brilliantly engineered by the Radicals, they wouldn't have just a crowd of undisciplined Zonies to deal with. The advancing army would include a mass of trained, educated, disciplined urban conspirators, guided by a functioning Council and led by the General. The Zonies are only foot soldiers, harmless without a brain.

Intel should have reported the plot through the proper channels the moment they discovered it? Yes? And then what? Then the pie-eyed social engineers would have slapped a few wrists and designed a few more stupid ways to coddle men. Until one day some group of plotters somewhere would succeed, and somebody like the General would lord it over the world again.

The Radicals have a lot of explaining to do, but they also have chaos on their side. The Zonies have to be dealt with right away, that much is obvious, so the toughest units have to be dispatched to the border, and there's no time to sort out which officers are loyal to whom, and one couldn't dispense with those loyal to the Radicals even if one could identify them. The same thing is true of Security. Every available techie is needed to track down the glitch and bring the systems back up ASAP. Rigging the men's HUE bands was quite a feat; you can't do without that caliber of talent in a situation like this. It's hard to argue with the case the Radicals are making. Gender Amity and Social Engineering can sputter all they want; the fact remains that, without the armbands, their protégés would be rampaging through the city's streets right now wreaking mayhem.

Ironically, despite the fact that their coup was preempted, this hour belongs to the Radicals, and Nadine knows it. She has the floor, and a frowning Lavinia Tree can only listen obediently.

"This panic atmosphere is uncalled for," Nadine says. "The Zonies can be taken care of, we're ready for them. The rest of the guys are down for the count. We'll have security back soon, the best people are working on it. We were lucky this time, but we can't count on that always being the case, as I hope we are all realizing. Now is the time to learn our lesson. Were we right about not trusting men? Yes, we were. Were we right to prepare the wristbands? Yes, we were. Please listen. We have a proposal, and we are right again."

Some cabinet members mutter that the extremists are receiving altogether too much of a hearing, but Lavinia waves them back. She will listen.

Nadine takes a deep breath. "Men aren't constructed for equality," she says. "They can't handle it. Not even with each other. Look at them: they always have to have bosses, leaders, hierarchies. Gender amity, gender equality, that's bunk. It's a fantasy. I wish it could be that way. Balance, equality, fairness, everybody holding up half the sky—that would be nice, but it won't happen, not while men are involved. It will never, never be that way. They don't have a middle ground. They can either be on the top, or be on the bottom. It's them or us, and the world is a better place if it's us."

She won't get much argument there.

"All right. Now, for one gender to dominate the other, the one that's going to be subordinate has to be made to feel like a minority. It has to believe itself to be weaker, dumber, and dependent on the other. They did it to us for thousands of years."

Cleo relaxes a little; this sounds like one of her teachers talking, and a teacher talking is an eminently normal situation. She looks around; several of the women are nodding, and there's a lot less tension in the room than there was before.

"Now, how did they do it to us? They used a combination of violence, physical intimidation, and psychological warfare. For the latter, they merely had to work with what they knew to be our weak points: a desire to be liked, a need for connection, and a weak ego. So, how do we reverse that? We have to neutralize their physical advantages and work on their weak points. There's not much you can do to their ego: their gargantuan self-esteem is impervious even to facts, let alone to artificial attempts to undermine it. They *are* vulnerable to sexual manipulation, and Special Operations, Manipulative Gender Psychology, is one of our most successful branches. That's useful, but we hardly want to base our entire society on it. The bottom line is, you have to make them feel like a minority to get them to behave like a minority, and it's going to be very difficult to accomplish that with force or manipulation alone. However, we have another option. They can actually *be* a minority."

She's lost Cleo, who looks around and sees from the uncomprehending faces that she is not alone in her bewilderment. Nadine takes another deep breath; they're going to make her spell it out.

"The wristband has a lethality function. Right now it's set on stun, but it can be advanced forward."

Some are still at sea, but not Lavinia.

"You're suggesting that we kill them," she states, evenly.

"Not all of them," Nadine says. "We don't suggest killing all of them. We just want to reconfigure the demographic proportions to a more manageable level. We propose a population ratio of 70 percent to 30 percent."

All hell breaks loose.

"And we could try 60 percent to 40 percent and see how that goes," she adds, raising her voice above the din.

Cleo doesn't know where to look first. Everyone is on their feet, yelling, gesticulating.

The lead demographer is saying something about the destabilizing effect of severe gender imbalances; two colleagues are disagreeing; the head of Security is pointing out that societal problems will indeed plummet once men are a minority; Social Engineering is saying that Nadine's portrayal is slanderous, and that men would already have turned the corner to enlightenment if only one had approved their bureau's last budget increase.

Amidst all of this, Cleo hears a familiar voice; it's her mother, who must have come in late and been hidden in the crush, but is now struggling forward. Theresa is waving a paper that explains how this indubitably more desirable gender ratio can be achieved more gradually, without actual murder, just by doctoring the drinking water.

If I were Lavinia, I'd be near a breakdown, but she's made of sterner stuff, which is why she's a Founding Mother and I'm not.

However, I am guessing that she is as relieved as I am to know that the male population is out of commission during this debate. Not only does this spare them the anxiety of knowing that their fate hangs so perilously in the balance, not only does it save them the embarrassment of hearing their developmental prospects so dismally assayed and all these nasty things being said about them, I especially would not want them to witness the degree of confusion, the vituperation, the disarray in the ranks.

Lavinia lets the debate ebb and flow for a while, then she taps a button and a gong sounds, demanding silence.

Here's what I think. I think she knows what she wants to do, but she's looking for a stylish way to do it. She surveys the crowd of flustered, agitated faces and zeroes in on the youngest.

"You," she says. "The young girl over there. Yes, you in the big T-shirt. Move forward, dear. Let her through, please."

Cleo gulps, but Riva nudges her, and she advances a few steps.

"Do you understand what we're talking about, dear?" Lavinia asks, in her gravelly voice.

Cleo nods.

"Go ahead, tell me," Lavinia urges.

"Well," Cleo mumbles, "I guess we're talking about whether we should, whether it would be a good idea to . . ." She pauses.

"Speak up, dear. Finish your thought," Lavinia instructs.

"To kill a whole bunch of the men while they're asleep," Cleo says.

Lavinia nods. "To kill a whole bunch of the men while they're asleep," she repeats, and lets the sentence hang there for a moment, harsher for the idiom. "Precisely, my dear. That is exactly what is being contemplated here. And what about you? Do you think that would be a good idea?"

"I think that would be really mean," Cleo says. "And I don't think we should do that at all."

Some mouths open wide to annotate this, but Lavinia sounds her gong again and looks sternly into the audience.

"The drinking water," Theresa calls out, thinking the moment ideal to repeat her alternative suggestion, but under Lavinia's sternly frosty gaze, her suggestion fades to a croaking whisper.

Lavinia Tree stands up. She isn't very tall; she's obviously tired; still she has a regal presence, and can command a room. Under the power of her charisma, the hall becomes so quiet that she can speak softly, as though she were thinking out loud.

"I know that some of you want me to step down," she says, "so you can push forward faster with the changes you want to make. And I know that some of you want me to crack down on the Radicals, for following their own agenda and disregarding the rules." The Radicals start to protest this version, but she turns to address them directly.

"No, don't try to defend yourselves, it's not necessary. You won't be punished," she says. "We were reckless with our safety, and you pointed it out in time. Nothing you said is untrue. Men cannot rule again; they have too few scruples, and too easily ride roughshod over the lives of others. Maybe someday . . . but not very soon . . ."

The ongoing computer breakdown has wreaked havoc with the automatic lighting; it has a chlorophylly green tint that makes everyone look mossy, as though they lived underwater, and gives Lavinia's face a sad and bitter cast. She looks down at the table, and her voice lowers, almost as though she had forgotten where she was, and were talking to herself.

"We're not a very nice species," she muses, wearily. "Could anyone claim that women are fundamentally good? That could not be claimed. But I suppose that, as hands go, ours are a little bit cleaner.

"Where did that little girl in the big shirt go?" she asks, peering into the crowd. Hands push Cleo forward from the cover she had once again sought in the crowd, and Lavinia relaxes visibly as soon as she spots her. "Yes," she murmurs. "There's the new generation, grown under different circumstances entirely, maybe they'll see the way forward. All we need to do is hold on to things until we can hand over to them. That's the most anyone should expect of us. We've done enough, we've gone far enough. Try to keep your hands clean, dear," she murmurs.

And that is how the male population gets its collective butt saved, not that they're ever grateful for anything women do to give them a nice life on this planet.

Things go back to normal, with some important revisions.

The leaderless Zonies are rounded up and pushed back behind their restored and heavily reinforced borders.

Heads roll, but in line with Lavinia's guiding precepts, they don't roll very far. The Radicals are reprimanded but promoted, and if you're planning to give me any grief on that, I have only three things to say: Yitzhak Rabin, Yasir Arafat, Ollie North. Terrorists into world leaders, mavericks into talk show hosts: that's the way of the world. Psych Ops and Intel are given new, less sanguine directors. Security is restructured and put under tighter command. Harmony's members, male and female, are shipped to rehabilitation centers. Vera is hospitalized, probably for good. The housekeeping fleet is retired and replaced with strictly commercial cleaning services.

The General is brought before a panel of psychologists and declared nonrehabilitatable, which greatly resembles what we used to call a life sentence without possibility of parole; he'll be confined to a closed facility until death do him part. Not that he minds. As part of his social reparations, he is made into a consultant. He gets to wear a uniform, receives a medal every year or so, and is as happy as a lark. Soon his high-security cell is plastered with maps, all divided into sectors, stuck with pins, and bristling with planned anti-missile batteries. Current disks of all the international arms gazettes are delivered punctually to his cell's compuscreen. He teleconferences with ministerial committees and military experts; he refers to his cell neighbor as his attaché, and sometimes gets him to salute.

Brett tries to squeeze some mileage out of his belated abortive attempt to report the plot, but hard-hearted hard-liners are running the show now, and he finds himself in the same boat and on the same floor as the General, though with a milder sentence. His new book, *Locked into Masculinity,* inspires hundreds of women to offer to personally supervise his eventual rehabilitation, Lisa not among them.

Theresa is ordered to abandon both her sex-selection drinking water and her prenatal testosterone projects, but never mind, she's got lots of other ideas.

In deference to his traumatic experiences, and in recognition of his service to the nation, Justin is amnestied for his basement activities and excused from the rest of the evaluation process. The Residential Suites, hotbed of sedition, are temporarily closed down while the Men's Bureau comes up with a better plan for supervising errant gendermates. Nadine is their new supervisor, so they'd better look sharp. Seems like Will is going to have a career, too; after Justin told every interviewer how the brilliant leadership of this unhewn jewel of masculinity saved him from the Harmony mob, Will is being trained as a re-ed liaison officer.

The closure of the Residential Suites threatens to put Justin in a hostel until he can save enough money to get his own place, but Violet says that she and Anita have "tons of room" in their loft, and could use his company, instead of "rattling around all by themselves" in that "big old place." We'll have to see how that goes. If I were Justin, I'd worry about the way Anita narrowed her eyes when Violet made that offer—but, honey, those weren't the eyes he was looking deeply and soulfully into, so I guess he missed it.

As for Lisa, the Ministry of Thought puts her on permanent payroll with a promotion, even though she won't officially graduate for another year. Also, they still want her to finish the project. After all the excitement, it's a letdown to be working on sex again, and she'll miss Justin now that his stint is over, but she has a new assistant, Alex. Sort of. He has a day job as a trainer in Wilderness Survival and Small Arms, which is now a mandatory part of the Women's Evaluation Program, but he's generously volunteered to serve as Lisa's unsalaried after-hours assistant. He says he can be requisitioned for consultations at any time; experiments, too, if she wishes. I expect her research to experience major advances soon; after all, no matter what the theorists believe, nothing can take the place of fieldwork.

Which brings us to Alex's father. He's doing well. He's got a grief counselor and a reintegration adviser and his own personal Fostering Transgenerational Understanding buddy, a whole tribe of empathetic individuals who don't mind if he asks them a million questions and finds almost anything they say "fascinating, fascinating."

The Female Genocide memorial, now called Forget-Us-Not Park, is under construction as planned, except for the field of rock salt, which has been replaced by a playground after all. The Rosa Parks interactive monument is also back. It is basically a giant jungle gym in the shape of a bus. It's a lot of fun, and the children love it. The bus seats spin, bounce, and rock, you can climb up onto the roof and slide out the windows, the hand straps ring chimes, and the steps are piano keys that play tunes when you jump on them. The bus driver is Rosa Parks. To my knowledge, Mrs. Parks never drove a bus or wanted to; she merely wanted to sit down in one. Having her as the driver makes very little sense, but I like it. A little black lady, cast in bronze, wearing a hat, driving a rambunctious crew of bouncing, jumping, laughing children into the future—yes, I like it.

Mac almost died, to give our story a touch of tragedy, but Cleo loves him so much that I couldn't go through with it. So Mackie's back, by popular acclaim. We'll have him recover from his battle wounds. He'll limp a bit, and become a canine revolutionary folk hero. He'll inspire a line of stuffed animals and a series of children's books, and give his name to a special pet area next to the interactive playground. Besides a grassy patch for their more prosaic and odiferous activities, Mac's Corner will also include an obstacle course for dogs, which will feature a hologram of Mac jumping its hurdles once a day, at dusk. It will be a popular attraction. Every evening, you will hear the pitiful pleading of exhausted parents impatient to take their children home to dinner and bath and bed, and the assertive protests of their children that they won't leave, not yet. Not before they've seen Mackie jump.